WHITE LIES

MORE WILDSIDE CLASSICS

Please see www.wildsidepress.com for a complete list!

WHITE LIES

CHARLES READE

WILDSIDE PRESS

WHITE LIES

This edition published in 2006 by Wildside Press, LLC.
www.wildsidepress.com

CHAPTER I.

Towards the close of the last century the Baron de Beaurepaire lived in the chateau of that name in Brittany. His family was of prodigious antiquity; seven successive barons had already flourished on this spot when a younger son of the house accompanied his neighbor the Duke of Normandy in his descent on England, and was rewarded by a grant of English land, on which he dug a mote and built a chateau, and called it Beaurepaire (the worthy Saxons turned this into Borreper without delay). Since that day more than twenty gentlemen of the same lineage had held in turn the original chateau and lands, and handed them down to their present lord.

Thus rooted in his native Brittany, Henri Lionel Marie St. Quentin de Beaurepaire was as fortunate as any man can be pronounced before he dies. He had health, rank, a good income, a fair domain, a goodly house, a loving wife, and two lovely young daughters, all veneration and affection. Two months every year he visited the Faubourg St. Germain and the Court. At both every gentleman and every lacquey knew his name, and his face: his return to Brittany after this short absence was celebrated by a rustic fete.

Above all, Monsieur de Beaurepaire possessed that treasure of treasures, content. He hunted no heart-burns. Ambition did not tempt him; why should he listen to long speeches, and court the unworthy, and descend to intrigue, for so precarious and equivocal a prize as a place in the Government, when he could be De Beaurepaire without trouble or loss of self-respect? Social ambition could get little hold of him; let parvenus give balls half in doors, half out, and light two thousand lamps, and waste their substance battling and manoeuvring for fashionable distinction; he had nothing to gain by such foolery, nothing to lose by modest living; he was the twenty-ninth Baron of Beaurepaire. So wise, so proud, so little vain, so strong in health and wealth and honor, one would have said nothing less than an earthquake could shake this gentleman and his house. Yet both were shaken, though rooted by centuries to the soil; and by no vulgar earthquake.

For years France had bowed in silence beneath two galling burdens — a selfish and corrupt monarchy, and a multitudinous, privileged, lazy, and oppressive aristocracy, by whom the peasant was handled like a Russian serf. [Said peasant is now the principal proprietor of the soil.]

The lower orders rose upon their oppressors, and soon

showed themselves far blacker specimens of the same breed. Law, religion, humanity, and common sense, hid their faces; innocent blood flowed in a stream, and terror reigned. To Monsieur de Beaurepaire these republicans — murderers of women, children, and kings — seemed the most horrible monsters nature had ever produced; he put on black, and retired from society; he felled timber, and raised large sums of money upon his estate. And one day he mounted his charger, and disappeared from the chateau.

Three months after this, a cavalier, dusty and pale, rode into the courtyard of Beaurepaire, and asked to see the baroness. She came to him; he hung his head and held her out a letter.

It contained a few sad words from Monsieur de Laroche-jaquelin. The baron had just fallen in La Vendee, fighting for the Crown.

From that hour till her death the baroness wore black.

The mourner would have been arrested, and perhaps be-headed, but for a friend, the last in the world on whom the family reckoned for any solid aid. Dr. Aubertin had lived in the chateau twenty years. He was a man of science, and did not care a button for money; so he had retired from the practice of medicine, and pursued his researches at ease under the baron's roof. They all loved him, and laughed at his occasional reveries, in the days of prosperity; and now, in one great crisis, the protege became the protector, to their astonishment and his own. But it was an age of ups and downs. This amiable theorist was one of the oldest verbal republicans in Europe. And why not? In theory a republic is the perfect form of government: it is merely in practice that it is impossible; it is only upon going off paper into reality, and trying actually to self-govern limited nations, after heating them white hot with the fire of politics and the bellows of bombast — that the thing resolves itself into bloodshed silvered with moonshine.

Dr. Aubertin had for years talked and written speculative republicanism. So they applied to him whether the baroness shared her husband's opinions, and he boldly assured them she did not; he added, "She is a pupil of mine." On this audacious statement they contented themselves with laying a heavy fine on the lands of Beaurepaire.

Assignats were abundant, but good mercantile paper, a noto-rious coward, had made itself wings and fled, and specie was creeping into strong boxes like a startled rabbit into its hole. The fine was paid; but Beaurepaire had to be heavily mortgaged, and the loan bore a high rate of interest. This, with the baron's pre-vious mortgages, swamped the estate.

The baroness sold her carriage and horses, and she and her daughters prepared to deny themselves all but the bare necessaries of life, and pay off their debts if possible. On this their dependants fell away from them; their fair-weather friends came no longer near them; and many a flush of indignation crossed their brows, and many an aching pang their hearts, as adversity revealed the baseness and inconstancy of common people high or low.

When the other servants had retired with their wages, one Jacintha remained behind, and begged permission to speak to the baroness.

"What would you with me, my child?" asked that lady, with an accent in which a shade of surprise mingled with great politeness.

"Forgive me, madame," began Jacintha, with a formal courtesy; "but how can I leave you, and Mademoiselle Josephine, and Mademoiselle Rose? I was born at Beaurepaire; my mother died in the chateau: my father died in the village; but he had meat every day from the baron's own table, and fuel from the baron's wood, and died blessing the house of Beaurepaire. I *cannot* go. The others are gone because prosperity is here no longer. Let it be so; I will stay till the sun shines again upon the chateau, and then you shall send me away if you are bent on it; but not now, my ladies — oh, not now! Oh! oh! oh!" And the warm-hearted girl burst out sobbing ungracefully.

"My child," said the baroness, "these sentiments touch me, and honor you. But retire, if you please, while I consult my daughters."

Jacintha cut her sobs dead short, and retreated with a formal reverence.

The consultation consisted of the baroness opening her arms, and both her daughters embracing her at once. Proud as they were, they wept with joy at having made one friend amongst all their servants. Jacintha stayed.

As months rolled on, Rose de Beaurepaire recovered her natural gayety in spite of bereavement and poverty; so strong are youth, and health, and temperament. But her elder sister had a grief all her own: Captain Dujardin, a gallant young officer, wellborn, and his own master, had courted her with her parents' consent; and, even when the baron began to look coldly on the soldier of the Republic, young Dujardin, though too proud to encounter the baron's irony and looks of scorn, would not yield love to pique. He came no more to the chateau, but he would wait hours and hours on the path to the little oratory in the park, on the bare chance of a passing word or even a kind look from Josephine. So much devotion gradually won a heart which in happier times she had been half encouraged to give him; and, when he left her on a military service of uncommon danger, the woman's reserve melted, and, in that moment of mutual grief and passion, she vowed she loved him better than all the world.

Letters from the camp breathing a devotion little short of worship fed her attachment; and more than one public mention of his name and services made her proud as well as fond of the fiery young soldier.

Still she did not open her heart to her parents. The baron, alive at that time, was exasperated against the Republic, and all who served it; and, as for the baroness, she was of the old school: a passionate love in a lady's heart before marriage was contrary to her notions of etiquette. Josephine loved Rose very tenderly; but shrank with modest delicacy from making her a confidante of feelings, the bare relation of which leaves the female hearer a child no longer.

So she hid her heart, and delicious first love nestled deep in her nature, and thrilled in every secret vein and fibre.

They had parted two years, and he had joined the army of the Pyrenees about one month, when suddenly all correspondence ceased on his part.

Restless anxiety rose into terror as this silence continued; and starting and trembling at every sound, and edging to the window at every footstep, Josephine expected hourly the tidings of her lover's death.

Months rolled on in silence.

Then a new torture came. He must not be dead but unfaithful. At this all the pride of her race was fired in her.

The struggle between love and ire was almost too much for nature: violently gay and moody by turns she alarmed both her mother and the good Dr. Aubertin. The latter was not, I think, quite without suspicion of the truth; however, he simply prescribed change of air and place; she must go to Frejus, a watering-place distant about five leagues. Mademoiselle de Beaurepaire yielded a languid assent. To her all places were alike.

But when they returned from Frejus a change had taken place. Rose had extracted her sister's secret, and was a changed girl. Pity, and the keen sense of Josephine's wrong, had raised her sisterly love to a passion. The great-hearted girl hovered about her lovely, suffering sister like an angel, and paid her the tender attentions of a devoted lover, and hated Camille Dujardin with all her heart: hated him all the more that she saw Josephine shrink even from her whenever she inveighed against him.

At last Rose heard some news of the truant lover. The fact is, this young lady was as intelligent as she was inexperienced; and she had asked Jacintha to tell Dard to talk to every soldier that passed through the village, and ask him if he knew anything about Captain Dujardin of the 17th regiment. Dard cross-examined about a hundred invalided warriors, who did not even recognize the captain's name; but at last, by extraordinary luck, he actually did fall in with two, who told him strange news about Captain Dujardin. And so then Dard told Jacintha; and Jacintha soon had the men into the kitchen and told Rose. Rose ran to tell Josephine; but stopped in the passage, and turned suddenly very cold. Her courage failed her; she feared Josephine would not take the news as she ought; and perhaps would not love her so well if *she* told her; so she thought to herself she would let the soldiers tell their own tale. She went into the room where Josephine was reading to the baroness and Dr. Aubertin; she sat quietly down; but at the first opportunity made Josephine one of those imperceptible signals which women, and above all, sisters, have reduced to so subtle a system. This done, she went carelessly out: and Josephine in due course followed her, and found her at the door.

"What is it?" said Josephine, earnestly.

"Have you courage?" was Rose's reply.

"He is dead?" said Josephine, turning pale as ashes.

"No, no;" said Rose hastily; "he is alive. But you will need all your courage."

"Since he lives I fear nothing," said Josephine; and stood there and quivered from head to foot. Rose, with pitying looks, took her by the hand and drew her in silence towards the kitchen.

Josephine yielded a mute submission at first; but at the very door hung back and faltered, "He loves another; he is married: let me go." Rose made no reply, but left her there and went into the kitchen and found two dragoons seated round a bottle of wine. They rose and saluted her.

"Be seated, my brave men," said she; "only please tell me what you told Jacintha about Captain Dujardin."

"Don't stain your mouth with the captain, my little lady. He is a traitor."

"How do you know?"

"Marcellus! mademoiselle asks us how we know Captain Dujardin to be a traitor. Speak."

Marcellus, thus appealed to, told Rose after his own fashion that he knew the captain well: that one day the captain rode out of the camp and never returned: that at first great anxiety was felt on his behalf, for the captain was a great favorite, and passed for the smartest soldier in the division: that after awhile anxiety gave place to some very awkward suspicions, and these suspicions it was his lot and his comrade's here to confirm. About a month later he and the said comrade and two more were sent, well mounted, to reconnoitre a Spanish village. At the door of a little inn they caught sight of a French uniform. This so excited their curiosity that he went forward nearer than prudent, and distinctly recognized Captain Dujardin seated at a table drinking between two guerillas; then he rode back and told the others, who then came up and satisfied themselves it was so: that if any of the party had entertained a doubt, it was removed in an unpleasant way; he, Marcellus, disgusted at the sight of a French uniform drinking among Spaniards, took down his carabine and fired at the group as carefully as a somewhat restive horse permitted: at this, as if by magic, a score or so of guerillas poured out from Heaven knows where, musket in hand, and delivered a volley; the officer in command of the party fell dead, Jean Jacques here got a broken arm, and his own horse was wounded in two places, and fell from loss of blood a few furlongs from the French camp, to the neighborhood of which the vagabonds pursued them, hallooing and shouting and firing like barbarous banditti as they were.

"However, here I am," concluded Marcellus, "invalided for awhile, my lady, but not expended yet: we will soon dash in among them again for death or glory. Meantime," concluded he, filling both glasses, "let us drink to the eyes of beauty (military salute); and to the renown of France; and double damnation to all her traitors, like that Captain Dujardin; whose neck may the devil twist."

Ere they could drink to this energetic toast, a low wail at the door, like a dying hare's, arrested the glasses on their road, and the rough soldiers stood transfixed, and looked at one another in some dismay. Rose flew to the door with a face full of concern.

Josephine was gone.

Then Rose had the tact and resolution to say a few kind, encouraging words to the soldiers, and bid Jacintha be hospitable to them. This done she darted up-stairs after Josephine; she reached the main corridor just in time to see her creep along it with the air and carriage of a woman of fifty, and enter her own room.

Rose followed softly with wet eyes, and turned the handle gently. But the door was locked.

"Josephine! Josephine!"

No answer.

"I want to speak to you. I am frightened. Oh, do not be alone."

A choking voice answered, "Give me a little while to draw my breath." Rose sank down at the door, and sat close to it, with her head against it, sobbing bitterly. She was hurt at not being let in; such a friend as she had proved herself. But this personal feeling was only a fraction of her grief and anxiety.

A good half hour elapsed ere Josephine, pale and stern as no one had ever seen her till that hour, suddenly opened the door. She started at sight of Rose couched sorrowful on the threshold; her stern look relaxed into tender love and pity; she sank, blushing, on her knees, and took her sister's head quickly to her bosom. "Oh, my little love, have you been here all this time?" — "Oh! oh! oh!" was all the little love could reply. Then the deserted one, still kneeling, took Rose in her lap, and caressed and comforted her, and poured words of gratitude and affection over her like a warm shower.

They rose hand in hand.

Then Rose suddenly seized Josephine, and looked long and anxiously down into her eyes. They flashed fire under the scrutiny. "Yes, it is all over; I could not despise and love. I am dead to him, as he is dead to France."

This was joyful news to Rose. "I hoped it would be so," said she; "but you frightened me. My noble sister, were I ever to lose your esteem, I should die. Oh, how awful yet how beautiful is your scorn. For worlds I would not be that Cam" — Josephine laid her hand imperiously on Rose's mouth. "To mention his name to me will be to insult me; De Beaurepaire I am, and a Frenchwoman. Come, dear, let us go down and comfort our mother."

They went down; and this patient sufferer, and high minded conqueror, of her own accord took up a commonplace book, and read aloud for two mortal hours to her mother and Aubertin. Her voice only wavered twice.

To feel that life is ended; to wish existence, too, had ceased; and so to sit down, an aching hollow, and take a part and sham an interest in twaddle to please others; such are woman's feats. How like nothing at all they look!

A man would rather sit on the buffer of a steam-engine and ride at the Great Redan.

Rose sat at her elbow, a little behind her, and turned the leaves, and on one pretence or other held Josephine's hand nearly all the rest of the day. Its delicate fibres remained tense, like a greyhound's sinews after a race, and the blue veins rose to sight in it, though her voice and eyes were mastered.

So keen was the strife, so matched the antagonists, so hard the victory.

For ire and scorn are mighty. And noble blood in a noble heart is heroic. And Love is a giant.

CHAPTER II.

The French provinces were now organized upon a half military plan, by which all the local authorities radiated towards a centre of government. By-the-by, this feature has survived subsequent revolutions and political changes.

In days of change, youth is at a premium; because, though experience is valuable, the experience of one order of things unfits ordinary men for another order of things. So a good many old fogies in office were shown the door, and a good deal of youth and energy infused into the veins of provincial government. For instance, Edouard Riviere, who had but just completed his education with singular eclat at a military school, was one fine day ordered into Brittany to fill a responsible post under Commandant Raynal, a blunt, rough soldier, that had risen from the ranks, and bore a much higher character for zeal and moral integrity than for affability.

This officer was the son of a widow that kept a grocer's shop in Paris. She intended him for spice, but he thirsted for glory, and vexed her. So she yielded, as mothers will.

In the armies of the republic a good soldier rose with unparalleled certainty, and rapidity, too; for when soldiers are being mowed down like oats, it is a glorious time for such of them as keep their feet. Raynal mounted fast, and used to write to his mother, and joke her about the army being such a bad profession; and, as he was all for glory, not money, he lived with Spartan frugality, and saved half his pay and all his prize money for the old lady in Paris.

But this prosperous man had to endure a deep disappointment; on the very day he was made commandant and one of the general's aides-de-camp, came a letter into the camp. His mother was dead after a short illness. This was a terrible blow to the simple, rugged soldier, who had never had much time nor inclination to flirt with a lot of girls, and toughen his heart. He came back to Paris honored and rich, but downcast. The old home, empty of his mother, seemed to him not to have the old look. It made him sadder. To cheer him up they brought him much money. The widow's trade had taken a wonderful start the last few years, and she had been playing the same game as he had, living on ten-pence a day, and saving all for him. This made him sadder, if anything.

"What," said he, "have we both been scraping all this dross together for? I would give it all to sit one hour by the fire, with her hand in mine, and hear her say, 'Scamp, you made me unhappy when you were young, but I have lived to be proud of you.'"

He applied for active service, no matter what: obtained at once this post in Brittany, and threw himself into it with that honest zeal and activity, which are the best earthly medicine for all our griefs. He was busy writing, when young Riviere first presented himself. He looked up for a moment, and eyed him, to take his measure; then put into his hand a report by young Nicole, a subordinate filling a post of the same nature as Riviere's; and bade him analyze that report on the spot: with this he instantly resumed his own work.

Edouard Riviere was an adept at this sort of task, and soon handed him a neat analysis. Raynal ran his eye over it, nodded cold approval, and told him to take this for the present as a guide as to his own duties. He then pointed to a map on which Riviere's district was marked in blue ink, and bade him find the centre of it. Edouard took a pair of compasses off the table, and soon discovered that the village of Beaurepaire was his centre. "Then quarter yourself at Beaurepaire; and good-day," said Raynal.

The chateau was in sight from Riviere's quarters, and he soon learned that it belonged to a royalist widow and her daughters, who all three held themselves quite aloof from the rest of the world. "Ah," said the young citizen, "I see. If these rococo citizens play that game with me, I shall have to take them down." Thus a fresh peril menaced this family, on whose hearts and fortunes such heavy blows had fallen.

One evening our young official, after a day spent in the service of the country, deigned to take a little stroll to relieve the cares of administration. He imprinted on his beardless face the expression of a wearied statesman, and strolled through an admiring village. The men pretended veneration from policy; the women, whose views of this great man were shallower but more sincere, smiled approval of his airs; and the young puppy affected to take no notice of either sex.

Outside the village, Publicola suddenly encountered two young ladies, who resembled nothing he had hitherto met with in his district; they were dressed in black, and with extreme simplicity; but their easy grace and composure, and the refined sentiment of their gentle faces, told at a glance they belonged to the high nobility. Publicola divined them at once, and involuntarily raised his hat to so much beauty and dignity, instead of poking it with a finger as usual. On this the ladies instantly courtesied to him after the manner of their party, with a sweep and a majesty, and a precision of politeness, that the pup would have laughed at if he had heard of it; but seeing it done, and well done, and by lovely women of rank, he was taken aback by it, and lifted his hat again, and bowed again after he had gone by, and was generally flustered. In short, instead of a member of the Consular Government saluting private individuals of a decayed party that existed only by sufferance, a handsome, vain, good-natured boy had met two self-possessed young ladies of distinction and breeding, and had cut the usual figure.

For the next hundred yards his cheeks burned and his vanity cooled. But bumptiousness is elastic in France, as in England, and doubtless among the Esquimaux. "Well, they are pretty girls," says he to himself. "I never saw two such pretty girls together; they will do for me to flirt with while I am banished to this Arcadia." Banished from school, I beg to observe.

And "awful beauty" being no longer in sight, Mr. Edouard resolved he would flirt with them to their hearts' content. But there are ladies with whom a certain preliminary is required before you can flirt with them. You must be on speaking terms. How was this to be managed?

He used to watch at his window with a telescope, and whenever the sisters came out of their own grounds, which unfortunately was not above twice a week, he would throw himself in their way by the merest accident, and pay them a dignified and courteous salute, which he had carefully got up before a mirror in the privacy of his own chamber.

One day, as he took off his hat to the young ladies, there broke from one of them a smile, so sudden, sweet, and vivid, that he seemed to feel it smite him first on the eyes then in the heart. He could not sleep for this smile.

Yet he had seen many smilers; but to be sure most of them smiled without effect, because they smiled eternally; they seemed cast with their mouths open, and their pretty teeth forever in sight; and this has a saddening influence on a man of sense — when it has any. But here a fair, pensive face had brightened at sight of him; a lovely countenance, on which circumstances, not nature, had impressed gravity, had sprung back to its natural gayety for a moment, and had thrilled and bewitched the beholder.

The next Sunday he went to church — and there worshipped — whom? Cupid. He smarted for his heathenism; for the young ladies went with higher motives, and took no notice of him. They lowered their long silken lashes over one breviary, and scarcely observed the handsome citizen. Meantime he, contemplating their pious beauty with earthly eyes, was drinking long draughts of intoxicating passion. And when after the service they each took an arm of Dr. Aubertin, and he with the air of an admiral convoying two ships choke-full of specie, conducted his precious charge away home, our young citizen felt jealous, and all but hated the worthy doctor.

This went on till he became listless and dejected on the days he did not see them. Then he asked himself whether he was not a cowardly fool to keep at such a distance. After all he was a man in authority. His friendship was not to be despised, least of all by a family suspected of disaffection to the state.

He put on his glossy beaver with enormous brim, high curved; his blue coat with brass buttons; his white waistcoat, gray breeches, and top-boots; and marched up to the chateau of Beaurepaire, and sent in his card with his name and office inscribed.

Jacintha took it, bestowed a glance of undisguised admiration on the young Adonis, and carried it to the baroness. That lady sent her promptly down again with a black-edged note to this effect.

Highly flattered by Monsieur de Riviere's visit, the baroness must inform him that she receives none but old acquaintances, in the present grief of the family, and of the *kingdom*.

Young Riviere was cruelly mortified by this rebuff. He went off hurriedly, grinding his teeth with rage.

"Cursed aristocrats! We have done well to pull you down, and we will have you lower still. How I despise myself for giving any one the chance to affront me thus. The haughty old fool; if she had known her interest, she would have been too glad to make a powerful friend. These royalists are in a ticklish position; I can tell her that. She calls me De Riviere; that implies nobody without a 'De' to their name would have the presumption to visit her old tumbledown house. Well, it is a lesson; I am a republican, and the Commonwealth trusts and honors me; yet I am so ungrateful as to go out of the way to be civil to her enemies, to royalists; as if those worn-out creatures had hearts, as if they could comprehend the struggle that took place in my mind between duty, and generosity to the fallen, before I could make the first overture to their acquaintance; as if they could understand the politeness of the heart, or anything nobler than curving and ducking and heartless etiquette. This is the last notice I will ever take of that old woman, unless it is to denounce her."

He walked home to the town very fast, his heart boiling, and his lips compressed, and his brow knitted.

To this mood succeeded a sullen and bitter one. He was generous, but vain, and his love had humiliated him so bitterly, he resolved to tear it out of his heart. He absented himself from church; he met the young ladies no more. He struggled fiercely with his passion; he went about dogged, silent, and sighing. Presently he devoted his leisure hours to shooting partridges instead of ladies. And he was right; partridges cannot shoot back; whereas beautiful women, like Cupid, are all archers more or less, and often with one arrow from eye or lip do more execution than they have suffered from several discharges of our small shot.

In these excursions, Edouard was generally accompanied by a thick-set rustic called Dard, who, I believe, purposes to reveal his own character to you, and so save me that trouble.

One fine afternoon, about four o'clock, this pair burst remorselessly through a fence, and landed in the road opposite Bigot's Auberge; a long low house, with "*Ici on loge a pied et a cheval*," written all across it in gigantic letters. Riviere was for moving homeward, but Dard halted and complained dismally of "the soldier's gripes." The statesman had never heard of that complaint, so Dard explained that the *vulgar* name for it was hunger. "And only smell," said he, "the soup is just fit to come off the fire."

Riviere smiled sadly, but consented to deign to eat a morsel in the porch. Thereat Dard dashed wildly into the kitchen.

They dined at one little round table, each after his fashion. When Dard could eat no more, he proceeded to drink; and to talk in proportion. Riviere, lost in his own thoughts, attended to him as men of business do to a babbling brook; until suddenly from the mass of twaddle broke forth a magic word — Beaurepaire; then the languid lover pricked up his ears and found Mr. Dard was abusing that noble family right and left. Young Riviere inquired what ground of offence they had given *him*. "I'll tell you," said Dard; "they impose on Jacintha; and so she imposes on me." Then observing he had at last gained his employer's ear, he became prodigiously loquacious, as such people generally are when once they get upon their own griefs.

"These Beaurepaire aristocrats," said he, with his hard peasant good-sense, "are neither the one thing nor the other; they cannot keep up nobility, they have not the means; they will not come down off their perch, they have not the sense. No, for as small as they are, they must look and talk as big as ever. They can only afford one servant, and I don't believe they pay her; but they must be attended on just as obsequious as when they had a dozen. And this is fatal to all us little people that have the misfortune to be connected with them."

"Why, how are you connected with them?"

"By the tie of affection."

"I thought you hated them."

"Of course I do; but I have the ill-luck to love Jacintha, and she loves these aristocrats, and makes me do little odd jobs for them." And at this Dard's eyes suddenly glared with horror.

"Well, what of that?" asked Riviere.

"What of it, citizen, what? you do not know the fatal meaning of those accursed words?"

"Why, I never heard of a man's back being broken by little odd jobs."

"Perhaps not his back, citizen, but his heart? if little odd jobs will not break that, why nothing will. Torn from place to place, and from trouble to trouble; as soon as one tiresome thing begins to go a bit smooth, off to a fresh plague, in-doors work when it is dry, out-a-doors when it snows; and then all bustle; no taking one's work quietly, the only way it agrees with a fellow. 'Milk the cow, Dard, but look sharp; the baroness's chair wants mending. Take these slops to the pig, but you must not wait to see him enjoy them: you are wanted to chop billets.' Beat the mats, take down the curtains, walk to church (best part of a league), and heat the pew cushions; come back and cut the cabbages, paint the door, and wheel the old lady about the terrace, rub quicksilver on the little dog's back, — mind he don't bite you to make hisself sick, — repair the ottoman, roll the gravel, scour the kettles, carry half a ton of water up two purostairs, trim the turf, prune the vine, drag the fish-pond; and when you *are* there, go in and gather water lilies for Mademoiselle Josephine while you are drowning the puppies; that is little odd jobs: may Satan twist her neck who invented them!"

"Very sad all this," said young Riviere.

Dard took the little sneer for sympathy, and proceeded to "the cruellest wrong of all."

"When I go into their kitchen to court Jacintha a bit, instead of finding a good supper there, which a man has a right to, courting a cook, if I don't take one in my pocket, there is no supper, not to say supper, for either her or me. I don't call a salad and a bit of cheese-rind — *supper.* Beggars in silk and satin! Every sou they have goes on to their backs, instead of into their bellies."

"I have heard their income is much reduced," said Edouard gently.

"Income! I would not change with them if they'd throw me in half a pancake a day. I tell you they are the poorest family for leagues round; not that they need be quite so starved, if they could swallow a little of their pride. But no, they must have china and plate and fine linen at dinner; so their fine plates are always bare, and their silver trays empty. Ask the butcher, if you don't believe *me*. Just you ask him whether he does not go three times to the smallest shopkeeper, for once he goes to Beaurepaire. Their tenants send them a little meal and eggs, and now and then a hen; and their great garden is chock full of fruit and vegetables, and Jacintha makes me dig in it gratis; and so they muddle on. But, bless your heart, coffee! they can't afford it; so they roast a lot of horse-beans that cost nothing, and grind them, and serve up the liquor in a silver coffee-pot, on a silver salver. Haw, haw, haw!"

"Is it possible? reduced to this?" said Edouard gravely.

"Don't you be so weak as to pity them," cried the remorseless plebeian. "Why don't they melt their silver into soup, and cut down their plate into rashers of bacon? why not sell the superfluous, and buy the needful, which it is grub? And, above all, why don't they let their old tumble-down palace to some rich grocer, and that accursed garden along with it, where I sweat gratis, and live small and comfortable, and pay honest men for their little odd jobs, and" —

Here Riviere interrupted him, and asked if it was really true about the beans.

"True?" said Dard, "why, I have seen Rose doing it for the old woman's breakfast: it was Rose invented the move. A girl of nineteen beginning already to deceive the world! But they are all tarred with the same stick. Down with the aristocrats!"

"Dard," said Riviere, "you are a brute."

"Me, citizen?" inquired Dard with every appearance of genuine surprise.

Edouard Riviere rose from his seat in great excitement. Dard's abuse of the family he was lately so bitter against had turned him right round. He pitied the very baroness herself, and forgave her declining his visit.

"Be silent," said he, "for shame! There is such a thing as noble poverty; and you have described it. I might have disdained these people in their prosperity, but I revere them in their affliction. And I'll tell you what, don't you ever dare to speak slightly of them again in my presence, or" —

He did not conclude his threat, for just then he observed that a strapping girl, with a basket at her feet, was standing against the corner of the Auberge, in a mighty careless attitude, but doing nothing, so most likely listening with all her ears and soul. Dard, however, did not see her, his back being turned to her as he sat; so he replied at his ease, —

"I consent," said he very coolly: "that is your affair; but permit me," and here he clenched his teeth at remembrance of his wrongs, "to say that I will no more be a scullery man without wages to these high-minded starvelings, these illustrious beggars." Then he heated himself red-hot. "I will not even be their galley slave. Next, I have done my last little odd job in this world," yelled the now infuriated factotum, bouncing up to his feet in brief fury. "Of two things one: either Jacintha quits those aristos, or I leave Jacin — eh? — ah! — oh! — ahem! How — 'ow d'ye do, Jacintha?" And his roar ended in a whine, as when a dog runs barking out, and receives in full career a cut from his master's whip, his generous rage turns to whimper with ludicrous abruptness. "I was just talking of you, Jacintha," quavered Dard in conclusion.

"I heard you, Dard," replied Jacintha slowly, softly, grimly. Dard withered.

It was a lusty young woman, with a comely peasant face somewhat freckled, and a pair of large black eyes surmounted by coal-black brows. She stood in a bold attitude, her massive but well-formed arms folded so that the pressure of each against the other made them seem gigantic, and her cheek red with anger, and her eyes glistening like basilisks upon citizen Dard. She looked so grand, with her lowering black brows, that even Riviere felt a little uneasy. As for Jacintha, she was evidently brooding with more ire than she chose to utter before a stranger. She just slowly unclasped her arms, and, keeping her eye fixed on Dard, pointed with a domineering gesture towards Beaurepaire. Then the doughty Dard seemed no longer master of his limbs: he rose slowly, with his eyes fastened to hers, and was moving off like an ill-oiled automaton in the direction indicated; but at that a suppressed snigger began to shake Riviere's whole body till it bobbed up and down on the seat. Dard turned to him for sympathy.

"There, citizen," he cried, "do you see that imperious gesture? That means you promised to dig in the aristocrat's garden this afternoon, so march! Here, then, is one that has gained nothing by kings being put down, for I am ruled with a mopstick of iron. Thank your stars, citizen, that you are not in may place."

"Dard," retorted Jacintha, "if you don't like your place, I'd quit it. There are two or three young men down in the village will be glad to take it."

"I won't give them the chance, the vile egotists!" cried Dard. And he returned to the chateau and little odd jobs.

Jacintha hung behind, lowered her eyes, put on a very deferential manner, and thanked Edouard for the kind sentiments he had uttered; but at the same time she took the liberty to warn him against believing the extravagant stories Dard had been telling about her mistress's poverty. She said the simple fact was that the baron had contracted debts, and the baroness, being the soul of honor, was living in great economy to pay them off. Then, as to Dard getting no supper up at Beaurepaire, a complaint that appeared to sting her particularly, she assured him she was alone to blame: the baroness would be very angry if she knew it. "But," said she, "Dard is an egotist. Perhaps you may have noticed that trait in him."

"Glimpses of it," replied Riviere, laughing.

"Monsieur, he is so egotistic that he has not a friend in the world but me. I forgive him, because I know the reason; he has never had a headache or a heartache in his life."

Edouard, aged twenty, and a male, did not comprehend this piece of feminine logic one bit: and, while he puzzled over it in silence, Jacintha went on to say that if she were to fill her egotist's paunch, she should never know whether he came to Beaurepaire for her, or himself. "Now, Dard," she added, "is no beauty, monsieur; why, he is three inches shorter than I am."

"You are joking! he looks a foot," said Edouard.

"He is no scholar neither, and I have had to wipe up many a sneer and many a sarcasm on his account; but up to now I have always been able to reply that this five feet one of egotism loves me sincerely; and the moment I doubt this, I give him the sack, — poor little fellow!"

"In a word," said Riviere, a little impatiently, "the family at Beaurepaire are not in such straits as he pretends?"

"Monsieur, do I look like one starved?"

"By Jove, no! by Ceres, I mean."

"Are my young mistresses wan, and thin?"

"Treason! blasphemy! ah, no! By Venus and Hebe, no!"

Jacintha smiled at this enthusiastic denial, and also because her sex is apt to smile when words are used they do not understand.

"Dard is a fool," suggested Riviere, by way of general solution. He added, "And yet, do you know I wish every word he said had been true." (Jacintha's eyes expressed some astonishment.) "Because then you and I would have concerted means to do them kindnesses, secretly; for I see you are no ordinary servant; you love your young mistresses. Do you not?"

These simple words seemed to touch a grander chord in Jacintha's nature.

"Love them?" said she, clasping her hands; "ah, sir, do not be offended; but, believe me, it is no small thing to serve an old, old family. My grandfather lived and died with them; my father was their gamekeeper, and fed to his last from off the poor baron's plate (and now they have killed him, poor man); my mother died in the house and was buried in the sacred ground near the family chapel. They put an inscription on her tomb praising her fidelity and probity. Do you think these things do not sink into the heart of the poor? — praise on her tomb, and not a word on their own, but just the name, and when each was born and died, you know. Ah! the pride of the mean is dirt; but the pride of the noble is gold."

"For, look you, among parvenues I should be a servant, and nothing more; in this proud family I am a humble friend; of course they are not always gossiping with me like vulgar masters and mistresses; if they did, I should neither respect nor love them; but they all smile on me whenever I come into the room, even the baroness herself. I belong to them, and they belong to me, by ties without number, by the many kind words in many troubles, by the one roof that sheltered us a hundred years, and the grave where our bones lie together till the day of judgment."[1]

Jacintha clasped her hands, and her black eyes shone out warm through the dew. Riviere's glistened too.

"That is well said," he cried; "it is nobly said: yet, after all, these are ties that owe their force to the souls they bind. How often have such bonds round human hearts proved ropes of sand! They grapple *you* like hooks of steel; because you are steel yourself to the backbone. I admire you, Jacintha. Such women as you have a great mission in France just now."

Jacintha shook her head incredulously. "What can we poor women do?"

"Bring forth heroes," cried Publicola with fervor. "Be the mothers of great men, the Catos and the Gracchi of the future!"

---

1   The French peasant often thinks half a sentence, and utters the other half aloud, and so breaks air in the middle of a thought. Probably Jacintha's whole thought, if we had the means of knowing it, would have run like this — "Besides, I have another reason: I could not be so comfortable myself elsewhere — for, look you" —

Jacintha smiled. She did not know the Gracchi nor their politics; but the name rang well. "Gracchi!" Aristocrats, no doubt. "That would be too much honor," replied she modestly. "At present, I must say adieu!" and she moved off an inch at a time, in an uncertain hesitating manner, not very difficult to read; but Riviere, you must know, had more than once during this interview begged her to sit down, and in vain; she had always thanked him, but said she had not a moment to stay. So he made no effort to detain her now. The consequence was — she came slowly back of her own accord, and sat down in a corner of the porch, where nobody could see her, and then she sighed deeply.

"What is the matter now?" said Edouard, opening his eyes.

She looked at him point-blank for one moment; and her scale turned.

"Monsieur," said she timidly, "you have a good face, and a good heart. All I told you was — give me your honor not to betray us."

"I swear it," said Edouard, a little pompously.

"Then — Dard was not so far from the truth; it was but a guess of his, for I never trusted my own sweetheart as I now trust a stranger. But to see what I see every day, and have no one I dare breathe a word to, oh, it is very hard! But on what a thread things turn! If any one had told me an hour ago it was you I should open my heart to! It's not economy: it's not stinginess; they are not paying off their debts. They never can. The baroness and the Demoiselles de Beaurepaire — are paupers."

"Paupers, Jacintha?"

"Ay, paupers! their debts are greater than their means. They live here by sufferance. They have only their old clothes to wear. They have hardly enough to eat. Just now our cow is in full milk, you know; so that is a great help: but, when she goes dry, Heaven knows what we shall do; for I don't. But that is not the worst; better a light meal than a broken heart. Your precious government offers the chateau for sale. They might as well send for the guillotine at once, and cut off all our heads. You don't know my mistress as I do. Ah, butchers, you will drag nothing out of that but her corpse. And is it come to this? the great old family to be turned adrift like beggars. My poor mistress! my pretty demoiselles that I played with and nursed ever since I was a child! (I was just six when Josephine was born) and that I shall love with my last breath" —

She could say no more, but choked by the strong feeling so long pent up in her own bosom, fell to sobbing hysterically, and trembling like one in an ague.

The statesman, who had passed all his short life at school and college, was frightened, and took hold of her and pulled her, and cried, "Oh! don't, Jacintha; you will kill yourself, you will die; this is frightful: help here! help!" Jacintha put her hand to his mouth, and, without leaving off her hysterics, gasped out, "Ah! don't expose me." So then he didn't know what to do; but he seized a tumbler and filled it with wine, and forced it between her lips. All she did was to bite a piece out of the glass as clean as if a diamond had cut it. This did her a world of good: destruction of sacred household property gave her another turn. "There, I've broke your glass now," she cried, with a marvellous change of tone; and she came-to and cried quietly like a reasonable person, with her apron to her eyes.

When Edouard saw she was better, he took her hand and said proudly, "Secret for secret. I choose this moment to confide to you that I love Mademoiselle Rose de Beaurepaire. Love her? I did love her; but now you tell me she is poor and in distress, I adore her." The effect of this declaration on Jacintha was magical, comical. Her apron came down from one eye, and that eye dried itself and sparkled with curiosity: the whole countenance speedily followed suit and beamed with sacred joy. What! an interesting love affair confided to her all in a moment! She lowered her voice to a whisper directly. "Why, how did you manage? She never goes into company."

"No; but she goes to church. Besides, I have met her eleven times out walking with her sister, and twice out of the eleven she smiled on me. O Jacintha! a smile such as angels smile; a smile to warm the heart and purify the soul and last forever in the mind."

"Well, they say 'man is fire and woman tow:' but this beats all. Ha! ha!"

"Oh! do not jest. I did not laugh at you. Jacintha, it is no laughing matter; I revere her as mortals revere the saints; I love her so that were I ever to lose all hope of her I would not live a day. And now that you have told me she is poor and in sorrow, and I think of her walking so calm and gentle — always in black, Jacintha, — and her low courtesy to me whenever we met, and her sweet smile to me though her heart must be sad, oh! my heart yearns for her. What can I do for her? How shall I surround her with myself unseen — make her feel that a man's love waits upon her feet every step she takes — that a man's love floats in the air round that lovely head?" Then descending to earth for a moment, "but I say, you promise not to betray me; come, secret for secret."

"I will not tell a soul; on the honor of a woman," said Jacintha.

The form of protestation was quite new to Edouard, and not exactly the one his study of the ancient writers would have led him to select. But the tone was convincing: he trusted her. They parted sworn allies; and, at the very moment of parting, Jacintha, who had cast many a furtive glance at the dead game, told Edouard demurely, Mademoiselle Rose was very fond of roast partridge. On this he made her take the whole bag; and went home on wings. Jacintha's revelation roused all that was noble and forgiving in him. His understanding and his heart expanded from that hour, and his fancy spread its pinions to the sun of love. Ah! generous Youth, let who will betray thee; let who will sneer at thee; let me, though young no longer, smile on thee and joy in thee! She he loved was sad, was poor, was menaced by many ills; then she needed a champion. He would be her unseen friend, her guardian angel. A hundred wild schemes whirled in his beating heart and brain. He could not go in-doors, indeed, no room could contain him: he made for a green lane he knew at the back of the village, and there he walked up and down for hours. The sun set, and the night came, and the stars glittered; but still he walked alone, inspired, exalted, full of generous and loving schemes: of sweet and tender fancies: a heart on fire; and youth the fuel, and the flame vestal.

CHAPTER III.

This very day was the anniversary of the baron's death.

The baroness kept her room all the morning, and took no nourishment but one cup of spurious coffee Rose brought her. Towards evening she came down-stairs. In the hall she found two chaplets of flowers; they were always placed there for her on this sad day. She took them in her hand, and went into the little oratory that was in the park; there she found two wax candles burning, and two fresh chaplets hung up. Her daughters had been there before her.

She knelt and prayed many hours for her husband's soul; then she rose and hung up one chaplet and came slowly away with the other in her hand. At the gate of the park, Josephine met her with tender anxiety in her sapphire eyes, and wreathed her arms round her, and whispered, "But you have your children still."

The baroness kissed her and they came towards the house together, the baroness leaning gently on her daughter's elbow.

Between the park and the angle of the chateau was a small plot of turf called at Beaurepaire the Pleasance, a name that had descended along with other traditions; and in the centre of this Pleasance, or Pleasaunce, stood a wonderful oak-tree. Its circumference was thirty-four feet. The baroness came to this ancient tree, and hung her chaplet on a mutilated limb called the "knights' bough."

The sun was setting tranquil and red; a broad ruby streak lingered on the deep green leaves of the prodigious oak. The baroness looked at it awhile in silence.

Then she spoke slowly to it and said, "You were here before us: you will be here when we are gone."

A spasm crossed Josephine's face, but she said nothing at the time. And so they went in together.

Now as this tree was a feat of nature, and, above all, played a curious part in our story, I will ask you to stay a few minutes and look at it, while I say what was known about it; not the thousandth part of what it could have told, if trees could speak as well as breathe.

The baroness did not exaggerate; the tree was far older than even this ancient family. They possessed among other archives a manuscript written by a monk, a son of the house, about four hundred years before our story, and containing many of the oral traditions about this tree that had come down to him from remote antiquity. According to this authority, the first Baron of Beaurepaire had pitched his tent under a fair oak-tree that stood prope rivum, near a brook. His grandson built a square tower hard by, and dug a moat that enclosed both tree and tower, and received the waters of the brook aforesaid.

At this time the tree seems only to have been remarked for its height. But, a century and a half before the monk wrote, it had become famous in all the district for its girth, and in the monk's own day had ceased to grow; but not begun to decay. The mutilated arm I have mentioned was once a long sturdy bough, worn smooth as velvet in one part from a curious cause: it ran about as high above the ground as a full-sized horse, and the knights and squires used to be forever vaulting upon it, the former in armor; the monk, when a boy, had seen them do it a thousand times. This bough broke in two, A.D. 1617: but the mutilated limb was still called the knights' bough, nobody knew why. So do names survive their ideas.

What had not this tree seen since first it came green and tender as a cabbage above the soil, and stood at the mercy of the first hare or rabbit that should choose to cut short its frail existence!

Since then eagles had perched on its crown, and wild boars fed without fear of man upon its acorns. Troubadours had sung beneath it to lords and ladies seated round, or walking on the grass and commenting the minstrel's tales of love by exchange of amorous glances. Mediaeval sculptors had taken its leaves, and wisely trusting to nature, had adorned churches with those leaves cut in stone.

It had seen a Norman duke conquer England, and English kings invade France and be crowned at Paris. It had seen a girl put knights to the rout, and seen the warrior virgin burned by envious priests with common consent both of the curs she had defended and the curs she had defeated.

Why, in its old age it had seen the rise of printing, and the first dawn of national civilization in Europe. It flourished and decayed in France; but it sprung in Gaul. And more remarkable still, though by all accounts it may see the world to an end, it was a tree in ancient history: its old age awaits the millennium; its first youth belonged to that great tract of time which includes the birth of Christ, the building of Rome, and the siege of Troy.

The tree had, ere this, mingled in the fortunes of the family. It had saved their lives and taken their lives. One lord of Beaurepaire, hotly pursued by his feudal enemies, made for the tree, and hid himself partly by a great bough, partly by the thick screen of leaves. The foe darted in, made sure he had taken to the house, ransacked it, and got into the cellar, where by good-luck was a store of Malvoisie: and so the oak and the vine saved the quaking baron. Another lord of Beaurepaire, besieged in his castle, was shot dead on the ramparts by a cross-bowman who had secreted himself unobserved in this tree a little before the dawn.

A young heir of Beaurepaire, climbing for a raven's nest to the top of this tree, lost his footing and fell, and died at its foot: and his mother in her anguish bade them cut down the tree that had killed her boy. But the baron her husband refused, and spake in this wise: "ytte ys eneugh that I lose mine sonne, I will nat alsoe lose mine Tre." In the male you see the sober sentiment of the proprietor outweighed the temporary irritation of the parent. Then the mother bought fifteen ells of black velvet, and stretched a pall from the knights' bough across the west side to another branch, and cursed the hand that should remove it, and she herself "wolde never passe the Tre neither going nor coming, but went still about." And when she died and should have been carried past the tree to the park, her dochter did cry from a window to the bearers, "Goe about! goe about!" and they went about, and all the company. And in time the velvet pall rotted, and was torn and driven away by the winds: and when the hand of Nature, and no human hand, had thus flouted and dispersed the trappings of the mother's grief, two pieces were picked up and preserved among the family relics: but the black velvet had turned a rusty red.

So the baroness did nothing new in this family when she hung her chaplet on the knights' bough; and, in fact, on the west side, about eighteen feet from the ground, there still mouldered one corner of an Atchievement an heir of Beaurepaire had nailed there two centuries before, when his predecessor died: "For," said he, "the chateau is of yesterday, but the tree has seen us all come and go." The inside of the oak was hollow as a drum; and on its east side yawned a fissure as high as a man and as broad as a street-door. Dard used to wheel his wheelbarrow into the tree at a trot, and there leave it.

Yet in spite of excavation and mutilation not life only but vigor dwelt in this wooden shell. The extreme ends of the longer boughs were firewood, touchwood, and the crown was gone this many a year: but narrow the circle a very little to where the indomitable trunk could still shoot sap from its cruse deep in earth, and there on every side burst the green foliage in its season countless as the sand. The leaves carved centuries ago from these very models, though cut in stone, were most of them mouldered, blunted, notched, deformed: but the delicate types came back with every summer, perfect and lovely as when the tree was but their elder brother: and greener than ever: for, from what cause nature only knows, the leaves were many shades richer than any other tree could show for a hundred miles round; a deep green, fiery, yet soft; and then their multitude — the staircases of foliage as you looked up the tree, and could scarce catch a glimpse of the sky. An inverted abyss of color, a mound, a dome, of flake emeralds that quivered in the golden air.

And now the sun sets; the green leaves are black; the moon rises: her cold light shoots across one half that giant stem.

How solemn and calm stands the great round tower of living wood, half ebony, half silver, with its mighty cloud above of flake jet leaves tipped with frosty fire!

Now is the still hour to repeat in a whisper the words of the dame of Beaurepaire, "You were here before us: you will be here when we are gone."

We leave the hoary king of trees standing in the moonlight, calmly defying time, and follow the creatures of a day; for, what they were, we are.

A spacious saloon panelled; dead but showy white picked out sparingly with gold. Festoons of fruits and flowers finely carved in wood on some of the panels. These also not smothered in gilding, but as it were gold speckled here and there, like tongues of flame winding among insoluble snow. Ranged against the walls were sofas and chairs covered with rich stuffs well worn. And in one little distant corner of the long room a gray-haired gentleman and two young ladies sat round a small plain table, on which burned a solitary candle; and a little way apart in this candle's twilight an old lady sat in an easy-chair, thinking of the past, scarce daring to inquire the future. Josephine and Rose were working: not fancy-work but needle-work; Dr. Aubertin writing. Every now and then he put the one candle nearer the girls. They raised no objection: only a few minutes after a white hand would glide from one or other of them like a serpent, and smoothly convey the light nearer to the doctor's manuscript.

"Is it not supper-time?" he inquired. "I have an inward monitor; and I think our dinner was more ethereal than usual."

"Hush!" said Josephine, and looked uneasily towards her mother. "Wax is so dear."

"Wax? — ah! — pardon me:" and the doctor returned hastily to his work. But Rose looked up and said, "I wonder Jacintha does not come; it is certainly past the hour;" and she pried into the room as if she expected to see Jacintha on the road. But she saw in fact very little of anything, for the spacious room was impenetrable to her eye; midway from the candle to the distant door its twilight deepened, and all became shapeless and sombre. The prospect ended sharp and black, as in those out-o'-door closets imagined and painted by a certain great painter, whose Nature comes to a full stop as soon as he has no further commercial need of her, instead of melting by fine expanse and exquisite gradation into genuine distance, as nature does in Claude and in nature. To reverse the picture, if you stood at the door you looked across forty feet of black, and the little corner seemed on fire, and the fair heads about the candle shone like the St. Cecilias and Madonnas in an antique stained-glass window.

At last the door opened, and another candle fired Jacintha's comely peasant face in the doorway. She put down her candle outside the door, and started as crow flies for the other light. After glowing a moment in the doorway she dived into the shadow and emerged into light again close to the table with napkins on her arm. She removed the work-box reverentially, the doctor's manuscript unceremoniously, and proceeded to lay a cloth: in which operation she looked at Rose a point-blank glance of admiration: then she placed the napkins; and in this process she again cast a strange look of interest upon Rose. The young lady noticed it this time, and looked inquiringly at her in return, half expecting some communication; but Jacintha lowered her eyes and bustled about the table. Then Rose spoke to her with a sort of instinct of curiosity, on the chance of drawing her out.

"Supper is late *tonight*, is it not, Jacintha?"

"Yes, mademoiselle; I have had more cooking than usual," and with this she delivered another point-blank look as before, and dived into the palpable obscure, and came to light in the doorway.

Her return was anxiously expected; for, if the truth must be told, they were very hungry. So rigorous was the economy in this decayed but honorable house that the wax candles burned *today* in the oratory had scrimped their dinner, unsubstantial as it was wont to be. Think of that, you in fustian jackets who grumble after meat. The door opened, Jacintha reappeared in the light of her candle a moment with a tray in both hands, and, approaching, was lost to view; but a strange and fragrant smell heralded her. All their eyes turned with curiosity towards the unwonted odor, and Jacintha dawned with three roast partridges on a dish.

They were wonder-struck, and looked from the birds to her in mute surprise, that was not diminished by a certain cynical indifference she put on. She avoided their eyes, and forcibly excluded from her face everything that could imply she did not serve up partridges to this family every night of her life.

"The supper is served, madame," said she, with a respectful courtesy and a mechanical tone, and, plunging into the night, swam out at her own candle, shut the door, and, unlocking her face that moment, burst out radiant, and so to the kitchen, and, with a tear in her eye, set-to and polished all the copper stewpans with a vigor and expedition unknown to the new-fangled domestic.

"Partridges, mamma! What next?"

"Pheasants, I hope," cried the doctor, gayly. "And after them hares; to conclude with royal venison. Permit me, ladies." And he set himself to carve with zeal.

Now nature is nature, and two pair of violet eyes brightened and dwelt on the fragrant and delicate food with demure desire; for all that, when Aubertin offered Josephine a wing, she declined it. "No partridge?" cried the savant, in utter amazement.

"Not *today*, dear friend; it is not a feast day *today*."

"Ah! no; what was I thinking of?"

"But you are not to be deprived," put in Josephine, anxiously. "We will not deny ourselves the pleasure of seeing you eat some."

"What!" remonstrated Aubertin, "am I not one of you?"

The baroness had attended to every word of this. She rose from her chair, and said quietly, "Both you and he and Rose will be so good as to let me see you eat."

"But, mamma," remonstrated Josephine and Rose in one breath.

"Je le veux," was the cold reply.

These were words the baroness uttered so seldom that they were little likely to be disputed.

The doctor carved and helped the young ladies and himself.

When they had all eaten a little, a discussion was observed to be going on between Rose and her sister. At last Aubertin caught these words, "It will be in vain; even you have not influence enough for that, Rose."

"We shall see," was the reply, and Rose put the wing of a partridge on a plate and rose calmly from her chair. She took the plate and put it on a little work-table by her mother's side. The others pretended to be all mouths, but they were all ears. The baroness looked in Rose's face with an air of wonder that was not very encouraging. Then, as Rose said nothing, she raised her aristocratic hand with a courteous but decided gesture of refusal.

Undaunted Rose laid her palm softly on the baroness's shoulder, and said to her as firmly as the baroness herself had just spoken, —

"Il le veut."

The baroness was staggered. Then she looked with moist eyes at the fair young face, then she reflected. At last she said, with an exquisite mixture of politeness and affection, "It is his daughter who has told me 'Il le veut.' I obey."

Rose returning like a victorious knight from the lists, saucily exultant, and with only one wet eyelash, was solemnly kissed and petted by Josephine and the doctor.

Thus they loved one another in this great, old, falling house. Their familiarity had no coarse side; a form, not of custom but affection, it went hand-in-hand with courtesy by day and night.

The love of the daughters for their mother had all the tenderness, subtlety, and unselfishness of womanly natures, together with a certain characteristic of the female character. And whither that one defect led them, and by what gradations, it may be worth the reader's while to observe.

The baroness retired to rest early; and she was no sooner gone than Josephine leaned over to Rose, and told her what their mother had said to the oak-tree. Rose heard this with anxiety; hitherto they had carefully concealed from their mother that the government claimed the right of selling the chateau to pay the creditors, etc.; and now both sisters feared the old lady had discovered it somehow, or why that strange thing she had said to the oak-tree? But Dr. Aubertin caught their remarks, and laid down his immortal MS. on French insects, to express his hope that they were putting a forced interpretation on the baroness's words.

"I think," said he, "she merely meant how short-lived are we all compared with this ancient oak. I should be very sorry to adopt the other interpretation; for if she knows she can at any moment be expelled from Beaurepaire, it will be almost as bad for her as the calamity itself; *that*, I think, would kill her."

"Why so?" said Rose, eagerly. "What is this house or that? Mamma will still have her daughters' love, go where she will."

Aubertin replied, "It is idle to deceive ourselves; at her age men and women hang to life by their habits; take her away from her chateau, from the little oratory where she prays every day for the departed, from her place in the sun on the south terrace, and from all the memories that surround her here; she would soon pine, and die."

Here the savant seeing a hobby-horse near, caught him and jumped on. He launched into a treatise upon the vitality of human beings, and proved that it is the mind which keeps the body of a man alive for so great a length of time as fourscore years; for that he had in the earlier part of his studies carefully dissected a multitude of animals, — frogs, rabbits, dogs, men, horses, sheep, squirrels, foxes, cats, etc., — and discovered no peculiarity in man's organs to account for his singular longevity, except in the brain or organ of mind. Thence he went to the longevity of men with contented minds, and the rapid decay of the careworn. Finally he succeeded in convincing them the baroness was so constituted, physically and mentally, that she would never move from Beaurepaire except into her grave. However, having thus terrified them, he proceeded to console them. "You have a friend," said he, "a powerful friend; and here in my pocket — somewhere — is a letter that proves it."

The letter was from Mr. Perrin the notary. It appeared by it that Dr. Aubertin had reminded the said Perrin of his obligations to the late baron, and entreated him to use all his influence to keep the estate in this ancient family.

Perrin had replied at first in a few civil lines; but his present letter was a long and friendly one. It made both the daughters of Beaurepaire shudder at the peril they had so narrowly escaped. For by it they now learned for the first time that one Jaques Bonard, a small farmer, to whom they owed but five thousand francs, had gone to the mayor and insisted, as he had a perfect right, on the estate being put up to public auction. This had come to Perrin's ears just in time, and he had instantly bought Bonard's debt, and stopped the auction; not, however, before the very bills were printed; for which he, Perrin, had paid, and now forwarded the receipt. He concluded by saying that the government agent was personally inert, and would never move a step in the matter unless driven by a creditor.

"But we have so many," said Rose in dismay. "We are not safe a day."

Aubertin assured her the danger was only in appearance. "Your large creditors are men of property, and such men let their funds lie unless compelled to move them. The small mortgagee, the petty miser, who has, perhaps, no investment to watch but one small loan, about which he is as anxious and as noisy as a hen with one chicken, he is the clamorous creditor, the harsh little egoist, who for fear of risking a crown piece would bring the Garden of Eden to the hammer. Now we are rid of that little wretch, Bonard, and have Perrin on our side; so there is literally nothing to fear."

The sisters thanked him warmly, and Rose shared his hopes; and said so; but Josephine was silent and thoughtful. Nothing more worth recording passed that night. But the next day was the first of May, Josephine's birthday.

Now they always celebrated this day as well as they could; and used to plant a tree, for one thing. Dard, well spurred by Jacintha, had got a little acacia; and they were all out in the Pleasaunce to plant it. Unhappily, they were a preposterous time making up their feminine minds where to have it set; so Dard turned rusty and said the park was the best place for it. There it could do no harm, stick it where you would.

"And who told you to put in your word?" inquired Jacintha. "You're here to dig the hole where mademoiselle chooses; not to argufy."

Josephine whispered Rose, "I admire the energy of her character. Could she be induced to order once for all where the poor thing is to be planted?"

"Then where *will* you have it, mademoiselle?" asked Dard, sulkily.

"Here, I think, Dard," said Josephine sweetly.

Dard grinned malignantly, and drove in his spade. "It will never be much bigger than a stinging nettle," thought he, "for the roots of the oak have sucked every atom of heart out of this." His black soul exulted secretly.

Jacintha stood by Dard, inspecting his work; the sisters intertwined, a few feet from him. The baroness turned aside, and went to look for a moment at the chaplet she had placed yesterday on the oak-tree bough. Presently she uttered a slight ejaculation; and her daughters looked up directly.

"Come here, children," said she. They glided to her in a moment; and found her eyes fixed upon an object that lay on the knights' bough.

It was a sparkling purse.

I dare say you have noticed that the bark on the boughs of these very ancient trees is as deeply furrowed as the very stem of an oak tree that boasts but a few centuries; and in one of these deep furrows lay a green silk purse with gold coins glittering through the glossy meshes.

Josephine and Rose eyed it a moment like startled deer; then Rose pounced on it. "Oh, how heavy!" she cried. This brought up Dard and Jacintha, in time to see Rose pour ten shining gold pieces out of the purse into her pink-white palm, while her face flushed and her eyes glittered with excitement. Jacintha gave a scream of joy; "Our luck is turned," she cried, superstitiously. Meanwhile, Josephine had found a slip of paper close to the purse. She opened it with nimble fingers; it contained one line in a hand like that of a copying clerk: *From a friend: in part payment of a great debt.*

Keen, piquant curiosity now took the place of surprise. Who could it be? The baroness's suspicion fell at once on Dr. Aubertin. But Rose maintained he had not ten gold pieces in the world. The baroness appealed to Josephine. She only blushed in an extraordinary way, and said nothing. They puzzled, and puzzled, and were as much in the dark as ever, when lo! one of the suspected parties delivered himself into the hands of justice with ludicrous simplicity. It happened to be Dr. Aubertin's hour of out-a-door study; and he came mooning along, buried in a book, and walked slowly into the group — started, made a slight apology, and was mooning off, lost in his book again. Then the baroness, who had eyed him with grim suspicion all the time, said with well-affected nonchalance, "Doctor, you dropped your purse; we have just picked it up." And she handed it to him. "Thank you, madame," said he, and took it quietly without looking at it, put it in his pocket, and retired, with his soul in his book. They stared comically at one another, and at this cool hand. "It's no more his than it's mine," said Jacintha, bluntly. Rose darted after the absorbed student, and took him captive. "Now, doctor," she cried, "be pleased to come out of the clouds." And with the word she whipped the purse out of his coat pocket, and holding it right up before his eye, insisted on his telling her whether that was his purse or not, money and all. Thus adjured, he disowned the property mighty coolly, for a retired physician, who had just pocketed it.

"No, my dear," said he; "and, now I think of it, I have not carried a purse this twenty years."

The baroness, as a last resource, appealed to his honor whether he had not left a purse and paper on the knights' bough. The question had to be explained by Josephine, and then the doctor surprised them all by being rather affronted — for once in his life.

"Baroness," said he, "I have been your friend and pensioner nearly twenty years; if by some strange chance money were to come into my hands, I should not play you a childish trick like this. What! have I not the right to come to you, and say, 'My old friend, here I bring you back a very small part of all I owe you?'"

"What geese we are," remarked Rose. "Dear doctor, *you* tell us who it is."

Dr. Aubertin reflected a single moment; then said he could make a shrewd guess.

"Who? who? who?" cried the whole party.

"Perrin the notary."

It was the baroness's turn to be surprised; for there was nothing romantic about Perrin the notary. Aubertin, however, let her know that he was in private communication with the said Perrin, and this was not the first friendly act the good notary had done her in secret.

While he was converting the baroness to his view, Josephine and Rose exchanged a signal, and slipped away round an angle of the chateau.

"Who is it?" said Rose.

"It is some one who has a delicate mind."

"Clearly, and therefore not a notary."

"Rose, dear, might it not be some person who has done us some wrong, and is perhaps penitent?"

"Certainly; one of our tenants, or creditors, you mean; but then, the paper says 'a friend.' Stay, it says a debtor. Why a debtor? Down with enigmas!"

"Rose, love," said Josephine, coaxingly, "think of some one that might — since it is not the doctor, nor Monsieur Perrin, might it not be — for after all, he would naturally be ashamed to appear before me."

"Before you? Who do you mean?" asked Rose nervously, catching a glimpse now.

"He who once pretended to love me."

"Josephine, you love that man still."

"No, no. Spare me!"

"You love him just the same as ever. Oh, it is wonderful; it is terrible; the power he has over you; over your judgment as well as your heart."

"No! for I believe he has forgotten my very name; don't you think so?"

"Dear Josephine, can you doubt it? Come, you do doubt it."

"Sometimes."

"But why? for what reason?"

"Because of what he said to me as we parted at that gate; the words and the voice seem still to ring like truth across the weary years. He said, 'I am to join the army of the Pyrenees, so fatal to our troops; but say to me what you never yet have said, Camille, I love you: and I swear I will come back alive.' So then I said to him, 'I love you,' — and he never came back."

"How could he come here? a deserter, a traitor!"

"It is not true; it is not in his nature; inconstancy may be. Tell me that he never really loved me, and I will believe you; but not that he is a traitor. Let me weep over my past love, not blush for it."

"Past? You love him *today* as you did three years ago."

"No," said Josephine, "no; I love no one. I never shall love any one again."

"But him. It is that love which turns your heart against others. Oh, yes, you love him, dearest, or why should you fancy our secret benefactor *could* be that Camille?"

"Why? Because I was mad: because it is impossible; but I see my folly. I am going in."

"What! don't you care to know who I think it was, perhaps?"

"No," said Josephine sadly and doggedly; she added with cold nonchalance, "I dare say time will show." And she went slowly in, her hand to her head.

"Her birthday!" sighed Rose.

The donor, whoever he was, little knew the pain he was inflicting on this distressed but proud family, or the hard battle that ensued between their necessities and their delicacy. The ten gold pieces were a perpetual temptation: a daily conflict. The words that accompanied the donation offered a bait. Their pride and dignity declined it; but these bright bits of gold cost them many a sharp pang. You must know that Josephine and Rose had worn out their mourning by this time; and were obliged to have recourse to gayer materials that lay in their great wardrobes, and were older, but less worn. A few of these gold pieces would have enabled the poor girls to be neat, and yet to mourn their father openly. And it went through and through those tender, simple hearts, to think that they must be disunited, even in so small a thing as dress; that while their mother remained in her weeds, they must seem no longer to share her woe.

The baroness knew their feeling, and felt its piety, and yet could not bow her dignity to say, "Take five of these bits of gold, and let us all look what we are — one." Yet in this, as in everything else, they supported each other. They resisted, they struggled, and with a wrench they conquered day by day. At last, by general consent, Josephine locked up the tempter, and they looked at it no more. But the little bit of paper met a kinder fate. Rose made a little frame for it, and it was kept in a drawer, in the salon: and often looked at and blessed. Just when they despaired of human friendship, this paper with the sacred word "friend" written on it, had fallen all in a moment on their aching hearts.

They could not tell whence it came, this blessed word.

But men dispute whence comes the dew?

Then let us go with the poets, who say it comes from heaven.

And even so that sweet word, friend, dropped like the dew from heaven on these afflicted ones.

So they locked the potent gold away from themselves, and took the kind slip of paper to their hearts.

The others left off guessing: Aubertin had it all his own way: he upheld Perrin as their silent benefactor, and bade them all observe that the worthy notary had never visited the chateau openly since the day the purse was left there. "Guilty conscience," said Aubertin dryly.

One day in his walks he met a gaunt figure ambling on a fat pony: he stopped him, and, holding up his finger, said abruptly, "We have found you out, Maitre Perrin."

The notary changed color.

"Oh, never be ashamed," said Aubertin; "a good action done slyly is none the less a good action."

The notary wore a puzzled air.

Aubertin admired his histrionic powers in calling up this look.

"Come, come, don't overdo it," said he. "Well, well; they cannot profit by your liberality; but you will be rewarded in a better world, take my word for that."

The notary muttered indistinctly. He was a man of moderate desires; would have been quite content if there had been no other world in perspective. He had studied this one, and made it pay: did not desire a better; sometimes feared a worse.

"Ah!" said Aubertin, "I see how it is; we do not like to hear ourselves praised, do we? When shall we see you at the chateau?"

"I propose to call on the baroness the moment I have good news to bring," replied Perrin; and to avoid any more compliments spurred the dun pony suddenly; and he waddled away.

Now this Perrin was at that moment on the way to dine with a character who plays a considerable part in the tale — Commandant Raynal. Perrin had made himself useful to the commandant, and had become his legal adviser. And, this very day after dinner, the commandant having done a good day's work permitted himself a little sentiment over the bottle, and to a man he thought his friend. He let out that he had a heap of money he did not know what to do with, and almost hated it now his mother was gone and could not share it.

The man of law consoled him with oleaginous phrases: told

him he very much underrated the power of money. His hoard, directed by a judicious adviser, would make him a landed proprietor, and the husband of some young lady, all beauty, virtue, and accomplishment, whose soothing influence would soon heal the sorrow caused by an excess of filial sentiment.

"Halt!" shouted Raynal: "say that again in half the words."

Perrin was nettled, for he prided himself on his colloquial style.

"You can buy a fine estate and a chaste wife with the money," snapped this smooth personage, substituting curt brutality for honeyed prolixity.

The soldier was struck by the propositions the moment they flew at him small and solid, like bullets.

"I've no time," said he, "to be running after women. But the estate I'll certainly have, because you can get that for me without my troubling my head."

"Is it a commission, then?" asked the other sharply.

"Of course. Do you think I speak for the sake of talking?"

And so Perrin received formal instructions to look out for a landed estate; and he was to receive a handsome commission as agent.

Now to settle this affair, and pocket a handsome percentage for himself, he had only to say "Beaurepaire."

Well, he didn't. Never mentioned the place; nor the fact that it was for sale.

Such are all our agents, when rival speculators. Mind that. Still it is a terrible thing to be so completely in the power of any man of the world, as from this hour Beaurepaire was in the power of Perrin the notary.

CHAPTER IV.

Edouard Riviere was unhappy. She never came out now. This alone made the days dark to him. And then he began to fear it was him she shunned. She must have seen him lie in wait for her; and so she would come out no more. He prowled about and contrived to fall in with Jacintha; he told her his grief. She assured him the simple fact was their mourning was worn out, and they were ashamed to go abroad in colors. This revelation made his heart yearn still more.

"O Jacintha," said he, "if I could only make a beginning; but here we might live a century in the same parish, and not one chance for a poor wretch to make acquaintance."

Jacintha admitted this, and said gentlefolks were to be pitied. "Why, if it was the likes of me, you and I should have made friends long before now."

Jacintha herself was puzzled what to do; she would have told Rose if she had felt sure it would be well received; but she could not find out that the young lady had even noticed the existence of Edouard. But her brain worked, and lay in wait for an opportunity.

One came sooner than she expected. One morning at about six o'clock, as she came home from milking the cow, she caught sight of young Riviere trying to open the iron gate. "What is up now?" thought she; suddenly the truth flashed upon her, clear as day. She put her pail down and stole upon him. "You want to leave us another purse," said she. He colored all over and panted.

"How did you know? how could you know? you won't betray me? you won't be so cruel? you promised."

"Me betray you," said Jacintha; "why, I'll help you; and then they will be able to buy mourning, you know, and then they will come out, and give you a chance. You can't open that gate, for it's locked. But you come round to the lane, and I'll get you the key; it is hanging up in the kitchen."

The key was in her pocket. But the sly jade wanted him away from that gate; it commanded a view of the Pleasaunce. He was no sooner safe in the lane, than she tore up-stairs to her young ladies, and asked them with affected calm whether they would like to know who left the purse.

"Oh, yes, yes!" screamed Rose.

"Then come with me. You *are* dressed; never mind your bonnets, or you will be too late."

Questions poured on her; but she waived all explanation, and did not give them time to think, or Josephine, for one, she knew would raise objections. She led the way to the Pleasaunce, and, when she got to the ancestral oak, she said hurriedly, "Now, mesdemoiselles, hide in there, and as still as mice. You'll soon know who leaves the purses."

With this she scudded to the lane, and gave Edouard the key. "Look sharp," said she, "before they get up; it's almost their dressing time."

"*You'll soon know who leaves the purses!*"

Curiosity, delicious curiosity, thrilled our two daughters of Eve.

This soon began to alternate with chill misgivings at the novelty of the situation.

"She is not coming back," said Josephine ruefully.

"No," said Rose, "and suppose when we pounce out on him, it should be a stranger."

"Pounce on him? surely we are not to do that?"

"Oh, y-yes; that is the p-p-programme," quavered Rose.

A key grated, and the iron gate creaked on its hinges. They ran together and pinched one another for mutual support, but did not dare to speak.

Presently a man's shadow came slap into the tree. They crouched and quivered, and expected to be caught instead of catching, and wished themselves safe back in bed, and all this a nightmare, and no worse.

At last they recovered themselves enough to observe that this shadow, one half of which lay on the ground, while the head and shoulders went a little way up the wall of the tree, represented a man's profile, not his front face. The figure, in short, was standing between them and the sun, and was contemplating the chateau, not the tree.

The shadow took off its hat to Josephine, in the tree. Then would she have screamed if she had not bitten her white hand instead, and made a red mark thereon.

It wiped its brow with a handkerchief; it had walked fast, poor thing! The next moment it was away.

They looked at one another and panted. They scarcely dared do it before. Then Rose, with one hand on her heaving bosom, shook her little white fist viciously at where the figure must be, and perhaps a comical desire of vengeance stimulated her curiosity. She now glided through the fissure like a cautious panther from her den; and noiseless and supple as a serpent began to wind slowly round the tree. She soon came to a great protuberance in the tree, and twining and peering round it with diamond eye, she saw a very young, very handsome gentleman, stealing on tiptoe to the nearest flower-bed. Then she saw him take a purse out of his bosom, and drop it on the bed. This done, he came slowly past the tree again, and was even heard to vent a little innocent chuckle of intense satisfaction: but of brief duration; for, when Rose saw the purse leave his hand, she made a rapid signal to Josephine to wheel round the other side of the tree, and, starting together with admirable concert, both the daughters of Beaurepaire glided into sight with a vast appearance of composure.

Two women together are really braver than fifteen separate; but still, most of this tranquillity was merely put on, but so admirably that Edouard Riviere had no chance with them. He knew nothing about their tremors; all he saw or heard was, a rustle, then a flap on each side of him as of great wings, and two lovely women were upon him with angelic swiftness. "Ah!" he cried out with a start, and glanced from the first-comer, Rose, to the gate. But Josephine was on that side by this time, and put up her hand, as much as to say, "You can't pass here." In such situations, the mind works quicker than lightning. He took off his hat, and stammered an excuse — "Come to look at the oak." At this moment Rose pounced on the purse, and held it up to Josephine. He was caught. His only chance now was to bolt for the mark and run; but it was not the notary, it was a novice who lost his presence of mind, or perhaps thought it rude to run when a lady told him to stand still. All he did was to crush his face into his two hands, round which his cheeks and neck now blushed red as blood. Blush? they could both see the color rush like a wave to the very roots of his hair and the tips of his fingers.

The moment our heroines, who, in that desperation which is one of the forms of cowardice, had hurled themselves on the foe, saw this, flash — the quick-witted poltroons exchanged purple lightning over Edouard's drooping head, and enacted lionesses in a moment.

It was with the quiet composure of lofty and powerful natures that Josephine opened on him. "Compose yourself, sir; and be so good as to tell us who you are." Edouard must answer. Now he could not speak through his hands; and he could not face a brace of tranquil lionesses: so he took a middle course, removed one hand, and shading himself from Josephine with the other, he gasped out, "I am — my name is Riviere; and I — I — ladies!"

"I am afraid we frighten you," said Josephine, demurely.

"Don't be frightened," said Rose, majestically; "we are not

very angry, only a *little* curious to know why you water our flowers with gold."

At this point-blank thrust, and from her, Edouard was so confounded and distressed, they both began to pity him. He stammered out that he was so confused he did not know what to say. He couldn't think how ever he could have taken such a liberty; might he be permitted to retire? and with this he tried to slip away.

"Let me detain you one instant," said Josephine, and made for the house.

Left alone so suddenly with the culprit, the dignity, and majesty, and valor of Rose seemed to ooze gently out; and she stood blushing, and had not a word to say; no more had Edouard. But he hung his head, and she hung her head. And, somehow or other, whenever she raised her eyes to glance at him, he raised his to steal a look at her, and mutual discomfiture resulted.

This awkward, embarrassing delirium was interrupted by Josephine's return. She now held another purse in her hand, and quietly poured the rest of the coin into it. She then, with a blush, requested him to take back the money.

At that he found his tongue. "No, no," he cried, and put up his hands in supplication. "Ladies, do let me speak *one* word to you. Do not reject my friendship. You are alone in the world; your father is dead; your mother has but you to lean on. After all, I am your neighbor, and neighbors should be friends. And I am your debtor; I owe you more than you could ever owe me; for ever since I came into this neighborhood I have been happy. No man was ever so happy as I, ever since one day I was walking, and met for the first time an angel. I don't say it was you, Mademoiselle Rose. It might be Mademoiselle Josephine."

"How pat he has got our names," said Rose, smiling.

"A look from that angel has made me so good, so happy. I used to vegetate, but now I live. Live! I walk on wings, and tread on roses. Yet you insist on declining a few miserable louis d'or from him who owes you so much. Well, don't be angry; I'll take them back, and throw them into the nearest pond, for they are really no use to me. But then you will be generous in your turn. You will accept my devotion, my services. You have no brother, you know; well, I have no sisters; let me be your brother, and your servant forever."

At all this, delivered in as many little earnest pants as there were sentences, the water stood in the fair eyes he was looking into so piteously.

Josephine was firm, but angelical. "We thank you, Monsieur

Riviere," said she, softly, "for showing us that the world is still embellished with hearts like yours. Here is the money;" and she held it out in her creamy hand.

"But we are very grateful," put in Rose, softly and earnestly.

"That we are," said Josephine, "and we beg to keep the purse as a souvenir of one who tried to do us a kindness without mortifying us. And now, Monsieur Riviere, you will permit us to bid you adieu."

Edouard was obliged to take the hint. "It is I who am the intruder," said he. "Mesdemoiselles, conceive, if you can, my pride and my disappointment." He then bowed low; they courtesied low to him in return; and he retired slowly in a state of mixed feeling indescribable.

With all their sweetness and graciousness, he felt overpowered by their high breeding, their reserve, and their composure, in a situation that had set his heart beating itself nearly out of his bosom. He acted the scene over again, only much more adroitly, and concocted speeches for past use, and was very hot and very cold by turns.

I wish he could have heard what passed between the sisters as soon as ever he was out of earshot. It would have opened his eyes, and given him a little peep into what certain writers call "the sex."

"Poor boy," murmured Josephine, "he has gone away unhappy."

"Oh, I dare say he hasn't gone far," replied Rose, gayly. "I shouldn't if I was a boy."

Josephine held up her finger like an elder sister; then went on to say she really hardly knew why she had dismissed him.

"Well, dear," said Rose, dryly, "since you admit so much, I must say I couldn't help thinking — while you were doing it — we were letting 'the poor boy' off ridiculously cheap."

"At least I did my duty?" suggested Josephine, inquiringly.

"Magnificently; you overawed even me. So now to business, as the gentlemen say. Which of us two takes him?"

"Takes whom?" inquired Josephine, opening her lovely eyes.

"Edouard," murmured Rose, lowering hers.

Josephine glared on the lovely minx with wonder and comical horror.

"Oh! you shall have him," said Rose, "if you like. You are the eldest, you know."

"Fie!"

"Do now; *to oblige me.*"

"For shame! Rose. Is this you? talking like that!"

"Oh! there's no compulsion, dear; I never force young ladies' inclinations. So you decline him?"

"Of course I decline him."

"Then, oh, you dear, darling Josephine, this is the prettiest present you ever made me," and she kissed her vehemently.

Josephine was frightened now. She held Rose out at arm's length with both hands, and looked earnestly into her, and implored her not to play with fire. "Take warning by me."

Rose recommended her to keep her pity for Monsieur Riviere, "who had fallen into nice hands," she said. That no doubt might remain on that head, she whispered mysteriously, but with much gravity and conviction, "I am an Imp;" and aimed at Josephine with her forefinger to point the remark. For one second she stood and watched this important statement sink into her sister's mind, then set-to and gambolled elfishly round her as she moved stately and thoughtful across the grass to the chateau.

Two days after this a large tree was blown down in Beaurepaire park, and made quite a gap in the prospect. You never know what a big thing a leafy tree is till it comes down. And this ill wind blew Edouard good; for it laid bare the chateau to his inquiring telescope. He had not gazed above half an hour, when a female figure emerged from the chateau. His heart beat. It was only Jacintha. He saw her look this way and that, and presently Dard appeared, and she sent him with his axe to the fallen tree. Edouard watched him hacking away at it. Presently his heart gave a violent leap; for why? two ladies emerged from the Pleasaunce and walked across the park. They came up to Dard, and stood looking at the tree and Dard hacking it, and Edouard watched them greedily. You know we all love to magnify her we love. And this was a delightful way of doing it. It is "a system of espionage" that prevails under every form of government. How he gazed, and gazed, on his now polar star; studied every turn, every gesture, with eager delight, and tried to gather what she said, or at least the nature of it.

But by and by they left Dard and strolled towards the other end of the park. Then did our astronomer fling down his tube, and come running out in hopes of intercepting them, and seeming to meet them by some strange fortuity. Hope whispered he should be blessed with a smile; perhaps a word even. So another minute and he was running up the road to Beaurepaire. But his good heart was doomed to be diverted to a much humbler object than his idol; as he came near the fallen tree he heard loud cries for help, followed by groans of pain. He bounded over the hedge, and there was Dard hanging over his axe, moaning. "What is the matter? what is the matter?" cried Edouard, running to him.

"Oh! oh! cut my foot. Oh!"

Edouard looked, and turned sick, for there was a gash right through Dard's shoe, and the blood welling up through it. But, recovering himself by an effort of the will, he cried out, "Courage, my lad! don't give in. Thank Heaven there's no artery there. Oh, dear, it is a terrible cut! Let us get you home, that is the first thing. Can you walk?"

"Lord bless you, no! nor stand neither without help."

Edouard flew to the wheelbarrow, and, reversing it, spun a lot of billet out. "Ye must not do that," said Dard with all the energy he was capable of in his present condition. "Why, that is Jacintha's wood." — "To the devil with Jacintha and her wood too!" cried Edouard, "a man is worth more than a fagot. Come, I shall wheel you home: it is only just across the park."

With some difficulty he lifted him into the barrow. Luckily he had his shooting-jacket on with a brandy-flask in it: he administered it with excellent effect.

The ladies, as they walked, saw a man wheeling a barrow across the park, and took no particular notice; but, as Riviere was making for the same point they were, though at another angle, presently the barrow came near enough for them to see Dard's head and arms in it. Rose was the first to notice this. "Look! look! if he is not wheeling Dard in the barrow now."

"Who?"

"Can you ask? Who provides all our excitement?"

Josephine instantly divined there was something amiss. "Consider," said she, "Monsieur Riviere would not wheel Dard all across the park for amusement."

Rose assented; and in another minute, by a strange caprice of fate, those Edouard had come to intercept, quickened their pace to intercept him. As soon as he saw their intention he thrilled all over, but did not slacken his pace. He told Dard to take his coat and throw it over his foot, for here were the young ladies coming.

"What for?" said Dard sulkily. "No! let them see what they have done with their little odd jobs: this is my last for one while. I sha'n't go on two legs again this year."

The ladies came up with them.

"O monsieur!" said Josephine, "what is the matter?"

"We have met with a little accident, mademoiselle, that is all. Dard has hurt his foot; nothing to speak of, but I thought he would be best at home."

Rose raised the coat which Riviere, in spite of Dard, had flung over his foot.

"He is bleeding! Dard is bleeding! Oh, my poor Dard. Oh! oh!"

"Hush, Rose!"

"No, don't put him out of heart, mademoiselle. Take another pull at the flask, Dard. If you please, ladies, I must have him home without delay."

"Oh yes, but I want him to have a surgeon," cried Josephine. "And we have no horses nor people to send off as we used to have."

"But you have me, mademoiselle," said Edouard tenderly. "Me, who would go to the world's end for you." He said this to Josephine, but his eye sought Rose. "I'm a famous runner," he added, a little bumptiously; "I'll be at the town in half an hour, and send a surgeon up full gallop."

"You have a good heart," said Rose simply.

He bowed his blushing, delighted face, and wheeled Dard to his cottage hard by with almost more than mortal vigor. How softly, how nobly, that frolicsome girl could speak! Those sweet words rang in his ears and ran warm round and round his heart, as he straightened his arms and his back to the work. When they had gone about a hundred yards, a single snivel went off in the wheelbarrow. Five minutes after, Dard was at home in charge of his grandmother, his shoe off, his foot in a wet linen cloth; and Edouard, his coat tied round the neck, squared his shoulders, and ran the two short leagues out. He ran them in forty minutes, found the surgeon at home, told the case, pooh-poohed that worthy's promise to go to the patient presently, darted into his stable, saddled the horse, brought him round, saw the surgeon into the saddle, started him, dined at the restaurateur's, strolled back, and was in time to get a good look at the chateau of Beaurepaire just as the sun set on it.

Jacintha came into Dard's cottage that evening.

"So you have been at it, my man," cried she cheerfully and rather roughly, then sat down and rocked herself, with her apron over her head. She explained this anomalous proceeding to his grandmother privately. "I thought I would keep his heart up anyway, but you see I was not fit."

Next morning, as Riviere sat writing, he received an unexpected visit from Jacintha. She came in with her finger to her lips, and said, "You prowl about Dard's cottage. They are sure to go and see him every day, and him wounded in their service."

"Oh, you good girl! you dear girl!" cried Edouard.

She did not reply in words, but, after going to the door, returned and gave him a great kiss without ceremony. "Dare say you know what that's for," said she, and went off with a clear conscience and reddish cheeks.

Dard's grandmother had a little house, a little land, a little money, and a little cow. She could just maintain Dard and herself, and her resources enabled Dard to do so many little odd jobs for love, yet keep his main organ tolerably filled.

"Go to bed, my little son, since you have got hashed," said she. — "Bed be hanged," cried he. "What good is bed? That's a silly old custom wants doing away with. It weakens you: it turns you into train oil: it is the doctor's friend, and the sick man's bane. Many a one dies through taking to bed, that could have kept his life if he had kept his feet like a man. If I had cut myself in two I would not go to bed, — till I go to the bed with a spade in it. No! sit up like Julius Caesar; and die as you lived, in your clothes: don't strip yourself: let the old women strip you; that is their delight laying out a chap; that is the time they brighten up, the old sorceresses." He concluded this amiable rhapsody, the latter part of which was levelled at a lugubrious weakness of his grandmother's for the superfluous embellishment of the dead, by telling her it was bad enough to be tied by the foot like an ass, without settling down on his back like a cast sheep. "Give me the armchair. I'll sit in it, and, if I have any friends, they will show it now: they will come and tell me what is going on in the village, for I can't get out to see it and hear it, they must know that."

Seated in state in his granny's easy-chair, the loss of which after thirty years' use made her miserable, she couldn't tell why, le Sieur Dard awaited his friends.

They did not come.

The rain did, and poured all the afternoon. Night succeeded, and solitude. Dard boiled over with bitterness. "They are a lot of pigs then, all those fellows I have drunk with at Bigot's and Simmet's. Down with all fair-weather friends."

The next day the sun shone, the air was clear, and the sky blue. "Ah! let us see now," cried Dard.

Alas! no fellow-drinkers, no fellow-smokers, came to console their hurt fellow. And Dard, who had boiled with anger yesterday, was now sad and despondent. "Down with egotists," he groaned.

About three in the afternoon came a tap at the door.

"Ah! at last," cried Dard: "come in!"

The door was slowly opened, and two lovely faces appeared at the threshold. The demoiselles De Beaurepaire wore a tender look of interest and pity when they caught sight of Dard, and on the old woman courtesying to them they courtesied to her and Dard. The next moment they were close to him, one a little to his right, the other to his left, and two pair of sapphire eyes with the mild lustre of sympathy playing down incessantly upon him. How was he? How had he slept? Was he in pain? Was he in much pain? tell the truth now. Was there anything to eat or drink he could fancy? Jacintha should make it and bring it, if it was within their means. A prince could not have had more solicitous attendants, nor a fairy king lovelier and less earthly ones.

He looked in heavy amazement from one to the other. Rose bent, and was by some supple process on one knee, taking the measure of the wounded foot. When she first approached it he winced: but the next moment he smiled. He had never been touched like this — it was contact and no contact — she treated his foot as the zephyr the violets — she handled it as if it had been some sacred thing. By the help of his eye he could just know she was touching him. Presently she informed him he was measured for a list shoe: and she would run home for the materials. During her absence came a timid tap to the door; and Edouard Riviere entered. He was delighted to see Josephine, and made sure Rose was not far off. It was Dard who let out that she was gone to Beaurepaire for some cloth to make him a shoe. This information set Edouard fidgeting on his chair. He saw such a chance as was not likely to occur again. He rose with feigned nonchalance, and saying, "I leave you in good hands; angel visitors are best enjoyed alone," slowly retired, with a deep obeisance. Once outside the door, dignity vanished in alacrity; he flew off into the park, and ran as hard as he could towards the chateau. He was within fifty yards of the little gate, when sure enough Rose emerged. They met; his heart beat violently. "Mademoiselle," he faltered.

"Ah! it is Monsieur Riviere, I declare," said Rose, coolly; all over blushes though.

"Yes, mademoiselle, and I am so out of breath. Mademoiselle Josephine awaits you at Dard's house."

"She sent you for me?" inquired Rose, demurely.

"Not positively. But I could see I should please her by coming for you; there is, I believe, a bull or so about."

"A bull or two! don't talk in that reckless way about such things. She has done well to send you; let us make haste."

"But I am a little out of breath."

"Oh, never mind that! I abhor bulls."

"But, mademoiselle, we are not come to them yet, and the faster we go now the sooner we shall."

"Yes; but I always like to get a disagreeable thing over as soon as possible," said Rose, slyly.

"Ah," replied Edouard, mournfully, "in that case let us make haste."

After a little spurt, mademoiselle relaxed the pace of her own accord, and even went slower than before. There was an awkward silence. Edouard eyed the park boundary, and thought, "Now what I have to say I must say before we get to you;" and being thus impressed with the necessity of immediate action, he turned to lead.

Rose eyed him and the ground, alternately, from under her long lashes.

At last he began to color and flutter. She saw something was coming, and all the woman donned defensive armor.

"Mademoiselle."

"Monsieur."

"Is it quite decided that your family refuse my acquaintance, my services, which I still — forgive me — press on you? Ah! Mademoiselle Rose, am I never to have the happiness of — of — even speaking to you?"

"It seems so," said Rose, ironically.

"Have you then decided against me too?"

"I?" asked Rose. "What have I to do with questions of etiquette? I am only a child: so considered at least."

"You a child — an angel like you?"

"Ask any of them, they will tell you I am a child; and it is to that I owe this conversation, no doubt; if you did not look on me as a child, you would not take this liberty with me," said the young cat, scratching without a moment's notice.

"Mademoiselle, do not be angry. I was wrong."

"Oh! never mind. Children are little creatures without reserve, and treated accordingly, and to notice them is to honor them."

"Adieu then, mademoiselle. Try to believe no one respects you more than I do."

"Yes, let us part, for there is Dard's house; and I begin to suspect that Josephine never sent you."

"I confess it."

"There, he confesses it. I thought so all along; *What a dupe i have been!*"

"I will offend no more," said poor silly Edouard. "Adieu,

mademoiselle. May you find friends as sincere as I am, and more to your taste!"

"Heaven hear your prayers!" replied the malicious thing, casting up her eyes with a mock tragic air.

Edouard sighed; a chill conviction that she was both heartless and empty fell on him. He turned away without another word. She called to him with a sudden airy cheerfulness that made him start. "Stay, monsieur, I forgot — I have a favor to ask you."

"I wish I could believe that:" and his eyes brightened.

Rose stopped, and began to play with her parasol. "You seem," said she softly, "to be pretty generous in bestowing your acquaintance on strangers. I should be glad if I might secure you for a dear friend of mine, Dr. Aubertin. He will not discredit my recommendation; and he will not make so many difficulties as we do; shall I tell you why? Because he is really worth knowing. In short, believe me, it will be a valuable acquaintance for you — and for him," added she with all the grace of the De Beaurepaires.

Many a man, inferior in a general way to Edouard Riviere, would have made a sensible reply to this. Such as, "Oh, any friend of yours, mademoiselle, must be welcome to me," or the like. But the proposal caught Edouard on his foible, his vanity, to wit; and our foibles are our manias. He was mortified to the heart's core. "She refuses to know me herself," thought he, "but she will use my love to make me amuse that old man." His heart swelled against her injustice and ingratitude, and his crushed vanity turned to strychnine. "Mademoiselle," said he, bitterly and doggedly, but sadly, "were I so happy as to have your esteem, my heart would overflow, not only on the doctor but on every honest person around. But if I must not have the acquaintance I value more than life, suffer me to be alone in the world, and never to say a word either to Dr. Aubertin, or to any human creature if I can help it."

The imperious young beauty drew herself up directly. "So be it, monsieur; you teach me how a child should be answered that forgets herself, and asks a favor of a stranger — a perfect stranger," added she, maliciously.

Could one of the dog-days change to mid-winter in a second, it would hardly seem so cold and cross as Rose de Beaurepaire turned from the smiling, saucy fairy of the moment before. Edouard felt as it were a portcullis of ice come down between her and him. She courtesied and glided away. He bowed and stood frozen to the spot.

He felt so lonely and so bitter, he must go to Jacintha for comfort.

He took advantage of the ladies being with Dard, and marched boldly into the kitchen of Beaurepaire.

"Well, I never," cried Jacintha. "But, after all, why not?"

He hurled himself on the kitchen table (clean as china), and told her it was all over. "She hates me now; but it is not my fault," and so poured forth his tale, and feeling sure of sympathy, asked Jacintha whether it was not bitterly unjust of Rose to refuse him her own acquaintance, yet ask him to amuse that old fogy.

Jacintha stood with her great arms akimbo, taking it all in, and looking at him with a droll expression of satirical wonder.

"Now you listen to a parable," said she. "Once there was a little boy madly in love with raspberry jam."

"A thing I hate."

"Don't tell me! Who hates raspberry jam? He came to the store closet, where he knew there were jars of it, and — oh! misery — the door was locked. He kicked the door, and wept bitterly. His mamma came and said, 'Here is the key,' and gave him the key. And what did he do? Why, he fell to crying and roaring, and kicking the door. 'I don't wa-wa-wa-wa-nt the key-ey-ey. I wa-a-ant the jam — oh! oh! oh! oh!'" and Jacintha mimicked, after her fashion, the mingled grief and ire of infancy debarred its jam. Edouard wore a puzzled air, but it was only for a moment; the next he hid his face in his hands, and cried, "Fool!"

"I shall not contradict you," said his Mentor.

"She was my best friend. Once acquainted with the doctor, I could visit at Beaurepaire."

"Parbleu!"

"She had thought of a way to reconcile my wishes with this terrible etiquette that reigns here."

"She thinks to more purpose than you do; that is clear."

"Nothing is left now but to ask her pardon, and to consent; I am off."

"No, you are not," and Jacintha laid a grasp of iron on him. "Will you be quiet? — is not one blunder a day enough? If you go near her now, she will affront you, and order the doctor not to speak to you."

"O Jacintha! your sex then are fiends of malice?"

"While it lasts. Luckily with us nothing lasts very long. Now you don't go near her till you have taken advantage of her hint, and made the doctor's acquaintance; that is easy done. He walks two hours on the east road every day, with his feet in the puddles and his head in the clouds. Them's *his* two tastes."

"But how am I to get him out of the clouds and the puddles?"

inquired Riviere half peevishly.

"How?" asked Jacintha, with a dash of that contempt uneducated persons generally have for any one who does not know some little thing they happen to know themselves. "How? Why, with the nearest blackbeetle, to be sure."

"A blackbeetle?"

"Black or brown; it matters little. Have her ready for use in your handkerchief: pull a long face: and says you — 'Excuse me, sir, I have *the misfortune* not to know the Greek name of this merchandise here.' Say that, and behold him launched. He will christen you the beast in Hebrew and Latin as well as Greek, and tell you her history down from the flood: next he will beg her of you, and out will come a cork and a pin, and behold the creature impaled. For that is how men love beetles. He has a thousand pinned down at home — beetles, butterflies, and so forth. When I go near the rubbish with my duster he trembles like an aspen. I pretend to be going to clean them, but it is only to see the face he makes, for even a domestic must laugh now and then — or die. But I never do clean them, for after all he is more stupid than wicked, poor man: I have not therefore the sad courage to make him wretched."

"Let us return to our beetle — what will his tirades about its antiquity advance me?"

"Oh! one begins about a beetle, but one ends Heaven knows where."

Riviere profited by this advice. He even improved on it. In due course he threw himself into Aubertin's way. He stopped the doctor reverentially, and said he had heard he was an entomologist. *would* he be kind enough to tell him what was this enormous chrysalis he had just found?

"The death's head moth!" cried Aubertin with enthusiasm — "the death's head moth! a great rarity in this district. Where found you this?" Riviere undertook to show him the place.

It was half a league distant. Coming and going he had time to make friends with Aubertin, and this was the easier that the old gentleman, who was a physiognomist as well as ologist, had seen goodness and sensibility in Edouard's face. At the end of the walk he begged the doctor to accept the chrysalis. The doctor coquetted. "That would be a robbery. You take an interest in these things yourself — at least I hope so."

The young rogue confessed modestly to the sentiment of entomology, but "the government worked him so hard as to leave him no hopes of shining in so high a science," said he sorrowfully.

The doctor pitied him. "A young man of your attainments and tastes to be debarred from the everlasting secrets of nature, by the fleeting politics of the day."

Riviere shrugged his shoulders. "Somebody must do the dirty work," said he, chuckling inwardly.

The chrysalis went to Beaurepaire in the pocket of a grateful man, who that same evening told the whole party his conversation with young Riviere, on whom he pronounced high encomiums. Rose's saucy eyes sparkled with fun: you might have lighted a candle at one and exploded a mine at the other; but not a syllable did she utter.

The doctor proved a key, and opened the enchanted castle. One fine day he presented his friend in the Pleasaunce to the baroness and her daughters.

They received him with perfect politeness. Thus introduced, and as he was not one to let the grass grow under his feet, he soon obtained a footing as friend of the family, which, being now advised by Josephine, he took care not to compromise by making love to Rose before the baroness. However, he insisted on placing his financial talent at their service. He surveyed and valued their lands, and soon discovered that all their farms were grossly underlet. Luckily most of the leases were run out. He prepared a new rent roll, and showed it Aubertin, now his fast friend. Aubertin at his request obtained a list of the mortgages, and Edouard drew a balance-sheet founded on sure data, and proved to the baroness that in able hands the said estate was now solvent.

This was a great comfort to the old lady: and she said to Aubertin, "Heaven has sent us a champion, a little republican — with the face of an angel."

Descending to practice, Edouard actually put three of the farms into the market, and let them at an advance of twenty per cent on the expired leases. He brought these leases signed; and the baroness had scarcely done thanking him, when her other secret friend, Monsieur Perrin, was announced. Edouard exchanged civilities with him, and then retired to the Pleasaunce. There he found both sisters, who were all tenderness and gratitude to him. By this time he had learned to value Josephine: she was so lovely and so good, and such a true womanly friend to him. Even Rose could not resist her influence, and was obliged to be kind to him, when Josephine was by. But let Josephine go, and instead of her being more tender, as any other girl would, left alone with her lover, sauciness resumed its empire till sweet Josephine returned. Whereof cometh an example; for the said Josephine was summoned to a final conference with the baroness and Monsieur Perrin.

"Don't be long," said Rose, as Josephine glided away, and (taking the precaution to wait till she was quite out of hearing), "I shall be so dull, dear, till you come back."

"I shall not though," said Edouard.

"I am not so sure of that. Now then."

"Now then, what?"

"Begin."

"Begin what?"

"Amusing me." And she made herself look sullen and unamusable all over.

"I will try," said Riviere. "I'll tell you what they say of you: that you are too young to love."

"So I am, much."

"No, no, no! I made a mistake. I mean too young to be loved."

"Oh, I am not too young for that, not a bit."

This point settled, she suggested that, if he could not amuse her, he had better do *the next best thing*, and that was, talk sense.

"I think I had better not talk at all," said he, "for I am no match for such a nimble tongue. And then you are so remorseless. I'll hold my tongue, and make a sketch of this magnificent oak."

"Ay, do: draw it as it appeared on a late occasion: with two ladies flying out of it, and you rooted with dismay."

"There is no need; that scene is engraved."

"Where? in all the shops?"

"No; on all our memories."

"Not on mine; not on mine. How terrified you were — ha, ha! and how terrified we should have been if you had not. Listen: once upon a time — don't be alarmed: it was long after Noah — a frightened hare ran by a pond; the frogs splashed in the water, smit with awe. Then she said, 'Ah ha! there are people in the world I frighten in my turn; I am the thunderbolt of war.' Excuse my quoting La Fontaine: I am not in 'Charles the Twelfth of Sweden' yet. I am but a child."

"And it's a great mercy, for when you grow up, you will be too much for me, that is evident. Come, then, Mademoiselle the Quizzer, come and adorn my sketch."

"Monsieur, shall I make you a confession? You will not be angry: I could not support your displeasure. I have a strange inclination to walk up and down this terrace while you go and draw that tree in the Pleasaunce."

"Resist that inclination; perhaps it will fly from you."

"No; you fly from me, and draw. I will rejoin you in a few minutes."

"Thank you, I'm not so stupid. You will step indoors directly."

"Do you doubt my word, sir?" asked she haughtily.

He had learned to obey all her caprices; so he went and placed himself on the west side of the oak and took out his sketch-book, and worked zealously and rapidly. He had done the outlines of the tree and was finishing in detail a part of the huge trunk, when his eyes were suddenly dazzled: in the middle of the rugged bark, deformed here and there with great wart-like bosses, and wrinkled, seamed, and ploughed all over with age, burst a bit of variegated color; bright as a poppy on a dungeon wall, it glowed and glittered out through a large hole in the brown bark; it was Rose's face peeping. To our young lover's eye how divine it shone! None of the half tints of common flesh were there, but a thing all rose, lily, sapphire, and soul. His pencil dropped, his mouth opened, he was downright dazzled by the glowing, bewitching face, sparkling with fun, in the gaunt tree. Tell me, ladies, did she know, even at that age, the value of that sombre frame to her brightness? The moment she found herself detected, the gaunt old tree rang musical with a crystal laugh, and out came the arch-dryad. "I have been there all the time. How solemn you looked! Now for the result of such profound study." He showed her his work; she altered her tone. "Oh, how clever!" she cried, "and how rapid! What a facility you have! Monsieur is an artist," said she gravely; "I will be more respectful," and she dropped him a low courtesy. "Mind you promised it me," she added sharply.

"You will accept it, then?"

"That I will, now it is worth having: dear me, I never reckoned on that. Finish it directly," cried this peremptory young person.

"First I must trouble you to stand out there near the tree."

"Me? what for?"

"Because art loves contrasts. The tree is a picture of age and gradual decay; by its side then I must place a personification of youth and growing loveliness."

She did not answer, but made a sort of defiant pirouette, and went where she was bid, and stood there with her back to the artist. "That will never do," said he; "you really must be so good as to turn round."

"Oh, very well." And when she came round, behold her color had risen mightily. Flattery is sweet.

This child of nature was delighted, and ashamed it should be seen that she was.

And so he drew her, and kept looking off the paper at her, and had a right in his character of artist to look her full in the face; and he did so with long lingering glances. To be sure, they all began severe and businesslike with half-closed eyes, and the peculiar hostile expression art puts on; but then they always ended open-eyed, and so full and tender, that she, poor girl, who was all real gold, though sham brass, blushed and blushed, and did not know which way to look not to be scorched up by his eye like a tender flower, or blandly absorbed like the pearly dew. Ah, happy hour! ah, happy days of youth and innocence and first love!

Trouble loves to intrude on these halcyon days.

The usually quiet Josephine came flying from the house, pale and agitated, and clung despairingly to Rose, and then fell to sobbing and lamenting piteously.

I shall take leave to relate in my own words what had just occurred to agitate her so. When she entered her mother's room, she found the baroness and Perrin the notary seated watching for her. She sat down after the usual civilities, and Perrin entered upon the subject that had brought him.

He began by confessing to them that he had not overcome the refractory creditor without much trouble; and that he had since learned there was another, a larger creditor, likely to press for payment or for sale of the estate. The baroness was greatly troubled by this communication: the notary remained cool as a cucumber, and keenly observant. After a pause he went on to say all this had caused him grave reflections. "It seems," said he with cool candor, "a sad pity the estate should pass from a family that has held it since the days of Charlemagne."

"Now God forbid!" cried the baroness, lifting her eyes and her quivering hands to heaven.

The notary held the republican creed in all its branches. "Providence, madame, does not interfere — in matters of business," said he. "Nothing but money can save the estate. Let us then be practical. Has any means occurred to you of raising money to pay off these incumbrances?"

"No. What means can there be? The estate is mortgaged to its full value: so they say, at least."

"And they say true," put in the notary quickly. "But do not distress yourself, madame: confide in me."

"Ah, my good friend, may Heaven reward you."

"Madame, up to the present time I have no complaint to make of Heaven. I am on the rise: here, mademoiselle, is a gimcrack they have given me;" and he unbuttoned his overcoat, and showed them a piece of tricolored ribbon and a clasp. "As for me, I look to 'the solid;' I care little for these things," said he, swelling visibly, "but the world is dazzled by them. However, I can show you something better." He took out a letter. "This is from the Minister of the Interior to a client of mine: a promise I shall be the next prefect; and the present prefect — I am happy to say — is on his death-bed. Thus, madame, your humble servant in a few short months will be notary no longer, but prefect; I shall then sell my office of notary: and I flatter myself when I am a prefect you will not blush to own me."

"Then, as now, monsieur," said the baroness politely, "we shall recognize your merit. But" —

"I understand, madame: like me you look to 'the solid.' Thus then it is; I have money."

"Ah! all the better for you."

"I have a good deal of money. But it is dispersed in a great many small but profitable investments: to call it in suddenly would entail some loss. Nevertheless, if you and my young lady there have ever so little of that friendly feeling towards me of which I have so much towards you, all my investments shall be called in, and two-thirds of your creditors shall be paid off at once. A single client of mine, no less a man than the Commandant Raynal, will, I am sure, advance me the remaining third at an hour's notice; and so Beaurepaire chateau, park, estate, and grounds, down to the old oak-tree, shall be saved; and no power shall alienate them from you, mademoiselle, and from the heirs of your body."

The baroness clasped her hands in ecstasy.

"But what are we to do for this?" inquired Josephine calmly, "for it seems to me that it can only be effected by a sacrifice on your part."

"I thank you, mademoiselle, for your penetration in seeing that I must make sacrifices. I would never have told you, but you have seen it; and I do not regret that you have seen it. Madame — mademoiselle — those sacrifices appear little to me; will seem nothing; will never be mentioned, or even alluded to after this day, if you, on your part, will lay me under a far heavier obligation, if in short" — here the contemner of things unsubstantial reopened his coat, and brought his ribbon to light again — "if you, madame, will accept me for your son-in-law — if you, mademoiselle, will take me for your husband."

The baroness and her daughter looked at one another in silence.

"Is it a jest?" inquired the former of the latter.

"Can you think so? Answer Monsieur Perrin. He has just done us a kind office, mother."

"I shall remember it. Monsieur, permit me to regret that having lately won our gratitude and esteem, you have taken this way of modifying those feelings. But after all," she added with gentle courtesy, "we may well put your good deeds against this — this error in judgment. The balance is in your favor still, provided you never return to this topic. Come, is it agreed?" The baroness's manner was full of tact, and the latter sentences were said with an open kindliness of manner. There was nothing to prevent Perrin from dropping the subject, and remaining good friends. A gentleman or a lover would have so done. Monsieur Perrin was neither. He said bitterly, "You refuse me, then."

The tone and the words were each singly too much for the baroness's pride. She answered coldly but civilly, —

"I do not refuse you. I do not take an affront into consideration."

"Be calm, mamma; no affront whatever was intended."

"Ah! here is one that is more reasonable," cried Perrin.

"There are men," continued Josephine without noticing him, "who look to but one thing — interest. It was an offer made politely in the way of business: decline it in the same spirit; that is what you have to do."

"Monsieur, you hear what mademoiselle says? She carries politeness a long way. After all it is a good fault. Well, monsieur, I need not answer you, since Mademoiselle de Beaurepaire has answered you; but I detain you no longer."

Strictly a weasel has no business with the temper of a tiger, but this one had, and the long vindictiveness of a Corsican. "Ah! my little lady, you turn me out of the house, do you?" cried he, grinding his teeth.

"Turn him out of the house? what a phrase! where has this man lived?"

"A man!" snarled Perrin, "whom none ever yet insulted without repenting it, and repenting in vain. You are under obligations to me, and you think to turn me out! You are at my mercy, and you think I will let you turn me to your door! In less than a mouth I will stand here, and say to you, Beaurepaire is mine. Begone from it!"

When he uttered these terrible words, each of which was like a sword-stroke to the baroness, the old lady, whose courage was not equal to her strength, shrank over the side of her armchair, and cried piteously — "He threatens me! he threatens me! I am fright-

ened;" and put up her trembling hands, for the notary's eloquence, being accompanied with abundance of gesture, bordered
upon physical violence. His brutality received an unexpected
check. Imagine that a sparrow-hawk had seized a trembling
pigeon, and that a royal falcon swooped, and with one lightning-
like stroke of body and wing, buffeted him away, and sent him
gaping and glaring and grasping at pigeonless air with his claws.
So swift and majestic, Josephine de Beaurepaire came from her
chair with one gesture of her body between her mother and the
notary, who was advancing with arms folded in a brutal, menacing
way — not the Josephine we have seen her, the calm languid
beauty, but the demoiselle de Beaurepaire — her great heart on
fire — her blood up — not her own only, but all the blood of all the
De Beaurepaires — pale as ashes with great wrath, her purple eyes
on fire, and her whole panther-like body full of spring. "Wretch!
you dare to insult her, and before me! Arriere miserable! or I soil
my hand with your face." And her hand was up with the word, up,
up, higher it seemed than ever a hand was raised before. And if he
had hesitated one moment, I really believe it would have come
down; not heavily, perhaps — the lightning is not heavy. But there
was no need. The towering threat and the flaming eye and the
swift rush buffeted the caitiff away: he recoiled. She followed him
as he went, strong, *for a moment or two*, as Hercules, beautiful and
terrible as Michael driving Satan. He dared not, or could not
stand before her: he writhed and cowered and recoiled all down
the room, while she marched upon him. But the driven serpent
hissed horribly as it wriggled away.

"You shall both be turned out of Beaurepaire by me, and forever; I swear it, parole de Perrin."

He had not been gone a minute when Josephine's courage
oozed away, and she ran, or rather tottered, into the Pleasaunce,
and clung like a drowning thing to Rose, and, when Edouard took
her hand, she clung to him. They had to gather what had happened how they could: the account was constantly interrupted
with her sobs and self-reproaches. She said she had ruined all she
loved: ruined her sister, ruined her mother, ruined the house of
Beaurepaire. Why was she ever born? Why had she not died three
years ago? (Query, what was the date at which Camille's letters
suddenly stopped?) "That coward," said she, "has the heart of a
fiend. He told us he never forgave an affront; and he holds our fate
in his hands. He will drive our mother from her home, and she
will die: murdered by her own daughter. After all, why did I refuse
him? What should I have sacrificed by marrying him? Rose, write

to him, and say — say — I was taken by surprise, I — I" — a violent flood of tears interrupted the sentence.

Rose flung her arms round her neck. "My beautiful Josephine marry that creature? Let house and lands go a thousand times sooner. I love my sister a thousand times better than the walls of this or any other house."

"Come, come," cried Edouard, "you are forgetting *me* all this time. Do you really think I am the sort of man to stand by with my hands in my pockets, and let her marry that cur, or you be driven out of Beaurepaire? Neither, while I live."

"Alas! dear boy," sighed Josephine, "what can you do?"

"I'll soon show you. From this hour forth it is a duel between that Perrin and me. Now, Josephine — Rose — don't you cry and fret like that: but just look quietly on, and enjoy the fight, both of you."

Josephine shook her head with a sad smile: but Rose delivered herself thus, after a sob, "La, yes; I forgot: we have got a gentleman now; that's one comfort."

Edouard rose to the situation: he saw that Perrin would lose no time; and that every day, or even hour, might be precious. He told them that the first thing he must do for them was to leave the company he loved best on earth, and run down to the town to consult Picard the rival notary: he would be back by supper-time, when he hoped they would do him the honor, in a matter of such importance, to admit him to a family council.

Josephine assented with perfect simplicity; Rose with a deep blush, for she was too quick not to see all the consequences of admitting so brisk a wooer into a family council.

It was a wet evening, and a sad and silent party sat round a wood fire in the great dining-hall. The baroness was almost prostrated by the scene with Perrin; and a sombre melancholy and foreboding weighed on all their spirits, when presently Edouard Riviere entered briskly, and saluted them all profoundly, and opened the proceedings with a little favorite pomposity. "Madame the baroness, and you Monsieur Aubertin, who honor me with your esteem, and you Mademoiselle de Beaurepaire, whom I adore, and you Mademoiselle Rose, whom I hoped to be permitted — you have this day done me the honor to admit me as your adviser. I am here to lay my plans before you. I believe, madame, I have already convinced you that your farms are underlet, and your property lowered in value by general mismanagement; this was doubtless known to Perrin, and set him scheming. Well, I rely on the same circumstance to defeat him. I have consulted Picard and shown him the rent-roll and balance-sheet I had already shown you. He has confessed that the estate is worth more than its debts, so capitalists can safely advance the money. Tomorrow morning, then, I ride to Commandant Raynal for a week's leave of absence; then, armed with Picard's certificate, shall proceed to my uncle and ask him to lend the money. His estate is very small compared with Beaurepaire, but he has always farmed it himself. 'I'll have no go-between,' says he, 'to impoverish both self and soil.' He is also a bit of a misanthrope, and has made me one. I have a very poor opinion of my fellow-creatures, very."

"Well, but," said Rose, "if he is all that, he will not sympathize with us, who have so mismanaged Beaurepaire. Will he not despise us?"

Edouard was a little staggered, but Aubertin came to his aid.

"Permit me, Josephine," said he. "Natural history steps in here, and teaches by me, its mouth-piece. A misanthrope hates all mankind, but is kind to every individual, generally too kind. A philanthrope loves the whole human race, but dislikes his wife, his mother, his brother, and his friends and acquaintances. Misanthrope is the potato: rough and repulsive outside, but good to the core. Philanthrope is a peach: his manner all velvet and bloom, his words sweet juice, his heart of hearts a stone. Let me read Philanthrope's book, and fall into the hands of Misanthrope."

Edouard admitted the shrewdness of this remark.

"And so," said he, "my misanthrope will say plenty of biting words, — which, by-the-by, will not hurt you, who will not hear them, only me, — and then he'll lend us the money, and Beaurepaire will be free, and I shall have had a hand in it. Hurrah!"

Then came a delicious hour to Edouard Riviere. Young and old poured out their glowing thanks and praises upon him till his checks burned like fire.

The baroness was especially grateful, and expressed a gentle regret that she could see no way of showing her gratitude except in words. "What can we do for this little angel?" said she, turning to Josephine.

"Leave that to me, mamma," replied Josephine, turning her lovely eyes full on Edouard, with a look the baroness misunderstood directly.

She sat and watched Josephine and Edouard with comical severity all the rest of the time she was there; and, when she retired, she kissed Rose affectionately, but whispered her eldest daughter, "I hope you are not serious. A mere boy compared with you."

"But such a sweet one," suggested Josephine, apologetically.

"What will the world come to?" said the baroness out loud, and retreated with a sour glance at all of them — except Rose.

She had not been gone five minutes when a letter came by messenger to Edouard. It was from Picard. He read it out.

"Perrin has been with me, to raise money. He wants it in forty-eight hours. Promises good legal security. I have agreed to try and arrange the matter for him."

They were all astonished at this.

"The double-faced traitor!" cried Edouard. "Stay; wait a minute. Let us read it to an end."

"This promise is, of course, merely to prevent his going elsewhere. At the end of the forty-eight hours I shall begin to make difficulties. Meantime, as Perrin is no fool, you had better profit to the full by this temporary delay."

"Well done, Picard!" shouted Edouard. "Notary cut notary. I won't lose an hour. I'll start at five; Commandant Raynal is an early riser himself."

Accordingly, at five he was on the road; Raynal's quarters lay in the direct line to his uncle's place. He found the commandant at home, and was well received. Raynal had observed his zeal, and liked his manners. He gave him the week's leave, and kept him to breakfast, and had his horse well fed. At eight o'clock Edouard rode out of the premises in high spirits. At the very gate he met a gaunt figure riding in on a squab pony. It was Perrin the notary coming in hot haste to his friend and employer, Commandant Raynal.

CHAPTER V.

After Edouard's departure, Josephine de Beaurepaire was sad, and weighed down with presentiments. She felt as soldiers sometimes feel who know the enemy is undermining them; no danger on the surface; nothing that can be seen, met, baffled, attacked, or evaded; in daily peril, all the more horrible that it imitates perfect serenity, they await the fatal match. She imparted her misgivings to Aubertin; but he assured her she exaggerated the danger.

"We have a friend still more zealous and active than our enemy; believe me, your depression is really caused by his absence; we all miss the contact of that young heroic spirit; we are a body, and he its soul."

Josephine was silent, for she said to herself, "Why should I dash their spirits? they are so happy and confident."

Edouard had animated Rose and Aubertin with his own courage, and had even revived the baroness.

It had been agreed between him and Picard that the latter should communicate with Dr. Aubertin direct, should anything fresh occur. And on the third day after Edouard's departure, Picard sent up a private message: "Perrin has just sent me a line to say he will not trouble us, as he is offered the money in another quarter."

This was a heavy blow, and sent them all to bed more or less despondent.

The next day brought a long letter from Edouard to Rose, telling her he had found his uncle crusty at first; but at last with a little patience, and the co-operation of Martha, his uncle's old servant, and his nurse, the old boy had come round. They might look on the affair as all but settled.

The contents of this letter were conveyed to the baroness. The house brightened under it: the more so that there was some hope of their successful champion returning in person next day. Meantime Perrin had applied to Raynal for the immediate loan of a large sum of money on excellent security. Raynal refused plump. Perrin rode away disconsolate.

But the next day he returned to the charge with another proposal: and the nature of this second proposal we shall learn from events.

The day Edouard was expected opened deliciously. It was a balmy morning, and tempted the sisters out before breakfast. They strolled on the south terrace with their arms round each other's waists, talking about Edouard, and wondering whether they should really see him before night. Rose owned she had missed him, and confessed for the first time she was a proud and happy girl.

"May I tell him so?" asked Josephine.

"Not for all the world. Would you dare?"

Further discussion of that nice point was stopped by the baroness coming out, leaning on Dr. Aubertin.

Then — how we young people of an unceremonious age should have stared — the demoiselles de Beaurepaire, inasmuch as this was their mother's first appearance, lowered their fair heads at the same time like young poplars bowing to the wind, and so waited reverently till she had slightly lifted her hands, and said, "God bless you, my children!"

It was done in a moment on both sides, but full of grace and piety, and the charm of ancient manners.

"How did our dear mother sleep?" inquired Josephine. Aubertin interposed with a theory that she slept very well indeed if she took what he gave her.

"Ay, IF," suggested Rose, saucily.

"I slept," said the baroness, "and I wish I had not for I dreamed an ugly dream." They all gathered round her, and she told her dream.

"I thought I was with you all in this garden. I was admiring the flowers and the trees, and the birds were singing with all their might. Suddenly a dark cloud came; it cleared almost directly; but flowers, trees, sky, and birds were gone now, and I could see the chateau itself no more. It means that I was dead. An ugly dream, my children, an ugly dream."

"But only a dream, dear mother," said Rose: then with a sweet, consoling smile, "See, here is your terrace and your chateau."

"And here are your daughters," said Josephine; and they both came and kissed her to put their existence out of doubt. "And here is your Aesculapius," said Aubertin. "And here is your Jacintha."

"Breakfast, madame," said Jacintha. "Breakfast, mesdemoiselles. Breakfast, monsieur:" dropping each a distinct courtesy in turn.

"She has turned the conversation very agreeably," said the baroness, and went in leaning on her old friend.

But the sisters lagged behind and took several turns in silence. Rose was the first to speak. "How superstitious of you!"

"I said nothing."

"No; but you looked volumes at me while mamma was telling

her dream. For my part I feel sure love is stronger than hate; and we shall stay all our days in this sweet place: and O Josey! am I not a happy girl that it's all owing to HIM!"

At this moment Jacintha came running towards them. They took it for a summons to breakfast, and moved to meet her. But they soon saw she was almost as white as her apron, and she came open-mouthed and wringing her hands. "What shall I do? what shall I do? Oh, don't let my poor mistress know!"

They soon got from her that Dard had just come from the town, and learned the chateau was sold, and the proprietor coming to take possession this very day. The poor girls were stupefied by the blow.

If anything, Josephine felt it worst. "It is my doing," she gasped, and tottered fainting. Rose supported her: she shook it off by a violent effort. "This is no time for weakness," she cried, wildly; "come to the Pleasaunce; there is water there. I love my mother. What will I not do for her? I love my mother."

Muttering thus wildly she made for the pond in the Pleasaunce. She had no sooner turned the angle of the chateau than she started back with a convulsive cry, and her momentary feebleness left her directly; she crouched against the wall and griped the ancient corner-stone with her tender hand till it powdered, and she spied with dilating eye into the Pleasaunce, Rose and Jacintha panting behind her. Two men stood with their backs turned to her looking at the oak-tree; one an officer in full uniform, the other the human snake Perrin. Though the soldier's back was turned, his off-handed, peremptory manner told her he was inspecting the place as its master.

"The baroness! the baroness!" cried Jacintha, with horror. They looked round, and the baroness was at their very backs.

"What is it?" cried she, gayly.

"Nothing, mamma."

"Let me see this nothing."

They glanced at one another, and, idle as the attempt was, the habit of sparing her prevailed, and they flung themselves between her and the blow.

"Josephine is not well," said Rose. "She wants to go in." Both girls faced the baroness.

"Jacintha," said the baroness, "fetch Dr. Aubertin. There, I have sent her away. So now tell me, why do you drive me back so? Something has happened," and she looked keenly from one to the other.

"O mamma! do not go that way: there are strangers in the

Pleasaunce."

"Let me see. So there are. Call Jacintha back that I may order these people out of my premises." Josephine implored her to be calm.

"Be calm when impertinent intruders come into my garden?"

"Mother, they are not intruders."

"What do you mean?"

"They have a right to be in our Pleasaunce. They have bought the chateau."

"It is impossible. *He* was to buy it for us — there is some mistake — what man would kill a poor old woman like me? I will speak to this gentleman: he wears a sword. Soldiers do not trample on women. Ah! that man."

The notary, attracted by her voice, was coming towards her, a paper in his hand.

Raynal coolly inspected the tree, and tapped it with his scabbard, and left Perrin to do the dirty work. The notary took off his hat, and, with a malignant affectation of respect, presented the baroness with a paper.

The poor old thing took it with a courtesy, the effect of habit, and read it to her daughters as well as her emotion permitted, and the language, which was as new to her as the dialect of Cat Island to Columbus.

"Jean Raynal, domiciled by right, and lodging in fact at the Chateau of Beaurepaire, acting by the pursuit and diligence of Master Perrin, notary; I, Guillaume Le Gras, bailiff, give notice to Josephine Aglae St. Croix de Beaurepaire, commonly called the Baroness de Beaurepaire, having no known place of abode" —

"Oh!"

"But lodging wrongfully at the said Chateau of Beaurepaire, that she is warned to decamp within twenty-four hours" —

"To decamp!"

"Failing which that she will be thereto enforced in the manner for that case made and provided with the aid of all the officers and agents of the public force."

"Ah! no, messieurs, pray do not use force. I am frightened enough already. I did not know I was doing anything wrong. I have been here thirty years. But, since Beaurepaire is sold, I comprehend perfectly that I must go. It is just. As you say, I am not in my own house. I will go, gentlemen, I will go. Whither shall I go, my children? The house where you were born to me is ours no longer. Excuse me, gentlemen — this is nothing to you. Ah! sir, you have revenged yourself on two weak women — may Heaven forgive you!"

The notary turned on his heel. The poor baroness, all whose pride the iron law, with its iron gripe, had crushed into dismay and terror, appealed to him. "O sir! send me from the house, but not from the soil where my Henri is laid! is there not in all this domain a corner where she who was its mistress may lie down and die? Where is the *new baron*, that I may ask this favor of him on my knees?"

She turned towards Raynal and seemed to be going towards him with outstretched arms. But Rose checked her with fervor. "Mamma! do not lower yourself. Ask nothing of these wretches. Let us lose all, but not forget ourselves."

The baroness had not her daughter's spirit. Her very person tottered under this blow. Josephine supported her, and the next moment Aubertin came out and hastened to her side. Her head fell back; what little strength she had failed her; she was half lifted, half led, into the house.

Commandant Raynal was amazed at all this, and asked what the deuce was the matter.

"Oh!" said the notary, "we are used to these little scenes in our business."

"But I am not," replied the soldier. "You never told me there was to be all this fuss."

He then dismissed his friend rather abruptly and strode up and down the Pleasaunce. He twisted his mustaches, muttered, and "pested," and was ill at ease. Accustomed to march gayly into a town, and see the regiment, that was there before, marching gayly out, or vice versa, and to strike tents twice a quarter at least, he was little prepared for such a scene as this. True, he did not hear all the baroness's words, but more than one tone of sharp distress reached him where he stood, and the action of the whole scene was so expressive, there was little need of words. He saw the notice given; the dismay it caused, and the old lady turn imploringly towards him with a speaking gesture, and above all he saw her carried away, half fainting, her hands clasped, her reverend face pale. He was not a man of quick sensibilities. He did not thoroughly take the scene in at first: it grew upon him afterwards.

"Confound it," thought he, "I am the proprietor. They all say so. Instead of which I feel like a thief. Fancy her getting so fond of a *place* as all this."

Presently it occurred to him that the shortness of the notice might have much to do with her distress. "These notaries," said he to himself, "understand nothing save law: women have piles of baggage, and can't strike tents directly the order comes, as we can. Perhaps if I were to give them twenty-four days instead of hours? — hum!"

With this the commandant fell into a brown study. Now each of us has his attitude of brown study. One runs about the room like hyena in his den; another stands stately with folded arms (this one seldom thinks to the purpose); another sits cross-legged, brows lowered: another must put his head into his hand, and so keep it up to thinking mark: another must twiddle a bit of string, or a key; grant him this, he can hatch an epic. This commandant must draw himself up very straight, and walk six paces and back very slowly, till the problem was solved: I suspect he had done a good bit of sentinel work in his time.

Now whilst he was guarding the old oak-tree, for all the world as if it had been the gate of the Tuileries or the barracks, Josephine de Beaurepaire came suddenly out from the house and crossed the Pleasaunce: her hair was in disorder, her manner wild: she passed swiftly into the park.

Raynal recognized her as one of the family; and after a moment's reflection followed her into the park with the good-natured intention of offering her a month to clear out instead of a day.

But it was not so easy to catch her: she flew. He had to take his scabbard in his left hand and fairly run after her. Before he could catch her, she entered the little chapel. He came up and had his foot on the very step to go in, when he was arrested by that he heard within.

Josephine had thrown herself on her knees and was praying aloud: praying to the Virgin with sighs and sobs and all her soul: wrestling so in prayer with a dead saint as by a strange perversity men cannot or will not wrestle with Him, who alone can hear a million prayers at once from a million different places, — can realize and be touched with a sense of all man's infirmities in a way no single saint with his partial experience of them can realize and be touched by them; who unasked suspended the laws of nature that had taken a stranger's only son, and she a widow; and wept at another great human sorrow, while the eyes of all the great saints that stood around it and Him were dry.

Well, the soldier stood, his right foot on the step and his sword in his left hand, transfixed: listening gravely to the agony of prayer the innocent young creature poured forth within: —

"O Madonna! hear me: it is for my mother's life. She will die — she will die. You know she cannot live if she is taken away from her house and from this holy place where she prays to you this many years. O Queen of Heaven! put out your hand to us unfortunates! Virgin, hear a virgin: mother, listen to a child who prays for her mother's life! The doctor says she will not live away from here. She is too old to wander over the world. Let them drive us forth: we are young, but not her, mother, oh, not her! Forgive the cruel men that do this thing! — they are like those who crucified your Son — they know not what they are doing. But you, Queen of Heaven, you know all; and, sweet mother, if you have kind sentiments towards me, poor Josephine, ah! show them now: for you know that it was I who insulted that wicked notary, and it is out of hatred to me he has sold our beloved house to a hard stranger. Look down on me, a child who loves her mother, yet will destroy her unless you pity me and help me. Oh! what shall I say? — what shall I do? mercy! mercy! for my poor mother, for me!"

Here her utterance was broken by sobs.

The soldier withdrew his foot quietly. Her words had knocked against his very breast-bone. He marched slowly to and fro before the chapel, upright as a dart, and stiff as a ramrod, and actually pale: for even our nerves have their habits; a woman's passionate grief shook him as a cannon fired over his head could not.

Josephine little thought who was her sentinel. She came to the door at last, and there he was marching backwards and forwards, upright and stiff. She gave a faint scream and drew back with a shudder at the sight of their persecutor. She even felt faintish at him, as women will in such cases.

Not being very quick at interpreting emotion, Raynal noticed her alarm, but not her repugnance; he saluted her with military precision by touching his cap as only a soldier can, and said rather gently for him, "A word with you, mademoiselle."

She replied only by trembling.

"Don't be frightened," said Raynal, in a tone not very reassuring. "I propose an armistice."

"I am at your disposal, sir," said Josephine, now assuming a calmness that was belied by the long swell of her heaving bosom.

"Of course you look on me as an enemy."

"How can I do otherwise, sir? yet perhaps I ought not. You did not know us. You just wanted an estate, I suppose — and — oh!"

"Well, don't cry; and let us come to the point, since I am a man of few words."

"If you please, sir. My mother may miss me."

"Well, I was in position on your flank when the notary delivered his fire. And I saw the old woman's distress."

"Ah, sir!"

"When you came flying out I followed to say a good word to you. I could not catch you. I listened while you prayed to the Virgin. That was not a soldier-like trick, you will say. I confess it."

"It matters little, sir, and you heard nothing I blush for."

"No! by St. Denis; quite the contrary. Well, to the point. Young lady, you love your mother."

"What has she on earth now but her children's love?"

"Now look here, young lady, I had a mother; I loved her in my humdrum way very dearly. She promised me faithfully not to die till I should be a colonel; and she went and died before I was a commandant, even; just before, too."

"Then I pity you," murmured Josephine; and her soft purple eye began to dwell on him with less repugnance.

"Thank you for that word, my good young lady," said Raynal. "Now, I declare, you are the first that has said that word to me about my losing the true friend, that nursed me on her knee, and pinched and pinched to make a man of me. I should like to tell you about her and me."

"I shall feel honored," said Josephine, politely, but with considerable restraint.

Then he told her all about how he had vexed her when he was a boy, and gone for a soldier, though she was all for trade, and how he had been the more anxious to see her enjoy his honors and success. "And, mademoiselle," said he, appealingly, "the day this epaulet was put on my shoulder in Italy, she died in Paris. Ah! how could you have the heart to do that, my old woman?"

The soldier's mustache quivered, and he turned away brusquely, and took several steps. Then he came back to Josephine, and to his infinite surprise saw that her purple eyes were thick with tears. "What? you are within an inch of crying for my mother, you who have your own trouble at this hour."

"Monsieur, our situations are so alike, I may well spare some little sympathy for your misfortune."

"Thank you, my good young lady. Well, then, to business; while you were praying to the Virgin, I was saying a word or two for my part to her who is no more."

"Sir!"

"Oh! it was nothing beautiful like the things you said to the other. Can I turn phrases? I saw her behind her little counter in the Rue Quincampoix; for she is a woman of the people, is my mother. I saw myself come to the other side of the counter, and I said, 'Look here, mother, here is the devil to pay about this new house. The old woman talks of dying if we take her from her home, and the young one weeps and prays to all the saints in paradise; what shall we do, eh?' Then I thought my old woman said to me, 'Jean, you are a soldier, a sort of vagabond; what do you want with a house in France? you who are always in a tent in Italy or Austria, or who knows where. Have you the courage to give honest folk so much pain for a caprice? Come now,' says she, 'the lady is of my age, say you, and I can't keep your fine house, because God has willed it otherwise; so give her my place; so then you can fancy it is me you have set down at your hearth: that will warm your heart up a bit, you little scamp,' said my old woman in her rough way. She was not well-bred like you, mademoiselle. A woman of the people, nothing more."

"She was a woman of God's own making, if she was like that," cried Josephine, the tears now running down her cheeks.

"Ah, that she was, she was. So between her and me it is settled — what are you crying for NOW? why, you have won the day; the field is yours; your mother and you remain; I decamp." He whipped his scabbard up with his left hand, and was going off without another word, if Josephine had not stopped him.

"But, sir, what am I to think? what am I to hope? it is impossible that in this short interview — and we must not forget what is due to you. You have bought the estate."

"True; well, we will talk over that, tomorrow; but being turned out of the house, that was the bayonet thrust to the old lady. So you run in and put her heart at rest about it. Tell her that she may live and die in this house for Jean Raynal; and tell her about the old woman in the Rue Quincampoix."

"God bless you, Jean Raynal!" cried Josephine, clasping her hands.

"Are you going?" said he, peremptorily.

"Oh, yes!" and she darted towards the chateau.

But when she had taken three steps she paused, and seemed irresolute. She turned, and in a moment she had glided to Raynal again and had taken his hand before he could hinder her, and pressed two velvet lips on it, and was away again, her cheeks scarlet at what she had done, and her wet eyes beaming with joy. She skimmed the grass like a lapwing; you would have taken her at this minute for Rose, or for Virgil's Camilla; at the gate she turned an instant and clasped her hands together, with such a look, to show Raynal she blessed him again, then darted into the house.

"Aha, my lady," said he, as he watched her fly, "behold you

changed a little since you came out." He was soon on the high road marching down to the town at a great rate, his sword clanking, and thus ran his thoughts: "This does one good; you are right, my old woman. Your son's bosom feels as warm as toast. Long live the five-franc pieces! And they pretend money cannot make a fellow happy. They lie; it is because they do not know how to spend it."

Meantime at the chateau, as still befalls in emergencies and trials, the master spirit came out and took its real place. Rose was now the mistress of Beaurepaire; she set Jacintha, and Dard, and the doctor, to pack up everything of value in the house. "Do it this moment!" she cried; "once that notary gets possession of the house, it may be too late. Enough of folly and helplessness. We have fooled away house and lands; our movables shall not follow them."

The moment she had set the others to work, she wrote a single line to Riviere to tell him the chateau and lands were sold, and would he come to Beaurepaire at once? She ran with it herself to Bigot's auberge, the nearest post-office, and then back to comfort her mother.

The baroness was seated in her armchair, moaning and wringing her hands, and Rose was nursing and soothing her, and bathing her temples with her last drop of eau de Cologne, and trying in vain to put some of her own courage into her, when in came Josephine radiant with happiness, crying "Joy! joy! joy!" and told her strange tale, with this difference, that she related her own share in it briefly and coldly, and was more eloquent than I about the strange soldier's goodness, and the interest her mother had awakened in his heart. And she told about the old woman in the Rue Quincampoix, her rugged phrases, and her noble, tender heart. The baroness, deaf to Rose's consolations, brightened up directly at Josephine's news, and at her glowing face, as she knelt pouring the good news, and hope, and comfort, point blank into her. But Rose chilled them both.

"It is a generous offer," said, she, "but one we cannot accept. We cannot live under so great an obligation. Is all the generosity to be on the side of this Bonapartist? Are we noble in name only? What would our father have said to such a proposal?"

Josephine hung her head. The baroness groaned.

"No, mother," continued Rose; "let house and land go, but honor and true nobility remain."

"What shall I do? you are cruel to me, Rose."

"Mamma," cried the enthusiastic girl, "we need depend on no

one. Josephine and I have youth and spirit."

"But no money."

"We have plenty of jewels, and pictures, and movables. We can take a farm."

"A farm!" shrieked the baroness.

"Why, his uncle has a farm, and we have had recourse to him for help: better a farmhouse than an almshouse, though that almshouse were a palace instead of a chateau."

Josephine winced and held up her hand deprecatingly. The baroness paled: it was a terrible stroke of language to come from her daughter. She said sternly, "There is no answer to that. We were born nobles, let us die farmers: only permit me to die first."

"Forgive me, mother," said Rose, kneeling. "I was wrong; it is for me to obey you, not to dictate. I speak no more." And, after kissing her mother and Josephine, she crept away, but she left her words sticking in both their consciences.

"*His* uncle," said the shrewd old lady. "She is no longer a child; and she says his uncle. This makes me half suspect it is her that dear boy — Josephine, tell me the truth, which of you is it?"

"Dear mother, who should it be? they are nearly of an age: and what man would not love our sweet Rose, that had eyes or a heart?"

The baroness sighed deeply; and was silent. After awhile she said, "The moment they have a lover, he detaches their hearts from their poor old mother. She is no longer what my Josephine is to me."

"Mamma, she is my superior. I see it more and more every day. She is proud: she is just; she looks at both sides. As for me, I am too apt to see only what will please those I love."

"And that is the daughter for me," cried the poor baroness, opening her arms wide to her.

The next morning when they were at breakfast, in came Jacintha to say the officer was in the dining-room and wanted to speak with the young lady he talked to yesterday. Josephine rose and went to him. "Well, mademoiselle," said he gayly, "the old woman was right. Here I have just got my orders to march: to leave France in a month. A pretty business it would have been if I had turned your mother out. So you see there is nothing to hinder you from living here."

"In your house, sir?"

"Why not, pray?"

"Forgive us. But we feel that would be unjust to you, humiliating to us: the poor are sometimes proud."

"Of course they are," said Raynal: "and I don't want to offend your pride. Confound the house: why did I go and buy it? It is no use to me except to give pain to worthy people." He then, after a moment's reflection, asked her if the matter could not be arranged by some third party, a mutual friend. "Then again," said he, "I don't know any friend of yours."

"Yes, sir," said Josephine; "we have one friend, who knows you, and esteems you highly."

She wanted to name Edouard; but she hesitated, and asked her conscience if it was fair to name him: and while she blushed and hesitated, lo and behold a rival referee hove in sight. Raynal saw him, suddenly opened a window, and shouted, "Hallo come in here: you are wanted."

Perrin had ridden up to complete the exodus of the De Beaurepaires, and was strolling about inspecting the premises he had expelled them from.

Here was a pretty referee!

Josephine almost screamed — "What are you doing? that is our enemy, our bitterest enemy. He has only sold you the estate to spite us, not for the love of you. I had — we had — we mortified his vanity. It was not our fault: he is a viper. Sir, pray, pray, pray be on your guard against his counsels."

These words spoken with rare fire and earnestness carried conviction: but it was too late to recall the invitation. The notary entered the room, and was going to bow obsequiously to Raynal, when he caught sight of Josephine, and almost started. Raynal, after Josephine's warning, was a little at a loss how to make him available; and even that short delay gave the notary's one foible time to lead him into temptation. "Our foibles are our manias."

"So," said he, "you have taken possession, commandant. These military men are prompt, are they not, mademoiselle?"

"Do not address yourself to me, sir, I beg," said Josephine quietly.

Perrin kept his self-command. "It is only as Commandant Raynal's agent I presume to address so distinguished a lady: in that character I must inform you that whatever movables you have removed are yours: those we find in the house on entering we keep."

"Come, come, not so fast," cried Raynal; "bother the chairs and tables! that is not the point."

"Commandant," said the notary with dignity, "have I done anything to merit this? have I served your interests so ill that you withdraw your confidence from me?"

"No, no, my good fellow; but you exceed your powers. Just now I want you to take orders, not give them."

"That is only just," said Perrin, "and I recall my hasty remark: excuse the susceptibility of a professional man, who is honored with the esteem of his clients; and favor me with your wishes."

"All right," said Raynal heartily. "Well, then — I want mademoiselle and her family to stay here while I go to Egypt with the First Consul. Mademoiselle makes difficulties; it offends her delicacy."

"Comedy!" said the notary contemptuously.

"Though her mother's life depends on her staying here."

"Comedy!" said Perrin. Raynal frowned.

"Her pride (begging her pardon) is greater than her affection."

"Farce!"

"I have pitched upon you to reconcile the two."

"Then you have pitched upon the wrong man," said Perrin bluntly. He added obsequiously, "I am too much your friend. She has been talking you over, no doubt; but you have a friend, an Ulysses, who is deaf to the siren's voice. I will be no party to such a transaction. I will not co-operate to humbug my friend and rob him of his rights."

If Josephine was inferior to the notary in petty sharpness, she was his superior in the higher kinds of sagacity; and particularly in instinctive perception of character. Her eye flashed with delight at the line Perrin was now taking with Raynal. The latter speedily justified her expectations: he just told Perrin to be off, and send him a more accommodating notary.

"A more accommodating notary!" screamed Perrin, stung to madness by this reproach. "There is not a more accommodating notary in Europe. Ungrateful man! is this the return for all my zeal, my integrity, my unselfishness? Is there another agent in the world who would have let such a bargain as Beaurepaire fall into your hands? It serves me right for deviating from the rules of business. Send me another agent — oh!"

The honest soldier was confused. The lawyer's eloquence overpowered him. He felt guilty. Josephine saw his simplicity, and made a cut with a woman's two-edged sword. "Sir," said she coolly, "do you not see it is an affair of money? This is his way of saying, Pay me handsomely for so unusual a commission."

"And I'll pay him double," cried Raynal, catching the idea; "don't be alarmed, I'll pay you for it."

"And my zeal, my devotion?"

"Put 'em in figures."

"And my prob —?"

"Add it up."

"And my integ —?"

"Add them together: and don't bother me."

"I see! I see! my poor soldier. You are no match for a woman's tongue."

"Nor, for a notary's. Go to hell, and send in your bill!" roared the soldier in a fury. "Well, will you go?" and he marched at him.

The notary scuttled out, with something between a snarl and a squeak.

Josephine hid her face in her hands.

"What is the matter with you?" inquired Raynal. "Not crying again, surely!"

"Me! I never cry — hardly. I hid my face because I could not help laughing. You frightened me, sir," said she: then very demurely, "I was afraid you were going to beat him."

"No, no; a good soldier never leathers a civilian if he can possibly help it; it looks so bad; and before a lady!"

"Oh, I would have forgiven you, monsieur," said Josephine benignly, and something like a little sun danced in her eye.

"Now, mademoiselle, since my referee has proved a pig, it is your turn. Choose you a mutual friend."

Josephine hesitated. "Ours is so young. You know him very well. You are doubtless the commandant of whom I once heard him speak with such admiration: his name is Riviere, Edouard Riviere."

"Know him? he is my best officer, out and out." And without a moment's hesitation he took Edouard's present address, and accepted that youthful Daniel as their referee; then looked at his watch and marched off to his public duties with sabre clanking at his heels.

The notary went home gnashing his teeth. His sweet revenge was turned to wormwood this day. Raynal's parting commissions rang in his ear; in his bitter mood the want of logical sequence in the two orders disgusted him.

So he inverted them.

He sent in a thundering bill the very next morning, but postponed the other commission till his dying day.

As for Josephine, she came into the drawing-room beaming with love and happiness, and after kissing both her mother and Rose with gentle violence, she let them know the strange turn things had taken.

And she whispered to Rose, "Only think, *your* Edouard to be *our* referee!"

Rose blushed and bent over her work; and wondered how Edouard would discharge so grave an office.

The matter approached a climax; for, as the reader is aware, Edouard was hourly expected at Beaurepaire.

He did not come; but it was not his fault. On receiving Rose's letter he declined to stay another hour at his uncle's.

He flung himself on his horse; and, before he was well settled on the stirrups, the animal shied violently at a wheelbarrow some fool had left there; and threw Edouard on the stones of the court-yard. He jumped up in a moment and laughed at Marthe's terror; meantime a farm-servant caught the nag and brought him back to his work.

But when Edouard went to put his hand on the saddle, he found it would not obey him. "Wait a minute," said he; "my arm is benumbed."

"Let me see!" said the farmer, and examined the limb himself; "benumbed? yes; and no wonder. Jacques, get on the brute and ride for the surgeon."

"Are you mad, uncle?" cried Edouard. "I can't spare my horse, and I want no surgeon; it will be well directly."

"It will be worse before it is better."

"I don't know what you mean, uncle; it is only numbed, ah! it hurts when I rub it."

"It is worse than numbed, boy; it is broken."

"Broken? nonsense:" and he looked at it in piteous bewilder-ment: "how can it be broken? it does not hurt except when I touch it."

"It *will* hurt: I know all about it. I broke mine fifteen years ago: fell off a haystack."

"Oh, how unfortunate I am!" cried Edouard, piteously. "But I will go to Beaurepaire all the same. I can have the thing mended there, as well as here."

"You will go to bed," said the old man, quietly; "that is where *you'll* go."

"I'll go to blazes sooner," yelled the young one.

The old man made a signal to his myrmidons, whom Marthe's cries had brought around, and four stout fellows took hold of Edouard by the legs and the left shoulder and carried him up-stairs raging and kicking; and deposited him on a bed.

Presently he began to feel faint, and so more reasonable. They cut his coat off, and put him in a loose wrapper, and after considerable delay the surgeon came, and set his arm skilfully, and behold this ardent spirit caged. He chafed and fretted sadly. Fortitude was not his forte.

It was two days after his accident. He was lying on his back, environed by slops and cursing his evil fate, and fretting his soul out of its fleshly prison, when suddenly he heard a cheerful trombone saying three words to Marthe, then came a clink-clank, and Marthe ushered into the sickroom the Commandant Raynal. The sick man raised himself in bed, with great surprise and joy.

"O commandant! this is kind to come and see your poor officer in purgatory."

"Ah," cried Raynal, "you see I know what it is. I have been chained down by the arm, and the leg, and all: it is deadly tiresome."

"Tiresome! it is — it is — oh, dear commandant, Heaven bless you for coming!"

"Ta! ta! ta! I am come on my own business."

"All the better. I have nothing to do; that is what kills me. I'm eating my own heart."

"Cannibal! Well, my lad, since you are in that humor, cheer up, for I bring you a job, and a tough one; it has puzzled me."

"What is it, commandant? What is it?"

"Well, do you know a house and a family called Beaurepaire?"

"Do I know Beaurepaire?"

And the pale youth turned very red; and stared with awe at this wizard of a commandant. He thought he was going to be called over the coals for frequenting a disaffected family. "Well," said Raynal, "I have been and bought this Beaurepaire."

Edouard uttered a loud exclamation. "It was *you* bought it! she never told me that."

"Yes," said Raynal, "I am the culprit; and we have fixed on you to undo my work without hurting their pride too much, poor souls; but let us begin with the facts."

Then Raynal told him my story after his fashion. Of course I shall not go and print his version; you might like his concise way better than my verbose; and I'm not here to hold up any man's coat-tails. Short as he made it, Edouard's eyes were moist more than once; and at the end he caught Raynal's hand and kissed it. Then he asked time to reflect; "for," said he, "I must try and be just."

"I'll give you an hour," said Raynal, with an air of grand munificence. The only treasure he valued was time.

In less than an hour Edouard had solved the knot, to his entire satisfaction; he even gave the commandant particular instructions for carrying out his sovereign decree. Raynal received these orders from his subordinate with that simplicity which formed part of his amazing character, and rode home relieved of all responsibility in the matter.

COMMANDANT RAYNAL TO
MADEMOISELLE DE BEAUREPAIRE.

Mademoiselle, — Before I could find time to write to our referee, news came in that he had just broken his arm; —

"Oh! oh, dear! our poor Edouard!"

And if poor Edouard had seen the pale faces, and heard the faltering accents, it would have reconciled him to his broken arm almost. This hand-grenade the commandant had dropped so coolly among them, it was a long while ere they could recover from it enough to read the rest of the letter, —

So I rode over to him, and found him on his back, fretting for want of something to do. I told him the whole story. He undertook the business. I have received his instructions, and next week shall be at his quarters to clear off his arrears of business, and make acquaintance with all your family, if they permit.

RAYNAL.

As the latter part of this letter seemed to require a reply, the baroness wrote a polite note, and Jacintha sent Dard to leave it for the commandant at Riviere's lodgings. But first they all sat down and wrote kind and pitying and soothing letters to Edouard. Need I say these letters fell upon him like balm?

They all inquired carelessly in their postscripts what he had decided as their referee. He replied mysteriously that they would know that in a week or two. Meantime, all he thought it prudent to tell them was that he had endeavored to be just to both parties.

"Little solemn puppy," said Rose, and was racked with curiosity.

Next week Raynal called on the baroness. She received him alone. They talked about Madame Raynal. The next day he dined with the whole party, and the commandant's manners were the opposite of what the baroness had inculcated. But she had a strong prejudice in his favor. Had her feelings been the other way his brusquerie would have shocked her. It amused her. If people's hearts are with you, *that* for their heads!

He came every day for a week, chatted with the baroness, walked with the young ladies; and when after work he came over in the evening, Rose used to cross-examine him, and out came such descriptions of battles and sieges, such heroism and such simplicity mixed, as made the evening pass delightfully. On these occasions the young ladies fixed their glowing eyes on him, and drank in his character as well as his narrative, in which were fewer "I's" than in anything of the sort you ever read or heard.

At length Rose contrived to draw him aside, and, hiding her curiosity under feigned nonchalance, asked him what the referee had decided. He told her that was a secret for the present.

"Well, but," said Rose, "not from me. Edouard and I have no secrets."

"Come, that's good," said Raynal. "Why, you are the very one he warned me against the most; said you were as curious as Mother Eve, and as sharp as her needle."

"Then he is a little scurrilous traitor," cried Rose, turning very red. "So that is how he talks of me behind my back, and calls me an angel to my face; I'll pay him for this. Do tell me, commandant; never mind what *he* says."

"What! disobey orders?"

"Orders? to you from that boy!"

"Oh!" said Raynal, "for that matter, we soldiers are used to command one moment, and obey the next."

In a word, this military pedant was impracticable, and Rose gave him up in disgust, and began to call up a sulky look when the other two sang his praises. For the old lady pronounced him charming, and Josephine said he was a man of crystal; never said a word he did not mean, and she wished she was like him. But the baroness thought this was going a little too far.

"No, thank you," said she hastily; "he is a man, a thorough man. He would make an intolerable woman. A fine life if one had a parcel of women about, all blurting out their real minds every moment, and never smoothing matters."

"Mamma, what a horrid picture!" chuckled Rose.

She then proposed that at his next visit they should all three make an earnest appeal to him to let them know what Edouard had decided.

But Josephine begged to be excused, feared it would be hardly delicate; and said languidly that for her part she felt they were in good hands, and prescribed patience. The baroness acquiesced, and poor Rose and her curiosity were baffled on every side.

At last, one fine day, her torments were relieved without any further exertion on her part. Jacintha bounced into the drawing-room with a notice that the commandant wanted to speak to Josephine a minute out in the Pleasaunce.

"How droll he is," said Rose; "fancy sending in for a young lady like that. Don't go, Josephine; how, he would stare."

"My dear, I no more dare disobey him than if I was one of his soldiers." And she laid down her work, and rose quietly to do what she was bid.

"Well," said Rose, superciliously, "go to your commanding officer. And, O Josephine, if you are worth anything at all, do get out of him what that Edouard has settled."

Josephine kissed her, and promised to try. After the first salutation, there was a certain hesitation about Raynal which Josephine had never seen a trace of in him before; so, to put him at his ease, and at the same time keep her promise to Rose, she asked timidly if their mutual friend had been able to suggest anything.

"What! don't you know that I have been acting all along upon his instructions?" answered Raynal.

"No, indeed! and you have not told us what he advised."

"Told you? why, of course not; they were secret instructions. I have obeyed one set, and now I come to the other; and there is the difficulty, being a kind of warfare I know nothing about."

"It must be savage warfare, then," suggested the lady politely.

"Not a bit of it. Now, who would have thought I was such a coward?"

Josephine was mystified; however, she made a shrewd guess. "Do you fear a repulse from any one of us? Then, I suppose, you meditate some extravagant act of generosity."

"Not I."

"Of delicacy, then."

"Just the reverse. Confound the young dog! why is he not here to help me?"

"But, after all," suggested Josephine, "you have only to carry out his instructions."

"That is true! that is true! but when a fellow is a coward, a poltroon, and all that sort of thing."

This repeated assertion of cowardice on the part of the living Damascus blade that stood bolt-upright before her, struck Josephine as so funny that she laughed merrily, and bade him fancy it was only a fort he was attacking instead of the terrible Josephine; whom none but heroes feared, she assured him.

This encouragement, uttered in jest, was taken in earnest. The soldier thanked her, and rallied visibly at the comparison. "All right," said he, "as you say, it is only a fort — so — mademoiselle!"

"Monsieur!"

"Hum! will you lend me your hand for a moment?"

"My hand! what for? there," and she put it out an inch a minute. He took it, and inspected it closely.

"A charming hand; the hand of a virtuous woman?"

"Yes," said Josephine as cool as a cucumber, too sublimely and absurdly innocent even to blush.

"Is it your own?"

"Sir!" She blushed at that, I can tell you.

"Because if it was, I would ask you to give it me. (I've fired the first shot anyway.)"

Josephine whipped her hand off his palm, where it lay like cream spilt on a trencher.

"Ah! I see; you are not free: you have a lover."

"No, no!" cried Josephine in distress; "I love nobody but my mother and sister: I never shall."

"Your mother," cried Raynal; "that reminds me; he told me to ask her; by Jove, I think he told me to ask her first;" and Raynal up with his scabbard and was making off.

Josephine begged him to do nothing of the kind.

"I can save you the trouble," said she.

"Ah, but my instructions! my instructions!" cried the military pedant, and ran off into the house, and left Josephine "planted there," as they say in France.

Raynal demanded a private interview of the baroness so significantly and unceremoniously that Rose had no alternative but to retire, but not without a glance of defiance at the bear. She ran straight, without her bonnet, into the Pleasaunce to slake her curiosity at Josephine. That young lady was walking pensively, but turned at sight of Rose, and the sisters came together with a clash of tongues.

"O Rose! he has" —

"Oh!"

So nimbly does the female mind run on its little beaten tracks, that it took no more than those syllables for even these innocent young women to communicate that Raynal had popped.

Josephine apologized for this weakness in a hero. "It wasn't his fault," said she. "It is your Edouard who set him to do it."

"My Edouard? Don't talk in that horrid way: I have no Edouard. You said 'no' of course."

"Something of the kind."

"What, did you not say 'no' plump?"

"I did not say it brutally, dear."

"Josephine, you frighten me. I know you can't say 'no' to any one; and if you don't say 'no' plump to such a man as this, you might as well say 'yes.'"

"Well, love," said Josephine, "you know our mother will relieve me of this; what a comfort to have a mother!"

They waited for Raynal's departure, to go to the baroness. They had to wait a long time. Moreover, when he did leave the chateau he came straight into the Pleasaunce. At sight of him Rose seized Josephine tight and bade her hold her tongue, as she could not say "no" plump to any one. Josephine was far from raising any objection to the arrangement.

"Monsieur," said Rose, before he could get a word out, "even if she had not declined, I could not consent."

Raynal tapped his forehead reflectively, and drew forth from memory that he had no instructions whatever to ask *her* consent.

She colored high, but returned to the charge.

"Is her own consent to be dispensed with too? She declined the honor, did she not?"

"Of course she did; but this was anticipated in my instructions. I am to be sure and not take the first two or three refusals."

"O Josephine, look at that insolent boy: he has found you out."

"Insolent boy!" cried Raynal; "why, it is the referee of your own choosing, and as well behaved a lad as ever I saw, and a zealous officer."

"My kind friends," put in Josephine with a sweet languor, "I cannot let you quarrel about a straw."

"It is not about a straw," said Raynal, "it is about you."

"The distinction involves a compliment, sir," said Josephine; then she turned to Rose, "Is it possible you do not see Monsieur Raynal's strange proposal in its true light? and you so shrewd in general. He has no personal feeling whatever in this eccentric proceeding: he wants to make us all happy, especially my mother, without seeming to lay us under too great an obligation. Surely good-nature was never carried so far before; ha, ha! Monsieur, I will encumber you with my friendship forever, if you permit me, but farther than that I will not abuse your generosity."

"Now look here, mademoiselle," began Raynal bluntly, "I did start with a good motive at first, that there's no denying. But, since I have been every day in your company, and seen how good and kind you are to all about you, I have turned selfish; and I say to myself, what a comfort such a wife as you would be to a soldier! Why, only to have you to write letters home to, would be worth half a fellow's pay. Do you know sometimes when I see the fellows writing their letters it gives me a knock here to think I have no one at all to write to."

Josephine sighed.

"So you see I am not so mighty disinterested. Now, mademoiselle, you speak so charmingly, I can't tell what you mean: can't tell whether you say 'no' because you could never like me, or whether it is out of delicacy, and you only want pressing. So I say no more at present: it is a standing offer. Take a day to consider. Take two if you like. I must go to the barracks; good-day."

"Oh! this must be put an end to at once," said Rose.

"With all my heart," replied Josephine; "but how?"

"Come to our mother, and settle that," said the impetuous sister, and nearly dragged the languid one into the drawing-room.

To their surprise they found the baroness walking up and down the room with unusual alacrity for a person of her years. She no sooner caught sight of Josephine than she threw her arms open to her with joyful vivacity, and kissed her warmly. "My love, you have saved us. I am a happy old woman. If I had all France to pick from I could not have found a man so worthy of my Josephine. He is brave, he is handsome, he is young, he is a rising man, he is a good son, and good sons make good husbands — and — I shall die at Beaurepaire, shall I not, Madame the Commandante?"

Josephine held her mother round the neck, but never spoke. After a silence she held her tighter, and cried a little.

"What is it?" asked the baroness confidentially of Rose, but without showing any very profound concern.

"Mamma! mamma! she does not love him."

"Love him? She would be no daughter of mine if she loved a man at sight. A modest woman loves her husband only."

"But she scarcely knows Monsieur Raynal."

"She knows more of him than I knew of your father when I married him. She knows his virtues and appreciates them. I have heard her, have I not, love? Esteem soon ripens into love when they are once fairly married."

"Mother, does her silence then tell you nothing? Her tears — are they nothing to you?"

"Silly child! These are tears that do not scald. The sweet soul weeps because she now for the first time sees she will have to leave her mother. Alas! my eldest, it is inevitable. Mothers are not immortal. While they are here it is their duty to choose good husbands for their daughters. My youngest, I believe, has chosen for herself — like the nation. But for my eldest I choose. We shall see which chooses the best. Meantime we stay at Beaurepaire, thanks to my treasure here."

"Josephine! Josephine! you don't say one word," cried Rose in dismay.

"What *can* I say? I love my mother and I love you. You draw me different ways. I want you to be both happy."

"Then if you will not speak out I must. Mother, do not deceive yourself: it is duty alone that keeps her silent: this match is odious to her."

"Then we are ruined. Josephine, is this match odious to you?"

"Not exactly odious: but I am very, very indifferent."

"There!" cried Rose triumphantly.

"There!" cried the baroness in the same breath, triumphantly. "She esteems his character; but his person is indifferent to her: in other words, she is a modest girl, and my daughter; and let me tell you, Rose, that but for the misfortunes of our house, both my daughters would be married as I was, without knowing half as much of their husbands as Josephine knows of this brave, honest, generous, filial gentleman."

"Well, then, since she will not speak out, I will. Pity me: I love her so. If this stranger, whom she does not love, takes her away from us, he will kill me. I shall die; oh!"

Josephine left her mother and went to console Rose.

The baroness lost her temper at this last stroke of opposition. "Now the truth comes out, Rose; this is selfishness. Do not deceive *your*self — selfishness!"

"Mamma!"

"You are only waiting to leave me yourself. Yet your eldest sister, forsooth, must be kept here for you, — till then." She added more gently, "Let me advise you to retire to your own room, and examine your heart fairly. You will find there is a strong dash of egoism in all this."

"If I do" —

"You will retract your opposition."

"My heart won't let me; but I will despise myself, and be silent."

And the young lady, who had dried her eyes the moment she was accused of selfishness, walked, head erect, from the room. Josephine cast a deprecating glance at her mother. "Yes, my angel!" said the latter, "I was harsh. But we are no longer of one mind, and I suppose never shall be again."

"Oh, yes, we shall. Be patient! Mother — you shall not leave Beaurepaire."

The baroness colored faintly at these four last words of her daughter, and hung her head.

Josephine saw that, and darted to her and covered her with kisses.

That day the doctor scolded them both. "You have put your mother into a high fever," said he; "here's a pulse; I do wish you would be more considerate."

The commandant did not come to dinner as usual. The evening passed heavily; their hearts were full of uncertainty.

"We miss our merry, spirited companion," said the baroness with a grim look at Rose. Both young ladies assented with ludicrous eagerness.

That night Rose came and slept with Josephine, and more than once she awoke with a start and seized Josephine convulsively and held her tight.

Accused of egoism! at first her whole nature rose in arms against the charge: but, after a while, coming as it did from so revered a person, it forced her to serious self-examination. The poor girl said to herself, "Mamma is a shrewd woman. Am I after all deceiving myself? Would she be happy, and am I standing in the way?" In the morning she begged her sister to walk with her in the park, so that they might be safe from interruption.

There, she said sadly, she could not understand her own sister. "Why are you so calm and cold, while am I in tortures of anxiety? Have you made some resolve and not confided it to your Rose?"

"No, love," was the reply; "I am scarce capable of a resolution; I am a mere thing that drifts."

"Let me put it in other words, then. How will this end?"

"I hardly know."

"Do you mean to marry Monsieur Raynal, then? answer me that."

"No; but I should not wonder if he were to marry *me*."

"But you said 'no.'"

"Yes, I said 'no' once."

"And don't you mean to say it again, and again, and again, till kingdom come?"

"What is the use? you heard him say he would not desist any the more, and I care too little about the matter to go on persisting, and persisting, and persisting."

"Why not, if he goes on pestering, and pestering, and pestering?"

"Ah, he is like you, all energy, at all hours; but I have so little where my heart is unconcerned: he seems, too, to have a wish! I have none either way, and my conscience says 'marry him!'"

"Your conscience say marry one man when you love another?"

"Heaven forbid! Rose, I love no one: I *have* loved; but now my heart is dead and silent; only my conscience says, 'You are the cause of all your mother's trouble; you are the cause that Beaurepaire was sold. Now you can repair that mischief, and at the same time make a brave man happy, our benefactor happy.' It is a great temptation: I hardly know why I said 'no' at all; surprise, perhaps — or to please you, pretty one."

Rose groaned: "Are you then worth so little that you would throw yourself away on a man who does not love you, nor want you, and is quite as happy single?"

"No; not happy; he is only stout-hearted and good, and therefore content; and he is a character that it would be easy — in short, I feel my power here: I could make that man happy; he has nobody to write to even, when he is away — poor fellow!"

"I shall lose all patience," cried Rose; "you are at your old trick, thinking of everybody but yourself: I let you do it in trifles, but I love you too well to permit it when the happiness of your whole life is at stake. I must be satisfied on one point, or else this marriage shall never take place: just answer me this; if Camille Dujardin stood on one side, and Monsieur Raynal on the other, and both asked your hand, which would you take?"

"That will never be. Whose? Not his whom I despise. Esteem might ripen into love, but what must contempt end in?"

This reply gave Rose great satisfaction. To exhaust all awkward contingencies, she said, "One question more, and I have done. Suppose Camille should turn out — be not quite — what shall I say — inexcusable?"

At this unlucky gush, Josephine turned pale, then red, then pale again, and cried eagerly, "Then all the world should not part us. Why torture me with such a question? Ah! you have heard something." And in a moment the lava of passion burst wildly through its thin sheet of ice. "I was blind. This is why you would save me from this unnatural marriage. You are breaking the good news to me by degrees. There is no need. Quick — quick — let me have it. I have waited three years; I am sick of waiting. Why don't you speak? Why don't you tell me? Then I will tell *you*. He is alive — he is well — he is coming. It was not he those soldiers saw;

they were so far off. How could they tell? They saw a uniform but not a face. Perhaps he has been a prisoner, and so could not write; could not come: but he is coming now. Why do you groan? why do you turn pale? ah! I see; I have once more deceived myself. I was mad. He I love is still a traitor to France and me, and I am wretched forever. Oh! that I were dead! oh! that I were dead! No; don't speak to me: never mind me; this madness will pass as it has before, and leave me a dead thing among the living. Ah! sister, why did you wake me from my dream? I was drifting so calmly, so peacefully, so dead, and painless, drifting over the dead sea of the heart towards the living waters of gratitude and duty. I was going to make more than one worthy soul happy; and seeing them happy, I should have been content and useful — what am I now? — and comforted other hearts, and died joyful — and young. For God is good; he releases the meek and patient from their burdens."

With this came a flood of tears; and she leaned against a bough with her forehead on her arm, bowed like a wounded lily.

"Accursed be that man's name, and *my* tongue if ever I utter it again in your hearing!" cried Rose, weeping bitterly. "You are wiser than I, and every way better. O my darling, dry your tears! Here he comes: look! riding across the park."

"Rose," cried Josephine, hastily, "I leave all to you. Receive Monsieur Raynal, and decline his offer if you think proper. It is you who love me best. My mother would give me up for a house; for an estate, poor dear."

"I would not give you for all the world."

"I know it. I trust all to you."

"Well, but don't go; stay and hear what I shall say."

"Oh, no; that poor man is intolerable to me NOW. Let me avoid his sight, and think of his virtues."

Rose was left alone, mistress of her sister's fate. She put her head into her hands and filled with anxiety and sudden doubt.

Like a good many more of us, she had been positive so long as the decision did not rest with her. But with power comes responsibility, with responsibility comes doubt. Easy to be an advocate in re incerta; hard to be the judge. And she had but a few seconds to think in; for Raynal was at hand. The last thing in her mind before he joined her was the terrible power of that base Camille over her sister. She despaired of curing Josephine, but a husband might. There's such divinity doth hedge a husband in innocent girls' minds.

"Well, little lady," began Raynal, "and how are you, and how is my mother-in-law that is to be — or is not to be, as your sister pleases; and how is *she*? have I frightened her away? There were two petticoats, and now there is but one."

"She left me to answer you."

"All the worse for me: I am not to your taste."

"Do not say that," said Rose, almost hysterically.

"Oh! it is no sacrilege. Not one in fifty likes me."

"But I do like you, sir."

"Then why won't you let me have your sister?"

"I have not quite decided that you shall not have her," faltered poor Rose. She murmured on, "I dare say you think me very unkind, very selfish; but put yourself in my place. I love my sister as no man can ever love her, I know: my heart has been one flesh and one soul with hers all my life. A stranger comes and takes her away from me as if she was I don't know what; his portmanteau; takes her to Egypt, oh! oh! oh!"

Raynal comforted her.

"What, do you think I am such a brute as to take that delicate creature about fighting with me? why, the hot sand would choke her, to begin. No. You don't take my manoeuvre. I have no family; I try for a wife that will throw me in a mother and sister. You will live all together the same as before, of course; only you must let me make one of you when I am at home. And how often will that be? Besides, I am as likely to be knocked on the head in Egypt as not; you are worrying yourself for nothing, little lady."

He uttered the last topic of consolation in a broad, hearty, hilarious tone, like a trombone impregnated with cheerful views of fate.

"Heaven forbid!" cried Rose: "and I will, for even I shall pray for you now. What you will leave her at home? forgive me for not seeing all your worth: of course I knew you were an angel, but I had no idea you were a duck. You are just the man for my sister. She likes to obey: you are all for commanding. So you see. Then she never thinks of herself; any other man but you would impose on her good-nature; but you are too generous to do that. So you see. Then she esteems you so highly. And one whom I esteem (between you and me) has chosen you for her."

"Then say yes, and have done with it," suggested the straight-forward soldier.

"Why should I say 'no?' you will make one another happy some day: you are both so good. Any other man but you would tear her from me; but you are too just, too kind. Heaven will reward you. No! I will. I will give you Josephine: ah, my dear brother-in-law, it is the most precious thing I have to give in the world."

"Thank you, then. So that is settled. Hum! no, it is not quite; I forgot; I have something for you to read; an anonymous letter. I got it this morning; it says your sister has a lover."

The letter ran to this tune: a friend who had observed the commandant's frequent visits at Beaurepaire wrote to warn him against traps. Both the young ladies of Beaurepaire were doubtless at the new proprietor's service to pick and choose from. But for all that each of them had a lover, and though these lovers had their orders to keep out of the way till monsieur should be hooked, he might be sure that if he married either, the man of her heart would come on the scene soon after, perhaps be present at the wedding.

In short, it was one of those poisoned arrows a coarse vindictive coward can shoot.

It was the first anonymous letter Rose had ever seen. It almost drove her mad on the spot. Raynal was sorry he had let her see it.

She turned red and white by turns, and gasped for breath.

"Why am I not a man? — why don't I wear a sword? I would pass it through this caitiff's heart. The cowardly slave! — the fiend! for who but a fiend could slander an angel like my Josephine? Hooked? Oh! she will never marry you if she sees this."

"Then don't let her see it: and why take it to heart like that? I don't trust to the word of a man who owns that his story is a thing he dares not sign his name to; at all events, I shall not put his word against yours. But it is best to understand one another in time. I am a plain man, but not a soft one. I should not be an easygoing husband like some I see about: I'd have no wasps round my honey; if my wife took a lover I would not lecture *the woman* — what is the use? — I'd kill *the man* then and there, in-doors or out, as I would kill a snake. If she took another, I'd send him after the first, and so on till one killed me."

"And serve the wretches right."

"Yes; but for my own sake I don't choose to marry a woman that loves any other man. So tell me the plain truth; come."

Rose turned chill in her inside. "I have no lover," she stammered. "I have a young fool that comes and teases me: but it is no secret. He is away, but why? he is on a sickbed, poor little fellow!"

"But your sister? She could not have a lover unknown to you."

"I defy her. No, sir; I have not seen her speak three words to any young man except Monsieur Riviere this three years past."

"That is enough;" and he tore the letter quietly to atoms.

Then Rose saw she could afford a little more candor. "Understand me; I can't speak of what happened when I was a child. But if ever she had a girlish attachment, he has not followed it up, or surely I should have seen something of him all these years."

"Of course. Oh! as for flirtations, let them pass: a lovely girl does not grow up without one or two whispering some nonsense into her ear. Why, I myself should have flirted no doubt; but I never had the time. Bonaparte gives you time to eat and drink, but not to sleep or flirt, and that reminds me I have fifty miles to ride, so good-by, sister-in-law, eh?"

"Adieu, brother-in-law."

Left alone, Rose had some misgivings. She had equivocated with one whose upright, candid nature ought to have protected him: but an enemy had accused Josephine; and it came so natural to shield her. "Did he really think I would expose my own sister?" said she to herself, angrily. Was not this anger secret self-discontent?

"Well, love," said Josephine, demurely, "have you dismissed him?"

"No."

Josephine smiled feebly. "It is easy to say 'say no;' but it is not so easy to say 'no,' especially when you feel you ought to say 'yes,' and have no wish either way except to give pleasure to others."

"But I am not such skim milk as all that," replied Rose: "I have always a strong wish where you are concerned, and your happiness. I hesitated whilst I was in doubt, but I doubt no longer: I have had a long talk with him. He has shown me his whole heart: he is the best, the noblest of creatures: he has no littleness or meanness. And then he is a thorough man; I know that by his being the very opposite of a woman in his ways. Now you are a thorough woman, and so you will suit one another to a T. I have decided: so no more doubts, love; no more tears; no more disputes. We are all of one mind, and I do think I have secured your happiness. It will not come in a day, perhaps, but it will come. So then in one little fortnight you marry Monsieur Raynal."

"What!" said Josephine, "you have actually settled that?"

"Yes."

"But are you sure I can make him as happy as he deserves?"

"Positive."

"I think so too; still" —

"It is settled, dear," said Rose soothingly.

"Oh, the comfort of that! you relieve me of a weight; you give me peace. I shall have duties; I shall do some good in the world. They were all for it but you before, were they not?"

"Yes, and now I am strongest for it of them all. Josephine, it is settled."

Josephine looked at her for a moment in silence, then said eagerly, "Bless you, dear Rose; you have saved your sister;" then, after a moment, in a very different voice, "O Camille! Camille! why have you deserted me?"

And with this she fell to sobbing terribly. Rose wept on her neck, but said nothing. She too was a woman, and felt that this was the last despairing cry of love giving up a hopeless struggle.

They sat twined together in silence till Jacintha came to tell them it was close upon dinner-time; so then they hastened to dry their tears and wash their red eyes, for fear their mother should see what they had been at, and worry herself.

"Well, mademoiselle, these two consent; but what do you say? for after all, it is you I am courting, and not them. Have you the courage to venture on a rough soldier like me?"

This delicate question was put point-blank before the three ladies.

"Sir," replied Josephine timidly, "I will be as frank, as straightforward as you are. I thank you for the honor you do me."

Raynal looked perplexed.

"And does that mean 'yes' or 'no'?"

"Which you please," said Josephine, hanging her sweet head.

The wedding was fixed for that day fortnight. The next morning wardrobes were ransacked. The silk, muslin, and lace of their prosperous days were looked out: grave discussions were held over each work of art. Rose was active, busy, fussy. The baroness threw in the weight of her judgment and experience.

Josephine managed to smile whenever either Rose or the baroness looked at all fixedly at her.

So glided the peaceful days. So Josephine drifted towards the haven of wedlock.

CHAPTER VI.

At Bayonne, a garrison town on the south frontier of France, two sentinels walked lethargically, crossing and recrossing before the governor's house. Suddenly their official drowsiness burst into energy; for a pale, grisly man, in rusty, defaced, dirty, and torn regimentals, was walking into the courtyard as if it belonged to him. The sentinels lowered their muskets, and crossed them with a clash before the gateway.

The scarecrow did not start back. He stopped and looked down with a smile at the steel barrier the soldiers had improvised for him, then drew himself a little up, carried his hand carelessly to his cap, which was nearly in two, and gave the name of an officer in the French army.

If you or I, dressed like a beggar who years ago had stolen regimentals and worn them down to civil garments, had addressed these soldiers with these very same words, the bayonets would have kissed closer, or perhaps the points been turned against our sacred and rusty person: but there is a freemasonry of the sword. The light, imperious hand that touched that battered cap, and the quiet clear tone of command told. The sentinels slowly recovered their pieces, but still looked uneasy and doubtful in their minds. The battered one saw this, and gave a sort of lofty smile; he turned up his cuffs and showed his wrists, and drew himself still higher.

The sentinels shouldered their pieces sharp, then dropped them simultaneously with a clatter and ring upon the pavement.

"Pass, captain."

The rusty figure rang the governor's bell. A servant came and eyed him with horror and contempt. He gave his name, and begged to see the governor. The servant left him in the hall, and went up-stairs to tell his master. At the name the governor reflected, then frowned, then bade his servant reach him down a certain book. He inspected it. "I thought so: any one with him?"

"No, your excellency."

"Load my pistols, put them on the table, show him in, and then order a guard to the door."

The governor was a stern veteran with a powerful brow, a shaggy eyebrow, and a piercing eye. He never rose, but leaned his chin on his hand, and his elbow on a table that stood between them, and eyed his visitor very fixedly and strangely. "We did not expect to see you on this side the Pyrenees," said he gravely.

"Nor I myself, governor."

"What do you come for?"

"A suit of regimentals, and money to take me to Paris."

"And suppose, instead of that, I turn out a corporal's guard, and bid them shoot you in the courtyard?"

"It would be the drollest thing you ever did, all things considered," said the other coolly, but bitterly.

The governor looked for the book he had lately consulted, found the page, handed it to the rusty officer, and watched him keenly: the blood rushed all over his face, and his lip trembled; but his eye dwelt stern yet sorrowful on the governor.

"I have read your book, now read mine." He drew off his coat and showed his wrists and arms, blue and waled. "Can you read that, sir?"

"No."

"All the better for you: Spanish fetters, general." He showed a white scar on his shoulder. "Can you read that? This is what I cut out of it," and he handed the governor a little round stone as big and almost as regular as a musket-ball.

"Humph! that could hardly have been fired from a French musket."

"Can you read this?" and he showed him a long cicatrix on his other arm.

"Knife I think," said the governor.

"You are right, sir: Spanish knife. Can you read this?" and opening his bosom he showed a raw wound on his breast.

"Oh, the devil!" cried the governor.

The wounded man put his rusty coat on again, and stood erect, and haughty, and silent.

The general eyed him, and saw his great spirit shining through this man. The more he looked the less could the scarecrow veil the hero from his practised eye. He said there must be some mistake, or else he was in his dotage; after a moment's hesitation, he added, "Be seated, if you please, and tell me what you have been doing all these years."

"Suffering."

"Not all the time, I suppose."

"Without intermission."

"But what? suffering what?"

"Cold, hunger, darkness, wounds, solitude, sickness, despair, prison, all that man can suffer."

"Impossible! a man would be dead at that rate before this."

"I should have died a dozen deaths but for one thing; I had promised her to live."

There was a pause. Then the old soldier said gravely, but more kindly, to the young one, "Tell me the facts, captain" (the first time he had acknowledged his visitor's military rank).

An hour had scarce elapsed since the rusty figure was stopped by the sentinels at the gate, when two glittering officers passed out under the same archway, followed by a servant carrying a furred cloak. The sentinels presented arms. The elder of these officers was the governor: the younger was the late scarecrow, in a brand-new uniform belonging to the governor's son. He shone out now in his true light; the beau ideal of a patrician soldier; one would have said he had been born with a sword by his side and drilled by nature, so straight and smart, yet easy he was in every movement. He was like a falcon, eye and all, only, as it were, down at the bottom of the hawk's eye lay a dove's eye. That compound and varying eye seemed to say, I can love, I can fight: I can fight, I can love, as few of you can do either.

The old man was trying to persuade him to stay at Bayonne, until his wound should be cured.

"No, general, I have other wounds to cure of longer standing than this one."

"Well, promise me to lay up at Paris."

"General, I shall stay an hour at Paris."

"An hour in Paris! Well, at least call at the War Office and present this letter."

That same afternoon, wrapped in the governor's furred cloak, the young officer lay at his full length in the coupe of the diligence, the whole of which the governor had peremptorily demanded for him, and rolled day and night towards Paris.

He reached it worn with fatigue and fevered by his wound, but his spirit as indomitable as ever. He went to the War Office with the governor's letter. It seemed to create some little sensation; one functionary came and said a polite word to him, then another. At last to his infinite surprise the minister himself sent down word he wished to see him; the minister put several questions to him, and seemed interested in him and touched by his relation.

"I think, captain, I shall have to send to you: where do you stay in Paris?"

"Nowhere, monsieur; I leave Paris as soon as I can find an easy-going horse."

"But General Bretaux tells me you are wounded."

"Not dangerously."

"Pardon me, captain, but is this prudent? is it just to yourself and your friends?"

"Yes, I owe it to those who perhaps think me dead."

"You can write to them."

"I grudge so great, so sacred a joy to a letter. No! after all I have suffered I claim to be the one to tell her I have kept my word: I promised to live, and I live."

"*Her*? then I say no more, only tell me what road you take."

"The road to Brittany."

As the young officer was walking his horse by the roadside about a league and a half from Paris, he heard a clatter behind him, and up galloped an aide-de-camp and drew up alongside, bringing his horse nearly on his haunches.

He handed him a large packet sealed with the arms of France. The other tore it open; and there was his brevet as colonel. His cheek flushed and his eye glittered with joy. The aide-de-camp next gave him a parcel: "Your epaulets, colonel! We hear you are going into the wilds where epaulets don't grow. You are to join the army of the Rhine as soon as your wound is well."

"Wherever my country calls me."

"Your address, then, colonel, that we may know where to put our finger on a tried soldier when we want one."

"I am going to Beaurepaire."

"Beaurepaire? I never heard of it."

"You never heard of Beaurepaire? it is in Brittany, forty-five leagues from Paris, forty-three leagues and a half from here."

"Good! Health and honor to you, colonel."

"The same to you, lieutenant; or a soldier's death."

The new colonel read the precious document across his horse's mane, and then he was going to put one of the epaulets on his right shoulder, bare at present: but he reflected.

"No; she should make him a colonel with her own dear hand. He put them in his pocket. He would not even look at them till she had seen them. Oh, how happy he was not only to come back to her alive, but to come back to her honored."

His wound smarted, his limbs ached, but no pain past or present could lay hold of his mind. In his great joy he remembered past suffering and felt present pain — yet smiled. Only every now and then he pined for wings to shorten the weary road.

He was walking his horse quietly, drooping a little over his saddle, when another officer well mounted came after him and passed him at a hand gallop with one hasty glance at his uniform, and went tearing on like one riding for his life.

"Don't I know that face?" said Dujardin.

He cudgelled his memory, and at last he remembered it was

the face of an old comrade. At least it strongly reminded him of one Jean Raynal who had saved his life in the Arno, when they were lieutenants together.

Yes, it was certainly Raynal, only bronzed by service in some hot country.

"Ah!" thought Camille; "I suppose I am more changed than he is; for he certainly did not recognize me at all. Now I wonder what that fellow has been doing all this time. What a hurry he was in! a moment more and I should have hailed him. Perhaps I may fall in with him at the next town."

He touched his horse with the spur, and cantered gently on, for trotting shook him more than he could bear. Even when he cantered he had to press his hand against his bosom, and often with the motion a bitterer pang than usual came and forced the water from his eyes; and then he smiled. His great love and his high courage made this reply to the body's anguish. And still his eyes looked straight forward as at some object in the distant horizon, while he came gently on, his hand pressed to his bosom, his head drooping now and then, smiling patiently, upon the road to Beaurepaire.

Oh! if anybody had told him that in five days his Josephine was to be married; and that the bronzed comrade, who had just galloped past him, was to marry her!

At Beaurepaire they were making and altering wedding-dresses. Rose was excited, and even Josephine took a calm interest. Dress never goes for nothing with her sex. The chairs and tables were covered, and the floor was littered. The baroness was presiding over the rites of vanity, and telling them what she wore at her wedding, under Louis XV., with strict accuracy, and what we men should consider a wonderful effort of memory, when the Commandant Raynal came in like a cannon-ball, without any warning, and stood among them in a stiff, military attitude. Exclamations from all the party, and then a kind greeting, especially from the baroness.

"We have been so dull without you, Jean."

"And I have missed you once or twice, mother-in-law, I can tell you. Well, I have got bad news; but you must consider we live in a busy time. Tomorrow I start for Egypt."

Loud ejaculations from the baroness and Rose. Josephine put down her work quietly.

The baroness sighed deeply, and the tears came into her eyes. "Oh, you must not be down-hearted, old lady," shouted Raynal. "Why, I am as likely to come back from Egypt as not. It is an even chance, to say the least."

This piece of consolation completed the baroness's unhappiness. She really had conceived a great affection for Raynal, and her heart had been set on the wedding.

"Take away all that finery, girls," said she bitterly; "we shall not want it for years. I shall not be alive when he comes home from Egypt. I never had a son — only daughters — the best any woman ever had; but a mother is not complete without a son, and I shall never live to have one now."

"I hate General Bonaparte," said Rose viciously.

"Hate my general?" groaned Raynal, looking down with a sort of superstitious awe and wonder at the lovely vixen. "Hate the best soldier the world ever saw?"

"What do I care for his soldiership? He has put off our wedding. For how many years did you say?"

"No; he has put it on."

In answer to the astonished looks this excited, he explained that the wedding was to have been in a week, but now it must be tomorrow at ten o'clock.

The three ladies set up their throats together. "Tomorrow?"

"Tomorrow. Why, what do you suppose I left Paris for yesterday? left my duties even."

"What, monsieur?" asked Josephine, timidly, "did you ride all that way, and leave your duties *merely to marry me?*" and she looked a little pleased.

"You are worth a great deal more trouble than that," said Raynal simply. "Besides, I had passed my word, and I always keep my word."

"So do I," said Josephine, a little proudly. "I will not go from it now, if you insist; but I confess to you, that such a proposal staggers me; so sudden — no preliminaries — no time to reflect; in short, there are so many difficulties that I must request you to reconsider the matter."

"Difficulties," shouted Raynal with merry disdain; "there are none, unless you sit down and make them; we do more difficult things than this every day of our lives: we passed the bridge of Arcola in thirteen minutes; and we had not the consent of the enemy, as we have yours — have we not?"

Her only reply was a look at her mother, to which the baroness replied by a nod; then turning to Raynal, "This empressement is very flattering; but I see no possibility: there is an etiquette we cannot altogether defy: there are preliminaries before a daughter of Beaurepaire can become a wife."

"There used to be all that, madam," laughed Raynal, putting her down good-humoredly; "but it was in the days when armies came out and touched their caps to one another, and went back into winter quarters. Then the struggle was who could go slowest; now the fight is who can go fastest. Time and Bonaparte wait for nobody; and ladies and other strong places are taken by storm, not undermined a foot a month as under Noah Quartorze: let me cut this short, as time is short."

He then drew a little plan of a wedding campaign. "The carriages will be here at 9 A.M.," said he; "they will whisk us down to the mayor's house by a quarter to ten: Picard, the notary, meets us there with the marriage contract, to save time; the contract signed, the mayor will do the marriage at quick step out of respect for me — half an hour — quarter past ten; breakfast in the same house an hour and a quarter: — we mustn't hurry a wedding breakfast — then ten minutes or so for the old fogies to waste in making speeches about our virtues — my watch will come out — my charger will come round — I rise from the table — embrace my dear old mother — kiss my wife's hand — into the saddle — canter to Paris — roll to Toulon — sail to Egypt. But I shall leave a wife and a mother behind me: they will both send me a kind word now and then; and I will write letters to you all from Egypt, and when I come home, my wife and I will make acquaintance, and we will all be happy together: and if I am killed out there, don't you go and fret your poor little hearts about it; it is a soldier's lot sooner or later. Besides, you will find I have taken care of you; nobody shall come and turn you out of your quarters, even though Jean Raynal should be dead; I have got to meet Picard at Riviere's on that very business — I am off."

He was gone as brusquely as he came.

"Mother! sister!" cried Josephine, "help me to love this man."

"You need no help," cried the baroness, with enthusiasm, "not love him, we should all be monsters."

Raynal came to supper looking bright and cheerful. "No more work *today*. I have nothing to do but talk; fancy that."

This evening Josephine de Beaurepaire, who had been silent and thoughtful, took a quiet opportunity, and purred in his ear, "Monsieur!"

"Mademoiselle!" rang the trombone.

"Am I not to go to Egypt?"

"No."

Josephine drew back at this brusque reply like a sensitive plant. But she returned to the attack.

"But is it not a wife's duty to be by her husband's side to look after his comfort — to console him when others vex him — to soothe him when he is harassed?"

"Her first duty is to obey him."

"Certainly."

"Well, when I am your husband, I shall bid you stay with your mother and sister while I go to Egypt."

"I shall obey you."

He told her bluntly he thought none the worse of her for making the offer; but should not accept it.

Camille Dujardin slept that night at a roadside inn about twelve miles from Beaurepaire, and not more than six from the town where the wedding was to take place next day.

It was a close race.

And the racers all unconscious of each other, yet spurred impartially by events that were now hurrying to a climax.

CHAPTER VII.

The next day at sharp nine two carriages were at the door.

But the ladies were not ready. Thus early in the campaign did they throw all into disorder. For so nicely had Raynal timed the several events that this threw him all into confusion. He stamped backwards and forwards, and twisted his mustaches, and swore. This enforced unpunctuality was a new torture to him. Jacintha told them he was angry, and that made them nervous and flurried, and their fingers strayed wildly among hooks and eyes, and all sorts of fastenings; they were not ready till half-past nine. Conscious they deserved a scolding, they sent Josephine down first to mollify. She dawned upon the honest soldier so radiant, so dazzling in her snowy dress, with her coronet of pearls (an heirloom), and her bridal veil parted, and the flush of conscious beauty on her cheek, that instead of scolding her, he actually blurted out, "Well! by St. Denis it was worth waiting half an hour for."

He recovered a quarter of an hour by making the driver gallop. Then occasional shrieks issued from the carriage that held the baroness. That ancient lady feared annihilation: she had not come down from a galloping age.

They drove into the town, drew up at the mayor's house, were received with great ceremony by that functionary and Picard, and entered the house.

When their carriages rattled into the street from the north side, Colonel Dujardin had already entered it from the south, and was riding at a foot's pace along the principal street. The motion of his horse now shook him past endurance. He dismounted at an inn a few doors from the mayor's house, and determined to do the rest of the short journey on foot. The landlord bustled about him obsequiously. "You are faint, colonel; you have travelled too far. Let me order you an excellent breakfast."

"No. I want a carriage; have you one?"

"I have two; but, unluckily, they are both engaged for the day, and by people of distinction. Commandant Raynal is married *today.*"

"Ah! I wish him joy," said Camille, heartily. He then asked the landlord to open the window, as he felt rather faint. The landlord insisted on breakfast, and Camille sat down to an omelet and a bottle of red wine. Then he lay awhile near the window, revived by the air, and watched the dear little street he had not seen for years. He felt languid, but happy, celestially happy.

She was a few doors from him, and neither knew it.

A pen was put into her white hand, and in another moment she had signed a marriage contract.

"Now to the church," cried the baroness, gayly. To get to the church, they must pass by the window Camille reclined at.

CHAPTER VIII.

"Oh! there's no time for that," said Raynal. And as the baroness looked horrified and amazed, Picard explained: "The state marries its citizens now, with reason: since marriage is a civil contract."

"Marriage a civil contract!" repeated the baroness. "What, is it then no longer one of the holy sacraments? What horrible impiety shall we come to next? Unhappy France! Such a contract would never be a marriage in my eyes: and what would become of an union the Church had not blessed?"

"Madame," said Picard, "the Church can bless it still; but it is only the mayor here that can *do* it."

All this time Josephine was blushing scarlet, and looking this way and that, with a sort of instinctive desire to fly and hide, no matter where, for a week or so.

"Haw! haw! haw!" roared Raynal; "here is a pretty mother. Wants her daughter to be unlawfully married in a church, instead of lawfully in a house. Give me the will!"

"Look here, mother-in-law: I have left Beaurepaire to my lawful wife."

"Otherwise," put in Picard, "in case of death, it would pass to his heir-at-law."

"And *he* would turn you all out, and that does not suit me. Now there stands the only man who can make mademoiselle my *lawful* wife. So quick march, monsieur the mayor, for time and Bonaparte wait for no man."

"Stay a minute, young people," said the mayor. "We should soothe respectable prejudices, not crush them. Madam, I am at least as old as you, and have seen many changes. I perfectly understand your feelings."

"Ah, monsieur! oh!"

"Calm yourself, dear madam; the case is not so bad as you think. It is perfectly true that in republican France the civil magistrate alone can bind French citizens in lawful wedlock. But this does not annihilate the religious ceremony. You can ask the Church's blessing on my work; and be assured you are not the only one who retains that natural prejudice. Out of every ten couples that I marry, four or five go to church afterwards and perform the ancient ceremonies. And they do well. For there before the altar the priest tells them what it is not my business to dilate upon — the grave moral and religious duties they have undertaken along with this civil contract. The state binds, but the

Church still blesses, and piously assents to that" —

"From which she has no power to dissent."

"Monsieur Picard, do you consider it polite to interrupt the chief magistrate of the place while he is explaining the law to a citizen?"

(This closed Picard.)

"I married a daughter last year," continued the worthy mayor.

"What, after this fashion?"

"I married her myself, as I will marry yours, if you will trust me with her. And after I have made them one, there is nothing to prevent them adjourning to the church."

"I beg your pardon," cried Raynal, "there are two things to prevent it: a couple that wait for no man: Time and Bonaparte. Come, sir; marry us, and have done with it."

The mayor assented. He invited Josephine to stand before him. She trembled and wept a little: Rose clung to her and wept, and the good mayor married the parties off hand.

"Is that all?" asked the baroness; "it is terribly soon done."

"It is done effectively, madam," said the mayor, with a smile. "Permit me to tell you that his Holiness the Pope cannot undo my work."

Picard grinned slyly, and whispered something into Raynal's ear.

"Oh! indeed," said Raynal aloud and carelessly. "Come, Madame Raynal, to breakfast: follow us, the rest of you."

They paired, and followed the bride and bridegroom into the breakfast-room.

The light words Picard whispered were five in number.

Now if the mayor had not snubbed Picard just before, he would have uttered those jocose but true words aloud. There was no particular reason why he should not. And if he had, — The threads of the web of life, how subtle they are! The finest cotton of Manchester, the finer meshes of the spider, seem three-inch cables by comparison with those moral gossamers which vulgar eyes cannot see at all, the "somethings, nothings," on which great fates have hung.

It was a cheerful breakfast, thanks to Raynal, who would be in high spirits, and would not allow a word of regret from any one. Madame Raynal sat by his side, looking up at him every now and then with innocent admiration. A merry wedding breakfast.

But if men and women could see through the walls of houses!

Two doors off sat the wounded colonel alone, recruiting the small remnant of his sore tried strength, that he might struggle on to Beaurepaire, and lose in one moment years of separation, pain, prison, anguish, martyrdom, in one great gush of joy without compare.

The wedding breakfast was ended. The time was drawing near to part. There was a silence. It was broken by Madame Raynal. She asked Raynal very timidly if he had reflected. "On what?" said he.

"About taking me to Egypt."

"No: I have not given it a thought since I said 'no.'"

"Yet permit me to say that it is my duty to be by your side, my husband." And she colored at this word, being the first time she had ever used it. Raynal was silent. She murmured on, "I would not be an encumbrance to you, sir: I should not be useless. Gentlemen, I could add more to his comfort than he gives me credit for."

Warm assent of the mayor and notary to this hint.

"I give you credit for being an angel," said Raynal warmly.

He hesitated. Rose was trembling, her fork shaking in her poor little hand.

She cast a piteous glance at him. He saw it.

"You shall go with me next time," said he. "Let us speak of it no more."

Josephine bowed her head. "At least give me something to do for you while you are away. Tell me what I can do for my absent friend to show my gratitude, my regard, my esteem."

"Well, let me think. I saw a plain gray dress at Beaurepaire."

"Yes, monsieur. My gray silk, Rose."

"I like that dress."

"Do you? Then the moment I reach home after losing you I shall put it on, and it shall be my constant wear. I see; you are right; gray becomes a wife whose husband is not dead, but is absent, and alas! in hourly danger."

"Now look at that!" cried Raynal to the company. "That is her all over: she can see six meanings where another would see but one. I never thought of that, I swear. I like modest colors, that is all. My mother used to be all for modest wives wearing modest colors."

"I am of her mind, sir. Is there nothing more difficult you will be so good as give me to do?"

"No; there is only one order more, and that will be easier still to such a woman as you. I commit to your care the name of Raynal. It is not so high a name as yours, but it is as honest. I am proud of it: I am jealous of it. I shall guard it for you in Egypt: you guard it in France for me."

"With my life," cried Josephine, lifting her eyes and her hand to heaven.

Soon after this Raynal ordered his charger.

The baroness began to cry. "The young people may hope to see you again," said she; "but there are two chances against your poor old mother."

"Courage, mother!" cried the stout soldier. "No, no; you won't play me such a trick: once is enough for that game."

"Brother!" cried Rose, "do not go without kissing your little sister, who loves you and thanks you." He kissed her. "Bravo, generous soul!" she cried, with her arms round his neck. "God protect you, and send you back safe to us!"

"Amen!" cried all present by one impulse, even the cold notary.

Raynal's mustache quivered. He kissed Josephine hastily on the brow, the baroness on both cheeks; shook the men's hands warmly but hastily, and strode out without looking behind him. He was moved for once.

They all followed him to the door of the house. He was tightening his horse's girths. He flung himself with all the resolution of his steel nature into the saddle, and, with one grand wave of his cocked hat to the tearful group, he spurred away for Egypt.

CHAPTER IX.

The baroness took the doctor a-shopping; she must buy Rose a gray silk. In doing this she saw many other tempting things. I say no more.

But the young ladies went up to Beaurepaire in the other carriage, for Josephine wished to avoid the gaze of the town, and get home and be quiet. The driver went very fast. He had drunk the bride's health at the mayor's, item the bridegroom's, the bridesmaid's, the mayor's, etc., and "a spur in the head is worth two in the heel," says the proverb. The sisters leaned back on the soft cushions, and enjoyed the smooth and rapid motion once so familiar to them, so rare of late.

Then Rose took her sister gently to task for having offered to go to Egypt. She had forgotten her poor sister.

"No, love," replied Josephine, "did you not see I dared not look towards you? I love you better than all the world; but this was my duty. I was his wife: I had no longer a feeble inclination and a feeble disinclination to decide between, but right on one side, wrong on the other."

"Oh! I know where your ladyship's strength lies: my force is — in — my inclinations."

"Yes, Rose," continued Josephine thoughtfully, "duty is a great comfort: it is so tangible; it is something to lay hold of for life or death; a strong tower for the weak but well disposed."

Rose assented, and they were silent a minute; and when she spoke again it was to own she loved a carriage. "How fast we glide! Now lean back with me, and take my hand, and as we glide shut your eyes and think: whisper me all your feelings, every one of them."

"Well, then," said Josephine, half closing her eyes, "in the first place I feel a great calm, a heavenly calm. My fate is decided. No more suspense. My duties are clear. I have a husband I am proud of. There is no perfidy with him, no deceit, no disingenuousness, no shade. He is a human sun. He will make me a better, truer woman, and I him a happier man. Yes, is it not nice to think that great and strong as he is I can teach him a happiness he knows not as yet?" And she smiled with the sense of her delicate power, but said no more; for she was not the one to talk much about herself. But Rose pressed her. "Yes, go on, dear," she said, "I seem to see your pretty little thoughts rising out of your heart like a bubbling fountain: go on."

Thus encouraged, Josephine thought on aloud, "And then,

gratitude!" said she. "I have heard it said, or read it somewhere, that gratitude is a burden: I cannot understand that sentiment; why, to me gratitude is a delight, gratitude is a passion. It is the warmest of all the tender feelings I have for dear Monsieur Raynal. I feel it glow here, in my bosom. I think I shall love him as I ought long before he comes back."

"BEFORE?"

"Yes," murmured Josephine, her eyes still half closed. "His virtues will always be present to me. His little faults of manner will not be in sight. Good Raynal! The image of those great qualities I revere so, perhaps because I fail in them myself, will be before my mind; and ere he comes home I shall love him dearly. I'll tell you one reason why I wished to go home at once was — no — you must guess."

"Guess?" said Rose, contemptuously. "As if I did not see it was to put on your gray silk."

Josephine smiled assent, and said almost with fervor, "Good Raynal! I feel prouder of his honest name than of our noble one. And I am so calm, dear, thanks to you, so tranquil; so pleased that my mother's mind is at rest, so convinced all is for the best, so contented with my own lot; so hap — py."

A gentle tear stole from beneath her long lashes. Rose looked at her wistfully: then laid her cheek to hers. They leaned back hand in hand, placid and silent.

The carriage glided fast. Beaurepaire was almost in sight.

Suddenly Josephine's hand tightened on Rose's, and she sat up in the carriage like a person awakened from a strange dream.

"What is it?" asked Rose.

"Some one in uniform."

"Oh, is that all? Ah! you thought it was a message from Raynal."

"Oh! no! on foot — walking very slowly. Coming this way, too. Coming this way!" and she became singularly restless, and looked round in the carriage. It was one of those old chariots with no side windows, but a peep hole at the back. This aperture, however, had a flap over it. Josephine undid the flap with nimble though agitated fingers; and saw — nothing. The road had taken a turn. "Oh," said Rose, carelessly, "for that matter the roads are full of soldiers just now."

"Ay, but not of officers on foot."

Rose gave her such a look, and for the first time this many a day spoke sternly to her, and asked her what on earth she had to do with uniforms or officers except one, the noblest in the world, her husband.

A month ago that word was almost indifferent to Josephine, or rather she uttered it with a sort of mild complacency. Now she started at it, and it struck chill upon her. She did not reply, however, and the carriage rolled on.

"He seemed to be dragging himself along." This was the first word Josephine had spoken for some time. "Oh, did he?" replied Rose carelessly; "well, let him. Here we are, at home."

"I am glad of it," said Josephine, "very glad."

On reaching Beaurepaire she wanted to go up-stairs at once and put on her gray gown. But the day was so delightful that Rose begged her to stroll in the Pleasaunce for half an hour and watch for their mother's return. She consented in an absent way, and presently began to walk very fast, unconscious of her companion. Rose laid a hand upon her playfully to moderate her, and found her skin burning.

"Why, what is the matter?" said she, anxiously.

"Nothing, nothing," was the sharp reply.

"There's a fretful tone; and how excited you look, and feel too. Well, I thought you were unnaturally calm after such an event."

"I only saw his back," said Josephine. "Did not you see him?"

"See who? Oh, that tiresome officer. Why, how much more are we to hear about him? I don't believe there *was* one."

At this moment a cocked hat came in sight, bobbing up and down above the palings that divided the park from the road. Josephine pointed to it without a word.

Rose got a little cross at being practically confuted, and said coldly, "Come, let us go in; the only cocked hat we can see is on the way to Paris."

Josephine assented eagerly. But she had not taken two steps towards the house ere she altered her mind, and said she felt faint, she wanted air; no, she should stay out a little longer. "Look, Rose," said she, in a strangely excited way, "what a shame! They put all manner of rubbish into this dear old tree: I will have it all turned out." And she looked with feigned interest into the tree: but her eyes seemed turned inward.

Rose gave a cry of surprise. "He is waving his hat to me! What on earth does that mean?"

"Perhaps he takes you for me," said Josephine.

"Who is it? What do you mean?"

"*It is he*! I knew his figure at a glance." And she blushed and trembled with joy; she darted behind the tree and peered round at him unseen: turning round a moment she found Rose at her back pale and stern. She looked at her, and said with terrible simplicity, "Ah, Rose, I forgot."

"Are you mad, Josephine? Into the house this moment; if it *is* he, I will receive him and send him about his business."

But Josephine stood fascinated, and pale as ashes; for now the cocked hat stopped, and a pale face with eyes whose eager fire shone even at that distance, rose above the palings. Josephine crouched behind Rose, and gasped out, "Something terrible is coming, terrible! terrible!"

"Say something hateful," said Rose, trembling in her turn, but only with anger. "The heartless selfish traitor! He never notices you till you are married to the noblest of mankind; and then he comes here directly to ruin your peace. No; I have altered my mind. He shall not see you, of course; but *you* shall hear *him*. I'll soon make you know the wretch and loathe him as I do. There, now he has turned the corner; hide in the oak while he is out of sight. Hide, quick, quick." Josephine obeyed mechanically; and presently, through that very aperture whence her sister had smiled on her lover she hissed out, in a tone of which one would not have thought her capable, "Be wise, be shrewd; find out who is the woman that has seduced him from me, and has brought two wretches to this. I tell you it is some wicked woman's doing. He loved me once."

"Not so loud! — one word: you are a wife. Swear to me you will not let him see you, come what may."

"Oh! never! never!" cried Josephine with terror. "I would rather die. When you have heard what he has to say, then tell him I am dead. No, tell him I adore my husband, and went to Egypt this day with him. Ah! would to God I had!"

"Sh! sh!"

"Sh!"

Camille was at the little gate.

Rose stood still, and nerved herself in silence. Josephine panted in her hiding-place.

Rose's only thought now was to expose the traitor to her sister, and restore her peace. She pretended not to see Camille till he was near her. He came eagerly towards her, his pale face flushing with great joy, and his eyes like diamonds.

"Josephine! It is not Josephine, after all," said he. "Why, this must be Rose, little Rose, grown up to a fine lady, a beautiful lady."

"What do you come here for, sir?" asked Rose in a tone of icy indifference.

"What do I come here for? is that the way to speak to me? but I am too happy to mind. Dear Beaurepaire! do I see you once again!"

"And madame?"

"What madame?"

"Madame Dujardin that is or was to be."

"This is the first I have ever heard of her," said Camille, gayly.

"This is odd, for we have heard all about it."

"Are you jesting?"

"No."

"If I understand you right, you imply that I have broken faith with Josephine?"

"Certainly."

"Then you lie, Mademoiselle Rose de Beaurepaire."

"Insolent!"

"No. It is you who have insulted your sister as well as me. She was not made to be deserted for meaner women. Come, mademoiselle, affront me, and me alone, and you shall find me more patient. Oh! who would have thought Beaurepaire would receive me thus?"

"It is your own fault. You never sent her a line for all these years."

"Why, how could I?"

"Well, sir, the information you did not supply others did. We know that you were seen in a Spanish village drinking between two guerillas."

"That is true," said Camille.

"An honest French soldier fired at you. Why, he told us so himself."

"He told you true," said Camille, sullenly. "The bullet grazed my hand; see, here is the mark. Look!" She did look, and gave a little scream; but recovering herself, said she wished it had gone through his heart. "Why prolong this painful interview?" said she; "the soldier told us all."

"I doubt that," said Camille. "Did he tell you that under the table I was chained tight down to the chair I sat in? Did he tell you that my hand was fastened to a drinking-horn, and my elbow to the table, and two fellows sitting opposite me with pistols quietly covering me, ready to draw the trigger if I should utter a cry? Did he tell you that I would have uttered that cry and died at that table but for one thing, I had promised her to live?"

"Not he; he told me nothing so incredible. Besides, what became of you all these years? You are a double traitor, to your country and to her."

Camille literally gasped for breath. "You are a most cruel young lady to insult me so," said he, and scalding tears forced themselves from his eyes.

Rose eyed him with merciless scorn.

He fought manfully against this weakness, with which his wound and his fatigue had something to do, as well as Rose's bitter words; and after a gallant struggle he returned her her haughty stare, and addressed her thus: "Mademoiselle, I feel myself blush, but it is for you I blush, not for myself. This is what *became* of me. I went out alone to explore; I fell into an ambuscade; I shot one of the enemy, and pinked another, but my arm being broken by a bullet, and my horse killed under me, the rascals got me. They took me about, tried to make a decoy of me as I have told you, and ended by throwing me into a dungeon. They loaded me with chains, too, though the walls were ten feet thick, and the door iron, and bolted and double-bolted outside. And there for months and years, in spite of wounds, hunger, thirst, and all the tortures those cowards made me suffer, I lived, because, Rose, I had promised some one at that gate there (and he turned suddenly and pointed to it) that I would come back alive. At last, one night, my jailer came to my cell drunk. I seized him by the throat and throttled him till he was insensible; his keys unlocked my fetters, and locked him in the cell, and I got safely outside. But there a sentinel saw me, and fired at me. He missed me but ran after me, and caught me. You see I was stiff, confined so long. He gave me a thrust of his bayonet; I flung my heavy keys fiercely in his face; he staggered; I wrested his piece from him, and disabled him."

"Ah!"

"I crossed the frontier in the night, and got to Bayonne; and thence, day and night, to Paris. There I met a reward for all my anguish. They gave me the epaulets of a colonel. See, here they are. France does not give these to traitors, young lady." He held them out to her in both hands. She eyed them half stupidly; all her thoughts were on the oak-tree hard by. She began to shudder. Camille was telling the truth. She felt that; she saw it; and Josephine was hearing it. "Ay! look at them, you naughty girl," said Camille, trying to be jocose over it all with his poor trembling lip. He went on to say that from the moment he had left dark Spain, and entered fair France everybody was so kind, so sympathizing. "They felt for the poor worn soldier coming back to his love. All but you, Rose. You told me I was a traitor to her and to France."

"I was told so," said Rose, faintly. She was almost at her wits' end what to say or do.

"Well, are you sorry or not sorry for saying such a cruel thing to a poor fellow?"

"Sorry, very sorry," whispered Rose. She could not persist in injustice, yet she did not want Josephine to hear.

"Then say no more about it; there's my hand. You are not a soldier, and did not know what you were talking about."

"I am very sorry I spoke so harshly to you. But you understand. How you look; how you pant."

"There, I will show you I forgive you. These epaulets, dear, I have never put them on. I said, no; Josephine shall put them on for me. I will take honor as well as happiness from her dear hand. But you are her sister, and what are epaulets compared with what she will give me? You shall put them on, dear. Come, then you will be sure I bear no malice."

Rose, faint at heart, consented in silence, and fastened on the epaulets. "Yes, Camille!" she cried, with sudden terror, "think of glory, now; nothing but glory."

"No one thinks of it more. But *today* how can I think of it, how can I give her a rival? Today I am all love. Rose, no man ever loved a human creature as I love Josephine. Your mother is well, dear? All are well at Beaurepaire? Oh, where is she all this time? in the house?" He was moving quickly towards the house; but Rose instinctively put out her hand to stop him. He recoiled a little and winced.

"What is the matter?" cried she.

"Nothing, dear girl; you put your hand on my wound, that is all. What is that noise in the tree? Anybody listening to us?"

"I'll see," said Rose, with all a woman's wit, and whipped hastily round to hinder Camille from going. She found Josephine white as death, apparently fainting, and clutching at the tree convulsively with her nails. Such was the intensity of the situation that she left her beloved sister in that piteous state, and even hoped she would faint dead away, and so hear no more. She came back white, and told Camille it was only a bird got into the tree. "And to think you should be wounded," said she, to divert his attention from the tree.

"Yes," said he, "and it is rather inflamed, and has worried me all the way. You need not go telling Josephine, though. They wanted me to stop and lay up at Bayonne. How could I? And again at Paris. How could I? They said, 'You will die.' — 'Not before I get to Beaurepaire,' said I. I could bear the motion of a horse no longer, so at the nearest town I asked for a carriage. Would you believe it? both his carriages were *out at a wedding*. I could not wait till they came back. I had waited an eternity. I came on foot. I dragged my self along; the body was weak, but the heart was strong. A little way from here my wound seemed inclined to open. I pressed it together tight with my hand; you see I could not afford to lose any more blood, and so struggled on. 'Die?' said I, 'not before Beaurepaire.' And, O Rose! now I could be content to die — at her feet; for I am happy. Oh! I am happy beyond words to utter. What I have gone through! But I kept my word, and this is Beaurepaire. Hurrah!" and his pale cheek flushed, and his eye gleamed, and he waved his hat feebly over his head, "hurrah! hurrah! hurrah!"

"Oh, don't! — don't! — don't!" cried Rose wild with pity and dismay.

"How can I help? — I am mad with joy — hurrah! hurrah! hurrah!"

"No! no! no! no! no!"

"What is the matter?"

"And must I stab you worse than all your enemies have stabbed you?" sighed Rose, and tears of womanly pity now streamed down her cheeks.

Camille's mind began to misgive him. What was become of Josephine? she did not appear. He faltered out, "Your mother is well; all are well I hope. Oh, where is she?" and receiving no reply, began to tremble visibly with the fear of some terrible calamity.

Rose, with a sister fainting close by, and this poor lover trembling before her, lost all self-command, and began to wring her hands and cry wildly. "Camille," she almost screamed, "there is but one thing for you to do; leave Beaurepaire on the instant: fly from it; it is no place for you."

"She is dead," said Camille, very quietly.

When he said that, with an unnatural and monotonous calm such as precedes deliberate suicide, it flashed in one moment across Rose that it was much best he should think so.

She did not reply; but she drooped her head and let him think it.

"She would have come to me ere this if she was alive," said he. "You are all in white: they mourn in white for angels like her, that go to heaven, virgins. Oh! I was blind. You might have told me at once; you see I can bear it. What does it matter to one who loves as I love? It is only to give her one more proof I lived only for her. I would have died a hundred times but for my promise to her. Yes, I am coming, love; I am coming."

He fell on his knees and smiled, and whispered, "I am coming, Josephine, I am coming."

A sob and a moan as of a creature dying in anguish answered him.

Rose screamed with terror when she heard it.

Camille rose to his feet, awestruck. "That was her voice, behind this tree," he whispered.

"No, no," cried Rose; "it was me."

But at that moment a rustle and a rush was heard of some one darting out of the tree.

Camille darted furiously round it in the same direction. Rose tried to stop him, but was too late. The next moment Raynal's wife was in his arms.

CHAPTER X.

Josephine wrestled long and terribly with nature in that old oak-tree. But who can so struggle forever? Anguish, remorse, horror, despair, and love wrenched her to and fro; and O mysterious human heart! gleams of a mad fitful joy shot through her, coming quick as lightning, going as quickly, and leaving the despair darker. And then the fierce struggle of the soul to make itself heard! More than once she had to close her mouth with her hand: more than once she seized her throat not to cry out. But as the struggle endured, she got weaker and weaker, and nature mightier and mightier. And when the wounded hero fell on his knees so close to her; when he who had resisted death so bravely for her, prepared to give up life calmly for her, her bosom rose beyond all control: it seemed to fill to choking, then to split wide open and give the struggling soul passage in one gasping sob and heart-stricken cry. Could she have pent this in she must have died.

It betrayed her. She felt it had: so then came the woman's instinct — flight: the coward's impulse — flight: the chaste wife's inspiration — flight. She rushed from her hiding-place and made wildly for the house.

But, unluckily, Camille was at that moment darting round the tree: she ran right into the danger she meant to flee. He caught her in his arms. He held her irresistibly. "I have got her; I have got her," he shouted in wild triumph. "No! I will not let you go. None but God shall ever take you from me, and he has spared you to me. You are not dead: you have kept faith as I have: you have lived. See! look at me. I am alive, I am well, I am happy. I told Rose that I suffered. If I had suffered I should remember it. It is all gone at sight of you, my love! my love! Oh, my Josephine! my love!"

His arm was firm round her waist. His glowing eyes poured love upon her. She felt his beating heart.

All that passed in her then, what mortal can say? She seemed two women: that part of her which could not get away from his strong arm lost all strength to resist, it yielded and thrilled under his embrace, her bosom heaving madly: all that was free writhed away from him; her face was averted with a glare of terror, and both her hands put up between his eyes and it.

"You turn away your head. Rose, she turns away. Speak for me. Scold her; for I don't know how to scold her. No answer from either; oh, what has turned your hearts against me so?"

"Camille," cried Rose — the tears streaming down her cheeks — "my poor Camille! leave Beaurepaire. Oh, leave it at once."

Returned towards her with a look of inquiry.

At that Josephine, like some feeble but nimble wild creature on whom a grasp has relaxed, writhed away from him and got free: "Farewell! Farewell!" she cried, in despair's own voice, and made swiftly for the house.

Camille stood aghast, and did not follow her.

Now ere she had gone many steps who should meet her right in front but Jacintha.

"Madame Raynal, the baroness's carriage is just in sight. I thought you'd like to know." Then she bawled proudly to Rose, "I was the first to call her madame;" and off went Jacintha convinced she had done something very clever.

This blow turned those three to stone.

Josephine had no longer the power or the wish to fly. "Better so," she thought, and she stood cowering.

The great passions that had spoken so loud were struck dumb, and a deep silence fell upon the place. Madame Raynal's quivering eye turned slowly and askant towards Camille, but stopped in terror ere it could see him. For she knew by this fearful stillness that the truth was creeping on Camille. And so did Rose.

At last Camille spoke one word in a low whisper.

"Madame?"

Dead silence.

"White? both in white?"

Rose came between him and Josephine, and sobbed out, "Camille, it was our doing. We drove her to it. O sir, look how afraid of you she is. Do not reproach her, if you are a man."

He waved her out of his way as if she had been some idle feather, and almost staggered up to Josephine.

"It is for you to speak, my betrothed: are you married?"

The poor creature, true to her nature, was thinking more of him than herself. Even in her despair it flashed across her, "If he knew all, he too would be wretched for life. If I let him think ill of me he may be happy one day." She cowered the picture of sorrow and tongue-tied guilt.

"Are you a wife?"

"Yes."

He winced and quivered as if a bullet had pierced him.

"This is how I came to be suspected; she I loved was false."

"Yes, Camille."

"No, no!" cried Rose; "don't believe *her*: she never suspected you. We have brought her to this, we alone."

"Be silent, Rose! oh, be silent!" gasped Josephine.

"I lived for you: I would have died for you; you could not even wait for me."

A low moan, but not a word of excuse.

"What can I do for you now?"

"Forget me, Camille," said she despairingly, doggedly.

"Forget you? never, never! there is but one thing I can do to show you how I loved you: I will forgive you, and begone. Whither shall I go? whither shall I go now?"

"Camile, your words stab her."

"Let none speak but I," said Camille; "none but I have the right to speak. Poor weak angel that loved yet could not wait: I forgive you. Be happy, if you can; I bid you be hap-py."

The quiet, despairing tones died away, and with them life seemed to end to her, and hope to go out. He turned his back quickly on her. He cried hoarsely, "To the army! Back to the army, and a soldier's grave!" Then with a prodigious effort he drew himself haughtily up in marching attitude. He took three strides, erect and fiery and bold.

At the next something seemed to snap asunder in the great heart, and the worn body that heart had held up so long, rolled like a dead log upon the ground with a tremendous fall.

CHAPTER XI.

The baroness and Aubertin were just getting out of their carriage, when suddenly they heard shrieks of terror in the Pleasaunce. They came with quaking hearts as fast as their old limbs would carry them. They found Rose and Josephine crouched over the body of a man, an officer.

Rose was just tearing open his collar and jacket. Dard and Jacintha had run from the kitchen at the screams. Camille lay on his back, white and motionless.

The doctor was the first to come up. "Who! what is this? I seem to know his face." Then shaking his head, "Whoever it is, it is a bad case. Stand away, ladies. Let me feel his pulse."

Whilst the old man was going stiffly down on one knee, Jacintha uttered a cry of terror. "See, see! his shirt! that red streak! Ah, ah! it is getting bigger and bigger:" and she turned faint in a moment, and would have fallen but for Dard.

The doctor looked. "All the better," said he firmly. "I thought he was dead. His blood flows; then I will save him. Don't clutch me so, Josephine; don't cling to me like that. Now is the time to show your breed: not turn sick at the sight of a little blood, like that foolish creature, but help me save him."

"Take him in-doors," cried the baroness.

"Into our house, mamma?" gasped Rose; "no, no."

"What," said the baroness, "a wounded soldier who has fought for France! leave him to lie and die outside my door: what would my son say to that? He is a soldier himself."

Rose cast a hasty look at Josephine. Josephine's eyes were bent on the ground, and her hands clenched and trembling.

"Now, Jacintha, you be off," said the doctor. "I can't have cowards about him to make the others as bad. Go and stew down a piece of good beef for him. Stew it in red wine and water."

"That I will: poor thing!"

"Why, I know him," said the baroness suddenly; "it is an old acquaintance, young Dujardin: you remember, Josephine. I used to suspect him of a fancy for you, poor fellow! Why, he must have come here to see us, poor soul."

"No matter who it is; it is a man. Now, girls, have you courage, have you humanity? Then come one on each side of him and take hands beneath his back, while I lift his head and Dard his legs."

"And handle him gently whatever you do," said Dard. "I know what it is to be wounded."

These four carried the lifeless burden very slowly and gently across the Pleasaunce to the house, then with more difficulty and caution up the stairs.

All the while the sisters' hands griped one another tight beneath the lifeless burden, and spoke to one another. And Josephine's arm upheld tenderly but not weakly the hero she had struck down. She avoided Rose's eye, her mother's, and even the doctor's: one gasping sob escaped her as she walked with head half averted, and vacant, terror-stricken eyes, and her victim on her sustaining arm.

The doctor selected the tapestried chamber for him as being most airy. Then he ordered the women out, and with Dard's help undressed the still insensible patient.

Josephine sat down on the stairs in gloomy silence, her eyes on the ground, like one waiting for her deathblow.

Rose, sick at heart, sat silent too at some distance. At last she said faintly, "Have we done well?"

"I don't know," said Josephine doggedly. Her eyes never left the ground.

"We could not let him die for want of care."

"He will not thank us. Better for him to die than live. Better for me."

At this instant Dard came running down. "Good news, mesdemoiselles, good news! the wound runs all along; it is not deep, like mine was. He has opened his eyes and shut them again. The dear good doctor stopped the blood in a twinkle. The doctor says he'll be bound to save him. I must run and tell Jacintha. She is taking on in the kitchen."

Josephine, who had risen eagerly from her despairing posture, clasped her hands together, then lifted up her voice and wept. "He will live! he will live!"

When she had wept a long while, she said to Rose, "Come, sister, help your poor Josephine."

"Yes, love, what shall we do?"

"My duty," faltered Josephine. "An hour ago it seemed so sweet," and she fell to weeping patiently again. They went to Josephine's room. She crept slowly to a wardrobe, and took out a gray silk dress.

"Oh, never mind for *today*," cried Rose.

"Help me, Rose. It is for myself as well; to remind me every moment I am Madame Raynal."

They put the gray gown on her, both weeping patiently. It will be known at the last day, all that honest women have suffered weeping silently in this noisy world.

Camille soon recovered his senses and a portion of his strength: then the irritation of his wound brought on fever. This in turn retired before the doctor's remedies and a sound constitution, but it left behind it a great weakness and general prostration. And in this state the fate of the body depends greatly on the mind.

The baroness and the doctor went constantly to see him, and soothe him: he smiled and thanked them, but his eager eyes watched the door for one who came not.

When he got well enough to leave his bed the largest couch was sent up to him from the saloon; a kind hand lined the baron's silk dressing-gown for him warm and soft and nice; and he would sit or lie on his couch, or take two turns in the room leaning upon Rose's shoulder, and glad of the support; and he looked piteously in her eyes when she came and when she went. Rose looked down; she could do nothing, she could say nothing.

With his strength, Camille lost a portion of his pride: he pined for a sight of her he no longer respected; pined for her, as the thirsty pine for water in Sahara.

At last one day he spoke out. "How kind you are to me, Rose! how kind you all are — but one."

He waited in hopes she would say something, but she held her tongue.

"At least tell me why it is. Is she ashamed? Is she afraid?"

"Neither."

"She hates me: it is true, then, that we hate those whom we have wounded. Cruel, cruel Josephine! Oh, heart of marble against which my heart has wrecked itself forever!"

"No, no! She is anything but cruel: but she is Madame Raynal."

"Ah! I forgot. But have I no claim on her? Nearly four years she has been my betrothed. What have I done? Was I ever false to her? I could forgive her for what she has done to me, but she cannot forgive me. Does she mean never to see me again?"

"Ask yourself what good could come of it."

"Very well," said Camille, with a malicious smile. "I am in her way. I see what she wants; she shall have it."

Rose carried these words to Josephine. They went through her like a sword.

Rose pitied her. Rose had a moment's weakness.

"Let us go to him," she said; "anything is better than this."

"Rose, I dare not," was the wise reply.

But the next day early, Josephine took Rose to a door outside the house, a door that had long been disused. Nettles grew before it. She produced a key and with great difficulty opened this door. It led to the tapestried chamber, and years ago they used to steal up it and peep into the room.

Rose scarcely needed to be told that she was to watch Camille, and report to her. In truth, it was a mysterious, vague protection against a danger equally mysterious. Yet it made Josephine easier. But so unflinching was her prudence that she never once could be prevailed on to mount those stairs, and peep at Camille herself. "I must starve my heart, not feed it," said she. And she grew paler and more hollow-eyed day by day.

Yet this was the same woman who showed such feebleness and irresolution when Raynal pressed her to marry him. But then dwarfs feebly drew her this way and that. Now giants fought for her. Between a feeble inclination and a feeble disinclination her dead heart had drifted to and fro. Now honor, duty, gratitude, — which last with her was a passion, — dragged her one way: love, pity, and remorse another.

Not one of these giants would relax his grasp, and nothing yielded except her vital powers. Yes; her temper, one of the loveliest Heaven ever gave a human creature, was soured at times.

Was it a wonder? There lay the man she loved pining for her; cursing her for her cruelty, and alternately praying Heaven to forgive him and to bless her: sighing, at intervals, all the day long, so loud, so deep, so piteously, as if his heart broke with each sigh; and sometimes, for he little knew, poor soul, that any human eye was upon him, casting aside his manhood in his despair, and flinging himself on the very floor, and muffling his head, and sobbing; he a hero.

And here was she pining in secret for him who pined for her? "I am not a woman at all," said she, who was all woman. "I am crueller to him than a tiger or any savage creature is to the victim she tears. I must cure him of his love for me; and then die; for what shall I have to live for? He weeps, he sighs, he cries for Josephine."

Her enforced cruelty was more contrary to this woman's nature than black is to white, or heat to cold, and the heart rebelled furiously at times. As when a rock tries to stem a current, the water fights its way on more sides than one, so insulted nature dealt with Josephine. Not only did her body pine, but her nerves were exasperated. Sudden twitches came over her, that almost made her scream. Her permanent state was utter despondency, but across it came fitful flashes of irritation; and then she was scarce mistress of herself.

Wherefore you, who find some holy woman cross and bitter,

stop a moment before you sum her up vixen and her religion naught: inquire the history of her heart: perhaps beneath the smooth cold surface of duties well discharged, her life has been, or even is, a battle against some self-indulgence the insignificant saint's very blood cries out for: and so the poor thing is cross, not because she is bad, but because she is better than the rest of us; yet only human.

Now though Josephine was more on her guard with the baroness than with Rose, or the doctor, or Jacintha, her state could not altogether escape the vigilance of a mother's eye.

But the baroness had not the clew we have; and what a difference that makes! How small an understanding, put by accident or instruction on the right track, shall run the game down! How great a sagacity shall wander if it gets on a false scent!

"Doctor," said the baroness one day, "you are so taken up with your patient you neglect the rest of us. Do look at Josephine! She is ill, or going to be ill. She is so pale, and so fretful, so peevish, which is not in her nature. Would you believe it, doctor, she snaps?"

"Our Josephine snap? This is new."

"And snarls."

"Then look for the end of the world."

"The other day I heard her snap Rose: and this morning she half snarled at me, just because I pressed her to go and console our patient. Hush! here she is. My child, I am accusing you to the doctor. I tell him you neglect his patient: never go near him."

"I will visit him one of these days," said Josephine, coldly.

"One of these days," said the baroness, shocked. "You used not to be so hard-hearted. A soldier, an old comrade of your husband's, wounded and sick, and you alone never go to him, to console him with a word of sympathy or encouragement."

Josephine looked at her mother with a sort of incredulous stare. Then, after a struggle, she replied with a tone and manner so spiteful and icy that it would have deceived even us who know her had we heard it. "He has plenty of nurses without me." She added, almost violently, "My husband, if he were wounded, would not have so many, perhaps not have one."

With this she rose and went out, leaving them aghast. She sat down in the passage on a window-seat, and laughed hysterically. Rose heard her and ran to her. Josephine told her what her mother had said to her. Rose soothed her. "Never mind, you have your sister who understands you: don't you go back till they have got some other topic."

Rose out of curiosity went in, and found a discussion going

on. The doctor was fathoming Josephine, for the benefit of his companion.

"It is a female jealousy, and of a mighty innocent kind. We are so taken up with this poor fellow, she thinks her soldier is forgotten."

"Surely, doctor, our Josephine would not be so unreasonable, so unjust," suggested her mother.

"She belongs to a sex, be it said without offending you, madame, among whose numberless virtues justice does not fill a prominent place."

The baroness shook her head. "That is not it. It is a piece of prudery. This young gentleman was a sort of admirer of hers, though she did not admire him much, as far as I remember. But it was four years ago; and she is married to a man she loves, or is going to love."

"Well, but, mamma, a trifling excess of delicacy is surely excusable." This from Rose.

"No, no; it is not delicacy; it is prudery. And when people are sick and suffering, an honest woman should take up her charity and lay down her prudery, or her coquetry: two things that I suspect are the same thing in different shapes."

Here Jacintha came in. "Mademoiselle, here is the colonel's broth; Madame Raynal has flavored it for him, and you are to take it up to him, and keep him company while he eats it."

"Come," cried the baroness, "my lecture has not been lost."

Rose followed Jacintha up-stairs.

Rose was heart and head on Raynal's side.

She had deceived him about Josephine's attachment, and felt all the more desirous to guard him against any ill consequences of it. Then he had been so generous to her: he had left her her sister, who would have gone to Egypt, and escaped this misery, but for her.

But on the other hand,

— Gentle pity
Tugged at her heartstrings with complaining cries.

This watching of Camille saddened even her. When she was with him his pride bore him up: but when he was alone as he thought, his anguish and despair were terrible, and broke out in so many ways that often Rose shrank in terror from her peep hole.

She dared not tell Josephine the half of what she saw: what she did tell her agitated her so terribly: and often Rose had it on the tip of her tongue to say, "Do pray go and see if you can say nothing that will do him good;" but she fought the impulse down. This battle of feeling, though less severe than her sister's, was constant; it destroyed her gayety. She, whose merry laugh used to ring like chimes through the house, never laughed now, seldom smiled, and often sighed.

Dr. Aubertin was the last to succumb to the deep depression, but his time came: and he had been for a day or two as grave and as sad as the rest, when one day that Rose was absent, spying on Camille, he took the baroness and Josephine into his confidence; and condescended finally to ask their advice.

"It is humiliating," said he, "after all my experience, to be obliged to consult unprofessional persons. Forty years ago I should have been *too wise* to do so. But since then I have often seen science baffled and untrained intelligences throw light upon hard questions: and your sex in particular has luminous instincts and reads things by flashes that we men miss with a microscope. Our dear Madame Raynal suspected that plausible notary, and to this day I believe she could not tell us why."

Josephine admitted as much very frankly.

"There you see," said the doctor. "Well, then, you must help me in this case. And this time I promise to treat your art with more respect."

"And pray who is it she is to read now?" asked the baroness.

"Who should it be but my poor patient? He puzzles me. I never knew a patient so faint-hearted."

"A soldier faint-hearted!" exclaimed the baroness. "To be sure these men that storm cities, and fire cannon, and cut and hack one another with so much spirit, are poor creatures compared with us when they have to lie quiet and suffer."

The doctor walked the room in great excitement. "It is not his wound that is killing him, there's something on his mind. You, Josephine, with your instincts do help me: do pray, for pity's sake, throw off that sublime indifference you have manifested all along to this man's fate."

"She has not," cried the baroness, firing up. "Did I not see her lining his dressing-gown for him? and she inspects everything that he eats: do you not?"

"Yes, mother." She then suggested in a faltering voice that time would cure the patient, and time alone.

"Time! you speak as if time was a quality: time is only a measure of events, favorable or unfavorable; it kills as many as it cures."

"Why, you surely would not imply his life is in any danger?" This was the baroness.

"Madame, if the case was not grave, should I take this unusual step? I tell you if some change does not take place soon, he will be a dead man in another fortnight. That is all *time* will do for him."

The baroness uttered an exclamation of pity and distress. Josephine put her hand to her bosom, and a creeping horror came over her, and then a faintness. She sat working mechanically, and turning like ice within. After a few minutes of this, she rose with every appearance of external composure and left the room. In the passage she met Rose coming hastily towards the salon laughing: the first time she had laughed this many a day. Oh, what a contrast between the two faces that met there — the one pale and horror stricken, the other rosy and laughing!

"Well, dear, at last I am paid for all my trouble, and yours, by a discovery; he never drinks a drop of his medicine; he pours it into the ashes under the grate; I caught him in the fact."

"Then this is too much: I can resist no longer. Come with me," said Josephine doggedly.

"Where?"

"To him."

CHAPTER XII.

Josephine paused on the landing, and laid her hand on Rose's shoulder. It was so cold it made Rose shudder, and exacted a promise from her not to contradict a word she should say to Camille. "I do not go to him for my pleasure, but for his life," she said; "I must deceive him and save him; and then let me lie down and die."

"Oh, that the wretch had never been born!" cried Rose, in despair. But she gave the required promise, and offered to go and tell Camille Josephine was coming to visit him.

But Josephine declined this. "No," said she; "give me every advantage; I must think beforehand every word I shall say; but take him by surprise, coward and doubleface that I am."

Rose knocked at the door. A faint voice said, "Come in." The sisters entered the room very softly. Camille sat on the sofa, his head bowed over his hands. A glance showed Josephine that he was doggedly and resolutely thrusting himself into the grave. Thinking it was only Rose — for he had now lost all hope of seeing Josephine come in at the door — he never moved. Some one glided gently but rapidly up to him. He looked up. Josephine was kneeling to him.

He lifted his head with a start, and trembled all over.

She whispered, "I am come to you to beg your pity; to appeal to your generosity; to ask a favor; I who deserve so little of you."

"You have waited a long time," said Camille, agitated greatly; "and so have I."

"Camille, you are torturing one who loved you once, and who has been very weak and faithless, but not so wicked as she appears."

"How am I torturing you?"

"With remorse; do I not suffer enough? Would you make me a murderess?"

"Why have you never been near me?" retorted Camille. "I could forgive your weakness, but not your heartlessness."

"It is my duty. I have no right to seek your society. If you really want mine, you have only to get well, and so join us down-stairs a week or two before you leave us."

"How am I to get well? My heart is broken."

"Camille, be a man. Do not fling away a soldier's life because a fickle, worthless woman could not wait for you. Forgive me like a man, or else revenge yourself like a man. If you cannot forgive me, kill me. See, I kneel at your feet. I will not resist you. Kill me."

"I wish I could. Oh! if I could kill you with a look and myself with a wish! No man should ever take you from me, then. We would be together in the grave at this hour. Do not tempt me, I say;" and he cast a terrible look of love, and hatred, and despair upon her. Her purple eye never winced; it poured back tenderness and affection in return. He saw and turned away with a groan, and held out his hand to her. She seized it and kissed it. "You are great, you are generous; you will not strike me as a woman strikes; you will not die to drive me to despair."

"I see," said he, more gently, "love is gone, but pity remains. I thought that was gone, too."

"Yes, Camille," said Josephine, in a whisper, "pity remains, and remorse and terror at what I have done to a man of whom I was never worthy."

"Well, madame, as you have come at last to me, and even do me the honor to ask me a favor — I shall try — if only out of courtesy — to — ah, Josephine! Josephine! when did I ever refuse you anything?"

At this Josephine sank into a chair, and burst out crying. Camille, at this, began to cry too; and the two poor things sat a long way from one another, and sobbed bitterly.

The man, weakened as he was, recovered his quiet despair first.

"Don't cry so," said he. "But tell me what is your will, and I shall obey you as I used before any one came between us."

"Then, live, Camille. I implore you to live."

"Well, Josephine, since you care about it, I will try and live. Why did not you come before and ask me? I thought I was in your way. I thought you wanted me dead."

Josephine cast a look of wonder and anguish on Camille, but she said nothing. She rang the bell, and, on Jacintha coming up, despatched her to Dr. Aubertin for the patient's medicine.

"Tell the doctor," said she, "Colonel Dujardin has let fall the glass." While Jacintha was gone, she scolded Camille gently. "How could you be so unkind to the poor doctor who loves you so? Only think: to throw away his medicines! Look at the ashes; they are wet. Camille, are you, too, becoming disingenuous?"

Jacintha came in with the tonic in a glass, and retired with an obeisance. Josephine took it to Camille.

"Drink with me, then," said he, "or I will not touch it." Josephine took the glass. "I drink to your health, Camille, and to your glory; laurels to your brow, and some faithful woman to your heart, who will make you forget this folly: it is for her I am saving you." She put the glass with well-acted spirit to her lips; but in the very action a spasm seized her throat and almost choked her; she lowered her head that he might not see her face, and tried again; but the tears burst from her eyes and ran into the liquid, and her lips trembled over the brim, and were paralyzed.

"No, no! give it me!" he cried; "there is a tear of yours in it." He drank off the bitter remedy now as if it had been nectar.

Josephine blushed.

"If you wanted me to live, why did you not come here before?"

"I did not think you would be so foolish, so wicked, so cruel as to do what you have been doing."

"Come and shine upon me every day, and you shall have no fresh cause of complaint; things flourish in the sunshine that die in the dark: Rose, it is as if the sun had come into my prison; you are pale, but you are beautiful as ever — more beautiful; what a sweet dress! so quiet, so modest, it sets off your beauty instead of vainly trying to vie with it." With this he put out his hand and took her gray silk dress, and went to kiss it as a devotee kisses the altar steps.

She snatched it away with a shudder.

"Yes, you are right," said she; "thank you for noticing my dress; it is a beautiful dress — ha! ha! A dress I take a pride in wearing, and always shall, I hope. I mean to be buried in it. Come, Rose. Thank you, Camille; you are very good, you have once more promised me to live. Get well; come down-stairs; then you will see me every day, you know — there is a temptation. Good-by, Camille! — are you coming, Rose? What are you loitering for? God bless you, and comfort you, and help you to forget what it is madness to remember!"

With these wild words she literally fled; and in one moment the room seemed to darken to Camille.

Outside the door Josephine caught hold of Rose. "Have I committed myself?"

"Over and over again. Do not look so terrified; I mean to me, but not to him. How blind he is! and how much better you must know him than I do to venture on such a transparent deceit. He believes whatever you tell him. He is all ears and no eyes. Yes, love, I watched him keenly all the time. He really thinks it is pity and remorse, nothing more. My poor sister, you have a hard life to lead, a hard game to play; but so far you have succeeded; yet could look poor Raynal in the face if he came home *today*."

"Then God be thanked!" cried Josephine. "I am as happy *today* as I can ever hope to be. Now let us go through the farce of dressing — it is near dinner-time — and then the farce of talking, and, hardest of all, the farce of living."

From that hour Camille began to get better very slowly, yet perceptibly.

The doctor, afraid of being mistaken, said nothing for some days, but at last he announced the good news at the dinner-table. "He is to come down-stairs in three days," added the doctor.

But I am sorry to say that as Camille's body strengthened some of the worst passions in our nature attacked him. Fierce gusts of hate and love combined overpowered this man's high sentiments of honor and justice, and made him clench his teeth, and vow never to leave Beaurepaire without Josephine. She had been his four years before she ever saw this interloper, and she should be his forever. Her love would soon revive when they should meet every day, and she would end by eloping with him.

Then conscience pricked him, and reminded him how and why Raynal had married her: for Rose had told him all. Should he undermine an absent soldier, whose whole conduct in this had been so pure, so generous, so unselfish?

But this was not all. As I have already hinted, he was under a great personal obligation to his quondam comrade Raynal. Whenever this was vividly present to his mind, a great terror fell on him, and he would cry out in anguish, "Oh! that some angel would come to me and tear me by force from this place!" And the next moment passion swept over him like a flood, and carried away all his virtuous resolves. His soul was in deep waters; great waves drove it to and fro. Perilous condition, which seldom ends well. Camille was a man of honor. In no other earthly circumstance could he have hesitated an instant between right and wrong. But such natures, proof against all other temptations, have often fallen, and will fall, where sin takes the angel form of her they love. Yet, of all men, they should pray for help to stand; for when they fall they still retain one thing that divides them from mean sinners.

Remorse, the giant that rends the great hearts which mock at fear.

The day came in which the doctor had promised his patient he should come down-stairs. First his comfortable sofa was taken down into the saloon for his use: then the patient himself came down leaning on the doctor's arm, and his heart palpitating at the thought of the meeting. He came into the room; the baroness was alone. She greeted him kindly, and welcomed him. Rose came in soon after and did the same. But no Josephine. Camille felt sick at heart. At last dinner was announced; "She will surely join us at dinner," thought he. He cast his eyes anxiously on the table; the napkins were laid for four only. The baroness carelessly explained this to him as they sat down. "Madame Raynal dines in her own room. I am sorry to say she is indisposed."

Camille muttered polite regrets: the rage of disappointment drove its fangs into him, and then came the heart-sickness of hope deferred. The next day he saw her, but could not get a word with her alone. The baroness tortured him another way. She was full of Raynal. She loved him. She called him her son; was never weary of descanting on his virtues to Camille. Not a day passed that she did not pester Camille to make a calculation as to the probable period of his return, and he was obliged to answer her. She related to him before Josephine and Rose, how this honest soldier had come to them like a guardian angel and saved the whole family. In vain he muttered that Rose had told him.

"Let me have the pleasure of telling it you my way," cried she, and told it diffusely, and kept him writhing.

The next thing was, Josephine had received no letter from him this month; the first month he had missed. In vain did Rose represent that he was only a few days over his time. The baroness became anxious, communicated her anxieties to Camille among the rest; and, by a torturing interrogatory, compelled him to explain to her before Josephine and them all, that ships do not always sail to a day, and are sometimes delayed. But oh! he winced at the man's name; and Rose observed that he never mentioned it, nor acknowledged the existence of such a person as Josephine's husband, except when others compelled him. Yet they were acquainted; and Rose sometimes wondered that he did not detract or sneer.

"I should," said she; "I feel I should."

"He is too noble," said Josephine, "and too wise. For, if he did, I should respect him less, and my husband more than I do — if possible."

Certainly Camille was not the sort of nature that detracts, but the reason he avoided Raynal's name was simply that his whole internal battle was to forget such a man existed. From this dream he was rudely awakened every hour since he joined the family, and the wound his self-deceiving heart would fain have skinned over, was torn open. But worse than this was the torture of being tanta-lized. He was in company with Josephine, but never alone. Even if she left the room for an instant, Rose accompanied her and returned with her. Camille at last began to comprehend that Josephine had decided there should be no private interviews between her and him. Thus, not only the shadow of the absent Raynal stood between them, but her mother and sister in person, and worst of all, her own will. He called her a cold-blooded fiend in his rage. Then the thought of all her tenderness and goodness came to rebuke him. But even in rebuking it maddened him. "Yes, it is her very nature to love; but since she can make her heart turn whichever way her honor bids, she will love her husband; she does not now; but sooner or later she will. Then she will have children — (he writhed with anguish and fury at this thought) — loving ties between him and her. He has everything on his side. I, nothing but memories she will efface from her heart. Will efface? She must have effaced them, or she could not have married him." I know no more pitiable state of mind than to love and hate the same creature. But when the two feelings are both intense, and meet in an ardent bosom, such a man would do well to spend a day or two upon his knees, praying for grace divine. For he who with all his soul loves and hates one woman is next door to a maniac, and is scarcely safe an hour together from suicide or even from homicide; this truth the newspapers tell us, by examples, every month; but are wonderfully little heeded, because newspapers do not, nor is it their business to, analyze and dwell upon the internal feelings of the despairing lover, whose mad and bloody act they record. With such a tempest in his heart did Camille one day wander into the park. And soon an irresistible attraction drew him to the side of the stream that flowed along one side of it. He eyed it gloomily, and wherever the stagnant water indicated a deeper pool than usual he stopped, and looked, and thought, "How calm and peaceful you are!"

He sat down at last by the water-side, his eyes bent on a calm, green pool.

It looked very peaceful; and it could give peace. He thought, oh! what a blessing; to be quit of rage, jealousy, despair, and life, all in a minute!

Yet that was a sordid death for a soldier to die, who had seen great battles. Could he not die more nobly than that? With this he suddenly felt in his pocket; and there sure enough fate had placed his pistols. He had put them into this coat; and he had not worn this coat until *today*. He had armed himself unconsciously. "Ah!" said he; "it is to be; all these things are preordained." (This notion of fate has strengthened many a fatal resolution.) Then he had a cruel regret. To die without a word; a parting word. Then he thought to himself, it was best so; for perhaps he should have taken her with him.

"Sir! colonel!" uttered a solemn voice behind him.

Absorbed and strung up to desperation as he was, this voice seemed unnaturally loud, and discordant with Camille's mood; a sudden trumpet from the world of small things.

It was Picard, the notary.

"Can you tell me where Madame Raynal is?"

"No. At the chateau, I suppose."

"She is not there; I inquired of the servant. She was out. You have not seen her, colonel?"

"Not I; I never see her."

"Then perhaps I had better go back to the chateau and wait for her: stay, are you a friend of the family? Colonel, suppose I were to tell you, and ask you to break it to Madame Raynal, or, better still, to the baroness, or Mademoiselle Rose."

"Monsieur," said Camille coldly, "charge me with no messages, for I cannot deliver them. *I am going another way.*"

"In that case, I will go to the chateau once more; for what I have to say must be heard."

Picard returned to the chateau wondering at the colonel's strange manner.

Camille, for his part, wondered that any one could be so mad as to talk to him about trifles; to him, a man standing on the brink of eternity. Poor soul, it was he who was mad and unlucky. He should have heard what Picard had to say. The very gentleness and solemnity of manner ought to have excited his curiosity.

He watched Picard's retiring form. When he was out of sight, then he turned round and resumed his thoughts as if Picard had been no more than a fly that had buzzed and then gone.

"Yes, I should have taken her with me," he said. He sat gloomy and dogged like a dangerous maniac in his cell; never moved, scarce thought for more than half an hour; but his deadly purpose grew in him. Suddenly he started. A lady was at the style, about a hundred yards distant. He trembled. It was Josephine.

She came towards him slowly, her eyes bent on the ground in a deep reverie. She stopped about a stone's throw from him, and looked at the river long and thoughtfully; then casting her eye around, she caught sight of Camille. He watched her grimly. He saw her give a little start, and half turn round; but if this was an impulse to retreat, it was instantly suppressed; for the next moment she pursued her way.

Camille stood gloomy and bitter, awaiting her in silence. He planted himself in the middle of the path, and said not a word.

She looked him all over, and her color came and went.

"Out so far as this," she said kindly; "and without your cap."

He put his hand to his head, and discovered that he was bare-headed.

"You will catch your death of cold. Come, let us go in and get your cap."

She made as if she would pass him. He planted himself right before her.

"No."

"Camille!"

"Why do you shun me as if I was a viper?"

"I do not shun you. I but avoid conferences that can lead to no good; it is my duty."

"You are very wise; cold-hearted people can be wise."

"Am I cold-hearted, Camille?"

"As marble."

She looked him in the face; the water came into her eyes; after awhile she whispered, sorrowfully, "Well, Camille, I am."

"But with all your wisdom and all your coldness," he went on to say, "you have made a mistake; you have driven me to madness and despair."

"Heaven forbid!" said she.

"Your prayer comes too late; you have done it."

"Camille, let me go to the oratory, and pray for you. You terrify me."

"It is no use. Heaven has no mercy for me. Take my advice; stay where you are; don't hurry; for what remains of your life you gave to pass with me, do you understand that?"

"Ah!" And she turned pale.

"Can you read my riddle?"

She looked him in the face. "I can read your eyes, and I know you love me. I think you mean to kill me. I have heard men kill the thing they love."

"Of course they do; sooner than another should have it, they kill it — they kill it."

"God has not made them patient like us women. Poor Camille!"

"Patience dies when hope dies. Come, Madame Raynal, say a prayer, for you are going to die."

"God bless you, Camille!" said the poor girl, putting her hands together in her last prayer. At this sweet touch of affection, Camille hung his head, and sobbed. Then suddenly lashing himself into fury, he cried, —

"You are my betrothed! you talk of duty; but you forget your duty to me. Are you not my betrothed this four years? Answer me that."

"Yes, Camille, I was."

"Did I not suffer death a hundred times for you, to keep faith with you, you cold-blooded traitress with an angel's face?"

"Ah, Camille! can you speak so bitterly to me? Have I denied your right to kill me? You shall never dishonor me, but you shall kill me, if it is your pleasure. I do not resist. Why, then, speak to me like that; must the last words I hear from your mouth be words of anger, cruel Camille?"

"I was wrong. But it is so hard to kill her I love in cold blood. I want anger as well as despair to keep me to it. Come, turn your head away from me, and all our troubles shall end."

"No, Camille, let me look at you. Then you will be the last thing I shall see on earth."

At this he hesitated a moment; then, with a fierce stamp at what he thought was weakness, he levelled a pistol at her.

She put up her hands with a piteous cry, "Oh! not my face, Camille! pray do not disfigure my face. Here — kill me here — in my bosom — my heart that loved you well, when it was no sin to love you."

"I can't shoot you. I can't spill your blood. The river will end all, and not disfigure your beauty, that has driven me mad, and cost you, poor wretch, your life."

"Thank you, dear Camille. The water does not frighten me as a pistol does; it will not hurt me; it will only kill me."

"No, it is but a plunge, and you will be at peace forever; and so shall I. Come, take my hand, Madame Raynal, Madame Raynal."

She gave him her hand with a look of infinite love. She only said, "My poor mother!" That word did not fall to the ground. It flashed like lightning at night across the demented lover, and lighted up his egotism (suicide, like homicide, is generally a fit of maniacal egotism), even to his eyes blinded by fury.

"Wretch that I am," he shrieked. "Fly, Josephine, fly! escape this moment, that my better angel whispers to me. Do you hear? begone, while it is time."

"I will not leave you, Camille."

"I say you shall. Go to your mother and Rose; go to those you love, and I can pity; go to the chapel and thank Heaven for your escape."

"Yes, but not without you, Camille. I am afraid to leave you."

"You have more to fear if you stay. Well, I can't wait any

longer. Stay, then, and live; and learn from me how to love Jean Raynal."

He levelled the pistol at himself.

Josephine threw herself on him with a cry, and seized his arm. With the strength excitement lent her she got the better, and all but overpowered him. But, as usual, the man's strength lasted longer, and with a sustained effort he threw her off; then, pale and panting, raised the pistol to take his life. This time she moved neither hand nor foot; but she palsied his rash hand with a word.

"No; *I love you.*"

CHAPTER XIII.

There lie the dead corpses of those words on paper; but my art is powerless to tell you how they were uttered, those words, potent as a king's, for they saved a life.

They were a cry of terror and a cry of reproach and a cry of love unfathomable.

The weapon shook in his hand. He looked at her with growing astonishment and joy; she at him fixedly and anxiously, her hands clasped in supplication.

"As you used to love me?"

"More, far more. Give me the pistol. I love you, dearest. I love you."

At these delicious words he lost all power of resistance, she saw; and her soft and supple hand stole in and closed upon his, and gently withdrew the weapon, and threw it into the water. "Good Camille! now give me the other."

"How do you know there is another?"

"I know you are not the man to kill a woman and spare yourself. Come."

"Josephine, have pity on me, do not deceive me; pray do not take this, my only friend, from me, unless you really love me."

"I love you; I adore you," was her reply.

She leaned her head on his shoulder, but with her hand she sought his, and even as she uttered those loving words she coaxed the weapon from his now unresisting grasp.

"There, it is gone; you are saved from death — saved from crime." And with that, the danger was over, she trembled for the first time, and fell to sobbing hysterically.

He threw himself at her knees, and embraced them again and again, and begged her forgiveness in a transport of remorse and self-reproach.

She looked down with tender pity on him, and heard his cries of penitence and shame.

"Rise, Camille, and go home with me," said she faintly.

"Yes, Josephine."

They went slowly and in silence. Camille was too ashamed and penitent to speak; too full of terror too at the abyss of crime from which he had been saved. The ancients feigned that a virgin could subdue a lion; perhaps they meant that a pure gentle nature can subdue a nature fierce but generous. Lion-like Camille walked by Josephine's side with his eyes bent on the ground, the picture of humility and penitence.

"This is the last walk you and I shall take together," said Josephine solemnly.

"I know it," said he humbly. "I have forfeited all right to be by your side."

"My poor, lost love," sighed Josephine, "will you never understand me? You never stood higher in my esteem than at this moment. It is the avowal you have forced from *me* that parts us. The man to whom I have said 'I' — must not remain beneath my husband's roof. Does not your sense of honor agree with mine?"

"It does," faltered he.

"Tomorrow you must leave the chateau."

"I will obey you."

"What, you do not resist, you do not break my heart by complaints, by reproaches?"

"No, Josephine, all is changed. I thought you unfeeling: I thought you were going to be *happy* with him; that was what maddened me."

"I pray daily *you* may be happy, no matter how. But you and I are not alike, dear as we are to one another. Well, do not fear: I shall never be happy — will that soothe you, Camille?"

"Yes, Josephine, all is changed; the words you have spoken have driven the fiends out of my heart. I have nothing to do now but to obey, you to command: it is your right. Since you love me a little still, dispose of me. Bid me live: bid me die: bid me stay: bid me go. I shall never disobey the angel who loves me, my only friend upon the earth."

A single deep sob from Josephine was all the answer.

Then he could not help asking her why she had not trusted him?

"Why did you not say to me long ago, 'I love you, but I am a wife; my husband is an honest soldier, absent, and fighting for France: I am the guardian of his honor and my own; be just, be generous, be self-denying; depart and love me only as angels love'? Perhaps this might have helped me to show you that I too am a man of honor."

"Perhaps I was wrong," sighed Josephine. "I think I should have trusted more to you. But then, who would have thought you could really doubt my love? You were ill; I could not bear you to go till you were well, quite well. I saw no other way to keep you but this, to treat you with feigned coldness. You saw the coldness, but not what it cost me to maintain it. Yes, I was unjust; and inconsiderate, for I had many furtive joys to sustain me: I had you in my house under my care — that thought was always sweet — I had a hand in everything that was for your good, for your comfort. I helped Jacintha make your soup and your chocolate every day. I had the delight of lining the dressing-gown you were to wear. I had always some little thing or other to do for you. These kept me up: I forgot in my selfishness that you had none of these supports, and that I was driving you to despair. I am a foolish, disingenuous woman: I have been very culpable. Forgive me!"

"Forgive you, angel of purity and goodness? I alone am to blame. What right had I to doubt your heart? I knew the whole story of your marriage; I saw your sweet pale face; but I was not pure enough to comprehend angelic virtue and unselfishness. Well, I am brought to my senses. There is but one thing for me to do — you bade me leave you tomorrow."

"I was very cruel."

"No! not cruel, wise. But I will be wiser. I shall go *tonight*."

"*Tonight*, Camille?" said Josephine, turning pale.

"Ay! for *tonight* I am strong; tomorrow I may be weak. *Tonight* everything thrusts me on the right path. *Tomorrow* everything will draw me from it. Do not cry, beloved one; you and I have a hard fight. We must be true allies; whenever one is weak, then is the time for the other to be strong. I have been weaker than you, to my shame be it said; but this is my hour of strength. A light from heaven shows me my path. I am full of passion, but like you I have honor. You are Raynal's wife, and — Raynal saved my life."

"Ah! is it possible? When? where? may Heaven bless him for it!"

"Ask HIM; and say I told you of it — I have not strength to tell it you, but I will go *tonight*."

Then Josephine, who had resisted till all her strength was gone, whispered with a blush that it was too late to get a conveyance.

"I need none to carry my sword, my epaulets, and my love for you. I shall go on foot."

Josephine said nothing, but she began to walk slower and slower. And so the unfortunate pair came along creeping slowly with drooping heads towards the gate of the Pleasaunce. There their last walk in this world must end. Many a man and woman have gone to the scaffold with hearts less heavy and more hopeful than theirs.

"Dry your eyes, Josephine," said Camille with a deep sigh. "They are all out on the Pleasaunce."

"No, I will not dry my eyes," cried Josephine, almost violently. "I care for nothing now."

The baroness, the doctor, and Rose, were all in the Pleasaunce: and as the pair came in, lo! every eye was bent on Josephine.

She felt this, and her eyes sought the ground: benumbed as she was with despondency, she began now to dread some fresh stroke or other.

Camille felt doubly guilty and confused. How they all look at us, he thought. Do they know what a villain I have been? He determined to slip away, and pack up, and begone. However, nobody took any notice of him. The baroness drew Josephine apart. And Rose followed her mother and sister with eyes bent on the ground.

There was a strange solemnity about them all.

Aubertin remained behind. But even he took no notice of Camille, but walked up and down with his hands behind him, and a sad and troubled face. Camille felt his utter desolation. He was nothing to any of them. He resolved to go at once, and charge Aubertin with his last adieus to the family. It was a wise and manly resolve. He stopped Aubertin in the middle of his walk, and said in a faint voice of the deepest dejection, —

"Doctor, the time is come that I must once more thank you for all your goodness to me, and bid you all farewell."

"What, going before your strength is re-established?" said the doctor politely, but not warmly.

"I am out of all danger, thanks to your skill."

"Colonel, at another time I should insist upon your staying a day or two longer; but now I think it would be unadvisable to press you to stay. Ah, colonel, you came to a happy house, but you leave a sad one. Poor Madame Raynal!"

"Sir!"

"You saw the baroness draw her aside."

"Y-yes."

"By this time she knows it."

"In Heaven's name what do you mean?" asked Camille.

"I forgot; you are not aware of the calamity that has fallen upon our beloved Josephine; on the darling of the house."

Camille turned cold with vague apprehension. But he contrived to stammer out, "No; tell me! for Heaven's sake tell me."

The doctor thus pressed revealed all in a very few words. "My poor friend," said he solemnly, "her husband — is dead."

CHAPTER XIV.

The baroness, as I have said, drew Josephine aside, and tried to break to her the sad news: but her own grief overcame her, and bursting into tears she bewailed the loss of her son. Josephine was greatly shocked. Death! — Raynal dead — her true, kind friend dead — her benefactor dead. She clung to her mother's neck, and sobbed with her. Presently she withdrew her face and suddenly hid it in both her hands.

She rose and kissed her mother once more: and went to her own room: and then, though there was none to see her, she hid her wet, but burning, cheeks in her hands.

Josephine confined herself for some days to her own room, leaving it only to go to the chapel in the park, where she spent hours in prayers for the dead and in self-humiliation. Her "tender conscience" accused herself bitterly for not having loved this gallant spirit more than she had.

Camille realized nothing at first; he looked all confused in the doctor's face, and was silent. Then after awhile he said, "Dead? Raynal dead?"

"Killed in action."

A red flush came to Camille's face, and his eyes went down to the ground at his very feet, nor did he once raise them while the doctor told him how the sad news had come. "Picard the notary brought us the Moniteur, and there was Commandant Raynal among the killed in a cavalry skirmish." With this, he took the journal from his pocket, and Camille read it, with awe-struck, and other feelings he would have been sorry to see analyzed. He said not a word; and lowered his eyes to the ground.

"And now," said Aubertin, "you will excuse me. I must go to my poor friend the baroness. She had a mother's love for him who is no more: well she might."

Aubertin went away, and left Dujardin standing there like a statue, his eyes still glued to the ground at his feet.

The doctor was no sooner out of sight, than Camille raised his eyes furtively, like a guilty person, and looked irresolutely this way and that: at last he turned and went back to the place where he had meditated suicide and murder; looked down at it a long while, then looked up to heaven — then fell suddenly on his knees: and so remained till night-fall. Then he came back to the chateau.

He whispered to himself, "And I am afraid it is too late to go away *tonight*." He went softly into the saloon. Nobody was there but Rose and Aubertin. At sight of him Rose got up and left the room. But I suppose she went to Josephine; for she returned in a few minutes, and rang the bell, and ordered some supper to be brought up for Colonel Dujardin.

"You have not dined, I hear," said she, very coldly.

"I was afraid you were gone altogether," said the doctor: then turning to Rose, "He told me he was going this evening. You had better stay quiet another day or two," added he, kindly.

"Do you think so?" said Camille, timidly.

He stayed upon these terms. And now he began to examine himself. "Did I wish him dead? I hope I never formed such a thought! I don't remember ever wishing him dead." And he went twice a day to that place by the stream, and thought very solemnly what a terrible thing ungoverned passion is; and repented — not eloquently, but silently, sincerely.

But soon his impatient spirit began to torment itself again. Why did Josephine shun him now? Ah! she loved Raynal now that he was dead. Women love the thing they have lost; so he had heard say. In that case, the very sight of him would of course be odious to her: he could understand that. The absolute, unreasoning faith he once had in her had been so rudely shaken by her marriage with Raynal, that now he could only believe just so much as he saw, and he saw that she shunned him.

He became moody, sad, and disconsolate: and as Josephine shunned him, so he avoided all the others, and wandered for hours by himself, perplexed and miserable. After awhile, he became conscious that he was under a sort of surveillance. Rose de Beaurepaire, who had been so kind to him when he was confined to his own room, but had taken little notice of him since he came down, now resumed her care of him, and evidently made it her business to keep up his heart. She used to meet him out walking in a mysterious way, and in short, be always falling in with him and trying to cheer him up: with tolerable success.

Such was the state of affairs when the party was swelled and matters complicated by the arrival of one we have lost sight of.

Edouard Riviere retarded his cure by an impatient spirit: but he got well at last, and his uncle drove him in the cabriolet to his own quarters. The news of the house had been told him by letter, but, of course, in so vague and general a way that, thinking he knew all, in reality he knew nothing.

Josephine had married Raynal. The marriage was sudden, but no doubt there was an attachment: he had some reason to believe in sudden attachments. Colonel Dujardin, an old acquaintance, had come back to France wounded, and the good doctor had undertaken his cure: this incident appeared neither strange nor any way important. What affected him most deeply was the death of Raynal, his personal friend and patron. But when his tyrants, as he called the surgeon and his uncle, gave him leave to go home, all feelings were overpowered by his great joy at the prospect of seeing Rose. He walked over to Beaurepaire, his arm in a sling, his heart beating. He was coming to receive the reward of all he had done, and all he had attempted. "I will surprise them," thought he. "I will see her face when I come in at the door: oh, happy hour! this pays for all." He entered the house without announcing himself; he went softly up to the saloon; to his great disappointment he found no one but the baroness: she received him kindly, but not with the warmth he expected. She was absorbed in her new grief. He asked timidly after her daughters. "Madame Raynal bears up, for the sake of others. You will not, however, see her: she keeps her room. My daughter Rose is taking a walk, I believe." After some polite inquiries, and sympathy with his accident, the baroness retired to indulge her grief, and Edouard thus liberated ran in search of his beloved.

He met her at the gate of the Pleasaunce, but not alone. She was walking with an officer, a handsome, commanding, haughty, brilliant officer. She was walking by his side, talking earnestly to him.

An arrow of ice shot through young Riviere; and then came a feeling of death at his heart, a new symptom in his young life.

The next moment Rose caught sight of him. She flushed all over and uttered a little exclamation, and she bounded towards him like a little antelope, and put out both her hands at once. He could only give her one.

"Ah!" she cried with an accent of heavenly pity, and took his hand with both hers.

This was like the meridian sun coming suddenly on a cold place. He was all happiness.

When Josephine heard he was come her eye flashed, and she said quickly, "I will come down to welcome him — dear Edouard!"

The sisters looked at one another. Josephine blushed. Rose smiled and kissed her. She colored higher still, and said, "No, she was ashamed to go down."

"Why?"

"Look at my face."

"I see nothing wrong with it, except that it eclipses other people's, and I have long forgiven you that."

"Oh, yes, dear Rose: look what a color it has, and a fortnight ago it was pale as ashes."

"Never mind; do you expect me to regret that?"

"Rose, I am a very bad woman."

"Are you, dear? then hook this for me."

"Yes, love. But I sometimes think you would forgive me if you knew how hard I pray to be better. Rose, I do try so to be as unhappy as I ought; but I can't, I can't. My cold heart seems as dead to unhappiness as once it was to happiness. Am I a heartless woman after all?"

"Not altogether," said Rose dryly. "Fasten my collar, dear, and don't torment yourself. You have suffered much and nobly. It was Heaven's will: you bowed to it. It was not Heaven's will that you should be blighted altogether. Bow in this, too, to Heaven's will: take things as they come, and do cease to try and reconcile feelings that are too opposite to live together."

"Ah! these are such comfortable words, Rose; but mamma will see this dreadful color in my cheek, and what can I say to her?"

"Ten to one it will not be observed; and if it should, I will say it is the excitement of seeing Edouard. Leave all to me."

Josephine greeted Edouard most affectionately, drew from him his whole history, and petted him and sympathized with him deliciously, and made him the hero of the evening. Camille, who was not naturally of a jealous temper, bore this very well at first, but at last he looked so bitter at her neglect of him, that Rose took him aside to soothe him. Edouard, missing the auditor he most valued, and seeing her in secret conference with the brilliant colonel, felt a return of the jealous pangs that had seized him at first sight of the man; and so they played at cross purposes.

At another period of the evening the conversation became more general; and Edouard took a dislike to Colonel Dujardin. A young man of twenty-eight nearly always looks on a boy of twenty-one with the air of a superior, and this assumption, not being an ill-natured one, is apt to be so easy and so undefined that the younger hardly knows how to resent or to resist it. But Edouard was a little vain as we know; and the Colonel jarred him terribly. His quick haughty eye jarred him. His regimentals jarred him: they fitted like a glove. His mustache and his manner jarred him, and, worst of all, his cool familiarity with Rose, who seemed to court him rather than be courted by him. He put this act of Rose's to the colonel's account, according to the custom of lovers, and revenged himself in a small way by telling Josephine in her ear "that the colonel produced on his mind the effect of an intolerable puppy."

Josephine colored up and looked at him with a momentary surprise. She said quietly, "Military men do give themselves some airs, but he is very amiable at bottom. You must make a better acquaintance with him, and then he will reveal to you his nobler qualities." — "Oh! I have no particular desire," sneered unlucky Edouard. Sweet as Josephine was, this was too much for her: she said nothing; but she quietly turned Edouard over to Aubertin, and joined Rose, and under cover of her had a sweet timid chat with her falsely accused.

This occupied the two so entirely that Edouard was neglected. This hurt his foible, and seemed to be so unkind on the very first day of his return that he made his adieus to the baroness, and marched off in dudgeon unobserved.

Rose missed him first, but said nothing.

When Josephine saw he was gone, she uttered a little exclamation, and looked at Rose. Rose put on a mien of haughty indifference, but the water was in her eyes.

Josephine looked sorrowful.

When they talked over everything together at night, she reproached herself. "We behaved ill to poor Edouard: we neglected him."

"He is a little cross, ill-tempered fellow," said Rose pettishly.

"Oh, no! no!"

"And as vain as a peacock."

"Has he not some right to be vain in this house?"

"Yes, — no. I am very angry with him. I won't hear a word in his favor," said Rose pouting: then she gave his defender a kiss. "Yes, dear," said Josephine, answering the kiss, and ignoring the words, "he is a dear; and he is not cross, nor so very vain, poor boy! now don't you see what it was?"

"No."

"Yes, you do, you little cunning thing: you are too shrewd not to see everything."

"No, indeed, Josephine; do tell me, don't keep me waiting: I can't bear that."

"Well, then — jealous! A little."

"Jealous? Oh, what fun! Of Camille? Ha! ha! Little goose!"

"And," said Josephine very seriously, "I almost think he would be jealous of any one that occupied your attention. I watched him more or less all the evening."

"All the better. I'll torment my lord."

"Heaven forbid you should be so cruel."

"Oh! I will not make him unhappy, but I'll tease him a little; it is not in nature to abstain."

This foible detected in her lover, Rose was very gay at the prospect of amusement it afforded her.

And I think I have many readers who at this moment are awaiting unmixed enjoyment and hilarity from the same source.

I wish them joy of their prospect.

Edouard called the next day: he wore a gloomy air. Rose met this with a particularly cheerful one; on this, Edouard's face cleared up, and he was himself again; agreeable as this was, Rose felt a little disappointed. "I am afraid he is not very jealous after all," thought she.

Josephine left her room this day and mingled once more with the family. The bare sight of her was enough for Camille at first, but after awhile he wanted more. He wanted to be often alone with her; but several causes co-operated to make her shy of giving him many such opportunities: first, her natural delicacy, coupled with her habit of self-denial; then her fear of shocking her mother, and lastly her fear of her own heart, and of Camille, whose power over her she knew. For Camille, when he did get a sweet word alone with her, seemed to forget everything except that she was his betrothed, and that he had come back alive to marry her. He spoke to her of his love with an ardor and an urgency that made her thrill with happiness, but at the same time shrink with a certain fear and self-reproach. Possessed with a feeling no stronger than hers, but single, he did not comprehend the tumult, the trouble, the daily contest in her heart. The wind seemed to him to be always changing, and hot and cold the same hour. Since he did not even see that she was acting in hourly fear of her mother's eye, he was little likely to penetrate her more hidden sentiments; and then he had not touched her key-note, — self-denial.

Women are self-denying and uncandid. Men are self-indulgent and outspoken.

And this is the key to a thousand double misunderstandings; for believe me, good women are just as stupid in misunderstanding men as honest men are in misunderstanding women.

To Camille, Josephine's fluctuations, joys, tremors, love, terror, modesty, seemed one grand total, caprice. The component parts of it he saw not; and her caprice tortured him almost to madness. Too penitent to give way again to violent passion, he gently fretted. His health retrograded and his temper began to sour. The eye of timid love that watched him with maternal anxiety from under its long lashes saw this with dismay, and Rose, who looked into her sister's bosom, devoted herself once more to soothe him without compromising Josephine's delicacy. Matters were not so bad but what a fine sprightly girl like Rose could cheer up a dejected but manly colonel; and Rose was generally successful.

But then, unfortunately, this led to a fresh mystification. Riviere's natural jealousy revived, and found constant food in the attention Rose paid Camille, a brilliant colonel living in the house while he, poor wretch, lived in lodgings. The false position of all the parties brought about some singular turns. I give from their number one that forms a link, though a small one, in my narrative.

One day Edouard came to tell Rose she was making him unhappy; he had her alone in the Pleasaunce; she received him with a radiant smile, and they had a charming talk, — a talk all about HIM: what the family owed him, etc.

On this, his late jealousy and sense of injury seemed a thing of three years ago, and never to return. So hard it is for the loving heart to resist its sun.

Jacintha came with a message from the colonel: "Would it be agreeable to Mademoiselle Rose to walk with him at the usual hour?"

"Certainly," said Rose.

As Jacintha was retiring Edouard called to her to stop a minute.

Then, turning to Rose, he begged her very ceremoniously to reconsider that determination.

"What determination?"

"To sacrifice me to this Colonel Dujardin." Still politely, only a little grimly.

Rose opened her eyes. "Are you mad?" inquired she with quiet hauteur.

"Neither mad nor a fool," was the reply. "I love you too well to share your regard with any one, upon any terms; least of all upon these, that there is to be a man in the world at whose beck and call you are to be, and at whose orders you are to break off an interview with me. Perdition!"

"Dear Edouard, what folly! Can you suspect me of discourtesy, as well as of — I know not what. Colonel Dujardin will join us, that is all, and we shall take a little walk with him."

"Not I. I decline the intrusion; you are engaged with me, and I have things to say to you that are not fit for that puppy to hear. So choose between me and him, and choose forever."

Rose colored. "I should be very sorry to choose either of you forever; but for this afternoon I choose you."

"Oh, thank you — my whole life shall prove my gratitude for this preference."

Rose beckoned Jacintha, and sent her with an excuse to Colonel Dujardin. She then turned with an air of mock submission to Edouard. "I am at monsieur's *orders*."

Then this unhappy novice, being naturally good-natured, thanked her again and again for her condescension in setting his heart at rest. He proposed a walk, since his interference had lost her one. She yielded a cold assent. This vexed him, but he took it for granted it would wear off before the end of the walk. Edouard's heart bounded, but he loved her too sincerely to be happy unless he could see her happy too; the malicious thing saw this, or perhaps knew it by instinct, and by means of this good feeling of his she revenged herself for his tyranny. She tortured him as only a woman can torture, and as even she can torture only a worthy man, and one who loves her. In the course of that short walk this inexperienced girl, strong in the instincts and inborn arts of her sex, drove pins and needles, needles and pins, of all sorts and sizes, through her lover's heart.

She was everything by turns, except kind, and nothing for long together. She was peevish, she was ostentatiously patient and submissive, she was inattentive to her companion and seemingly wrapped up in contemplation of absent things and persons, the colonel to wit; she was dogged, repulsive, and cold; and she never was herself a single moment. They returned to the gate of the Pleasaunce. "Well, mademoiselle," said Riviere very sadly, "that interloper might as well have been with us."

"Of course he might, and you would have lost nothing by permitting me to be courteous to a guest and an invalid. If you had not played the tyrant, and taken the matter into your own hands, I should have found means to soothe your jeal — I mean your vanity; but you preferred to have your own way. Well, you have had it."

"Yes, mademoiselle, you have given me a lesson; you have shown me how idle it is to attempt to force a young lady's inclinations in anything."

He bade her good-day, and went away sorrowful.

She cut Camille dead for the rest of the day.

Next morning, early, Edouard called expressly to see her. "Mademoiselle Rose," said he, humbly, "I called to apologize for the ungentlemanly tone of my remonstrances yesterday."

"Fiddle-dee," said Rose. "Don't do it again; that is the best apology."

"I am not likely to offend so again," said he sadly. "I am going away. I am sorry to say I am promoted; my new post is ten leagues. *He will have it all his own way now.* But perhaps it is best. Were I to stay here, I foresee you would soon lose whatever friendly feeling you have for me."

"Am I so changeable? I am not considered so," remonstrated Rose, gently.

Riviere explained; "I am not vain," said he, with that self-knowledge which is so general an attribute of human beings; "no man less so, nor am I jealous; but I respect myself, and I could never be content to share your time and your regard with Colonel Dujardin, nor with a much better man. See now; he has made me arrogant. Was I ever so before?"

"No! no! no! and I forgive you now, my poor Edouard."

"He has made you cold as ice to me."

"No! that was my own wickedness and spitefulness."

"Wickedness, spitefulness! they are not in your nature. It is all that wretch's doing."

Rose sighed, but she said nothing; for she saw that to excuse Camille would only make the jealous one more bitter against him.

"Will you deign to write to me at my new post? once a month? in answer to my letters?"

"Yes, dear. But you will ride over sometimes to see us."

"Oh, yes; but for some little time I shall not be able. The duties of a new post."

"Perhaps in a month — a fortnight?"

"Sooner perhaps; the moment I hear that man is out of the house."

Edouard went away, dogged and sad; Rose shut herself up in her room and had a good cry. In the afternoon Josephine came and remonstrated with her. "You have not walked with him at all *today.*"

"No; you must pet him yourself for once. I hate the sight of him; it has made mischief between Edouard and me, my being so attentive to him. Edouard is jealous, and I cannot wonder. After all, what right have I to mystify him who honors me with his affection?"

Then, being pressed with questions by Josephine, she related to her all that had passed between Edouard and her, word for word.

"Poor Camille!" sighed Josephine the just.

"Oh, dear, yes! poor Camille! who has the power to make us all miserable, and who does it, and will go on doing it until he is happy himself."

"Ah! would to Heaven I could make him as happy as he deserves to be."

"You could easily make him much happier than that. And why not do it?"

"O Rose," said Josephine, shocked, "how can you advise me so?"

She then asked her if she thought it possible that Camille could be ignorant of her heart.

"Josephine," replied Rose, angrily, "these men are absurd: they believe only what they see. I have done what I can for you and Camille, but it is useless. Would you have him believe you love him, you must yourself be kind to him; and it would be a charitable action: you would make four unhappy people happy, or, at least, put them on the road; *now* they are off the road, and, by what I have seen *today*, I think, if we go on so much longer, it will be too late to try to return. Come, Josephine, for my sake! Let me go and tell him you will consent — to all our happinesses. There, the crime is mine." And she ran off in spite of Josephine's faint and hypocritical entreaties. She returns the next minute looking all aghast. "It is too late," said she. "He is going away. I am sure he is, for he is packing up his things to go. I spied through the old place and saw him. He was sighing like a furnace as he strapped his portmanteau. I hate him, of course, but I was sorry for him. I could not help being. He sighed so all the time, piteously."

Josephine turned pale, and lifted her hands in surprise and dismay.

"Depend on it, Josephine, we are wrong," said Rose, firmly: "these wretches will not stand our nonsense above a certain time: they are not such fools. We are mismanaging: one gone, the other going; both losing faith in us."

Josephine's color returned to her cheek, and then mounted high. Presently she smiled, a smile full of conscious power and furtive complacency, and said quietly, "He will not go."

Rose was pleased, but not surprised, to hear her sister speak so confidently, for she knew her power over Camille. "That is right," said she, "go to him, and say two honest words: 'I bid you stay.'"

"O Rose! no!"

"Poltroon! You know he would go down on his knees, and stay directly."

"No: I should blush all my life before you and him. I *could* not.

I should let him go sooner, almost. Oh, no! I will never ask a man to stay who wishes to leave me. But just you go to him, and say Madame Raynal is going to take a little walk: will he do her the honor to be her companion? Not a word more, if you love me."

"I'll go. Hypocrite!"

Josephine received Camille with a bright smile. She seemed in unusually good spirits, and overflowing with kindness and innocent affection. On this his high gloomy brow relaxed, and all his prospects brightened as by magic. Then she communicated to him a number of little plans for next week and the week after. Among the rest he was to go with her and Rose to Frejus. "Such a sweet place: I want to show it you. You will come?"

He hesitated a single moment: a moment of intense anxiety to the smiling Josephine.

"Yes! he would come: it was a great temptation, he saw so little of her."

"Well, you will see more of me now."

"Shall I see you every day — alone, I mean?"

"Oh, yes, if you wish it," replied Josephine, in an off-hand, indifferent way.

He seized her hand and devoured it with kisses. "Foolish thing!" murmured she, looking down on him with ineffable tenderness. "Should I not be always with you if I consulted my inclination? — let me go."

"No! consult your inclination a little longer."

"Must I?"

"Yes; that shall be your punishment."

"For what? What have I done?" asked she with an air of great innocence.

"You have made me happy, me who adore you," was the evasive reply.

Josephine came in from her walk with a high color and beaming eyes, and screamed, "Run, Rose!"

On this concise, and to us not very clear instruction, Rose slipped up the secret stair. She saw Camille come in and gravely unpack his little portmanteau, and dispose his things in the drawers with soldier-like neatness, and hum an agreeable march. She came and told Josephine.

"Ah!" said Josephine with a little sigh of pleasure, and a gentle triumph in her eyes.

She had not only got her desire, but had arrived at it her way, — woman's way, round about.

This adroit benevolence led to more than she bargained for.

She and Camille were now together every day: and their hearts, being under restraint in public, melted together all the more in their stolen interviews.

At the third delicious interview the modest Camille begged Josephine to be his wife directly.

Have you noticed those half tame deer that come up to you in a park so lovingly, with great tender eyes, and, being now almost within reach, stop short, and with bodies fixed like statues on pedestals, crane out their graceful necks for sugar, or bread, or a chestnut, or a pocket-handkerchief? Do but offer to put your hand upon them, away they bound that moment twenty yards, and then stand quite still, and look at your hand and you, with great inquiring, suspicious, tender eyes.

So Josephine started at Camille's audacious proposal. "Never mention such a thing to me again: or — or, I will not walk with you any more:" then she thrilled with pleasure at the obnoxious idea, "she Camille's wife!" and colored all over — with rage, Camille thought. He promised submissively not to renew the topic: no more he did till next day. Josephine had spent nearly the whole interval in thinking of it; so she was prepared to put him down by calm reasons. She proceeded to do so, gently, but firmly.

Lo and behold! what does he do, but meets her with just as many reasons, and just as calm ones: and urges them gently, but firmly.

Heaven had been very kind to them: why should they be unkind to themselves? They had had a great escape: why not accept the happiness, as, being persons of honor, they had accepted the misery? with many other arguments, differing in other things, but agreeing in this, that they were all sober, grave, and full of common-sense.

Finding him not defenceless on the score of reason, she shifted her ground and appealed to his delicacy. On this he appealed to her love, and then calm reason was jostled off the field, and passion and sentiment battled in her place.

In these contests day by day renewed, Camille had many advantages.

Rose, though she did not like him, had now declared on his side. She refused to show him the least attention. This threw him on Josephine: and when Josephine begged her to help reduce Camille to reason, her answer would be, —

"Hypocrite!" with a kiss: or else she would say, with a half comic petulance, "No! no! I am on his side. Give him his own way, or he will make us all four miserable."

Thus Josephine's ally went over to the enemy.

And then this coy young lady's very power of resistance began to give way. She had now battled for months against her own heart: first for her mother; then, in a far more terrible conflict for Raynal, for honor and purity; and of late she had been battling, still against her own heart, for delicacy, for etiquette, things very dear to her, but not so great, holy, and sustaining as honor and charity that were her very household gods: and so, just when the motives of resistance were lowered, the length of the resistance began to wear her out.

For nothing is so hard to her sex as a long steady struggle. In matters physical, this is the thing the muscles of the fair cannot stand; in matters intellectual and moral, the long strain it is that beats them dead.

Do not look for a Bacona, a Newtona, a Handella, a Victoria Huga.

Some American ladies tell us education has stopped the growth of these.

No! mesdames. These are not in nature.

They can bubble letters in ten minutes that you could no more deliver to order in ten days than a river can play like a fountain. They can sparkle gems of stories: they can flash little diamonds of poems. The entire sex has never produced one opera nor one epic that mankind could tolerate: and why? these come by long, high-strung labor. But, weak as they are in the long run of everything but the affections (and there giants), they are all overpowering while their gallop lasts. Fragilla shall dance any two of you flat on the floor before four o'clock, and then dance on till the peep of day.

Only you trundle off to your business as usual, and could dance again the next night, and so on through countless ages.

She who danced you into nothing is in bed, a human jelly tipped with headache.

What did Josephine say to Rose one day? "I am tired of saying 'No! no! no! no! no!' forever and ever to him I love."

But this was not all. She was not free from self-reproach. Camille's faith in her had stood firm. Hers in him had not. She had wronged him, first by believing him false, then by marrying another. One day she asked his pardon for this. He replied that he had forgiven that; but would she be good enough to make him forget it?

"I wish I could."

"You can. Marry me: then your relation to that man will seem but a hideous dream. I shall be able to say, looking at you, my wife, 'I was faithful: I suffered something for her; I came home: she loved me still; the proof is, she was my wife within three months of my return.'"

When he said that to her in the Pleasaunce, if there had been a priest at hand . . . In a word, Josephine longed to show him her love, yet wished not to shock her mother, nor offend her own sense of delicacy; but Camille cared for nothing but his love. To sacrifice love and happiness, even for a time, to etiquette, seemed to him to be trifling with the substance of great things for the shadow of petty things; and he said so: sometimes sadly, sometimes almost bitterly.

So Josephine was a beleagured fortress, attacked with one will, and defended by troops, one-third of which were hot on the side of the besiegers.

When singleness attacks division, you know the result beforehand. Why then should I spin words? I will not trace so illmatched a contest step by step, sentence by sentence: let me rather hasten to relate the one peculiarity that arose out of this trite contest, where, under the names of Camille and Josephine, the two great sexes may be seen acting the whole world-wide distich, —

> *"It's a man's part to try,*
> *And a woman's to deny [for a while?]."*

Finding her own resolutions oozing away, Josephine caught at another person.

She said to Camille before Rose, —

"Even if I could bring myself to snatch at happiness in this indelicate way — scarce a month after, oh!" And there ended the lady's sentence. In the absence of a legitimate full stop, she put one hand before her lovely face to hide it, and so no more. But some two minutes after she delivered the rest in the form and with the tone of a distinct remark, "No: my mother would never consent."

"Yes, she would if you could be brought to implore her as earnestly as I implore you."

"Now would she?" asked Josephine, turning quickly to her sister.

"No, never. Our mother would look with horror on such a proposal. A daughter of hers to marry within a twelvemonth of her widowhood!"

"There, you see, Camille."

"And, besides, she loved Raynal so; she has not forgotten him as we have, almost."

"Ungrateful creature that I am!" sighed Josephine!

"She mourns for him every day. Often I see her eyes suddenly fill; that is for him. Josephine's influence with mamma is very great: it is double mine: but if we all went on our knees to her, the doctor and all, she would never consent."

"There you see, Camille: and I could not defy my mother, even for you."

Camille sighed.

"I see everything is against me, even my love: for that love is too much akin to veneration to propose to you a clandestine marriage."

"Oh, thank you! bless you for respecting as well as loving me, dear Camille," said Josephine.

These words, uttered with gentle warmth, were some consolation to Camille, and confirmed him, as they were intended to do, in the above good resolution. He smiled.

"Maladroit!" muttered Rose.

"Why maladroit?" asked Camille, opening his eyes.

"Let us talk of something else," replied Rose, coolly.

Camille turned red. He understood that he had done something very stupid, but he could not conceive what. He looked from one sister to the other alternately. Rose was smiling ironically, Josephine had her eyes bent demurely on a handkerchief she was embroidering.

That evening Camille drew Rose aside, and asked for an explanation of her "maladroit."

"So it was," replied Rose, sharply.

But as this did not make the matter quite clear, Camille begged a little further explanation.

"Was it your part to make difficulties?"

"No, indeed."

"Was it for you to tell her a secret marriage would not be delicate? Do you think she will be behind you in delicacy? or that a love without respect will satisfy her? yet you must go and tell her you respected her too much to ask her to marry you secretly. In other words, situated as she is, you asked her not to marry you at all: she consented to that directly; what else could you expect?"

"Maladroit! indeed," said Camille, "but I would not have said it, only I thought" —

"You thought nothing would induce her to marry secretly, so you said to yourself, 'I will assume a virtue: I will do a bit of cheap self-denial: decline to the sound of trumpets what another will be sure to deny me if I don't — ha! ha!' — well, for your comfort, I am by no means so sure she might not have been brought to do *anything* for you, except openly defy mamma: but now of course" —

And here this young lady's sentence ended: for the sisters, unlike in most things, were one in grammar.

Camille was so disconcerted and sad at what he had done, that Rose began to pity him: so she rallied him a little longer in spite of her pity: and then all of a sudden gave him her hand, and said she would try and repair the mischief.

He began to smother her hand with kisses.

"Oh!" said she, "I don't deserve all that: I have a motive of my own; let me alone, child, do. Your unlucky speech will be quoted to me a dozen times. Never mind."

Rose went and bribed Josephine to consent.

"Come, mamma shall not know, and as for you, you shall scarcely move in the matter; only do not oppose me very violently, and all will be well."

"Ah, Rose!" said Josephine; "it is delightful — terrible, I mean — to have a little creature about one that reads one like this. What shall I do? What shall I do?"

"Why, do the best you can under all the circumstances. His wound is healed, you know; he must go back to the army; you have both suffered to the limits of mortal endurance. Is he to go away unhappy, in any doubt of your affection? and you to remain behind with the misery of self-reproach added to the desolation of absence? — think."

"It is cruel. But to deceive my mother!"

"Do not say deceive our mother; that is such a shocking phrase."

Rose then reminded Josephine that their confessor had told them a wise reticence was not the same thing as a moral deceit. She reminded her, too, how often they had acted on his advice and always with good effect; how many anxieties and worries they had saved their mother by reticence. Josephine assented warmly to this.

Was there not some reason to think they had saved their mother's very life by these reticences? Josephine assented. "And, Josephine, you are of age; you are your own mistress; you have a right to marry whom you please: and, sooner or later, you will certainly marry Camille. I doubt whether even our mother could prevail on you to refuse him altogether. So it is but a question of time, and of giving our mother pain, or sparing her pain. Dear mamma is old; she is prejudiced. Why shock her prejudices? She could not be brought to understand the case: these things never happened in her day. Everything seems to have gone by rule then. Let us do nothing to worry her for the short time she has to live. Let us take a course between pain to her and cruelty to you and Camille."

These arguments went far to convince Josephine: for her own heart supported them. She went from her solid objections to untenable ones — a great point gained. She urged the difficulty, the impossibility of a secret marriage.

Camille burst in here: he undertook at once to overcome these imaginary difficulties. "They could be married at a distance."

"You will find no priest who will consent to do such a wicked thing as marry us without my mother's knowledge," objected Josephine.

"Oh! as to that," said Rose, "you know the mayor marries people nowadays."

"I will not be married again without a priest," said Josephine, sharply.

"Nor I," said Camille. "I know a mayor who will do the civil forms for me, and a priest who will marry me in the sight of Heaven, and both will keep it secret for love of me till it shall please Josephine to throw off this disguise."

"Who is the priest?" inquired Josephine, keenly.

"An old cure: he lives near Frejus: he was my tutor, and the mayor is the mayor of Frejus, also an old friend of mine."

"But what on earth will you say to them?"

"That is my affair: I must give them some reasons which compel me to keep my marriage secret. Oh! I shall have to tell them some fibs, of course."

"There, I thought so! I will not have you telling fibs; it lowers you."

"Of course it does; but you can't have secrecy without a fib or two."

"Fibs that will injure no one," said Rose, majestically.

From this day Camille began to act as well as to talk. He bought a light caleche and a powerful horse, and elected factotum Dard his groom. Camille rode over to Frejus and told a made-up story to the old cure and the mayor, and these his old friends believed every word he said, and readily promised their services and strict secrecy.

He told the young ladies what he had done.

Rose approved. Josephine shook her head, and seeing matters going as her heart desired and her conscience did not quite approve, she suddenly affected to be next to nobody in the business — to be resigned, passive, and disposed of to her surprise by Queen Rose and King Camille, without herself taking any actual part in their proceedings.

At last the great day arrived on which Camille and Josephine were to be married at Frejus.

The mayor awaited them at eleven o'clock. The cure at twelve. The family had been duly prepared for this excursion by several smaller ones.

Rose announced their intention over night; a part of it.

"Mamma," said she, blushing a little, "Colonel Dujardin is good enough to take us to Frejus tomorrow. It is a long way, and we must breakfast early or we shall not be back to dinner."

"Do so, my child. I hope you will have a fine day: and mind you take plenty of wraps with you in case of a shower."

At seven o'clock the next morning Camille and the two ladies took a hasty cup of coffee together instead of breakfast, and then Dard brought the caleche round.

The ladies got in, and Camille had just taken the reins in his hand, when Jacintha screamed to him from the hall, "Wait a moment, colonel, wait a moment! The doctor! don't go without the doctor!" And the next moment Dr. Aubertin appeared with his cloak on his arm, and, saluting the ladies politely, seated himself quietly in the vehicle before the party had recovered their surprise.

The ladies managed to keep their countenances, but Dujardin's discomfiture was evident.

He looked piteously at Josephine, and then asked Aubertin if they were to set him down anywhere in particular.

"Oh, no; I am going with you to Frejus," was the quiet reply.

Josephine quaked. Camille was devoured with secret rage: he lashed the horse and away they went.

It was a silent party. The doctor seemed in a reverie. The others did not know what to think, much less to say. Aubertin sat by Camille's side; so the latter could hold no secret communication with either lady.

Now it was not the doctor's habit to rise at this time of the morning: yet there he was, going with them to Frejus uninvited.

Josephine was in agony; had their intention transpired through some imprudence of Camille?

Camille was terribly uneasy. He concluded the secret had transpired through female indiscretion. Then they all tortured themselves as to the old man's intention. But what seemed most likely was, that he was with them to prevent a clandestine marriage by his bare presence, without making a scene and shocking Josephine's pride: and if so, was he there by his own impulse? No, it was rather to be feared that all this was done by order of the baroness. There was a finesse about it that smacked of a feminine origin, and the baroness was very capable of adopting such a means as this, to spare her own pride and her favorite daughter's. "The clandestine" is not all sugar. A more miserable party never went along, even to a wedding.

After waiting a long time for the doctor to declare himself, they turned desperate, and began to chatter all manner of trifles. This had a good effect: it roused Aubertin from his reverie, and presently he gave them the following piece of information: "I told you the other day that a nephew of mine was just dead; a nephew I had not seen for many years. Well, my friends, I received last night a hasty summons to his funeral."

"At Frejus?"

"No, at Paris. The invitation was so pressing, that I was obliged to go. The letter informed me, however, that a diligence passes through Frejus, at eleven o'clock, for Paris. I heard you say you were going to Frejus; so I packed up a few changes of linen, and my MS., my work on entomology, which at my last visit to the capital all the publishers were mad enough to refuse: here it is. Apropos, has Jacintha put my bag into the carriage?"

On this a fierce foot-search, and the bag was found. Meantime, Josephine leaned back in her seat with a sigh of thankfulness. She was more intent on not being found out than on being married. But Camille, who was more intent on being married than on not being found out, was asking himself, with fury, how on earth they should get rid of Aubertin in time.

Well, of course, under such circumstances as these the diligence did not come to its time, nor till long after; and all the while, they were waiting for it they were failing their rendezvous with the mayor, and making their rendezvous with the curate impossible. But, above all, there was the risk of one or other of those friends coming up and blurting all out, taking for granted that the doctor must be in their confidence, or why bring him.

At last, at half-past eleven o'clock, to their great relief, up came the diligence. The doctor prepared to take his place in the interior, when the conductor politely informed him that the vehicle stopped there a quarter of an hour.

"In that case I will not abandon my friends," said the doctor, affectionately.

One of his friends gnashed his teeth at this mark of affection. But Josephine smiled sweetly.

At last he was gone; but it wanted ten minutes only to twelve.

Josephine inquired amiably, whether it would not be as well to postpone matters to another day — meaning forever. "My *ardor* is chilled," said she, and showed symptoms of crying at what she had gone through.

Camille replied by half dragging them to the mayor. That worthy received them with profound, though somewhat demure respect, and invited them to a table sumptuously served. The ladies, out of politeness, were about to assent, but Camille begged permission to postpone that part until after the ceremony.

At last, to their astonishment, they were married. Then, with a promise to return and dine with the mayor, they went to the cure. Lo and behold! he was gone to visit a sick person. "He had waited a long time for them," said the servant.

Josephine was much disconcerted, and showed a disposition to cry again. The servant, a good-natured girl, nosed a wedding, and offered to run and bring his reverence in a minute.

Presently there came an old silvery-haired man, who addressed them all as his children. He took them to the church, and blessed their union; and for the first time Josephine felt as if Heaven consented. They took a gentle farewell of him, and went back to the mayor's to dine; and at this stage of the business Rose and Josephine at last effected a downright simultaneous cry, apropos of nothing that was then occurring.

This refreshed them mightily, and they glowed at the mayor's table like roses washed with dew.

But oh! how glad at heart they all were to find themselves in the carriage once more going home to Beaurepaire.

Rose and Josephine sat intertwined on the back seat; Camille, the reins in his right hand, nearly turned his back on the horse, and leaned back over to them and purred to Rose and his wife with ineffable triumph and tenderness.

The lovers were in Elysium, and Rose was not a little proud of her good management in ending all their troubles. Their mother received them back with great, and as they fancied, with singular, affection. She was beginning to be anxious about them, she said. Then her kindness gave these happy souls a pang it never gave them before.

Since the above events scarce a fortnight had elapsed; but such a change! Camille sunburnt and healthy, and full of animation and confidence; Josephine beaming with suppressed happiness, and more beautiful than Rose could ever remember to have seen her. For a soft halo of love and happiness shone around her head; a new and indefinable attraction bloomed on her face. She was a wife. Her eye, that used to glance furtively on Camille, now dwelt demurely on him; dwelt with a sort of gentle wonder and admiration as well as affection, and, when he came or passed very near her, a keen observer might have seen her thrill.

She kept a good deal out of her mother's way; for she felt within that her face must be too happy. She feared to shock her mother's grief with her radiance. She was ashamed of feeling unmixed heaven. But the flood of secret bliss she floated in bore all misgivings away. The pair were forever stealing away together for hours, and on these occasions Rose used to keep out of her mother's sight, until they should return. So then the new-married couple could wander hand in hand through the thick woods of Beaurepaire, whose fresh green leaves were now just out, and hear the distant cuckoo, and sit on mossy banks, and pour love into one another's eyes, and plan ages of happiness, and murmur their deep passion and their bliss almost more than mortal; could do all this and more, without shocking propriety. These sweet duets passed for trios: for on their return Rose would be out looking for them, or would go and meet them at some distance, and all three would go up together to the baroness, as from a joint excursion. And when they went up to their bedrooms, Josephine would throw her arms round her sister's neck, and sigh, "It is not happiness, it is beatitude!"

Meantime, the baroness mourned for Raynal. Her grief showed no decrease. Rose even fancied at times she wore a gloomy and discontented look as well; but on reflection she attributed that to her own fancy, or to the contrast that had now sprung up in her sister's beaming complacency.

Rose, when she found herself left day after day alone for hours, was sad and thought of Edouard. And this feeling gained on her day by day.

At last, one afternoon, she locked herself in her own room, and, after a long contest with her pride, which, if not indomitable, was next door to it, she sat down to write him a little letter. Now, in this letter, in the place devoted by men to their after-thoughts, by women to their pretended after-thoughts; i. e., to what they have been thinking of all through the letter, she dropped a careless hint that all the party missed him very much, "even the obnoxious colonel, who, by-the-by, has transferred his services elsewhere. I have forgiven him that, because he has said civil things about you."

Rose was reading her letter over again, to make sure that all the principal expressions were indistinct, and that the composition generally, except the postscript, resembled a Delphic oracle, when there was a hasty footstep, and a tap at her door, and in came Jacintha, excited.

"He is come, mademoiselle," cried she, and nodded her head like a mandarin, only more knowingly; then she added, "So you may burn that." For her quick eye had glanced at the table.

"Who is come?" inquired Rose, eagerly.

"Why, your one?"

"My one?" asked the young lady, reddening, "my what?"

"The little one — Edouard — Monsieur Riviere."

"Oh, Monsieur Riviere," said Rose, acting nonchalance. "Why could you not say so? you use such phrases, who can conjecture what you mean? I will come to Monsieur Riviere directly; mamma will be so glad."

Jacintha gone, Rose tore up the letter and locked up the pieces, then ran to the glass. Etc.

Edouard had been so profoundly miserable he could stand it no longer; in spite of his determination not to visit Beaurepaire while it contained a rival, he rode over to see whether he had not tormented himself idly: above all, to see the beloved face.

Jacintha put him into the salle a manger. "By that you will see her alone," said the knowing Jacintha. He sat down, hat and whip in hand, and wondered how he should be received — if at all.

In glides Rose all sprightliness and good-humor, and puts out her hand to him; the which he kisses.

"How could I keep away so long?" asked he vaguely, and self-astonished.

"How indeed, and we missing you so all the time!"

"Have *you* missed me?" was the eager inquiry.

"Oh, no!" was the cheerful reply; "but all the rest have."

Presently the malicious thing gave a sudden start.

"Oh! such a piece of news; you remember Colonel Dujardin, the obnoxious colonel?"

No answer.

"Transferred his attentions. Fancy!"

"Who to?"

"To Josephine and mamma. But such are the military. He only wanted to get rid of you: this done (through your want of spirit), he scorns the rich prize; so now I scorn *him*. Will you come for a walk?"

"Oh, yes!"

"We will go and look for my deserter. I say, tell me now; cannot I write to the commander-in-chief about this? a soldier has no right to be a deserter, has he? tell me, you are a public man, and know everything except my heart."

"Is it not too bad to tease me *today*?"

"Yes! but please! I have had few amusements of late. I find it so dull without you to tease."

Formal permission to tease being conceded, she went that instant on the opposite tack, and began to tell him how she had missed him, and how sorry she had been anything should have occurred to vex their kind good friend. In short, Edouard spent a delightful day, for Rose took him one way to meet Josephine, who, she knew, was coming another. At night the last embers of jealousy got quenched, for Josephine was a wife now, and had already begun to tell Camille all her little innocent secrets; and she told him all about Edouard and Rose, and gave him his orders; so he treated Rose with great respect before Edouard; but paid her no marked attention; also he was affable to Riviere, who, having ceased to suspect, began to like him.

In the course of the evening, the colonel also informed the baroness that he expected every day an order to join the army of the Rhine.

Edouard pricked his ears.

The baroness said no more than politeness dictated. She did not press him to stay, but treated his departure as a matter of course. Riviere rode home late in the evening in high spirits.

The next day Rose varied her late deportment; she sang snatches of melody, going about the house; it was for all the world like a bird chirping. In the middle of one chirp Jacintha interfered. "Hush, mademoiselle, your mamma! she is at the bottom of the corridor."

"What was I thinking of?" said Rose.

"Oh! I dare say you know, mademoiselle," replied the privileged domestic.

A letter of good news came from Aubertin. That summons to his nephew's funeral was an era in his harmless life.

The said nephew was a rich man and an oddity; one of those who love to surprise folk. Moreover, he had no children, and detected his nephews and nieces being unnaturally civil to him. "Waiting to cut me up," was his generous reading of them. So with this he made a will, and there defied, as far as in him lay, the laws of nature; for he set his wealth a-flowing backwards instead of forwards; he handed his property up to an ancestor, instead of down to posterity.

All this the doctor's pen set down with some humor, and in the calm spirit with which a genuine philosopher receives prosperity as well as adversity. Yet one natural regret escaped him; that all this wealth, since it was to come, had not come a year or two sooner.

All at Beaurepaire knew what their dear old friend meant.

His other news to them was that they might expect him any moment.

So here was another cause of rejoicing.

"I am so glad," said Josephine. "Now, perhaps, he will be able to publish his poor dear entomology, that the booksellers were all so unkind, so unfeeling about."

I linger on the brink of painful scenes to observe that a sweet and loving friendship, such as this was between the good doctor and three persons of another sex, is one of the best treasures of the human heart. Poverty had strengthened it; yet now wealth could not weaken it. With no tie of blood it yet was filial, sisterly, brotherly, national, chivalrous; happy, unalloyed sentiment, free from ups and downs, from heats and chills, from rivalry, from caprice; and, indeed, from all mortal accidents but one — and why say one? methinks death itself does but suspend these gentle, rare, unselfish amities a moment, then waft them upward to their abiding home.

CHAPTER XV.

It was a fair morning in June: the sky was a bright, deep, lovely, speckless blue: the flowers and bushes poured perfume, and sprinkled song upon the balmy air. On such a day, so calm, so warm, so bright, so scented, so tuneful, to live and to be young is to be happy. With gentle hand it wipes all other days out of the memory; it smiles, it smells, it sings, and clouds and rain and biting wind seem as far off and impossible as grief and trouble.

Camille and Josephine had stolen out, and strolled lazily up and down close under the house, drinking the sweet air, fragrant with perfume and melody; the blue sky, and love.

Rose was in the house. She had missed them; but she thought they must be near; for they seldom took long walks early in the day. Meeting Jacintha on the landing of the great staircase, she asked her where her sister was.

"Madame Raynal is gone for a walk. She has taken the colonel with her. You know she always takes the colonel out with her now."

"That will do. You can finish your work."

Jacintha went into Camille's room.

Rose, who had looked as grave as a judge while Jacintha was present, bubbled into laughter. She even repeated Jacintha's words aloud, and chuckled over them. "You know she always takes the colonel out with her now — ha, ha, ha!"

"Rose!" sighed a distant voice.

She looked round, and saw the baroness at some distance in the corridor, coming slowly towards her, with eyes bent gloomily on the ground. Rose composed her features into a settled gravity, and went to meet her.

"I wish to speak with you," said the baroness; "let us sit down; it is cool here."

Rose ran and brought a seat without a back, but well stuffed, and set it against the wall. The old lady sat down and leaned back, and looked at Rose in silence a good while; then she said, —

"There is room for you; sit down, for I want to speak seriously to you."

"Yes, mamma; what is it?"

"Turn a little round, and let me see your face."

Rose complied; and began to feel a little uneasy.

"Perhaps you can guess what I am going to say to you?"

"I have no idea."

"Well, I am going to put a question to you."

"With all my heart, dear mamma."

"I invite you to explain to me the most singular, the most unaccountable thing that ever fell under my notice. Will you do this for your mother?"

"O mamma! of course I will do anything to please you that I can; but, indeed, I don't know what you mean."

"I am going to tell you."

The old lady paused. The young one, naturally enough, felt a chill of vague anxiety strike across her frame.

"Rose," said the old lady, speaking very gently but firmly, and leaning in a peculiar way on her words, while her eye worked like an ice gimlet on her daughter's face, "a little while ago, when my poor Raynal — our benefactor — was alive — and I was happy — you all chilled my happiness by your gloom: the whole house seemed a house of mourning — tell me now why was this."

"Mamma!" said Rose, after a moment's hesitation, "we could hardly be gay. Sickness in the house! And if Colonel Raynal was alive, still he was absent, and in danger."

"Oh! then it was out of regard for him we were all dispirited?"

"Why, I suppose so," said Rose, stoutly; but then colored high at her own want of candor. However, she congratulated herself that her mother's suspicion was confined to past events.

Her self-congratulation on that score was short; for the baroness, after eying her grimly for a second or two in silence, put her this awkward question plump.

"If so, tell me why is it that ever since that black day when the news of his *death* reached us, the whole house has gone into black, and has gone out of mourning?"

"Mamma," stammered Rose, "what *do* you mean?"

"Even poor Camille, who was so pale and wan, has recovered like magic."

"O mamma! is not that fancy?" said Rose, piteously. "Of what do you suspect me? Can you think I am unfeeling — ungrateful? I should not be *your* daughter."

"No, no," said the baroness, "to do you justice, you attempt sorrow; as you put on black. But, my poor child, you do it with so little skill that one sees a horrible gayety breaking through that thin disguise: you are no true mourners: you are like the mutes or the undertakers at a funeral, forced grief on the surface of your faces, and frightful complacency below."

"Tra la! lal! la! la! Tra la! la! la! Tra la! la!" carolled Jacintha, in the colonel's room hard by.

The ladies looked at one another: Rose in great confusion.

"Tra la! la! la! Tra lal! lal! la! la! la!"

"Jacintha!" screamed Rose angrily.

"Hush! not a word," said the baroness. "Why remonstrate with *her*? Servants are but chameleons: they take the color of those they serve. Do not cry. I wanted your confidence, not your tears, love. There, I will not twice in one day ask you for your heart: it would be to lower the mother, and give the daughter the pain of refusing it, and the regret, sure to come one day, of having refused it. I will discover the meaning of it all by myself." She went away with a gentle sigh; and Rose was cut to the heart by her words; she resolved, whatever it might cost her and Josephine, to make a clean breast this very day. As she was one of those who act promptly, she went instantly in search of her sister, to gain her consent, if possible.

Now, the said Josephine was in the garden walking with Camille, and uttering a wife's tender solicitudes.

"And must you leave me? must you risk your life again so soon; the life on which mine depends?"

"My dear, that letter I received from headquarters two days ago, that inquiry whether my wound was cured. A hint, Josephine — a hint too broad for any soldier not to take."

"Camille, you are very proud," said Josephine, with an accent of reproach, and a look of approval.

"I am obliged to be. I am the husband of the proudest woman in France."

"Hush! not so loud: there is Dard on the grass."

"Dard!" muttered the soldier with a word of meaning. "Josephine," said he after a pause, and a little peevishly, "how much longer are we to lower our voices, and turn away our eyes from each other, and be ashamed of our happiness?"

"Five months longer, is it not?" answered Josephine quietly.

"Five months longer!"

Josephine was hurt at this, and for once was betrayed into a serious and merited remonstrance.

"Is this just?" said she. "Think of two months ago: yes, but two months ago, you were dying. You doubted my love, because it could not overcome my virtue and my gratitude: yet you might have seen it was destroying my life. Poor Raynal, my husband, my benefactor, died. Then I could do more for you, if not with delicacy, at least with honor; but no! words, and looks, and tender offices of love were not enough, I must give stronger proof. Dear Camille, I have been reared in a strict school: and perhaps none of your sex can know what it cost me to go to Frejus that day with him I love."

"My own Josephine!"

"I made but one condition: that you would not rob me of my mother's respect: to her our hasty marriage would appear monstrous, heartless. You consented to be secretly happy for six months. One fortnight has passed, and you are discontented again."

"Oh, no! do not think so. It is every word true. I am an ungrateful villain."

"How dare you say so? and to me! No! but you are a man."

"So I have been told; but my conduct to you, sweet one, has not been that of a man from first to last. Yet I could die for you, with a smile on my lips. But when I think that once I lifted this sacrilegious hand against your life — oh!"

"Do not be silly, Camille. I love you all the better for loving me well enough to kill me. What woman would not? I tell you, you foolish thing, you are a man: monseigneur is one of the lordly sex, that is accustomed to have everything its own way. My love, in a world that is full of misery, here are two that are condemned to be secretly happy a few months longer: a hard fate for one of your sex, it seems: but it is so much sweeter than the usual lot of mine, that really I cannot share your misery," and she smiled joyously.

"Then share my happiness, my dear wife."

"I do; only mine is deep, not loud."

"Why, Dard is gone, and we are out of doors; will the little birds betray us?"

"The lower windows are open, and I saw Jacintha in one of the rooms."

"Jacintha? we are in awe of the very servants. Well, if I must not say it loud I will say it often," and putting his mouth to her ear, he poured a burning whisper of love into it — "My love! my angel! my wife! my wife! my wife!"

She turned her swimming eyes on him.

"My husband!" she whispered in return.

Rose came out, and found them billing and cooing. "You *must* not be so happy, you two," said she authoritatively.

"How can we help it?" asked Camille.

"You must and shall help it, somehow," retorted this little tyrant. "Mamma suspects. She has given me such a cross-examination, my blood runs cold. No, on second thoughts, kiss her again, and you may both be as happy as you like; for I am going to tell mamma all, and no power on earth shall hinder me."

"Rose," said Camille, "you are a sensible girl; and I always said so."

But Josephine was horrified. "What! tell my mother that within a month of my husband's death?" —

"Don't say your husband," put in Camille wincing; "the priest never confirmed that union; words spoken before a magistrate do not make a marriage in the sight of Heaven."

Josephine cut him short. "Amongst honorable men and women all oaths are alike sacred: and Heaven's eye is in a magistrate's room as in a church. A daughter of Beaurepaire gave her hand to him, and called herself his wife. Therefore, she was his wife: and is his widow. She owes him everything; the house you are all living in among the rest. She ought to be proud of her brief connection with that pure, heroic spirit, and, when she is so little noble as to disown him, then say that gratitude and justice have no longer a place among mankind."

"Come into the chapel," said Camille, with a voice that showed he was hurt.

They entered the chapel, and there they saw something that thoroughly surprised them: a marble monument to the memory of Raynal. It leaned at present against the wall below the place prepared to receive it. The inscription, short, but emphatic, and full of feeling, told of the battles he had fought in, including the last fatal skirmish, and his marriage with the heiress of Beaurepaire; and, in a few soldier-like words, the uprightness, simplicity, and generosity of his character.

They were so touched by this unexpected trait in Camille that they both threw their arms round his neck by one impulse. "Am I wrong to be proud of him?" said Josephine, triumphantly.

"Well, don't say too much to me," said Camille, looking down confused. "One tries to be good; but it is very hard — to some of us — not to you, Josephine; and, after all, it is only the truth that we have written on that stone. Poor Raynal! he was my old comrade; he saved me from death, and not a soldier's death — drowning; and he was a better man than I am, or ever shall be. Now he is dead, I can say these things. If I had said them when he was alive, it would have been more to my credit."

They all three went back towards the house; and on the way Rose told them all that had passed between the baroness and her. When she came to the actual details of that conversation, to the words, and looks, and tones, Josephine's uneasiness rose to an overpowering height; she even admitted that further concealment would be very difficult.

"Better tell her than let her find out," said Rose. "We must tell her some day."

At last, after a long and agitated discussion, Josephine consented; but Rose must be the one to tell. "So then, you at least will make your peace with mamma," argued Josephine, "and let us go in and do this before our courage fails; besides, it is going to rain, and it has turned cold. Where have all these clouds come from? An hour ago there was not one in the sky."

They went, with hesitating steps and guilty looks, to the saloon. Their mother was not there. Here was a reprieve.

Rose had an idea. She would take her to the chapel, and show her the monument, and that would please her with poor Camille. "After that," said Rose, "I will begin by telling her all the misery you have both gone through; and, when she pities you, then I will show her it was all my fault your misery ended in a secret marriage."

The confederates sat there in a chilly state, waiting for the baroness. At last, as she did not come, Rose got up to go to her. "When the mind is made up, it is no use being cowardly, and putting off," said she, firmly. For all that, her cheek had but little color left in it, when she left her chair with this resolve.

Now as Rose went down the long saloon to carry out their united resolve, Jacintha looked in; and, after a hasty glance to see who was present, she waited till Rose came up to her, and then whipped a letter from under her apron and gave it her.

"For my mistress," said she, with an air of mystery.

"Why not take it to her, then?" inquired Rose.

"I thought you might like to see it first, mademoiselle," said Jacintha, with quiet meaning.

"Is it from the dear doctor?" asked Josephine.

"La, no, mademoiselle, don't you know the doctor is come home? Why, he has been in the house near an hour. He is with my lady."

The doctor proved Jacintha correct by entering the room in person soon after; on this Rose threw down the letter, and she and the whole party were instantly occupied in greeting him.

When the ladies had embraced him and Camille shaken hands with him, they plied him with a thousand questions. Indeed, he had not half satisfied their curiosity, when Rose happened to catch sight of the letter again, and took it up to carry to the baroness. She now, for the first time, eyed it attentively, and the consequence was she uttered an exclamation, and took the first opportunity to beckon Aubertin.

He came to her; and she put the letter into his hand.

He put up his glasses, and eyed it. "Yes!" whispered he, "it is from *him*."

Josephine and Camille saw something was going on; they joined the other two, with curiosity in their faces.

Rose put her hand on a small table near her, and leaned a moment. She turned half sick at a letter coming from the dead. Josephine now came towards her with a face of concern, and asked what was the matter.

The reply came from Aubertin. "My poor friends," said he, solemnly, "this is one of those fearful things that you have not seen in your short lives, but it has been more than once my lot to witness it. The ships that carry letters from distant countries vary greatly in speed, and are subject to detaining accidents. Yes, this is the third time I have seen a letter come written by a hand known to be cold. The baroness is a little excited *today*, I don't know from what cause. With your approbation, Madame Raynal, I will read this letter before I let her see it."

"Read it, if you please."

"Shall I read it out?"

"Certainly. There may be some wish expressed in it; oh, I hope there is!"

Camille, from delicacy, retired to some little distance, and the doctor read the letter in a low and solemn voice.

"MY DEAR MOTHER, — I hope all are well at Beaurepaire, as I am, or I hope soon to be. I received a wound in our last skirmish; not a very severe one; but it put an end to my writing for some time."

"Poor fellow! it was his death wound. Why, when was this written? — why," and the doctor paused, and seemed stupefied: "why, my dears, has my memory gone, or" — and again he looked eagerly at the letter — "what was the date of the battle in which he was killed? for this letter is dated the 15th of May. Is it a dream? no! this was written since the date of his death."

"No, doctor," said Rose, "you deceive yourself."

"Why, what was the date of the Moniteur, then?" asked Aubertin, in great agitation.

"Considerably later than this," said Camille.

"I don't think so; the journal! where is it?"

"My mother has it locked up. I'll run."

"No, Rose; no one but me. Now, Josephine, do not you go and give way to hopes that may be delusive. I must see that journal directly. I will go to the baroness. I shall excuse her less than you would."

He was scarcely gone when a cry of horror filled the room, a cry as of madness falling like a thunderbolt on a human mind. It was Josephine, who up to this had not uttered one word. But now she stood, white as a corpse, in the middle of the room, and wrung her hands. "What have I done? What shall I do? It was the 3d of May. I see it before me in letters of fire; the 3d of May! the 3d of May! — and he writes the 15th."

"No! no!" cried Camille wildly. "It was long, long after time 3d."

"It was the 3d of May," repeated Josephine in a hoarse voice that none would have known for hers.

Camille ran to her with words of comfort and hope; he did not share her fears. He remembered about when the Moniteur came, though not the very day. He threw his arm lovingly round her as if to protect her against these shadowy terrors. Her dilating eyes seemed fixed on something distant in space or time, at some horrible thing coming slowly towards her. She did not see Camille approach her, but the moment she felt him she turned upon him swiftly.

"Do you love me?" still in the hoarse voice that had so little in it of Josephine. "I mean, does one grain of respect or virtue mingle in your love for me?"

"What words are these, my wife?"

"Then leave Raynal's house upon the instant. You wonder I can be so cruel? I wonder too; and that I can see my duty so clear in one short moment. But I have lived twenty years since that letter came. Oh! my brain has whirled through a thousand agonies. And I have come back a thousand times to the same thing; you and I must see each other's face no more."

"Oh!" cried Rose, "is there no way but this?"

"Take care," she screamed, wildly, to her and Camille, "I am on the verge of madness; is it for you two to thrust me over the precipice? Come, now, if you are a man of honor, if you have a spark of gratitude towards the poor woman who has given you all except her fair name — that she will take to the grave in spite of you all — promise that you will leave Raynal's house this minute if he is alive, and let me die in honor as I have lived."

"No, no!" cried Camille, terror-stricken; "it cannot be. Heaven is merciful, and Heaven sees how happy we are. Be calm! these are idle fears; be calm! I say. For if it is so I will obey you. I will stay; I will go; I will die; I will live; I will obey you."

"Swear this to me by the thing you hold most sacred," she

almost shrieked.

"I swear by my love for you," was his touching reply.

Ere they had recovered a miserable composure after this passionate outburst, all the more terrible as coming from a creature so tender as Josephine, agitated voices were heard at the door, and the baroness tottered in, followed by the doctor, who was trying in vain to put some bounds to her emotion and her hopes.

"Oh, my children! my children!" cried she, trembling violently. "Here, Rose, my hands shake so; take this key, open the cabinet, there is the Moniteur. What is the date?"

The journal was found, and rapidly examined. The date was the 20th of May.

"There!" cried Camille. "I told you!"

The baroness uttered a feeble moan. Her hopes died as suddenly as they had been born, and she sank drooping into a chair, with a bitter sigh.

Camille stole a joyful look at Josephine. She was in the same attitude looking straight before her as at a coming horror. Presently Rose uttered a faint cry, "The battle was BEFORE."

"To be sure," cried the doctor. "You forget, it is not the date of the paper we want, but of the battle it records. For Heaven's sake, when was the battle?"

"The 3d of May," said Josephine, in a voice that seemed to come from the tomb.

Rose's hands that held the journal fell like a dead weight upon her knees, journal and all. She whispered, "It was the 3d of May."

"Ah!" cried the baroness, starting up, "he may yet be alive. He must be alive. Heaven is merciful! Heaven would not take my son from me, a poor old woman who has not long to live. There was a letter; where is the letter?"

"Are we mad, not to read the letter?" said the doctor. "I had it; it has dropped from my old fingers when I went for the journal."

A short examination of the room showed the letter lying crumpled up near the door. Camille gave it to the baroness. She tried to read it, but could not.

"I am old," said she; "my hand shakes and my eyes are troubled. This young gentleman will read it to us. His eyes are not dim and troubled. Something tells me that when I hear this letter, I shall find out whether my son lives. Why do you not read it to me, Camille?" cried she, almost fiercely.

Camille, thus pressed, obeyed mechanically, and began to read Raynal's letter aloud, scarce knowing what he did, but urged and driven by the baroness.

"MY DEAR MOTHER, — I hope all are well at Beaurepaire, as I am, or I hope soon to be. I received a wound in our last skirmish; not a very severe one, but it put an end to my writing for some time."

"Go on, dear Camille! go on."

"The page ends there, madame."

The paper was thin, and Camille, whose hand trembled, had some difficulty in detaching the leaves from one another. He succeeded, however, at last, and went on reading and writhing.

"By the way, you must address your next letter to me as Colonel Raynal. I was promoted just before this last affair, but had not time to tell you; and my wound stopped my writing till now."

"There, there!" cried the baroness. "He was Colonel Raynal, and Colonel Raynal was not killed."

The doctor implored her not to interrupt.

"Go on, Camille. Why do you hesitate? what is the matter? Do for pity's sake go on, sir."

Camille cast a look of agony around, and put his hand to his brow, on which large drops of cold perspiration, like a death dew, were gathering; but driven to the stake on all sides, he gasped on rather than read, for his eye had gone down the page.

"A namesake of mine, Commandant Raynal," —

"Ah!"

"has not been — so fortunate. He" —

"Go on! go on!"

The wretched man could now scarcely utter Raynal's words; they came from him in a choking groan.

"He was killed, poor fellow! while heading a gallant charge upon the enemy's flank."

He ground the letter convulsively in his hand, then it fell all crumpled on the floor.

"Bless you, Camille!" cried the baroness, "bless you! bless you! I have a son still."

She stooped with difficulty, took up the letter, and, kissing it again and again, fell on her knees, and thanked Heaven aloud before them all. Then she rose and went hastily out, and her voice was heard crying very loud, "Jacintha! Jacintha!"

The doctor followed in considerable anxiety for the effects of this violent joy on so aged a person. Three remained behind, panting and pale like those to whom dead Lazarus burst the tomb, and came forth in a moment, at a word. Then Camille half kneeled, half fell, at Josephine's feet, and, in a voice choked with sobs, bade her dispose of him.

She turned her head away. "Do not speak to me; do not look at me; if we look at one another, we are lost. Go! die at your post, and I at mine."

He bowed his head, and kissed her dress, then rose calm as despair, and white as death, and, with his knees knocking under him, tottered away like a corpse set moving.

He disappeared from the house.

The baroness soon came back, triumphant and gay.

"I have sent her to bid them ring the bells in the village. The poor shall be feasted; all shall share our joy: my son was dead, and lives. Oh, joy! joy! joy!"

"Mother!" shrieked Josephine.

"Mad woman that I am, I am too boisterous. Help me, Rose! she is going to faint; her lips are white."

Dr. Aubertin and Rose brought a chair. They forced Josephine into it. She was not the least faint; yet her body obeyed their hands just like a dead body. The baroness melted into tears; tears streamed from Rose's eyes. Josephine's were dry and stony, and fixed on coming horror. The baroness looked at her with anxiety. "Thoughtless old woman! It was too sudden; it is too much for my dear child; too much for me," and she kneeled, and laid her aged head on her daughter's bosom, saying feebly through her tears, "too much joy, too much joy!"

Josephine took no notice of her. She sat like one turned to stone looking far away over her mother's head with rigid eyes fixed on the air and on coming horrors.

Rose felt her arm seized. It was Aubertin. He too was pale now, though not before. He spoke in a terrible whisper to Rose, his eye fixed on the woman of stone that sat there.

"Is this joy?"

Rose, by a mighty effort, raised her eyes and confronted his full. "What else should it be?" said she.

And with these words this Spartan girl was her sister's champion once more against all comers, friend or foe.

CHAPTER XVI.

Dr. Aubertin received one day a note from a publishing bookseller, to inquire whether he still thought of giving the world his valuable work on insects. The doctor was amazed. "My valuable work! Why, Rose, they all refused it, and this person in particular recoiled from it as if my insects could sting on paper."

The above led to a correspondence, in which the convert to insects explained that the work must be published at the author's expense, the publisher contenting himself with the profits. The author, thirsting for the public, consented. Then the publisher wrote again to say that the immortal treatise must be spiced; a little politics flung in: "Nothing goes down, else." The author answered in some heat that he would not dilute things everlasting with the fleeting topics of the day, nor defile science with politics. On this his Mentor smoothed him down, despising him secretly for not seeing that a book is a matter of trade and nothing else. It ended in Aubertin going to Paris to hatch his Phoenix. He had not been there a week, when a small deputation called on him, and informed him he had been elected honorary member of a certain scientific society. The compliment was followed by others, till at last certain ladies, with the pliancy of their sex, find out they had always secretly cared for butterflies. Then the naturalist smelt a rat, or, in other words, began to scent that entomology, a form of idiocy in a poor man, is a graceful decoration of the intellect in a rich one.

Philosopher without bile, he saw through this, and let it amuse, not shock him. His own species, a singularly interesting one in my opinion, had another trait in reserve for him.

He took a world of trouble to find out the circumstances of his nephew's nephews and nieces: then he made arrangements for distributing a large part of his legacy among them. His intentions and the proportions of his generosity transpired.

Hitherto they had been silent, but now they all fell-to and abused him: each looking only to the amount of his individual share, not at the sum total the doctor was giving way to an ungrateful lot.

The donor was greatly amused, and noted down the incident and some of the remarks in his commonplace book, under the general head of "Bestiarium;" and the particular head of "Homo."

Paris with its seductions netted the good doctor, and held him two or three months; would have detained him longer, but for alarming accounts the baroness sent of Josephine's health. These determined him to return to Beaurepaire; and, must I own it, the announcement was no longer hailed at Beaurepaire with universal joy as heretofore.

Josephine Raynal, late Dujardin, is by this time no stranger to my intelligent reader. I wish him to bring his knowledge of her character and her sensibility to my aid. Imagine, as the weary hours and days and weeks roll over her head, what this loving woman feels for her lover whom she has dismissed; what this grateful wife feels for the benefactor she has unwittingly wronged; but will never wrong with her eyes open; what this lady pure as snow, and proud as fire, feels at the seeming frailty into which a cruel combination of circumstances has entrapped her.

Put down the book a moment: shut your eyes: and imagine this strange and complicated form of human suffering.

Her mental sufferings were terrible; and for some time Rose feared for her reason. At last her agonies subsided into a listlessness and apathy little less alarming. She seemed a creature descending inch by inch into the tomb. Indeed, I fully believe she would have died of despair: but one of nature's greatest forces stepped into the arena and fought on the side of life. She was affected with certain bilious symptoms that added to Rose's uneasiness, but Jacintha assured her it was nothing, and would retire and leave the sufferer better. Jacintha, indeed, seemed now to take a particular interest in Josephine, and was always about her with looks of pity and interest.

"Good creature!" thought Rose, "she sees my sister is unhappy: and that makes her more attentive and devoted to her than ever."

One day these three were together in Josephine's room. Josephine was mechanically combing her long hair, when all of a sudden she stretched out her hand and cried, "Rose!"

Rose ran to her, and coming behind her saw in the glass that her lips were colorless. She screamed to Jacintha, and between them they supported Josephine to the bed. She had hardly touched it when she fainted dead away. "Mamma! mamma!" cried Rose in her terror.

"Hush!" cried Jacintha roughly, "hold your tongue: it is only a faint. Help me loosen her: don't make any noise, whatever." They loosened her stays, and applied the usual remedies, but it was some time before she came-to. At last the color came back to her lips, then to her cheek, and the light to her eye. She smiled feebly on Jacintha and Rose, and asked if she had not been insensible.

"Yes, love, and frightened us — a little — not much — oh,

dear! oh, dear!"

"Don't be alarmed, sweet one, I am better. And I will never do it again, since it frightens you." Then Josephine said to her sister in a low voice, and in the Italian language, "I hoped it was death, my sister; but he comes not to the wretched."

"If you hoped that," replied Rose in the same language, "you do not love your poor sister who so loves you."

While the Italian was going on, Jacintha's dark eyes glanced suspiciously on each speaker in turn. But her suspicions were all wide of the mark.

"Now may I go and tell mamma?" asked Rose.

"No, mademoiselle, you shall not," said Jacintha. "Madame Raynal, do take my side, and forbid her."

"Why, what is it to you?" said Rose, haughtily.

"If it was not something to me, should I thwart my dear young lady?"

"No. And you shall have your own way, if you will but condescend to give me a reason."

This to some of us might appear reasonable, but not to Jacintha: it even hurt her feelings.

"Mademoiselle Rose," she said, "when you were little and used to ask me for anything, did I ever say to you, 'Give me a *reason* first'?"

"There! she is right," said Josephine. "We should not make terms with tried friends. Come, we will pay her devotion this compliment. It is such a small favor. For my part I feel obliged to her for asking it."

Josephine's health improved steadily from that day. Her hollow cheeks recovered their plump smoothness, and her beauty its bloom, and her person grew more noble and statue-like than ever, and within she felt a sense of indomitable vitality. Her appetite had for some time been excessively feeble and uncertain, and her food tasteless; but of late, by what she conceived to be a reaction such as is common after youth has shaken off a long sickness, her appetite had been not only healthy but eager. The baroness observed this, and it relieved her of a large portion of her anxiety. One day at dinner her maternal heart was so pleased with Josephine's performance that she took it as a personal favor, "Well done, Josephine," said she; "that gives your mother pleasure to see you eat again. Soup and bouillon: and now twice you have been to Rose for some of that pate, which does you so much credit, Jacintha."

Josephine colored high at this compliment.

"It is true," said she, "I eat like a pig;" and, with a furtive glance at the said pate, she laid down her knife and fork, and ate no more of anything. The baroness had now a droll misgiving.

"The doctor will be angry with me," said she: "he will find her as well as ever."

"Madame," said Jacintha hastily, "when does the doctor come, if I may make so bold, that I may get his room ready, you know?"

"Well thought of, Jacintha. He comes the day after tomorrow, in the afternoon."

At night when the young ladies went up to bed, what did they find but a little cloth laid on a little table in Josephine's room, and the remains of the pate she had liked. Rose burst out laughing. "Look at that dear duck of a goose, Jacintha! Our mother's flattery sank deep: she thinks we can eat her pates at all hours of the day and night. Shall I send it away?"

"No," said Josephine, "that would hurt her culinary pride, and perhaps her affection: only cover it up, dear, for just now I am not in the humor: it rather turns me."

It was covered up. The sisters retired to rest. In the morning Rose lifted the cover and found the plate cleared, polished. She was astounded.

The large tapestried chamber, once occupied by Camille Dujardin, was now turned into a sitting-room, and it was a favorite on account of the beautiful view from the windows.

One day Josephine sat there alone with some work in her hand; but the needle often stopped, and the fair head drooped. She heaved a deep sigh. To her surprise it was echoed by a sigh that, like her own, seemed to come from a heart full of sighs.

She turned hastily round and saw Jacintha.

Now Josephine had all a woman's eye for reading faces, and she was instantly struck by a certain gravity in Jacintha's gaze, and a flutter which the young woman was suppressing with tolerable but not complete success.

Disguising the uneasiness this discovery gave her, she looked her visitor full in the face, and said mildly, but a little coldly, "Well, Jacintha?"

Jacintha lowered her eyes and muttered slowly, —

"The doctor — comes — *today*," then raised her eyes all in a moment to take Josephine off her guard; but the calm face was impenetrable. So then Jacintha added, "to our misfortune," throwing in still more meaning.

"To our misfortune? A dear old friend — like him?"

Jacintha explained. "That old man makes me shake. You are never safe with him. So long as his head is in the clouds, you might take his shoes off, and on he'd walk and never know it; but every now and then he comes out of the clouds all in one moment, without a word of warning, and when he does his eye is on everything, like a bird's. Then he is so old: he has seen a heap. Take my word for it, the old are more knowing than the young, let them be as sharp as you like: the old have seen everything. *We* have only heard talk of the most part, with here and there a glimpse. To know life to the bottom you must live it out, from the soup to the dessert; and that is what the doctor has done, and now he is coming here. And Mademoiselle Rose will go telling him everything; and if she tells him half what she has seen, your secret will be no secret to that old man."

"My secret!" gasped Josephine, turning pale.

"Don't look so, madame: don't be frightened at poor Jacintha. Sooner or later you *must* trust somebody besides Mademoiselle Rose."

Josephine looked at her with inquiring, frightened eyes.

Jacintha drew nearer to her.

"Mademoiselle, — I beg pardon, madame, — I carried you in my arms when I was a child. When I was a girl you toddled at my side, and held my gown, and lisped my name, and used to put your little arms round my neck, and kissed me, you would; and if ever I had the least pain or sickness your dear little face would turn as sorrowful, and all the pretty color leave it for Jacintha; and now you are in trouble, in sore trouble, yet you turn away from me, you dare not trust me, that would be cut in pieces ere I would betray you. Ah, mademoiselle, you are wrong. The poor can feel: they have all seen trouble, and a servant is the best of friends where she has the heart to love her mistress; and do not I love you? Pray do not turn from her who has carried you in her arms, and laid you to sleep upon her bosom, many's and many's the time."

Josephine panted audibly. She held out her hand eloquently to Jacintha, but she turned her head away and trembled.

Jacintha cast a hasty glance round the room. Then she trembled too at what she was going to say, and the effect it might have on the young lady. As for Josephine, terrible as the conversation had become, she made no attempt to evade it: she remained perfectly passive. It was the best way to learn how far Jacintha had penetrated her secret, if at all.

Jacintha looked fearfully round and whispered in Josephine's ear, "When the news of Colonel Raynal's death came, you wept, but the color came back to your cheek. When the news of his life came, you turned to stone. Ah! my poor young lady, there has been more between you and *that man* than should be. Ever since one day you all went to Frejus together, you were a changed woman. I have seen you look at him as — as a wife looks at her man. I have seen *him*" —

"Hush, Jacintha! Do not tell me what you have seen: oh! do not remind me of joys I pray God to help me forget. He was my husband, then! — oh, cruel Jacintha, to remind me of what I have been, of what I am! Ah me! ah me! ah me!"

"Your husband!" cried Jacintha in utter amazement.

Then Josephine drooped her head on this faithful creature's shoulder, and told her with many sobs the story I have told you. She told it very briefly, for it was to a woman who, though little educated, was full of feeling and shrewdness, and needed but the bare facts: she could add the rest from her own heart and experience: could tell the storm of feelings through which these two unhappy lovers must have passed. Her frequent sighs of pity and sympathy drew Josephine on to pour out all her griefs. When the tale was ended she gave a sigh of relief.

"It might have been worse: I thought it was worse the more fool I. I deserve to have my head cut off." This was Jacintha's only comment at that time.

It was Josephine's turn to be amazed. "It could have been worse?" said she. "How? tell me," added she bitterly. "It would be a consolation to me, could I see that."

Jacintha colored and evaded this question, and begged her to go on, to keep nothing back from her. Josephine assured her she had revealed all. Jacintha looked at her a moment in silence.

"It is then as I half suspected. You do not know all that is before you. You do not see why I am afraid of that old man."

"No, not of him in particular."

"Nor why I want to keep Mademoiselle Rose from prattling to him?"

"No. I assure you Rose is to be trusted; she is wise — wiser than I am."

"You are neither of you wise. You neither of you know anything. My poor young mistress, you are but a child still. You have a deep water to wade through," said Jacintha, so solemnly that Josephine trembled. "A deep water, and do not see it even. You have told me what is past, now I must tell you what is coming. Heaven help me! But is it possible you have no misgiving? Tell the truth, now."

"Alas! I am full of them; at your words, at your manner, they fly around me in crowds."

"Have you no one?"

"No."

"Then turn your head from me a bit, my sweet young lady; I am an honest woman, though I am not so innocent as you, and I am forced against my will to speak my mind plainer than I am used to."

Then followed a conversation, to detail which might anticipate our story; suffice it to say, that Rose, coming into the room rather suddenly, found her sister weeping on Jacintha's bosom, and Jacintha crying and sobbing over her.

She stood and stared in utter amazement.

Dr. Aubertin, on his arrival, was agreeably surprised at Madame Raynal's appearance. He inquired after her appetite.

"Oh, as to her appetite," cried the baroness, "that is immense."

"Indeed!"

"It was," explained Josephine, "just when I began to get better, but now it is as much as usual." This answer had been arranged beforehand by Jacintha. She added, "The fact is, we wanted to see you, doctor, and my ridiculous ailments were a good excuse for tearing you from Paris." — "And now we have succeeded," said Rose, "let us throw off the mask, and talk of other things; above all, of Paris, and your eclat."

"For all that," persisted the baroness, "she was ill, when I first wrote, and very ill too."

"Madame Raynal," said the doctor solemnly, "your conduct has been irregular; once ill, and your illness announced to your medical adviser, etiquette forbade you to get well but by his prescriptions. Since, then, you have shown yourself unfit to conduct a malady, it becomes my painful duty to forbid you henceforth ever to be ill at all, without my permission first obtained in writing."

This badinage was greatly relished by Rose, but not at all by the baroness, who was as humorless as a swan.

He stayed a month at Beaurepaire, then off to Paris again: and being now a rich man, and not too old to enjoy innocent pleasures, he got a habit of running backwards and forwards between the two places, spending a month or so at each alternately. So the days rolled on. Josephine fell into a state that almost defies description; her heart was full of deadly wounds, yet it seemed, by some mysterious, half-healing balm, to throb and ache, but bleed no more. Beams of strange, unreasonable complacency would shoot across her; the next moment reflection would come, she would droop her head, and sigh piteously. Then all would merge in a wild terror of detection. She seemed on the borders of a river of bliss, new, divine, and inexhaustible: and on the other bank mocking malignant fiends dared her to enter that heavenly stream. The past to her was full of regrets; the future full of terrors, and empty of hope. Yet she did not, could not succumb. Instead of the listlessness and languor of a few months back, she had now more energy than ever; at times it mounted to irritation. An activity possessed her: it broke out in many feminine ways. Among the rest she was seized with what we men call a cacoethes of the needle: "a raging desire" for work. Her fingers itched for work. She was at it all day. As devotees retire to pray, so she to stitch. On a wet day she would often slip into the kitchen, and ply the needle beside Jacintha: on a dry day she would hide in the old oak-tree, and sit like a mouse, and ply the tools of her craft, and make things of no mortal use to man or woman; and she tried little fringes of muslin upon her white hand, and held it up in front of her, and smiled, and then moaned. It was winter, and Rose used sometimes to bring her out a thick shawl, as she sat in the old oak-tree stitching, but Josephine nearly always declined it. *She was nearly impervious to cold.*

Then, her purse being better filled than formerly, she visited the poor more than ever, and above all the young couples; and took a warm interest in their household matters, and gave them muslin articles of her own making, and sometimes sniffed the soup in a young housewife's pot, and took a fancy to it, and, if invited to taste it, paid her the compliment of eating a good plateful of it, and said it was much better soup than the chateau produced, and, what is stranger, thought so: and, whenever some peevish little brat set up a yell in its cradle and the father naturally enough shook his fist at the destroyer of his peace, Madame Raynal's lovely face filled with concern not for the sufferer but the pest, and she flew to it and rocked it and coaxed it and consoled it, till the young housewife smiled and stopped its mouth by other means. And, besides the five-franc pieces she gave the infants to hold, these visits of Madame Raynal were always followed by one from Jacintha with a basket of provisions on her stalwart arm, and honest Sir John Burgoyne peeping out at the corner. Kind and beneficent as she was, her temper deteriorated considerably, for it came down from angelic to human. Rose and Jacintha were struck with the change, assented to everything she said, and encouraged her in everything it pleased her caprice to do. Meantime the baroness lived on her son Raynal's letters (they came regularly twice a month). Rose too had a correspondence, a constant source of delight to her. Edouard Riviere was posted at a distance, and could not visit her; but their love advanced rapidly. Every day he wrote down for his Rose the acts of the day, and twice a week sent the budget to his sweetheart, and told her at the same time every feeling of his heart. She was less fortunate than he; she had to carry a heavy secret; but still she found plenty to tell him, and tender feelings too to vent on him in her own arch, shy, fitful way. Letters can enchain hearts; it was by letters that these two found themselves imperceptibly betrothed. Their union was looked forward to as certain, and not very distant. Rose was fairly in love.

One day, Dr. Aubertin, coming back from Paris to Beaurepaire rather suddenly, found nobody at home but the baroness. Josephine and Rose were gone to Frejus; had been there more than a week. She was ailing again; so as Frejus had agreed with her once, Rose thought it might again. "She would send for them back directly."

"No," said the doctor, "why do that? I will go over there and see them." Accordingly, a day or two after this, he hired a carriage, and went off early in the morning to Frejus. In so small a place he expected to find the young ladies at once; but, to his surprise, no one knew them nor had heard of them. He was at a nonplus, and just about to return home and laugh at himself and the baroness for this wild-goose chase, when he fell in with a face he knew, one Mivart, a surgeon, a young man of some talent, who had made his acquaintance in Paris. Mivart accosted him with great respect; and, after the first compliments, informed him that he had been settled some months in this little town, and was doing a fair stroke of business.

"Killing some, and letting nature cure others, eh?" said the doctor; then, having had his joke, he told Mivart what had brought him to Frejus.

"Are they pretty women, your friends? I think I know all the pretty women about," said Mivart with levity. "They are not pretty," replied Aubertin. Mivart's interest in them faded visibly out of his countenance. "But they are beautiful. The elder might pass for Venus, and the younger for Hebe."

"I know them then!" cried he; "they are patients of mine."

The doctor colored. "Ah, indeed!"

"In the absence of your greater skill," said Mivart, politely; "it is Madame Aubertin and her sister you are looking for, is it not?"

Aubertin groaned. "I am rather too old to be looking for a Madame Aubertin," said he; "no; it is Madame Raynal, and Mademoiselle de Beaurepaire."

Mivart became confidential. "Madame Aubertin and her sister," said he, "are so lovely they make me ill to look at them: the deepest blue eyes you ever saw, both of them; high foreheads; teeth like ivory mixed with pearl; such aristocratic feet and hands; and their arms — oh!" and by way of general summary the young surgeon kissed the tips of his fingers, and was silent; language succumbed under the theme. The doctor smiled coldly.

Mivart added, "If you had come an hour sooner, you might have seen Mademoiselle Rose; she was in the town."

"Mademoiselle Rose? who is that?"

"Why, Madame Aubertin's sister."

At this Dr. Aubertin looked first very puzzled, then very grave.

"Hum!" said he, after a little reflection, "where do these paragons live?"

"They lodge at a small farm; it belongs to a widow; her name is Roth." They parted. Dr. Aubertin walked slowly towards his carriage, his hands behind him, his eyes on the ground. He bade the driver inquire where the Widow Roth lived, and learned it was about half a league out of the town. He drove to the farmhouse; when the carriage drove up, a young lady looked out of the window on the first floor. It was Rose de Beaurepaire. She caught the doctor's eye, and he hers. She came down and welcomed him with a great appearance of cordiality, and asked him, with a smile, how he found them out.

"From your medical attendant," said the doctor, dryly.

Rose looked keenly in his face.

"He said he was in attendance on two paragons of beauty, blue eyes, white teeth and arms."

"And you found us out by that?" inquired Rose, looking still more keenly at him.

"Hardly; but it was my last chance of finding you, so I came. Where is Madame Raynal?"

"Come into this room, dear friend. I will go and find her."

Full twenty minutes was the doctor kept waiting, and then in came Rose, gayly crying, "I have hunted her high and low, and where do you think my lady was? sitting out in the garden — come."

Sure enough, they found Josephine in the garden, seated on a low chair. She smiled when the doctor came up to her, and asked after her mother. There was an air of languor about her; her color was clear, delicate, and beautiful.

"You have been unwell, my child."

"A little, dear friend; you know me; always ailing, and tormenting those I love."

"Well! but, Josephine, you know this place and this sweet air always set you up. Look at her now, doctor; did you ever see her look better? See what a color. I never saw her look more lovely."

"I never saw her look SO lovely; but I have seen her look better. Your pulse. A little languid?"

"Yes, I am a little."

"Do you stay at Beaurepaire?" inquired Rose; "if so, we will come home."

"On the contrary, you will stay here another fortnight," said the doctor, authoritatively.

"Prescribe some of your nice tonics for me, doctor," said Josephine, coaxingly.

"No! I can't do that; you are in the hands of another practitioner."

"What does that matter? You were at Paris."

"It is not the etiquette in our profession to interfere with another man's patients."

"Oh, dear! I am so sorry," began Josephine.

"I see nothing here that my good friend Mivart is not competent to deal with," said the doctor, coldly.

Then followed some general conversation, at the end of which the doctor once more laid his commands on them to stay another fortnight where they were, and bade them good-by.

He was no sooner gone than Rose went to the door of the kitchen, and called out, "Madame Jouvenel! Madame Jouvenel! you may come into the garden again."

The doctor drove away; but, instead of going straight to Beaurepaire, he ordered the driver to return to the town. He then walked to Mivart's house.

In about a quarter of an hour he came out of it, looking singularly grave, sad, and stern.

CHAPTER XVII.

Edouard Riviere contrived one Saturday to work off all arrears of business, and start for Beaurepaire. He had received a very kind letter from Rose, and his longing to see her overpowered him. On the road his eyes often glittered, and his cheek flushed with expectation. At last he got there. His heart beat: for four months he had not seen her. He ran up into the drawing-room, and there found the baroness alone; she welcomed him cordially, but soon let him know Rose and her sister were at Frejus. His heart sank. Frejus was a long way off. But this was not all. Rose's last letter was dated from Beaurepaire, yet it must have been written at Frejus. He went to Jacintha, and demanded an explanation of this. The ready Jacintha said it looked as if she meant to be home directly; and added, with cool cunning, "That is a hint for me to get their rooms ready."

"This letter must have come here enclosed in another," said Edouard, sternly.

"Like enough," replied Jacintha, with an appearance of sovereign indifference.

Edouard looked at her, and said, grimly, "I will go to Frejus."

"So I would," said Jacintha, faltering a little, but not perceptibly; "you might meet them on the road, if so be they come the same road; there are two roads, you know."

Edouard hesitated; but he ended by sending Dard to the town on his own horse, with orders to leave him at the inn, and borrow a fresh horse. "I shall just have time," said he. He rode to Frejus, and inquired at the inns and post-office for Mademoiselle de Beaurepaire. They did not know her; then he inquired for Madame Raynal. No such name known. He rode by the seaside upon the chance of their seeing him. He paraded on horseback throughout the place, in hopes every moment that a window would open, and a fair face shine at it, and call him. At last his time was up, and he was obliged to ride back, sick at heart, to Beaurepaire. He told the baroness, with some natural irritation, what had happened. She was as much surprised as he was.

"I write to Madame Raynal at the post-office, Frejus," said she.

"And Madame Raynal gets your letters?"

"Of course she does, since she answers them; you cannot have inquired at the post."

"Why, it was the first place I inquired at, and neither Mademoiselle de Beaurepaire nor Madame Raynal were known there."

Jacintha, who could have given the clew, seemed so puzzled herself, that they did not even apply to her. Edouard took a sorrowful leave of the baroness, and set out on his journey home.

Oh! how sad and weary that ride seemed now by what it had been coming. His disappointment was deep and irritating; and ere he had ridden half way a torturer fastened on his heart. That torture is suspicion; a vague and shadowy, but gigantic phantom that oppresses and rends the mind more terribly than certainty. In this state of vague, sickening suspicion, he remained some days: then came an affectionate letter from Rose, who had actually returned home. In this she expressed her regret and disappointment at having missed him; blamed herself for misleading him, but explained that their stay at Frejus had been prolonged from day to day far beyond her expectation. "The stupidity of the post-office was more than she could account for," said she. But, what went farthest to console Edouard, was, that after this contretemps she never ceased to invite him to come to Beaurepaire. Now, before this, though she said many kind and pretty things in her letters, she had never invited him to visit the chateau; he had noticed this. "Sweet soul," thought he, "she really is vexed. I must be a brute to think any more about it. Still" —

So this wound was skinned over.

At last, what he called his lucky star ordained that he should be transferred to the very post his Commandant Raynal had once occupied. He sought and obtained permission to fix his quarters in the little village near Beaurepaire, and though this plan could not be carried out for three months, yet the prospect of it was joyful all that time — joyful to both lovers. Rose needed this consolation, for she was very unhappy: her beloved sister, since their return from Frejus, had gone back. The flush of health was faded, and so was her late energy. She fell into deep depression and languor, broken occasionally by fits of nervous irritation.

She would sit for hours together at one window languishing and fretting. Can the female reader guess which way that window looked?

Now, Edouard was a favorite of Josephine's; so Rose hoped he would help to distract her attention from those sorrows which a lapse of years alone could cure.

On every account, then, his visit was looked forward to with hope and joy.

He came. He was received with open arms. He took up his quarters at his old lodgings, but spent his evenings and every leisure hour at the chateau.

He was very much in love, and showed it. He adhered to Rose like a leech, and followed her about like a little dog.

This would have made her very happy if there had been nothing great to distract her attention and her heart; but she had Josephine, whose deep depression and fits of irritation and terror filled her with anxiety; and so Edouard was in the way now and then. On these occasions he was too vain to see what she was too polite to show him offensively.

But on this she became vexed at his obtuseness.

"Does he think I can be always at his beck and call?" thought she.

"She is always after her sister," said he.

He was just beginning to be jealous of Josephine when the following incident occurred: —

Rose and the doctor were discussing Josephine. Edouard pretended to be reading a book, but he listened to every word.

Dr. Aubertin gave it as his opinion that Madame Raynal did not make enough blood.

"Oh! if I thought that!" cried Rose.

"Well, then, it is so, I assure you."

"Doctor," said Rose, "do you remember, one day you said healthy blood could be drawn from robust veins and poured into a sick person's?"

"It is a well-known fact," said Aubertin.

"I don't believe it," said Rose, dryly.

"Then you place a very narrow limit to science," said the doctor, coldly.

"Did you ever see it done?" asked Rose, slyly.

"I have not only seen it done, but have done it myself."

"Then do it for us. There's my arm; take blood from that for dear Josephine!" and she thrust a white arm out under his eye with such a bold movement and such a look of fire and love as never beamed from common eyes.

A keen, cold pang shot through the human heart of Edouard Riviere.

The doctor started and gazed at her with admiration: then he hung his head. "I could not do it. I love you both too well to drain either of life's current."

Rose veiled her fire, and began to coax. "Once a week; just once a week, dear, dear doctor; you know I should never miss it. I am so full of that health, which Heaven denies to her I love."

"Let us try milder measures first," said the doctor. "I have most faith in time."

"What if I were to take her to Frejus? hitherto, the sea has always done wonders for her."

"Frejus, by all means," said Edouard, mingling suddenly in the conversation; "and this time I will go with you, and then I shall find out where you lodged before, and how the boobies came to say they did not know you."

Rose bit her lip. She could not help seeing then how much dear Edouard was in her way and Josephine's. Their best friends are in the way of all who have secrets. Presently the doctor went to his study. Then Edouard let fall a mock soliloquy. "I wonder," said he, dropping out his words one by one, "whether any one will ever love me well enough to give a drop of their blood for me."

"If you were in sickness and sorrow, who knows?" said Rose, coloring up.

"I would soon be in sickness and sorrow if I thought that."

"Don't jest with such matters, monsieur."

"I am serious. I wish I was as ill as Madame Raynal is, to be loved as she is."

"You must resemble her in some other things to be loved as she is.

"You have often made me feel that of late, dear Rose."

This touched her. But she fought down the kindly feeling. "I am glad of it," said she, out of perverseness. She added after a while, "Edouard, you are naturally jealous."

"Not the least in the world, Rose, I assure you. I have many faults, but jealous I am not."

"Oh, yes, you are, and suspicious, too; there is something in your character that alarms me for our happiness."

"Well, if you come to that, there are things in *your* conduct I could wish explained."

"There! I said so. You have not confidence in me."

"Pray don't say that, dear Rose. I have every confidence in you; only please don't ask me to divest myself of my senses and my reason."

"I don't ask you to do that or anything else for me; good-by, for the present."

"Where are you going now? tic! tic! I never can get a word in peace with you."

"I am not going to commit murder. I'm only going up-stairs to my sister."

"Poor Madame Raynal, she makes it very hard for me not to dislike her."

"Dislike my Josephine?" and Rose bristled visibly.

"She is an angel, but I should hate an angel if it came forever between you and me."

"Excuse me, she was here long before you. It is you that came between her and me."

"I came because I was told I should be welcome," said Edouard bitterly, and equivocating a little; he added, "and I dare say I shall go when I am told I am one too many."

"Bad heart! who says you are one too many in the house? But you are too exigent, monsieur; you assume the husband, and you tease me. It is selfish; can you not see I am anxious and worried? you ought to be kind to me, and soothe me; that is what I look for from you, and, instead of that, I declare you are getting to be quite a worry."

"I should not be if you loved me as I love you. I give *you* no rival. Shall I tell you the cause of all this? you have secrets."

"What secrets?"

"Is it me you ask? am I trusted with them? Secrets are a bond that not even love can overcome. It is to talk secrets you run away from me to Madame Raynal. Where did you lodge at Frejus, Mademoiselle the Reticent?"

"In a grotto, dry at low water, Monsieur the Inquisitive."

"That is enough: since you will not tell me, I will find it out before I am a week older."

This alarmed Rose terribly, and drove her to extremities. She decided to quarrel.

"Sir," said she, "I thank you for playing the tyrant a little prematurely; it has put me on my guard. Let us part; you and I are not suited to each other, Edouard Riviere."

He took this more humbly than she expected. "Part!" said he, in consternation; "that is a terrible word to pass between you and me. Forgive me! I suppose I am jealous."

"You are; you are actually jealous of my sister. Well, I tell you plainly I love you, but I love my sister better. I never could love any man as I do her; it is ridiculous to expect such a thing."

"And do you think I could bear to play second fiddle to her all my life?"

"I don't ask you. Go and play first trumpet to some other lady."

"You speak your wishes so plainly now, I have nothing to do but to obey."

He kissed her hand and went away disconsolately.

Rose, instead of going to Josephine, her determination to do which had mainly caused the quarrel, sat sadly down, and leaned her head on her hand. "I am cruel. I am ungrateful. He has gone away broken-hearted. And what shall I do without him? — little fool! I love him better than he loves me. He will never forgive me. I have wounded his vanity; and they are vainer than we are. If we meet at dinner I will be so kind to him, he will forget it all. No! Edouard will not come to dinner. He is not a spaniel that you can beat, and then whistle back again. Something tells me I have lost him, and if I have, what shall I do? I will write him a note. I will ask him to forgive me."

She sat down at the table, and took a sheet of notepaper and began to write a few conciliatory words. She was so occupied in making these kind enough, and not too kind, that a light step approached her unobserved. She looked up and there was Edouard. She whipped the paper off the table.

A look of suspicion and misery crossed Edouard's face.

Rose caught it, and said, "Well, am I to be affronted any more?"

"No, Rose. I came back to beg you to forget what passed just now," said he.

Rose's eye flashed; his return showed her her power. She abused it directly.

"How can I forget it if you come reminding me?"

"Dear Rose, now don't be so unkind, so cruel — I have not come back to tease you, sweet one. I come to know what I can do to please you; to make you love me again?" and he was about to kneel graciously on one knee.

"I'll tell you. Don't come near me for a month."

Edouard started up, white as ashes with mortification and wounded love.

"This is how you treat me for humbling myself, when it is you that ought to ask forgiveness."

"Why should I ask what I don't care about?"

"What *do* you care about? — except that sister of yours? You have no heart. And on this cold-blooded creature I have wasted a love an empress might have been proud of inspiring. I pray Heaven some man may sport with your affections, you heartless creature, as you have played with mine, and make you suffer what I suffer now!"

And with a burst of inarticulate grief and rage he flung out of the room.

Rose sank trembling on the sofa a little while: then with a mighty effort rose and went to comfort her sister.

Edouard came no more to Beaurepaire.

There is an old French proverb, and a wise one, "Rien n'est certain que l'imprevu;" it means you can make sure of nothing but this, that matters will not turn as you feel sure they will. And, even for this reason, you, who are thinking of suicide because trade is declining, speculation failing, bankruptcy impending, or your life going to be blighted forever by unrequited love — *don't do it.* Whether you are English, American, French, or German, listen to a man that knows what is what, and *don't do it.* I tell you none of those horrors, when they really come, will affect you as you fancy they will. The joys we expect are not a quarter so bright, nor the troubles half so dark as we think they will be. Bankruptcy coming is one thing, come is quite another: and no heart or life was ever really blighted at twenty years of age. The love-sick girls that are picked out of the canal alive, all, without exception, marry another man, have brats, and get to screech with laughter when they think of sweetheart No. 1, generally a blockhead, or else a blackguard, whom they were fools enough to wet their clothes for, let alone kill their souls. This happens INVARIABLY. The love-sick girls that are picked out of the canal dead have fled from a year's misery to eternal pain, from grief that time never failed to cure, to anguish incurable. In this world "Rien n'est certain que l'imprevu."

Edouard and Rose were tender lovers, at a distance. How much happier and more loving they thought they should be beneath the same roof. They came together: their prominent faults of character rubbed: the secret that was in the house did its work: and altogether, they quarrelled. L'imprevu.

Dard had been saying to Jacintha for ever so long, "When granny dies, I will marry you."

Granny died. Dard took possession of her little property. Up came a glittering official, and turned him out; he was not her heir. Perrin, the notary, was. He had bought the inheritance of her two sons, long since dead.

Dard had not only looked on the cottage and cow, as his, but had spoken of them as such for years. The disappointment and the irony of comrades ate into him.

"I will leave this cursed place," said he.

Josephine instantly sent for him to Beaurepaire. He came, and was factotum with the novelty of a fixed salary. Jacintha accommodated him with a new little odd job or two. She set him to dance on the oak floors with a brush fastened to his right foot; and, after a rehearsal or two, she made him wait at table. Didn't he bang the things about: and when he brought a lady a dish, and she did not instantly attend, he gave her elbow a poke to attract attention: then she squeaked; and he grinned at her double absurdity in minding a touch, and not minding the real business of the table.

But his wrongs rankled in him. He vented antique phrases such as, "I want a change;" "This village is the last place the Almighty made," etc.

Then he was attacked with a moral disease: affected the company of soldiers. He spent his weekly salary carousing with the military, a class of men so brilliant that they are not expected to pay for their share of the drink; they contribute the anecdotes and the familiar appeals to Heaven: and is not that enough?

Present at many recitals, the heroes of which lost nothing by being their own historians, Dard imbibed a taste for military adventure. His very talk, which used to be so homely, began now to be tinselled with big swelling words of vanity imported from the army. I need hardly say these bombastical phrases did not elevate his general dialect: they lay fearfully distinct upon the surface, "like lumps of marl upon a barren soil, encumbering the ground they could not fertilize."

Jacintha took leave to remind him of an incident connected with warfare — wounds.

"Do you remember how you were down upon your luck when you did but cut your foot? Why, that is nothing in the army. They never go out to fight but some come back with arms off, and some with legs off and some with heads; and the rest don't come back at all: and how would you like that?"

This intrusion of statistics into warfare at first cooled Dard's impatience for the field. But presently the fighting half of his heart received an ally in one Sergeant La Croix (not a bad name for a military aspirant). This sergeant was at the village waiting to march with the new recruits to the Rhine. Sergeant La Croix was a man who, by force of eloquence, could make soldiering appear the most delightful as well as glorious of human pursuits. His tongue fired the inexperienced soul with a love of arms, as do the drums and trumpets and tramp of soldiers, and their bayonets glittering in the sun. He would have been worth his weight in fustian here, where we recruit by that and jargon; he was superfluous in France, where they recruited by force: but he was ornamental: and he set Dard and one or two more on fire. Indeed, so absorbing was his sense of military glory, that there was no room left in him for that mere verbal honor civilians call veracity.

To speak plainly, the sergeant was a fluent, fertile, interesting, sonorous, prompt, audacious liar: and such was his success, that

Dard and one or two more became mere human fiction pipes — of comparatively small diameter — irrigating a rural district with false views of military life, derived from that inexhaustible reservoir, La Croix.

At last the long-threatened conscription was levied: every person fit to bear arms, and not coming under the allowed exceptions, drew a number: and at a certain hour the numbers corresponding to these were deposited in an urn, and one-third of them were drawn in presence of the authorities. Those men whose numbers were drawn had to go for soldiers. Jacintha awaited the result in great anxiety. She could not sit at home for it; so she went down the road to meet Dard, who had promised to come and tell her the result as soon as known. At last she saw him approaching in a disconsolate way. "O Dard! speak! are we undone? are you a dead man?" cried she. "Have they made a soldier of you?"

"No such luck: I shall die a man of all work," grunted Dard.

"And you are sorry? you unnatural little monster! you have no feeling for me, then."

"Oh, yes, I have; but glory is No. 1 with me now."

"How loud the bantams crow! You leave glory to fools that be six feet high."

"General Bonaparte isn't much higher than I am, and glory sits upon his brow. Why shouldn't glory sit upon my brow?"

"Because it would weigh you down, and smother you, you little fool." She added, "And think of me, that couldn't bear you to be killed at any price, glory or no glory."

Then, to appease her fears, Dard showed her his number, 99; and assured her he had seen the last number in the functionary's hand before he came away, and it was sixty something.

This ocular demonstration satisfied Jacintha; and she ordered Dard to help her draw the water.

"All right," said he, "there is no immortal glory to be picked up *today*, so I'll go in for odd jobs."

While they were at this job a voice was heard hallooing. Dard looked up, and there was a rigid military figure, with a tremendous mustache, peering about. Dard was overjoyed. It was his friend, his boon-companion. "Come here, old fellow," cried he, "ain't I glad to see you, that is all?" La Croix marched towards the pair. "What are you skulking here for, recruit ninety-nine?" said he, sternly, dropping the boon-companion in the sergeant; "the rest are on the road."

"The rest, old fellow! what do you mean? why, I was not

drawn."

"Yes, you were."

"No, I wasn't."

"Thunder of war, but I say you were. Yours was the last number."

"That is an unlucky guess of yours, for I saw the last number. Look here," and he fumbled in his pocket, and produced his number.

La Croix instantly fished out a corresponding number.

"Well, and here you are; this was the last number drawn."

Dard burst out laughing.

"You goose!" said he, "that is sixty-six — look at it."

"Sixty-six!" roared the sergeant; "no more than yours is — they are both sixty-sixes when you play tricks with them, and turn them up like that; but they are both ninety-nines when you look at them fair."

Dard scratched his head.

"Come," said the corporal, briskly, "make up his bundle, girl, and let us be off; we have got our marching orders; going to the Rhine."

"And do you think that I will let him go?" screamed Jacintha. "No! I will say one word to Madame Raynal, and she will buy him a substitute directly."

Dard stopped her sullenly. "No! I have told all in the village that I would go the first chance: it is come, and I'll go. I won't stay to be laughed at about this too. If I was sure to be cut in pieces, I'd go. Give over blubbering, girl, and get us a bottle of the best wine, and while we are drinking it, the sergeant and I, you make up my bundle. I shall never do any good here."

Jacintha knew the obstinate toad. She did as she was bid, and soon the little bundle was ready, and the two men faced the wine; La Croix, radiant and bellicose; Dard, crestfallen but dogged (for there was a little bit of good stuff at the bottom of the creature); and Jacintha rocking herself, with her apron over her head.

"I'll give you a toast," said La Croix. "Here's gunpowder."

Jacintha promptly honored the toast with a flood of tears.

"Drop that, Jacintha," said Dard, angrily; "do you think that is encouraging? Sergeant, I told this poor girl all about glory before you came, but she was not ripe for it: say something to cheer her up, for I can't."

"I can," cried this trumpet of battle, emptying its glass. "Attention, young woman."

"Oh, dear! oh, dear! yes, sir."

"A French soldier is a man who carries France in his heart" —

"But if the cruel foreign soldiers kill him? Oh!"

"Why, in that case, he does not care a straw. Every man must die; horses likewise, and dogs, and donkeys, when they come to the end of their troubles; but dogs and donkeys and chaps in blouses can't die gloriously; as Dard may, if he has any luck at all: so, from this hour, if there was twice as little of him, be proud of him, for from this time he is a part of France and her renown. Come, recruit ninety-nine, shoulder your traps at duty's call, and let us go forth in form. Attention! Quick — march! Halt! is that the way I showed you to march? Didn't I tell you to start from the left? Now try again. *quick* — march! left — right — left — right — left — right — *now* you've — *got* it — *drat* ye, — *keep* it — left — right — left — right — left — right." And with no more ado the sergeant marched the little odd-job man to the wars.

VIVE LA FRANCE!

CHAPTER XVIII.

Edouard, the moment his temper cooled, became very sad. He longed to be friends again with Rose, but did not know how. His own pride held him back, and so did his fear that he had gone too far, and that his offended mistress would not listen to an offer of reconciliation from him. He sat down alone now to all his little meals. No sweet, mellow voices in his ear after the fatigues of the day. It was a dismal change in his life.

At last, one day, he received three lines from Josephine, requesting him to come and speak to her. He went over directly, full of vague hopes. He found her seated pale and languid in a small room on the ground floor.

"What has she been doing to you, dear?" began she kindly.

"Has she not told you, Madame Raynal?"

"No; she is refractory. She will tell me nothing, and that makes me fear she is the one in fault."

"Oh! if she does not accuse me, I am sure I will not accuse her. I dare say I am to blame; it is not her fault that I cannot make her love me."

"But you can. She does."

"Yes; but she loves others better, and she holds me out no hope it will ever be otherwise. On this one point how can I hope for your sympathy; unfortunately for me you are one of my rivals. She told me plainly she never could love me as she loves you."

"And you believed her?"

"I had good reason to believe her."

Josephine smiled sadly. "Dear Edouard," said she, "you must not attach so much importance to every word we say. Does Rose at her age know everything? Is she a prophet? Perhaps she really fancies she will always love her sister as she does now; but you are a man of sense; you ought to smile and let her talk. When you marry her you will take her to your own house; she will only see me now and then; she will have you and your affection always present. Each day some new tie between you and her. You two will share every joy, every sorrow. Your children playing at your feet, and reflecting the features of both parents, will make you one. Your hearts will melt together in that blessed union which raises earth so near to heaven; and then you will wonder you could ever be jealous of poor Josephine, who must never hope — ah, me!"

Edouard, wrapped up in himself, mistook Josephine's emotion at the picture she had drawn of conjugal love. He soothed her, and vowed upon his honor he never would separate Rose from her.

"Madame Raynal," said he, "you are an angel, and I am a fiend. Jealousy must be the meanest of all sentiments. I never will be jealous again, above all, of you, sweet angel. Why, you are my sister as well as hers, and she has a right to love you, for I love you myself."

"You make me very happy when you talk so," sighed Josephine. "Peace is made?"

"Never again to be broken. I will go and ask her pardon. What is the matter now?"

For Jacintha was cackling very loud, and dismissing with ignominy two beggars, male and female.

She was industry personified, and had no sympathy with mendicity. In vain the couple protested, Heaven knows with what truth, that they were not beggars, but mechanics out of work. "March! tramp!" was Jacintha's least word. She added, giving the rein to her imagination, "I'll loose the dog." The man moved away, the woman turned appealingly to Edouard. He and Josephine came towards the group. She had got a sort of large hood, and in that hood she carried an infant on her shoulders. Josephine inspected it. "It looks sickly, poor little thing," said she.

"What can you expect, young lady?" said the woman. "Its mother had to rise and go about when she ought to have been in her bed, and now she has not enough to give it."

"Oh, dear!" cried Josephine. "Jacintha, give them some food and a nice bottle of wine."

"That I will," cried Jacintha, changing her tone with courtier-like alacrity. "I did not see she was nursing."

Josephine put a franc into the infant's hand; the little fingers closed on it with that instinct of appropriation, which is our first and often our last sentiment. Josephine smiled lovingly on the child, and the child seeing that gave a small crow.

"Bless it," said Josephine, and thereupon her lovely head reared itself like a snake's, and then darted down on the child; and the young noble kissed the beggar's brat as if she would eat it.

This won the mother's heart more than even the gifts.

"Blessings on you, my lady!" she cried. "I pray the Lord not to forget this when a woman's trouble comes on you in your turn! It is a small child, mademoiselle, but it is not an unhealthy one. See." Inspection was offered, and eagerly accepted.

Edouard stood looking on at some distance in amazement, mingled with disgust.

"Ugh!" said he, when she rejoined him, "how could you kiss

that nasty little brat?"

"Dear Edouard, don't speak so of a poor little innocent. Who would pity them if we women did not? It had lovely eyes."

"Like saucers."

"Yes."

"It is no compliment when you are affectionate to anybody; you overflow with benevolence on all creation, like the rose which sheds its perfume on the first-comer."

"If he is not going to be jealous of me next," whined Josephine.

She took him to Rose, and she said, "There, whenever good friends quarrel, it is understood they were both in the wrong. Bygones are to be bygones; and when your time comes round to quarrel again, please consult me first, since it is me you will afflict." She left them together, and went and tapped timidly at the doctor's study.

Aubertin received her with none of that reserve she had seen in him. He appeared both surprised and pleased at her visit to his little sanctum. He even showed an emotion Josephine was at a loss to account for. But that wore off during the conversation, and, indeed, gave place to a sort of coldness.

"Dear friend," said she, "I come to consult you about Rose and Edouard." She then told him what had happened, and hinted at Edouard's one fault. The doctor smiled. "It is curious. You have come to draw my attention to a point on which it has been fixed for some days past. I am preparing a cure for the two young fools; a severe remedy, but in their case a sure one."

He then showed her a deed, wherein he had settled sixty thousand francs on Rose and her children. "Edouard," said he, "has a good place. He is active and rising, and with my sixty thousand francs, and a little purse of ten thousand more for furniture and nonsense, they can marry next week, if they like. Yes, marriage is a sovereign medicine for both of these patients. She does not love him quite enough. Cure: marriage. He loves her a little too much. Cure: marriage."

"O doctor!"

"Can't help it. I did not make men and women. We must take human nature as we find it, and thank God for it on the whole. Have you nothing else to confide to me?"

"No, doctor."

"Are you sure?"

"No, dear friend. But this is very near my heart," faltered Josephine.

The doctor sighed; then said gently, "They shall be happy: as happy as you wish them."

Meantime, in another room, a reconciliation scene was taking place, and the mutual concessions of two impetuous but generous spirits.

The baroness noticed the change in Josephine's appearance. She asked Rose what could be the matter.

"Some passing ailment," was the reply.

"Passing? She has been so, on and off, a long time. She makes me very anxious."

Rose made light of it to her mother, but in her own heart she grew more and more anxious day by day. She held secret conferences with Jacintha; that sagacious personage had a plan to wake Josephine from her deathly languor, and even soothe her nerves, and check those pitiable fits of nervous irritation to which she had become subject. Unfortunately, Jacintha's plan was so difficult and so dangerous, that at first even the courageous Rose recoiled from it; but there are dangers that seem to diminish when you look them long in the face.

The whole party was seated in the tapestried room: Jacintha was there, sewing a pair of sheets, at a respectful distance from the gentlefolks, absorbed in her work; but with both ears on full cock.

The doctor, holding his glasses to his eye, had just begun to read out the Moniteur.

The baroness sat close to him, Edouard opposite; and the young ladies each in her corner of a large luxurious sofa, at some little distance.

"'The Austrians left seventy cannon, eight thousand men, and three colors upon the field. Army of the North: General Menard defeated the enemy after a severe engagement, taking thirteen field-pieces and a quantity of ammunition.'"

The baroness made a narrow-minded renmark. "That is always the way with these journals," said she. "Austrians! Prussians! when it's Egypt one wants to hear about." — "No, not a word about Egypt," said the doctor; "but there is a whole column about the Rhine, where Colonel Dujardin is — and Dard. If I was dictator, the first nuisance I would put down is small type." He then spelled out a sanguinary engagement: "eight thousand of the enemy killed. We have some losses to lament. Colonel Dujardin" —

"Only wounded, I hope," said the baroness.

The doctor went coolly on. "At the head of the 24th brigade made a brilliant charge on the enemy's flank, that is described in the general order as having decided the fate of the battle."

"How badly you do read," said the old lady, sharply. "I thought he was gone; instead of that he has covered himself with glory; but it is all our doing, is it not, young ladies? We saved his life."

"We saved it amongst us, madame."

"What is the matter, Rose?" said Edouard.

"Nothing: give me the salts, quick."

She only passed them, as it were, under her own nostrils; then held them to Josephine, who was now observed to be trembling all over. Rose contrived to make it appear that this was mere sympathy on Josephine's part.

"Don't be silly, girls," cried the baroness, cheerfully; "there is nobody killed that we care about."

Dr. Aubertin read the rest to himself.

Edouard fell into a gloomy silence and tortured himself about Camille, and Rose's anxiety and agitation.

By and by the new servant brought in a letter. It was the long-expected one from Egypt.

"Here is something better than salts for you. A long letter, Josephine, and all in his own hand; so he is safe, thank Heaven! I was beginning to be uneasy again. You frightened me for that poor Camille: but this is worth a dozen Camilles; this is my son; I would give my old life for him." — "My dear Mother — ('Bless him!'), my dear wife, and my dear sister — ('Well! you sit there like two rocks!') — We have just gained a battle — fifty colors. ('What do you think of that?') All the enemy's baggage and ammunition are in our hands. ('This is something like a battle, this one.') Also the Pasha of Natolie. ('Ah! the Pasha of Natolie; an important personage, no doubt, though I never had the honor of hearing of him. Do you hear? — you on the sofa. My son has captured the Pasha of Natolie. He is as brave as Caesar.') But this success is not one of those that lead to important results ('Never mind, a victory is a victory'), and I should not wonder if Bonaparte was to dash home any day. If so, I shall go with him, and perhaps spend a whole day with you, on my way to the Rhine."

At this prospect a ghastly look passed quick as lightning between Rose and Josephine.

The baroness beckoned Josephine to come close to her, and read her what followed in a lower tone of voice.

"Tell my wife I love her more and more every day. I don't expect as much from her, but she will make me very happy if she can make shift to like me as well as her family do." — "No danger!

What husband deserves to be loved as he does? I long for his return, that his wife, his mother, and his sister may all combine to teach this poor soldier what happiness means. We owe him everything, Josephine, and if we did not love him, and make him happy, we should be monsters; now should we not?"

Josephine stammered an assent.

"*Now* you may read his letter: Jacintha and all," said the baroness graciously.

The letter circulated. Meantime, the baroness conversed with Aubertin in quite an undertone.

"My friend, look at Josephine. That girl is ill, or else she is going to be ill."

"Neither the one nor the other, madame," said Aubertin, looking her coolly in the face.

"But I say she is. Is a doctor's eye keener than a mother's?"

"Considerably," replied the doctor with cool and enviable effrontery.

The baroness rose. "Now, children, for our evening walk. We shall enjoy it now."

"I trust you may: but for all that I must forbid the evening air to one of the party — to Madame Raynal."

The baroness came to him and whispered, "That is right. Thank you. See what is the matter with her, and tell me." And she carried off the rest of the party.

At the same time Jacintha asked permission to pass the rest of the evening with her relations in the village. But why that swift, quivering glance of intelligence between Jacintha and Rose de Beaurepaire when the baroness said, "Yes, certainly"?

Time will show.

Josephine and the doctor were left alone. Now Josephine had noticed the old people whisper and her mother glance her way, and the whole woman was on her guard. She assumed a languid complacency, and by way of shield, if necessary, took some work, and bent her eyes and apparently her attention on it.

The doctor was silent and ill at ease.

She saw he had something weighty on his mind. "The air would have done me no harm," said she.

"Neither will a few words with me."

"Oh, no, dear friend. Only I think I should have liked a little walk this evening."

"Josephine," said the doctor quietly, "when you were a child I saved your life."

"I have often heard my mother speak of it. I was choked by the croup, and you had the courage to lance my windpipe."

"Had I?" said the doctor, with a smile. He added gravely, "It seems then that to be cruel is sometimes kindness. It is the nature of men to love those whose life they save."

"And they love you."

"Well, our affection is not perfect. I don't know which is most to blame, but after all these years I have failed to inspire you with confidence." The doctor's voice was sad, and Josephine's bosom panted.

"Pray do not say so," she cried. "I would trust you with my life."

"But not with your secret."

"My secret! What secret? I have no secrets."

"Josephine, you have now for full twelve months suffered in body and mind, yet you have never come to me for counsel, for comfort, for an old man's experience and advice, nor even for medical aid."

"But, dear friend, I assure you" —

"We *do not* deceive our friend. We *cannot* deceive our doctor."

Josephine trembled, but defended herself after the manner of her sex. "Dear doctor," said she, "I love you all the better for this. Your regard for me has for once blinded your science. I am not so robust as you have known me, but there is nothing serious the matter with me. Let us talk of something else. Besides, it is not interesting to talk about one's self."

"Very well; since there is nothing serious or interesting in your case, we will talk about something that is both serious and interesting."

"With all my heart;" and she smiled with a sense of relief.

But the doctor leaned over the table to her, and said in a cautious and most emphatic whisper, "We will talk about *your child*."

The work dropped from Josephine's hands: she turned her face wildly on Aubertin, and faltered out, "M — my child?"

"My words are plain," replied he gravely. "*Your child*."

When the doctor repeated these words, when Josephine looking in his face saw he spoke from knowledge, however acquired, and not from guess, she glided down slowly off the sofa and clasped his knees as he stood before her, and hid her face in an agony of shame and terror on his knees.

"Forgive me," she sobbed. "Pray do not expose me! Do not destroy me."

"Unhappy young lady," said he, "did you think you had deceived me, or that you are fit to deceive any but the blind? Your face, your anguish after Colonel Dujardin's departure, your languor, and then your sudden robustness, your appetite, your caprices, your strange sojourn at Frejus, your changed looks and loss of health on your return! Josephine, your old friend has passed many an hour thinking of you, divining your folly, following your trouble step by step. Yet you never invited him to aid you."

Josephine faltered out a lame excuse. If she had revered him less she could have borne to confess to him. She added it would be a relief to her to confide in him.

"Then tell me all," said he.

She consented almost eagerly, and told him — nearly all. The old man was deeply affected. He murmured in a broken voice, "Your story is the story of your sex, self-sacrifice, first to your mother, then to Camille, now to your husband."

"And he is well worthy of any sacrifice I can make," said Josephine. "But oh, how hard it is to live!"

"I hope to make it less hard to you ere long," said the doctor quietly. He then congratulated himself on having forced Josephine to confide in him. "For," said he, "you never needed an experienced friend more than at this moment. Your mother will not always be so blind as of late. Edouard is suspicious. Jacintha is a shrewd young woman, and very inquisitive."

Josephine was not at the end of her concealments: she was ashamed to let him know she had made a confidant of Jacintha and not of him. She held her peace.

"Then," continued Aubertin, "there is the terrible chance of Raynal's return. But ere I take on me to advise you, what are your own plans?"

"I don't know," said Josephine helplessly.

"You — don't — know!" cried the doctor, looking at her in utter amazement.

"It is the answer of a mad woman, is it not? Doctor, I am little better. My foot has slipped on the edge of a precipice. I close my eyes, and let myself glide down it. What will become of me?"

"All shall be well," said Aubertin, "provided you do not still love that man."

Josephine did not immediately reply: her thoughts turned inwards. The good doctor was proceeding to congratulate her on being cured of a fatal passion, when she stopped him with wonder in her face. "Not love him! How can I help loving him? I was his betrothed. I wronged him in my thoughts. War, prison, anguish, could not kill him; he loved me so. He struggled bleeding to my feet; and could I let him die, after all? Could I be crueller than prison, and torture, and despair?"

The doctor sighed deeply; but, arming himself with the necessary resolution, he sternly replied, "A woman of your name cannot vacillate between love and honor; such vacillations have but one end. I will not let you drift a moral wreck between passion and virtue; and that is what it will come to if you hesitate now."

"Hesitate! Who can say I have hesitated where my honor was concerned? You can read our bodies then, but not our hearts. What! you see me so pale, forlorn, and dead, and that does not tell you I have bid Camille farewell forever? That we might be safer still I have not even told him he is a father: was ever woman so cruel as I am? I have written him but one letter, and in that I must deceive him. I told him I thought I might one day be happy, if I could hear that he did not give way to despair. I told him we must never meet again in this world. So now come what will: show me my duty and I will do it. This endless deceit burns my heart. Shall I tell my husband? It will be but one pang more, one blush more for me. But my mother!" and, thus appealed to, Dr. Aubertin felt, for the first time, all the difficulty of the situation he had undertaken to cure. He hesitated, he was embarrassed.

"Ah," said Josephine, "you see." Then, after a short silence, she said despairingly, "This is my only hope: that poor Raynal will be long absent, and that ere he returns mamma will lie safe from sorrow and shame in the little chapel. Doctor, when a woman of my age forms such wishes as these, I think you might pity her, and forgive her ill-treatment of you, for she cannot be very happy. Ah me! ah me! ah me!"

"Courage, poor soul! All is now in my hands, and I will save you," said the doctor, his voice trembling in spite of him. "Guilt lies in the intention. A more innocent woman than you does not breathe. Two courses lay open to you: to leave this house with Camille Dujardin, or to dismiss him, and live for your hard duty till it shall please Heaven to make that duty easy (no middle course was tenable for a day); of these two paths you chose the right one, and, having chosen, I really think you are not called on to reveal your misfortune, and make those unhappy to whose happiness you have sacrificed your own for years to come."

"Forever," said Josephine quietly.

"The young use that word lightly. The old have almost ceased to use it. They have seen how few earthly things can conquer time."

He resumed, "You think only of others, Josephine, but I shall think of you as well. I shall not allow your life to be wasted in a needless struggle against nature." Then turning to Rose, who had glided into the room, and stood amazed, "Her griefs were as many before her child was born, yet her health stood firm. Why? because nature was on her side. Now she is sinking into the grave. Why? because she is defying nature. Nature intended her to be pressing her child to her bosom day and night; instead of that, a peasant woman at Frejus nurses the child, and the mother pines at Beaurepaire."

At this, Josephine leaned her face on her hands on the doctor's shoulder. In this attitude she murmured to him, "I have never seen him since I left Frejus." Dr. Aubertin sighed for her. Emboldened by this, she announced her intention of going to Frejus the very next day to see her little Henri. But to this Dr. Aubertin demurred. "What, another journey to Frejus?" said he, "when the first has already roused Edouard's suspicions; I can never consent to that."

Then Josephine surprised them both. She dropped her coaxing voice and pecked the doctor like an irritated pigeon. "Take care," said she, "don't be too cruel to me. You see I am obedient, resigned. I have given up all I lived for: but if I am never to have my little boy's arms round me to console me, then — why torment me any longer? Why not say to me, 'Josephine, you have offended Heaven; pray for pardon, and die'?"

Then the doctor was angry in his turn. "Oh, go then," said he, "go to Frejus; you will have Edouard Riviere for a companion this time. Your first visit roused his suspicions. So before you go tell your mother all; for since she is sure to find it out, she had better hear it from you than from another."

"Doctor, have pity on me," said Josephine.

"You have no heart," said Rose. "She shall see him though, in spite of you."

"Oh, yes! he has a heart," said Josephine: "he is my best friend. He will let me see my boy."

All this, and the tearful eyes and coaxing yet trembling voice, was hard to resist. But Aubertin saw clearly, and stood firm. He put his handkerchief to his eyes a moment: then took the pining young mother's hand. "And, do you think," said he, "I do not pity you and love your boy? Ah! he will never want a father whilst I live; and from this moment he is under my care. I will go to see him; I will bring you news, and all in good time; I will place him where you shall visit him without imprudence; but, for the present, trust a wiser head than yours or Rose's; and give me your sacred promise not to go to Frejus."

Weighed down by his good-sense and kindness, Josephine resisted no longer in words. She just lifted her hands in despair and began to cry. It was so piteous, Aubertin was ready to yield in turn, and consent to any imprudence, when he met with an unexpected ally.

"Promise," said Rose, doggedly.

Josephine looked at her calmly through her tears.

"Promise, dear," repeated Rose, and this time with an intonation so fine that it attracted Josephine's notice, but not the doctor's. It was followed by a glance equally subtle.

"I promise," said Josephine, with her eye fixed inquiringly on her sister.

For once she could not make the telegraph out: but she could see it was playing, and that was enough. She did what Rose bid her; she promised not to go to Frejus without leave.

Finding her so submissive all of a sudden, he went on to suggest that she must not go kissing every child she saw. "Edouard tells me he saw you kissing a beggar's brat. The young rogue was going to quiz you about it at the dinner-table; luckily, he told me his intention, and I would not let him. I said the baroness would be annoyed with you for descending from your dignity — and exposing a noble family to fleas — hush! here he is."

"Tiresome!" muttered Rose, "just when" —

Edouard came forward with a half-vexed face.

However, he turned it off into play. "What have you been saying to her, monsieur, to interest her so? Give me a leaf out of your book. I need it."

The doctor was taken aback for a moment, but at last he said slyly, "I have been proposing to her to name the day. She says she must consult you before she decides that."

"Oh, you wicked doctor! — and consult *him* of all people!"

"So be off, both of you, and don't reappear before me till it is settled."

Edouard's eyes sparkled. Rose went out with a face as red as fire.

It was a balmy evening. Edouard was to leave them for a week the next day. They were alone: Rose was determined he should go away quite happy. Everything was in Edouard's favor: he pleaded his cause warmly: she listened tenderly: this happy evening her piquancy and archness seemed to dissolve into tenderness as she and Edouard walked hand in hand under the moon: a tenderness all the more heavenly to her devoted lover, that she was not one of those angels who cloy a man by invariable sweetness.

For a little while she forgot everything but her companion. In that soft hour he won her to name the day, after her fashion.

"Josephine goes to Paris with the doctor in about three weeks," murmured she.

"And you will stay behind, all alone?"

"Alone? that shall depend on you, monsieur."

On this Edouard caught her for the first time in his arms.

She made a faint resistance.

"Seal me that promise, sweet one!"

"No! no! — there!"

He pressed a delicious first kiss upon two velvet lips that in their innocence scarcely shunned the sweet attack.

For all that, the bond was no sooner sealed after this fashion, than the lady's cheek began to burn.

"Suppose we go in NOW?" said she, dryly.

"Ah, not yet."

"It is late, dear Edouard."

And with these words something returned to her mind with its full force: something that Edouard had actually made her forget. She wanted to get rid of him now.

"Edouard," said she, "can you get up early in the morning? If you can, meet me here tomorrow before any of them are up; then we can talk without interruption."

Edouard was delighted.

"Eight o'clock?"

"Sooner if you like. Mamma bade me come and read to her in her room *tonight*. She will be waiting for me. Is it not tiresome?"

"Yes, it is."

"Well, we must not mind that, dear; in three weeks' time we are to have too much of one another, you know, instead of too little."

"Too much! I shall never have enough of you. I shall hate the night which will rob me of the sight of you for so many hours in the twenty-four."

"If you can't see me, perhaps you may hear me; my tongue runs by night as well as by day."

"Well, that is a comfort," said Edouard, gravely. "Yes, little quizzer, I would rather hear you scold than an angel sing. Judge, then, what music it is when you say you love me!"

"I love you, Edouard."

Edouard kissed her hand warmly, and then looked irresolutely at her face.

"No, no!" said she, laughing and blushing. "How rude you are. Next time we meet."

"That is a bargain. But I won't go till you say you love me again.

"Edouard, don't be silly. I am ashamed of saying the same thing so often — I won't say it any more. What is the use? You know I love you. There, I *have* said it: how stupid!"

"Adieu, then, my wife that is to be."

"Adieu! dear Edouard."

"My hus — go on — my hus —"

"My huswife that shall be."

Then they walked very slowly towards the house, and once more Rose left quizzing, and was all tenderness.

"Will you not come in, and bid them 'good-night'?"

"No, my own; I am in heaven. Common faces — common voices would bring me down to earth. Let me be alone; — your sweet words ringing in my ear. I will dilute you with nothing meaner than the stars. See how bright they shine in heaven; but not so bright as you shine in my heart."

"Dear Edouard, you flatter me, you spoil me. Alas! why am I not more worthy of your love?"

"More worthy! How can that be?"

Rose sighed.

"But I will atone for all. I will make you a better — (here she substituted a full stop for a substantive) — than you expect. You will see else."

She lingered at the door: a proof that if Edouard, at that particular moment, had seized another kiss, there would have been no very violent opposition or offence.

But he was not so impudent as some. He had been told to wait till the next meeting for that. He prayed Heaven to bless her, and so the affianced lovers parted for the night.

It was about nine o'clock. Edouard, instead of returning to his lodgings, started down towards the town, to conclude a bargain with the innkeeper for an English mare he was in treaty for. He wanted her for tomorrow's work; so that decided him to make the purchase. In purchases, as in other matters, a feather turns the balanced scale. He sauntered leisurely down. It was a very clear night; the full moon and the stars shining silvery and vivid. Edouard's heart swelled with joy. He was loved after all, deeply loved; and in three short weeks he was actually to be Rose's husband: her lord and master. How like a heavenly dream it all seemed — the first hopeless courtship, and now the wedding fixed! But it was no dream; he felt her soft words still murmur music at his heart, and the shadow of her velvet lips slept upon his own.

He had strolled about a league when he heard the ring of a horse's hoofs coming towards him, accompanied by a clanking noise; it came nearer and nearer, till it reached a hill that lay a little ahead of Edouard; then the sounds ceased; the cavalier was walking his horse up the hill.

Presently, as if they had started from the earth, up popped between Edouard and the sky, first a cocked hat that seemed in that light to be cut with a razor out of flint; then the wearer, phosphorescent here and there; so brightly the keen moonlight played on his epaulets and steel scabbard. A step or two nearer, and Edouard gave a great shout; it was Colonel Raynal.

After the first warm greeting, and questions and answers, Raynal told him he was on his way to the Rhine with despatches.

"To the Rhine?"

"I am allowed six days to get there. I made a calculation, and found I could give Beaurepaire half a day. I shall have to make up for it by hard riding. You know me; always in a hurry. It is Bonaparte's fault this time. He is always in a hurry too."

"Why, colonel," said Edouard, "let us make haste then. Mind they go early to rest at the chateau."

"But you are not coming my way, youngster?"

"Not coming your way? Yes, but I am. Yours is a face I don't see every day, colonel; besides I would not miss *their* faces, especially the baroness's and Madame Raynal's, at sight of you; and, besides," — and the young gentleman chuckled to himself, and thought of Rose's words, "the next time we meet;" well, this will be the next time. "May I jump up behind?"

Colonel Raynal nodded assent. Edouard took a run, and lighted like a monkey on the horse's crupper. He pranced and kicked at this unexpected addition; but the spur being promptly applied to his flanks, he bounded off with a snort that betrayed more astonishment than satisfaction, and away they cantered to Beaurepaire, without drawing rein.

"There," said Edouard, "I was afraid they would be gone to bed; and they are. The very house seems asleep — fancy — at half-past ten."

"That is a pity," said Raynal, "for this chateau is the stronghold of etiquette. They will be two hours dressing before they will come out and shake hands. I must put my horse into the stable. Go you and give the alarm."

"I will, colonel. Stop, first let me see whether none of them are up, after all."

And Edouard walked round the chateau, and soon discovered a light at one window, the window of the tapestried room. Running round the other way he came slap upon another light: this one was nearer the ground. A narrow but massive door, which he had always seen not only locked but screwed up, was wide open; and through the aperture the light of a candle streamed out and met the moonlight streaming in.

"Hallo!" cried Edouard.

He stopped, turned, and looked in.

"Hallo!" he cried again much louder.

A young woman was sleeping with her feet in the silvery moonlight, and her head in the orange-colored blaze of a flat candle, which rested on the next step above of a fine stone staircase, whose existence was now first revealed to the inquisitive Edouard.

Coming plump upon all this so unexpectedly, he quite started.

"Why, Jacintha!"

He touched her on the shoulder to wake her. No. Jacintha was sleeping as only tired domestics can sleep. He might have taken the candle and burnt her gown off her back. She had found a step that fitted into the small of her back, and another that supported her head, and there she was fast as a door.

At this moment Raynal's voice was heard calling him.

"There is a light in that bedroom."

"It is not a bedroom, colonel; it is our sitting-room now. We shall find them all there, or at least the young ladies; and perhaps the doctor. The baroness goes to bed early. Meantime I can show you one of our dramatis personae, and an important one too. She rules the roost."

He took him mysteriously and showed him Jacintha.

Moonlight by itself seems white, and candlelight by itself seems yellow; but when the two come into close contrast at night, candle turns a reddish flame, and moonlight a bluish gleam.

So Jacintha, with her shoes in this celestial sheen, and her face in that demoniacal glare, was enough to knock the gazer's eye out.

"Make a good sentinel — this one," said Raynal — "an outlying picket for instance, on rough ground, in front of the enemy's riflemen."

"Ha! ha! colonel! Let us see where this staircase leads. I have an idea it will prove a short cut."

"Where to?"

"To the saloon, or somewhere, or else to some of Jacintha's haunts. Serve her right for going to sleep at the mouth of her den."

"Forward then — no, halt! Suppose it leads to the bedrooms? Mind this is a thundering place for ceremony. We shall get drummed out of the barracks if we don't mind our etiquette."

At this they hesitated; and Edouard himself thought, on the whole, it would be better to go and hammer at the front door.

Now while they hesitated, a soft delicious harmony of female voices suddenly rose, and seemed to come and run round the walls. The men looked at one another in astonishment; for the effect was magical. The staircase being enclosed on all sides with stone walls and floored with stone, they were like flies inside a violoncello; the voices rang above, below, and on every side of the vibrating walls. In some epochs spirits as hardy as Raynal's, and wits as quick as Riviere's, would have fled then and there to the nearest public, and told over cups how they had heard the dames of Beaurepaire, long since dead, holding their revel, and the conscious old devil's nest of a chateau quivering to the ghostly strains.

But this was an incredulous age. They listened, and listened, and decided the sounds came from up-stairs.

"Let us mount, and surprise these singing witches," said Edouard.

"Surprise them! what for? It is not the enemy — for once. What is the good of surprising our friends?"

Storming parties and surprises were no novelty and therefore no treat to Raynal.

"It will be so delightful to see their faces at first sight of you. O colonel, for my sake! Don't spoil it by going tamely in at the front door, after coming at night from Egypt for half an hour."

Raynal grumbled something about its being a childish trick; but to please Edouard consented at last; only stipulated for a light: "or else," said he, "we shall surprise ourselves instead with a broken neck, going over ground we don't know to surprise the natives — our skirmishers got nicked that way now and then in Egypt."

"Yes, colonel, I will go first with Jacintha's candle." Edouard mounted the stairs on tiptoe. Raynal followed. The solid stone steps did not prate. The men had mounted a considerable way, when puff a blast of wind came through a hole, and out went Edouard's candle. He turned sharply round to Raynal. "Peste!" said he in a vicious whisper. But the other laid his hand on his shoulder and whispered, "Look to the front." He looked, and, his own candle being out, saw a glimmer on ahead. He crept towards it. It was a taper shooting a feeble light across a small aperture. They caught a glimpse of what seemed to be a small apartment. Yet Edouard recognized the carpet of the tapestried room — which was a very large room. Creeping a yard nearer, he discovered that it was the tapestried room, and that what had seemed the further wall was only the screen, behind which were lights, and two women singing a duet.

He whispered to Raynal, "It is the tapestried room."

"Is it a sitting-room?" whispered Raynal.

"Yes! yes! Mind and not knock your foot against the wood."

And Raynal went softly up and put his foot quietly through the aperture, which he now saw was made by a panel drawn back close to the ground; and stood in the tapestried chamber. The carpet was thick; the voices favored the stealthy advance; the floor of the old house was like a rock; and Edouard put his face through the aperture, glowing all over with anticipation of the little scream of joy that would welcome his friend dropping in so nice and suddenly from Egypt.

The feeling was rendered still more piquant by a sharp curiosity that had been growing on him for some minutes past. For why was this passage opened *tonight*? — he had never seen it opened before. And why was Jacintha lying sentinel at the foot of the stairs?

But this was not all. Now that they were in the room both men became conscious of another sound besides the ladies' voices — a very peculiar sound. It also came from behind the screen. They both heard it, and showed, by the puzzled looks they cast at one another, that neither could make out what on earth it was. It consisted of a succession of little rustles, followed by little thumps on the floor.

But what was curious, too, this rustle, thump — rustle, thump — fell exactly into the time of the music; so that, clearly, either the rustle thump was being played to the tune, or the tune sung to the rustle thump.

This last touch of mystery inflamed Edouard's impatience beyond bearing: he pointed eagerly and merrily to the corner of the screen. Raynal obeyed, and stepped very slowly and cautiously towards it.

Rustle, thump! rustle, thump! rustle, thump! with the rhythm of harmonious voices.

Edouard got his head and foot into the room without taking his eye off Raynal.

Rustle, thump! rustle, thump! rustle, thump!

Raynal was now at the screen, and quietly put his head round it, and his hand upon it.

Edouard was bursting with expectation.

No result. What is this? Don't they see him? Why does he not speak to them? He seems transfixed.

Rustle, thump! rustle, thump; accompanied now for a few notes by one voice only, Rose's.

Suddenly there burst a shriek from Josephine, so loud, so fearful, that it made even Raynal stagger back a step, the screen in his hand.

Then another scream of terror and anguish from Rose. Then a fainter cry, and the heavy helpless fall of a human body.

Raynal sprang forward whirling the screen to the earth in terrible agitation, and Edouard bounded over it as it fell at his feet. He did not take a second step. The scene that caught his eye stupefied and paralyzed him in full career, and froze him to the spot with amazement and strange misgivings.

CHAPTER XIX.

To return for a moment to Rose. She parted from Edouard, and went in at the front door: but the next moment she opened it softly and watched her lover unseen. "Dear Edouard!" she murmured: and then she thought, "how sad it is that I must deceive him, even *tonight*: must make up an excuse to get him from me, when we were so happy together. Ah! he little knows how I shall welcome our wedding-day. When once I can see my poor martyr on the road to peace and content under the good doctor's care. And oh! the happiness of having no more secrets from him I love! Dear Edouard! when once we are married, I never, never, will have a secret from you again — I swear it."

As a comment on these words she now stepped cautiously out, and peered in every direction.

"St — st!" she whispered. No answer came to this signal.

Rose returned into the house and bolted the door inside. She went up to the tapestried room, and found the doctor in the act of wishing Josephine good-night. The baroness, fatigued a little by her walk, had mounted no higher than her own bedroom, which was on the first floor just under the tapestried room. Rose followed the doctor out. "Dear friend, one word. Josephine talked of telling Raynal. You have not encouraged her to do that?"

"Certainly not, while he is in Egypt."

"Still less on his return. Doctor, you don't know that man. Josephine does not know him. But I do. He would kill her if he knew. He would kill her that minute. He would not wait: he would not listen to excuses: he is a man of iron. Or if he spared her he would kill Camille: and that would destroy her by the cruellest of all deaths! My friend, I am a wicked, miserable girl. I am the cause of all this misery!"

She then told Aubertin all about the anonymous letter, and what Raynal had said to her in consequence.

"He never would have married her had he known she loved another. He asked me was it so. I told him a falsehood. At least I equivocated, and to equivocate with one so loyal and simple was to deceive him. I am the only sinner: that sweet angel is the only sufferer. Is this the justice of Heaven? Doctor, my remorse is great. No one knows what I feel when I look at my work. Edouard thinks I love her so much better than I do him. He is wrong: it is not love only, it is pity: it is remorse for the sorrow I have brought on her, and the wrong I have done poor Raynal."

The high-spirited girl was greatly agitated: and Aubertin,

though he did not acquit her of all blame, soothed her, and made excuses for her.

"We must not always judge by results," said he. "Things turned unfortunately. You did for the best. I forgive you for one. That is, I will forgive you if you promise not to act again without my advice."

"Oh, never! never!"

"And, above all, no imprudence about that child. In three little weeks they will be together without risk of discovery. Well, you don't answer me."

Rose's blood turned cold. "Dear friend," she stammered, "I quite agree with you."

"Promise, then."

"Not to let Josephine go to Frejus?" said Rose hastily. "Oh, yes! I promise."

"You are a good girl," said Aubertin. "You have a will of your own. But you can submit to age and experience." The doctor then kissed her, and bade her farewell.

"I leave for Paris at six in the morning," he said. "I will not try your patience or hers unnecessarily. Perhaps it will not be three weeks ere she sees her child under her friend's roof."

The moment Rose was alone, she sat down and sighed bitterly. "There is no end to it," she sobbed despairingly. "It is like a spider's web: every struggle to be free but multiplies the fine yet irresistible thread that seems to bind me. And *tonight* I thought to be so happy; instead of that, he has left me scarce the heart to do what I have to do."

She went back to the room, opened a window, and put out a white handkerchief, then closed the window down on it.

Then she went to Josephine's bedroom-door: it opened on the tapestried room.

"Josephine," she cried, "don't go to bed just yet."

"No, love. What are you doing? I want to talk to you. Why did you say promise? and what did you mean by looking at me so? Shall I come out to you?"

"Not just yet," said Rose; she then glided into the corridor, and passed her mother's room and the doctor's, and listened to see if all was quiet. While she was gone Josephine opened her door; but not seeing Rose in the sitting-room, retired again.

Rose returned softly, and sat down with her head in her hand, in a calm attitude belied by her glancing eye, and the quick tapping of her other hand upon the table.

Presently she raised her head quickly; a sound had reached

her ear, — a sound so slight that none but a high-strung ear could have caught it. It was like a mouse giving a single scratch against a stone wall.

Rose coughed slightly.

On this a clearer sound was heard, as of a person scratching wood with the finger-nail. Rose darted to the side of the room, pressed against the wall, and at the same time put her other hand against the rim of one of the panels and pushed it laterally; it yielded, and at the opening stood Jacintha in her cloak and bonnet.

"Yes," said Jacintha, "under my cloak — look!"

"Ah! you found the things on the steps?"

"Yes! I nearly tumbled over them. Have you locked that door?"

"No, but I will." And Rose glided to the door and locked it. Then she put the screen up between Josephine's room and the open panel: then she and Jacintha were wonderfully busy on the other side the screen, but presently Rose said, "This is imprudent; you must go down to the foot of the stairs and wait till I call you."

Jacintha pleaded hard against this arrangement, and represented that there was no earthly chance of any one coming to that part of the chateau.

"No matter; I will be guarded on every side."

"Mustn't I stop and just see her happy for once?"

"No, my poor Jacintha, you must hear it from my lips."

Jacintha retired to keep watch as she was bid. Rose went to Josephine's room, and threw her arms round her neck and kissed her vehemently. Josephine returned her embrace, then held her out at arm's length and looked at her.

"Your eyes are red, yet your little face is full of joy. There, you smile."

"I can't help that; I am so happy."

"I am glad of it. Are you coming to bed?"

"Not yet. I invite you to take a little walk with me first. Come!" and she led the way slowly, looking back with infinite archness and tenderness.

"You almost frighten me," said Josephine; "it is not like you to be all joy when I am sad. Three whole weeks more!"

"That is it. Why are you sad? because the doctor would not let you go to Frejus. And why am I not sad? because I had already thought of a way to let you see Edouard without going so far."

"Rose! O Rose! O Rose!"

"This way — come!" and she smiled and beckoned with her

finger, while Josephine followed like one under a spell, her bosom heaving, her eye glancing on every side, hoping some strange joy, yet scarce daring to hope.

Rose drew back the screen, and there was a sweet little berceau that had once been Josephine's own, and in it, sunk deep in snow-white lawn, was a sleeping child, that lay there looking as a rose might look could it fall upon new-fallen snow.

At sight of it Josephine uttered a little cry, not loud but deep — ay, a cry to bring tears into the eye of the hearer, and she stood trembling from head to foot, her hands clasped, and her eye fascinated and fixed on the cradle.

"My child under this roof! What have you done?" but her eye, fascinated and fixed, never left the cradle.

"I saw you languishing, dying, for want of him."

"Oh, if anybody should come?" But her eye never stirred an inch from the cradle.

"No, no, no! the door is locked. Jacintha watches below; there is no dan — Ah, oh, poor sister!"

For, as Rose was speaking, the young mother sprang silently upon her child. You would have thought she was going to kill him; her head reared itself again and again like a crested snake's, and again and again and again and again plunged down upon the child, and she kissed his little body from head to foot with soft violence, and murmured, through her streaming tears, "My child! my darling! my angel! oh, my poor boy! my child! my child!"

I will ask my female readers of every degree to tell their brothers and husbands all the young noble did: how she sat on the floor, and had her child on her bosom; how she smiled over it through her tears; how she purred over it; how she, the stately one, lisped and prattled over it; and how life came pouring into her heart from it.

Before she had had it in her arms five minutes, her pale cheek was as red as a rose, and her eyes brighter than diamonds.

"Bless you, Rose! bless you! bless you! in one moment you have made me forget all I ever suffered in my life."

"There is a cold draught," cried she presently, with maternal anxiety; "close the panel, Rose."

"No, dear; or I could not call to Jacintha, or she to me; but I will shift the screen round between him and the draught. There, now, come to his aunt — a darling!"

Then Rose sat on the floor too, and Josephine put her boy on aunt's lap, and took a distant view of him. But she could not bear so vast a separation long. She must have him to her bosom again.

Presently my lord, finding himself hugged, opened his eyes, and, as a natural consequence, his mouth.

"Oh, that will never do," cried Rose, and they put him back in the cradle with all expedition, and began to rock it. Young master was not to be altogether appeased even by that. So Rose began singing an old-fashioned Breton chant or lullaby.

Josephine sang with her, and, singing, watched with a smile her boy drop off by degrees to sleep under the gentle motion and the lulling song. They sang and rocked till the lids came creeping down, and hid the great blue eyes; but still they sang and rocked, lulling the boy, and gladdening their own hearts; for the quaint old Breton ditty was tunable as the lark that carols over the green wheat in April; and the words so simple and motherly, that a nation had taken them to heart. Such songs bind ages together and make the lofty and the low akin by the great ties of music and the heart. Many a Breton peasant's bosom in the olden time had gushed over her sleeping boy as the young dame's of Beaurepaire gushed now — in this quaint, tuneful lullaby.

Now, as they kneeled over the cradle, one on each side, and rocked it, and sang that ancient chant, Josephine, who was opposite the screen, happening to raise her eyes, saw a strange thing.

There was the face of a man set close against the side of the screen, and peeping and peering out of the gloom. The light of her candle fell full on this face; it glared at her, set pale, wonder-struck, and vivid in the surrounding gloom.

Horror! It was her husband's face.

At first she was quite stupefied, and looked at it with soul and senses benumbed. Then she trembled, and put her hand to her eyes; for she thought it a phantom or a delusion of the mind. No: there it glared still. Then she trembled violently, and held out her left hand, the fingers working convulsively, to Rose, who was still singing.

But, at the same moment, the mouth of this face suddenly opened in a long-drawn breath. At this, Josephine uttered a violent shriek, and sprang to her feet, with her right hand quivering and pointing at that pale face set in the dark.

Rose started up, and, wheeling her head round, saw Raynal's gloomy face looking over her shoulder. She fell screaming upon her knees, and, almost out of her senses, began to pray wildly and piteously for mercy.

Josephine uttered one more cry, but this was the faint cry of nature, sinking under the shock of terror. She swooned dead away, and fell senseless on the floor ere Raynal could debarrass himself of the screen, and get to her.

This, then, was the scene that met Edouard's eyes. His affianced bride on her knees, white as a ghost, trembling, and screaming, rather than crying, for mercy. And Raynal standing over his wife, showing by the working of his iron features that he doubted whether she was worthy he should raise her.

One would have thought nothing could add to the terror of this scene. Yet it was added to. The baroness rang her bell violently in the room below. She had heard Josephine's scream and fall.

At the ringing of this shrill bell Rose shuddered like a maniac, and grovelled on her knees to Raynal, and seized his very knees and implored him to show some pity.

"O sir! kill us! we are culpable" —

Dring! dring! dring! dring! dring! pealed the baroness's bell again.

"But do not tell our mother. Oh, if you are a man! do not! do not! Show us some pity. We are but women. Mercy! mercy! mercy!"

"Speak out then," groaned Raynal. "What does this mean? Why has my wife swooned at sight of me? — whose is this child?"

"Whose?" stammered Rose. Till he said that, she never thought there *could* be a doubt whose child.

Dring! dring! dring! dring! dring!

"Oh, my God!" cried the poor girl, and her scared eyes glanced every way like some wild creature looking for a hole, however small, to escape by.

Edouard, seeing her hesitation, came down on her other side. "Whose is the child, Rose?" said he sternly.

"You, too? Why were we born? mercy! oh! pray let me go to my sister."

Dring! dring! dring! dring! dring! went the terrible bell.

The men were excited to fury by Rose's hesitation; they each seized an arm, and tore her screaming with fear at their violence, from her knees up to her feet between them with a single gesture.

"Whose is the child?"

"You hurt me!" said she bitterly to Edouard, and she left crying and was terribly calm and sullen all in a moment.

"Whose is the child?" roared Edouard and Raynal, in one raging breath. "Whose is the child?"

"It is mine."

CHAPTER XX.

These were not words; they were electric shocks.

The two arms that gripped Rose's arms were paralyzed, and dropped off them; and there was silence.

Then first the thought of all she had done with those three words began to rise and grow and surge over her. She stood, her eyes turned downwards, yet inwards, and dilating with horror.

Silence.

Now a mist began to spread over her eyes, and in it she saw indistinctly the figure of Raynal darting to her sister's side, and raising her head.

She dared not look round on the other side. She heard feet stagger on the floor. She heard a groan, too; but not a word.

Horrible silence.

With nerves strung to frenzy, and quivering ears, that magnified every sound, she waited for a reproach, a curse; either would have been some little relief. But no! a silence far more terrible.

Then a step wavered across the room. Her soul was in her ear. She could hear and feel the step totter, and it shook her as it went. All sounds were trebled to her. Then it struck on the stone step of the staircase, not like a step, but a knell; another step, another and another; down to the very bottom. Each slow step made her head ring and her heart freeze.

At last she heard no more. Then a scream of anguish and recall rose to her lips. She fought it down, for Josephine and Raynal. Edouard was gone. She had but her sister now, the sister she loved better than herself; the sister to save whose life and honor she had this moment sacrificed her own, and all a woman lives for.

She turned, with a wild cry of love and pity, to that sister's side to help her; and when she kneeled down beside her, an iron arm was promptly thrust out between the beloved one and her.

"This is my care, madame," said Raynal, coldly.

There was no mistaking his manner. The stained one was not to touch his wife.

She looked at him in piteous amazement at his ingratitude. "It is well," said she. "It is just. I deserve this from you."

She said no more, but drooped gently down beside the cradle, and hid her forehead in the clothes beside the child that had brought all this woe, and sobbed bitterly.

Then honest Raynal began to be sorry for her, in spite of himself. But there was no time for this. Josephine stirred; and, at the same moment, a violent knocking came at the door of the apartment, and the new servant's voice, crying, "Ladies, for Heaven's sake, what is the matter? The baroness heard a fall — she is getting up — she will be here. What shall I tell her is the matter?"

Raynal was going to answer, but Rose, who had started up at the knocking, put her hand in a moment right before his mouth, and ran to the door. "There is nothing the matter; tell mamma I am coming down to her directly." She flew back to Raynal in an excitement little short of frenzy. "Help me carry her into her own room," cried she imperiously. Raynal obeyed by instinct; for the fiery girl spoke like a general, giving the word of command, with the enemy in front. He carried the true culprit in his arms, and laid her gently on her bed.

"Now put *it* out of sight — take this, quick, man! quick!" cried Rose.

Raynal went to the cradle. "Ah! my poor girl," said he, as he lifted it in his arms, "this is a sorry business; to have to hide your own child from your own mother!"

"Colonel Raynal," said Rose, "do not insult a poor, despairing girl. C'est lache."

"I am silent, young woman," said Raynal, sternly. "What is to be done?"

"Take it down the steps, and give it to Jacintha. Stay, here is a candle; I go to tell mamma you are come; and, Colonel Raynal, I never injured *you*: if you tell my mother you will stab her to the heart, and me, and may the curse of cowards light on you! — may" —

"Enough!" said Raynal, sternly. "Do you take me for a babbling girl? I love your mother better than you do, or this brat of yours would not be here. I shall not bring her gray hairs down with sorrow to the grave. I shall speak of this villany to but one person; and to him I shall talk with this, and not with the idle tongue." And he tapped his sword-hilt with a sombre look of terrible significance.

He carried out the cradle. The child slept sweetly through it all.

Rose darted into Josephine's room, took the key from the inside to the outside, locked the door, put the key in her pocket, and ran down to her mother's room; her knees trembled under her as she went.

Meantime, Jacintha, sleeping tranquilly, suddenly felt her throat griped, and heard a loud voice ring in her ear; then she was lifted, and wrenched, and dropped. She found herself lying clear of the steps in the moonlight; her head was where her feet had been, and her candle out.

She uttered shriek upon shriek, and was too frightened to get up. She thought it was supernatural; some old De Beaurepaire had served her thus for sleeping on her post. A struggle took place between her fidelity and her superstitious fears. Fidelity conquered. Quaking in every limb, she groped up the staircase for her candle.

It was gone.

Then a still more sickening fear came over her.

What if this was no spirit's work, but a human arm — a strong one — some man's arm?

Her first impulse was to dart up the stairs, and make sure that no calamity had befallen through her mistimed drowsiness. But, when she came to try, her dread of the supernatural revived. She could not venture without a light up those stairs, thronged perhaps with angry spirits. She ran to the kitchen. She found the tinderbox, and with trembling hands struck a light. She came back shading it with her shaky hands; and, committing her soul to the care of Heaven, she crept quaking up the stairs. Then she heard voices above, and that restored her more; she mounted more steadily. Presently she stopped, for a heavy step was coming down. It did not sound like a woman's step. It came further down; she turned to fly.

"Jacintha!" said a deep voice, that in this stone cylinder rang like thunder from a tomb.

"Oh! saints and angels save me!" yelled Jacintha; and fell on her knees, and hid her head for security; and down went her candlestick clattering on the stone.

"Don't be a fool!" said the iron voice. "Get up and take this."

She raised her head by slow degrees, shuddering. A man was holding out a cradle to her; the candle he carried lighted up his face; it was Colonel Raynal.

She stared at him stupidly, but never moved from her knees, and the candle began to shake violently in her hand, as she herself trembled from head to foot.

Then Raynal concluded she was in the plot; but, scorning to reproach a servant, he merely said, "Well, what do you kneel there for, gaping at me like that? Take this, I tell you, and carry it out of the house."

He shoved the cradle roughly down into her hands, then turned on his heel without a word.

Jacintha collapsed on the stairs, and the cradle beside her, for all the power was driven out of her body; she could hardly support her own weight, much less the cradle.

She rocked herself, and moaned out, "Oh, what's this? oh, what's this?"

A cold perspiration came over her whole frame.

"What could this mean? What on earth had happened?"

She took up the candle, for it was lying burning and guttering on the stairs; scraped up the grease with the snuffers, and by force of habit tried to polish it clean with a bit of paper that shook between her fingers; she did not know what she was doing. When she recovered her wits, she took the child out of the cradle, and wrapped it carefully in her shawl; then went slowly down the stairs; and holding him close to her bosom, with a furtive eye, and brain confused, and a heart like lead, stole away to the tenantless cottage, where Madame Jouvenel awaited her.

Meantime, Rose, with quaking heart, had encountered the baroness. She found her pale and agitated, and her first question was, "What is the matter? what have you been all doing over my head?"

"Darling mother," replied Rose, evasively, "something has happened that will rejoice your heart. Somebody has come home."

"My son? eh, no! impossible! We cannot be so happy."

"He will be with you directly."

The old lady now trembled with joyful agitation.

"In five minutes I will bring him to you. Shall you be dressed? I will ring for the girl to help you."

"But, Rose, the scream, and that terrible fall. Ah! where is Josephine?"

"Can't you guess, mamma? Oh, the fall was only the screen; they stumbled over it in the dark."

"They! who?"

"Colonel Raynal, and — and Edouard. I will tell you, mamma, but don't be angry, or even mention it; they wanted to surprise us. They saw a light burning, and they crept on tiptoe up to the tapestried room, where Josephine and I were, and they did give us a great fright."

"What madness!" cried the baroness, angrily; "and in Josephine's weak state! Such a surprise might have driven her into a fit."

"Yes, it was foolish, but let it pass, mamma. Don't speak of it, for he is so sorry about it."

Then Rose slipped out, ordered a fire in the salon, and not in the tapestried room, and the next minute was at her sister's door. There she found Raynal knocking, and asking Josephine how she was.

"Pray leave her to me a moment," said she. "I will bring her down to you. Mamma is waiting for you in the salon."

Raynal went down. Rose unlocked the bedroom-door, went in, and, to her horror, found Josephine lying on the floor. She dashed water in her face, and applied every remedy; and at last she came back to life, and its terrors.

"Save me, Rose! save me — he is coming to kill me — I heard him at the door," and she clung trembling piteously to Rose.

Then Rose, seeing her terror, was almost glad at the suicidal falsehood she had told. She comforted and encouraged Josephine and — deceived her. (This was the climax.)

"All is well, my poor coward," she cried; "your fears are all imaginary; another has owned the child, and the story is believed."

"Another! impossible! He would not believe it."

"He does believe it — he shall believe it."

Rose then, feeling by no means sure that Josephine, terrified as she was, would consent to let her sister come to shame to screen her, told her boldly that Jacintha had owned herself the mother of the child, and that Raynal's only feeling towards *her* was pity, and regret at having so foolishly frightened her, weakened as she was by illness. "I told him you had been ill, dear. But how came you on the ground?"

"I had come to myself; I was on my knees praying. He tapped. I heard his voice. I remember no more. I must have fainted again directly."

Rose had hard work to make her believe that her guilt, as she called it, was not known; and even then she could not prevail on her to come down-stairs, until she said, "If you don't, he will come to you." On that Josephine consented eagerly, and with trembling fingers began to adjust her hair and her dress for the interview.

All this terrible night Rose fought for her sister. She took her down-stairs to the salon; she put her on the sofa; she sat by her and pressed her hand constantly to give her courage. She told the story of the surprise her own way, before the whole party, including the doctor, to prevent Raynal from being called on to tell it his way. She laughed at Josephine's absurdity, but excused it on account of her feeble health. In short, she threw more and more dust in all their eyes.

But by the time when the rising sun came faintly in and

lighted the haggard party, where the deceived were happy, the deceivers wretched, the supernatural strength this young girl had shown was almost exhausted. She felt an hysterical impulse to scream and weep: each minute it became more and more ungovernable. Then came an unexpected turn. Raynal after a long and tiring talk with his mother, as he called her, looked at his watch, and in a characteristic way coolly announced his immediate departure, this being the first hint he had given them that he was not come back for good.

The baroness was thunderstruck.

Rose and Josephine pressed one another's hands, and had much ado not to utter a loud cry of joy.

Raynal explained that he was the bearer of despatches. "I must be off: not an hour to lose. Don't fret, mother, I shall soon be back again, if I am not knocked on the head."

Raynal took leave of them all. When it came to Rose's turn, he drew her aside and whispered into her ear, "Who is the man?"

She started, and seemed dumfounded.

"Tell me, or I ask my wife."

"She has promised me not to betray me: I made her swear. Spare me now, brother; I will tell you all when you come back."

"That is a bargain: now hear *me* swear: he shall marry you, or he shall die by my hand."

He confirmed this by a tremendous oath.

Rose shuddered, but said nothing, only she thought to herself, "I am forewarned. Never shall you know who is the father of that child."

He was no sooner gone than the baroness insisted on knowing what this private communication between him and Rose was about.

"Oh," said Rose, "he was only telling me to keep up your courage and Josephine's till he comes back."

This was the last lie the poor entangled wretch had to tell that morning. The next minute the sisters, exhausted by their terrible struggle, went feebly, with downcast eyes, along the corridor and up the staircase to Josephine's room.

They went hand in hand. They sank down, dressed as they were, on Josephine's bed, and clung to one another and trembled together, till their exhausted natures sank into uneasy slumbers, from which each in turn would wake ever and anon with a convulsive start, and clasp her sister tighter to her breast.

Theirs was a marvellous love. Even a course of deceit had not yet prevailed to separate or chill their sister bosoms. But still in this deep and wonderful love there were degrees: one went a shade deeper than the other now — ay, since last night. Which? why, she who had sacrificed herself for the other, and dared not tell her, lest the sacrifice should be refused.

It was the gray of the morning, and foggy, when Raynal, after taking leave, went to the stable for his horse. At the stable-door he came upon a man sitting doubled up on the very stones of the yard, with his head on his knees. The figure lifted his head, and showed him the face of Edouard Riviere, white and ghastly: his hair lank with the mist, his teeth chattering with cold and misery. The poor wretch had walked frantically all night round and round the chateau, waiting till Raynal should come out. He told him so.

"But why didn't you? — Ah! I see. No! you could not go into the house after that. My poor fellow, there is but one thing for you to do. Turn your back on her, and forget she ever lived; she is dead to you."

"There is something to be done besides that," said Edouard, gloomily.

"What?"

"Vengeance."

"That is my affair, young man. When I come back from the Rhine, she will tell me who her seducer is. She has promised."

"And don't you see through that?" said Edouard, gnashing his teeth; "that is only to gain time: she will never tell you. She is young in years, but old in treachery."

He groaned and was silent a moment, then laying his hand on Raynal's arm said grimly, "Thank Heaven, we don't depend on her for information! I know the villain."

Raynal's eyes flashed: "Ah! then tell me this moment."

"It is that scoundrel Dujardin."

"Dujardin! What do you mean?"

"I mean that, while you were fighting for France, your house was turned into a hospital for wounded soldiers."

"And pray, sir, to what more honorable use could they put it?"

"Well, this Dujardin was housed by you, was nursed by your wife and all the family; and in return has seduced your sister, my affianced."

"I can hardly believe that. Camille Dujardin was always a man of honor, and a good soldier."

"Colonel, there has been no man near the place but this Dujardin. I tell you it is he. Don't make me tear my bleeding heart out: must I tell you how often I caught them together, how I suspected, and how she gulled me? blind fool that I was, to believe a woman's words before my own eyes. I swear to you he is the villain; the only question is, which of us two is to kill him."

"Where is the man?"

"In the army of the Rhine."

"Ah! all the better."

"Covered with glory and honor. Curse him! oh, curse him! curse him!"

"I am in luck. I am going to the Rhine."

"I know it. That is why I waited here all through this night of misery. Yes, you are in luck. But you will send me a line when you have killed him; will you not? Then I shall know joy again. Should he escape you, he shall not escape me."

"Young man," said Raynal, with dignity, "this rage is unmanly. Besides, we have not heard his side of the story. He is a good soldier; perhaps he is not all to blame: or perhaps passion has betrayed him into a sin that his conscience and honor disapprove: if so, he must not die. You think only of your wrong: it is natural: but I am the girl's brother; guardian of her honor and my own. His life is precious as gold. I shall make him marry her."

"What! reward him for his villany?" cried Edouard, frantically.

"A mighty reward," replied Raynal, with a sneer.

"You leave one thing out of the calculation, monsieur," said Edouard, trembling with anger, "that I will kill your brother-in-law at the altar, before her eyes."

"*You* leave one thing out of the calculation: that you will first have to cross swords, at the altar, with me."

"So be it. I will not draw on my old commandant. I could not; but be sure I will catch him and her alone some day, and the bride shall be a widow in her honeymoon."

"As you please," said Raynal, coolly. "That is all fair, as you have been wronged. I shall make her an honest wife, and then you may make her an honest widow. (This is what they call *love*, and sneer at me for keeping clear of it.) But neither he nor you shall keep *my sister* what she is now, a —" and he used a word out of camp.

Edouard winced and groaned. "Oh! don't call her by such a name. There is some mystery. She loved me once. There must have been some strange seduction."

"Now you deceive yourself," said Raynal. "I never saw a girl that could take her own part better than she can; she is not like her sister at all in character. Not that I excuse him; it was a dishonorable act, an ungrateful act to my wife and my mother."

"And to you."

"Now listen to me: in four days I shall stand before him. I shall not go into a pet like you; I am in earnest. I shall just say to him, 'Dujardin, I know all!' Then if he is guilty his face will show it directly. Then I shall say, 'Comrade, you must marry her whom you have dishonored.'"

"He will not. He is a libertine, a rascal."

"You are speaking of a man you don't know. He *will* marry her and repair the wrong he has done."

"Suppose he refuses?"

"Why should he refuse? The girl is not ugly nor old, and if she has done a folly, he was her partner in it."

"But *suppose* he refuses?"

Raynal ground his teeth. "Refuse? If he does, I'll run my sword through his carcass then and there, and the hussy shall go into a convent."

CHAPTER XXI.

The French army lay before a fortified place near the Rhine, which we will call Philipsburg.

This army knew Bonaparte by report only; it was commanded by generals of the old school.

Philipsburg was defended on three sides by the nature of the ground; but on the side that faced the French line of march there was only a zigzag wall, pierced, and a low tower or two at each of the salient angles.

There were evidences of a tardy attempt to improve the defences. In particular there was a large round bastion, about three times the height of the wall; but the masonry was new, and the very embrasures were not yet cut.

Young blood was for assaulting these equivocal fortifications at the end of the day's march that brought the French advanced guard in sight of the place; but the old generals would not hear of it; the soldiers' lives must not be flung away assaulting a place that could be reduced in twenty-one days with mathematical certainty. For at this epoch a siege was looked on as a process with a certain result, the only problem was in how many days would the place be taken; and even this they used to settle to a day or two on paper by arithmetic; so many feet of wall, and so many guns on the one side; so many guns, so many men, and such and such a soil to cut the trenches in on the other: result, two figures varying from fourteen to forty. These two figures represented the duration of the siege.

For all that, siege arithmetic, right in general, has often been terribly disturbed by one little incident, that occurs from time to time; viz., Genius INside. And, indeed, this is one of the sins of genius; it goes and puts out calculations that have stood the brunt of years. Archimedes and Todleben were, no doubt, clever men in their way and good citizens, yet one characteristic of delicate men's minds they lacked — veneration; they showed a sad disrespect for the wisdom of the ancients, deranged the calculations which so much learning and patient thought had hallowed, disturbed the minds of white-haired veterans, took sieges out of the grasp of science, and plunged them back into the field of wild conjecture.

Our generals then sat down at fourteen hundred yards' distance, and planned the trenches artistically, and directed them to be cut at artful angles, and so creep nearer and nearer the devoted town. Then the Prussians, whose hearts had been in their shoes at first sight of the French shakos, plucked up, and turned not the garrison only but the population of the town into engineers and masons. Their fortifications grew almost as fast as the French trenches.

The first day of the siege, a young but distinguished brigadier in the French army rode to the quarters of General Raimbaut, who commanded his division, and was his personal friend, and respectfully but firmly entreated the general to represent to the commander-in-chief the propriety of assaulting that new bastion before it should become dangerous. "My brigade shall carry it in fifteen minutes, general," said he.

"What! cross all that open under fire? One-half your brigade would never reach the bastion."

"But the other half would take it."

"That is not so certain."

General Raimbaut refused to forward the young colonel's proposal to headquarters. "I will not subject you to TWO refusals in one matter," said he, kindly.

The young colonel lingered. He said, respectfully, "One question, general, when that bastion cuts its teeth will it be any easier to take than now?"

"Certainly; it will always be easier to take it from the sap than to cross the open under fire to it, and take it. Come, colonel, to your trenches; and if your friend should cut its teeth, you shall have a battery in your attack that will set its teeth on edge. Ha! ha!"

The young colonel did not echo his chief's humor; he saluted gravely, and returned to the trenches.

The next morning three fresh tiers of embrasures grinned one above another at the besiegers. The besieged had been up all night, and not idle. In half these apertures black muzzles showed themselves.

The bastion had cut its front teeth.

Thirteenth day of the siege.

The trenches were within four hundred yards of the enemy's guns, and it was hot work in them. The enemy had three tiers of guns in the round bastion, and on the top they had got a long 48-pounder, which they worked with a swivel joint, or the like, and threw a great roaring shot into any part of the French lines.

As to the commander-in-chief and his generals, they were dotted about a long way in the rear, and no shot came as far as them; but in the trenches the men began now to fall fast, especially on the left attack, which faced the round bastion. Our young colonel had got his heavy battery, and every now and then he would divert the general efforts of the bastion, and compel it to concentrate its attention on him, by pounding away at it till it was all in sore places. But he meant it worse mischief than that. Still, as heretofore, regarding it as the key to Philipsburg, he had got a large force of engineers at work driving a mine towards it, and to this he trusted more than to breaching it; for the bigger holes he made in it by day were all stopped at night by the townspeople.

This colonel was not a favorite in the division to which his brigade belonged. He was a good soldier, but a dull companion. He was also accused of hauteur and of an unsoldierly reserve with his brother officers.

Some loose-tongued ones even called him a milk-sop, because he was constantly seen conversing with the priest — he who had nothing to say to an honest soldier.

Others said, "No, hang it, he is not a milk-sop: he is a tried soldier: he is a sulky beggar all the same." Those under his immediate command were divided in opinion about him. There was something about him they could not understand. Why was his sallow face so stern, so sad? and why with all that was his voice so gentle? somehow the few words that did fall from his mouth were prized. One old soldier used to say, "I would rather have a word from our brigadier than from the commander-in-chief." Others thought he must at some part of his career have pillaged a church, taken the altar-piece, and sold it to a picture-dealer in Paris, or whipped the earrings out of the Madonna's ears, or admitted the female enemy to quarter upon ungenerous conditions: this, or some such crime to which we poor soldiers are liable: and now was committing the mistake of remording himself about it. "Always alongside the chaplain, you see!"

This cold and silent man had won the heart of the most talkative sergeant in the French army. Sergeant La Croix protested with many oaths that all the best generals of the day had commanded him in turn, and that his present colonel was the first that had succeeded in inspiring him with unlimited confidence. "He knows every point of war — this one," said La Croix, "I heard him beg and pray for leave to storm this thundering bastion before it was armed: but no, the old muffs would be wiser than our colonel. So now here we are kept at bay by a place that Julius Caesar and Cannibal wouldn't have made two bites at apiece; no more would I if I was the old boy out there behind the hill." In such terms do sergeants denote commanders-in-chief — at a distance. A voluble sergeant has more influence with the men than the minister of war is perhaps aware: on the whole, the 24th brigade would have followed its gloomy colonel to grim death and a foot farther. One thing gave these men a touch of superstitious reverence for their commander. He seemed to them free from physical weakness. He never *sat down* to dinner, and seemed never to sleep. At no hour of the day or night were the sentries safe from his visits.

Very annoying. But, after awhile, it led to keen watchfulness: the more so that the sad and gloomy colonel showed by his manner he appreciated it. Indeed, one night he even opened his marble jaws, and told Sergeant La Croix that a watchful sentry was an important soldier, not to his brigade only, but to the whole army. Judge whether the maxim and the implied encomium did not circulate next morning, with additions.

Sixteenth day of the siege. The round bastion opened fire at eight o'clock, not on the opposing battery, but on the right of the French attack. Its advanced position enabled a portion of its guns to rake these trenches slant-wise: and depressing its guns it made the round shot strike the ground first and ricochet over.

On this our colonel opened on them with all his guns: one of these he served himself. Among his other warlike accomplishments, he was a wonderful shot with a cannon. He showed them capital practice this morning: drove two embrasures into one, and knocked about a ton of masonry off the parapet. Then taking advantage of this, he served two of his guns with grape, and swept the enemy off the top of the bastion, and kept it clear. He made it so hot they could not work the upper guns. Then they turned the other two tiers all upon him, and at it both sides went ding, dong, till the guns were too hot to be worked. So then Sergeant La Croix popped his head up from the battery, and showed the enemy a great white plate. This was meant to convey to them an invitation to dine with the French army: the other side of the table of course.

To the credit of Prussian intelligence be it recorded, that this pantomimic hint was at once taken and both sides went to dinner.

The fighting colonel, however, remained in the battery, and kept a detachment of his gunners employed cooling the guns and repairing the touch-holes. He ordered his two cutlets and his glass of water into the battery.

Meantime, the enemy fired a single gun at long intervals, as much as to say, "We had the last word."

Let trenches be cut ever so artfully, there will be a little space exposed here and there at the angles. These spaces the men are ordered to avoid, or whip quickly across them into cover.

Now the enemy had just got the range of one of these places with their solitary gun, and had already dropped a couple of shot right on to it. A camp follower with a tray, two cutlets, and a glass of water, came to this open space just as a puff of white smoke burst from the bastion. Instead of instantly seeking shelter till the shot had struck, he, in his inexperience, thought the shot must have struck, and all danger be over. He stayed there mooning instead of pelting under cover: the shot (eighteen-pound) struck him right on the breast, knocked him into spilikins, and sent the mutton cutlets flying.

The human fragments lay quiet, ten yards off. But a soldier that was eating his dinner kicked it over, and jumped up at the side of "Death's Alley" (as it was christened next minute), and danced and yelled with pain.

"Haw! haw! haw!" roared a soldier from the other side of the alley.

"What is that?" cried Sergeant La Croix. "What do you laugh at, Private Cadel?" said he sternly, for, though he was too far in the trench to see, he had heard that horrible sound a soldier knows from every other, the "thud" of a round shot striking man or horse.

"Sergeant," said Cadel, respectfully, "I laugh to see Private Dard, that got the wind of the shot, dance and sing, when the man that got the shot itself does not say a word."

"The wind of the shot, you rascal!" roared Private Dard: "look here!" and he showed the blood running down his face.

The shot had actually driven a splinter of bone out of the sutler into Dard's temple.

"I am the unluckiest fellow in the army," remonstrated Dard: and he stamped in a circle.

"Seems to me you are only the second unluckiest this time," said a young soldier with his mouth full; and, with a certain dry humor, he pointed vaguely over his shoulder with the fork towards the corpse.

The trenches laughed and assented.

This want of sympathy and justice irritated Dard. "You cursed fools!" cried he. "He is gone where we must all go — without any trouble. But look at me. I am always getting barked. Dogs of Prussians! they pick me out among a thousand. I shall have a headache all the afternoon, you see else."

Some of our heads would never have ached again: but Dard had a good thick skull.

Dard pulled out his spilikin savagely.

"I'll wrap it up in paper for Jacintha," said he. "Then that will learn her what a poor soldier has to go through."

Even this consolation was denied Private Dard.

Corporal Coriolanus Gand, a bit of an infidel from Lyons, who sometimes amused himself with the Breton's superstition, told him with a grave face, that the splinter belonged not to him, but to the sutler, and, though so small, was doubtless a necessary part of his frame.

"If you keep that, it will be a bone of contention between you two," said he; "especially at midnight. *He will be always coming back to you for it.*"

"There, take it away!" said the Breton hastily, "and bury it with the poor fellow."

Sergeant La Croix presented himself before the colonel with a rueful face and saluted him and said, "Colonel, I beg a thousand pardons; your dinner has been spilt — a shot from the bastion."

"No matter," said the colonel. "Give me a piece of bread instead."

La Croix went for it himself, and on his return found Cadel sitting on one side of Death's Alley, and Dard with his head bound up on the other. They had got a bottle which each put up in turn wherever he fancied the next round shot would strike, and they were betting their afternoon rations which would get the Prussians to hit the bottle first.

La Croix pulled both their ears playfully.

"Time is up for playing marbles," said he. "Be off, and play at duty," and he bundled them into the battery.

It was an hour past midnight: a cloudy night. The moon was up, but seen only by fitful gleams. A calm, peaceful silence reigned.

Dard was sentinel in the battery.

An officer going his rounds found the said sentinel flat instead of vertical. He stirred him with his scabbard, and up jumped Dard.

"It's all right, sergeant. O Lord! it's the colonel. I wasn't asleep, colonel."

"I have not accused you. But you will explain what you were doing."

"Colonel," said Dard, all in a flutter, "I was taking a squint at them, because I saw something. The beggars are building a wall, now."

"Where?"

"Between us and the bastion."

"Show me."

"I can't, colonel; the moon has gone in; but I did see it."

"How long was it?"

"About a hundred yards."

"How high?"

"Colonel, it was ten feet high if it was an inch."

"Have you good sight?"

"La! colonel, wasn't I a bit of a poacher before I took to the bayonet?"

"Good! Now reflect. If you persist in this statement, I turn out the brigade on your information."

"I'll stand the fire of a corporal's guard at break of day if I make a mistake now," said Dard.

The colonel glided away, called his captain and first lieutenants, and said two words in each ear, that made them spring off their backs.

Dard, marching to an fro, musket on shoulder, found himself suddenly surrounded by grim, silent, but deadly eager soldiers, that came pouring like bees into the open space behind the battery. The officers came round the colonel.

"Attend to two things," said he to the captains. "Don't fire till they are within ten yards: and don't follow them unless I lead you."

The men were then told off by companies, some to the battery, some to the trenches, some were kept on each side Death's Alley, ready for a rush.

They were not all of them in position, when those behind the parapet saw, as it were, something deepen the gloom of night, some fourscore yards to the front: it was like a line of black ink suddenly drawn upon a sheet covered with Indian ink.

It seems quite stationary. The novices wondered what it was. The veterans muttered — "Three deep."

Though it looked stationary, it got blacker and blacker. The soldiers of the 24th brigade griped their muskets hard, and set their teeth, and the sergeants had much ado to keep them quiet.

All of a sudden, a loud yell on the right of the brigade, two or three single shots from the trenches in that direction, followed by a volley, the cries of wounded men, and the fierce hurrahs of an attacking party.

Our colonel knew too well those sounds: the next parallel had been surprised, and the Prussian bayonet was now silently at work.

Disguise was now impossible. At the first shot, a guttural voice in front of Dujardin's men was heard to give a word of command. There was a sharp rattle and in a moment the thick black line was tipped with glittering steel.

A roar and a rush, and the Prussian line three deep came furiously like a huge steel-pointed wave, at the French lines. A tremendous wave of fire rushed out to meet that wave of steel: a crash of two hundred muskets, and all was still. Then you could see through the black steel-tipped line in a hundred frightful gaps, and the ground sparkled with bayonets and the air rang with the cries of the wounded.

A tremendous cheer from the brigade, and the colonel charged at the head of his column, out by Death's Alley.

The broken wall was melting away into the night. The colonel wheeled his men to the right: one company, led by the impetuous young Captain Jullien, followed the flying enemy.

The other attack had been only too successful. They shot the sentries, and bayoneted many of the soldiers in their tents: others escaped by running to the rear, and some into the next parallel.

Several, half dressed, snatched up their muskets, killed one Prussian, and fell riddled like sieves.

A gallant officer got a company together into the place of arms and formed in line.

Half the Prussian force went at them, the rest swept the trenches: the French company delivered a deadly volley, and the next moment clash the two forces crossed bayonets, and a silent deadly stabbing match was played: the final result of which was inevitable. The Prussians were five to one. The gallant officer and the poor fellows who did their duty so stoutly, had no thought left but to die hard, when suddenly a roaring cheer seemed to come from the rear rank of the enemy. "France! France!" Half the 24th brigade came leaping and swarming over the trenches in the Prussian rear. The Prussians wavered. "France!" cried the little party that were being overpowered, and charged in their turn with such fury that in two seconds the two French corps went through the enemy's centre like paper, and their very bayonets clashed together in more than one Prussian body.

Broken thus in two fragments the Prussian corps ceased to exist as a military force. The men fled each his own way back to the fort, and many flung away their muskets, for French soldiers were swarming in from all quarters. At this moment, bang! bang! bang! from the bastion.

"They are firing on my brigade," said our colonel. "Who has led his company there against my orders? Captain Neville, into the battery, and fire twenty rounds at the bastion! Aim at the flashes from their middle tier."

"Yes, colonel."

The battery opened with all its guns on the bastion. The right attack followed suit. The town answered, and a furious cannonade roared and blazed all down both lines till daybreak. Hell seemed broken loose.

Captain Jullien had followed the flying foe: but could not come up with them: and, as the enemy had prepared for every contingency, the fatal bastion, after first throwing a rocket or two to discover their position, poured showers of grape into them, killed many, and would have killed more but that Captain Neville and his gunners happened by mere accident to dismount one gun and to kill a couple of gunners at the others. This gave the remains of the company time to disperse and run back. When the men were mustered, Captain Jullien and twenty-five of his company did not answer to their names. At daybreak they were visible from the trenches lying all by themselves within eighty yards of the bastion.

A flag of truce came from the fort: the dead were removed on both sides and buried. Some Prussian officers strolled into the French lines. Civilities and cigars exchanged: "Bon jour," "Gooten daeg:" then at it again, ding dong all down the line blazing and roaring.

At twelve o'clock the besieged had got a man on horseback, on top of a hill, with colored flags in his hand, making signals.

"What are you up to now?" inquired Dard.

"You will see," said La Croix, affecting mystery; he knew no more than the other.

Presently off went Long Tom on the top of the bastion, and the shot came roaring over the heads of the speakers.

The flags were changed, and off went Long Tom again at an elevation.

Ten seconds had scarcely elapsed when a tremendous explosion took place on the French right. Long Tom was throwing red-hot shot; one had fallen on a powder wagon, and blown it to pieces, and killed two poor fellows and a horse, and turned an artillery man at some distance into a seeming nigger, but did him no great harm; only took him three days to get the powder out of his clothes with pipe clay, and off his face with raw potato-peel.

When the tumbril exploded, the Prussians could be heard to cheer, and they turned to and fired every iron spout they owned. Long Tom worked all day.

They got into a corner where the guns of the battery could not hit them or him, and there was his long muzzle looking towards the sky, and sending half a hundredweight of iron up into the clouds, and plunging down a mile off into the French lines.

And, at every shot, the man on horseback made signals to let the gunners know where the shot fell.

At last, about four in the afternoon, they threw a forty-eight-pound shot slap into the commander-in-chief's tent, a mile and a half behind trenches.

Down comes a glittering aide-de-camp as hard as he can gallop.

"Colonel Dujardin, what are you about, sir? *Your bastion* has thrown a round shot into the commander-in-chief's tent."

The colonel did not appear so staggered as the aide-de-camp expected.

"Ah, indeed!" said he quietly. "I observed they were trying distances."

"Must not happen again, colonel. You must drive them from the gun."

"How?"

"Why, where is the difficulty?"

"If you will do me the honor to step into the battery, I will show you," said the colonel.

"If you please," said the aide-de-camp stiffly.

Colonel Dujardin took him to the parapet, and began, in a calm, painstaking way, to show him how and why none of his guns could be brought to bear upon Long Tom.

In the middle of the explanation a melodious sound was heard in the air above them, like a swarm of Brobdingnag bees.

"What is that?" inquired the aide-de-camp.

"What? I see nothing."

"That humming noise."

"Oh, that? Prussian bullets. Ah, by-the-by, it is a compliment to your uniform, monsieur; they take you for some one of importance. Well, as I was observing" —

"Your explanation is sufficient, colonel; let us get out of this. Ha, ha! you are a cool hand, colonel, I must say. But your battery is a warm place enough: I shall report it so at headquarters."

The grim colonel relaxed.

"Captain," said he politely, "you shall not have ridden to my post in vain. Will you lend me your horse for ten minutes?"

"Certainly; and I will inspect your trenches meantime."

"Do so; oblige me by avoiding that angle; it is exposed, and the enemy have got the range to an inch."

Colonel Dujardin slipped into his quarters; off with his half-dress jacket and his dirty boots, and presently out he came full fig, glittering brighter than the other, with one French and two foreign orders shining on his breast, mounted the aide-de-camp's horse, and away full pelt.

Admitted, after some delay, into the generalissimo's tent, Dujardin found the old gentleman surrounded by his staff and wroth: nor was the danger to which he had been exposed his sole cause of ire.

The shot had burst through his canvas, struck a table on which was a large inkstand, and had squirted the whole contents over the despatches he was writing for Paris.

Now this old gentleman prided himself upon the neatness of his despatches: a blot on his paper darkened his soul.

Colonel Dujardin expressed his profound regret. The commander, however, continued to remonstrate. "I have a great deal of writing to do," said he, "as you must be aware; and, when I am writing, I expect to be quiet."

Colonel Dujardin assented respectfully to the justice of this. He then explained at full length why he could not bring a gun in the battery to silence "Long Tom," and quietly asked to be permitted to run a gun out of the trenches, and take a shot at the offender.

"It is a point-blank distance, and I have a new gun, with which a man ought to be able to hit his own ball at three hundred yards."

The commander hesitated.

"I cannot have the men exposed."

"I engage not to lose a man — except him who fires the gun. *He* must take his chance."

"Well, colonel, it must be done by volunteers. The men must not be *ordered* out on such a service as that."

Colonel Dujardin bowed, and retired.

"Volunteers to go out of the trenches!" cried Sergeant La Croix, in a stentorian voice, standing erect as a poker, and swelling with importance.

There were fifty offers in less than as many seconds.

"Only twelve allowed to go," said the sergeant; "and I am one," added he, adroitly inserting himself.

A gun was taken down, placed on a carriage, and posted near Death's Alley, but out of the line of fire.

The colonel himself superintended the loading of this gun; and to the surprise of the men had the shot weighed first, and then weighed out the powder himself.

He then waited quietly a long time till the bastion pitched one of its periodical shots into Death's Alley, but no sooner had the shot struck, and sent the sand flying past the two lanes of curious noses, than Colonel Dujardin jumped upon the gun and waved his cocked hat. At this preconcerted signal, his battery opened fire on the bastion, and the battery to his right opened on the wall that fronted them; and the colonel gave the word to run the gun out of the trenches. They ran it out into the cloud of smoke their own guns were belching forth, unseen by the enemy; but they had no sooner twisted it into the line of Long Tom, than the smoke was gone, and there they were, a fair mark.

"Back into the trenches, all but one!" roared Dujardin.

And in they ran like rabbits.

"Quick! the elevation."

Colonel Dujardin and La Croix raised the muzzle to the mark — hoo, hoo, hoo! ping, ping, ping! came the bullets about their ears.

"Away with you!" cried the colonel, taking the linstock from him.

Then Colonel Dujardin, fifteen yards from the trenches, in full blazing uniform, showed two armies what one intrepid soldier can do. He kneeled down and adjusted his gun, just as he would have done in a practising ground. He had a pot shot to take, and a pot shot he would take. He ignored three hundred muskets that were levelled at him. He looked along his gun, adjusted it, and re-adjusted it to a hair's breadth. The enemy's bullets pattered upon it: still he adjusted it delicately. His men were groaning and tearing their hair inside at his danger.

At last it was levelled to his mind, and then his movements were as quick as they had hitherto been slow. In a moment he stood erect in the half-fencing attitude of a gunner, and his linstock at the touch-hole: a huge tongue of flame, a volume of smoke, a roar, and the iron thunderbolt was on its way, and the colonel walked haughtily but rapidly back to the trenches; for in all this no bravado. He was there to make a shot; not to throw a chance of life away watching the effect.

Ten thousand eyes did that for him.

Both French and Prussians risked their own lives craning out to see what a colonel in full uniform was doing under fire from a whole line of forts, and what would be his fate; but when he fired the gun their curiosity left the man and followed the iron thunderbolt.

For two seconds all was uncertain; the ball was travelling.

Tom gave a rear like a wild horse, his protruding muzzle went up sky-high, then was seen no more, and a ring of old iron and a clatter of fragments was heard on the top of the bastion. Long Tom was dismounted. Oh! the roar of laughter and triumph from one end to another of the trenches; and the clapping of forty thousand hands that went on for full five minutes; then the Prussians, either through a burst of generous praise for an act so chivalrous and so brilliant, or because they would not be crowed over, clapped their tea thousand hands as loudly, and thus thundering, heart-thrilling salvo of applause answered salvo on both sides that terrible arena.

That evening came a courteous and flattering message from the commander-in-chief to Colonel Dujardin; and several officers visited his quarters to look at him; they went back disappointed. The cry was, "What a miserable, melancholy dog! I expected to see a fine, dashing fellow."

The trenches neared the town. Colonel Dujardin's mine was far advanced; the end of the chamber was within a few yards of the bastion. Of late, the colonel had often visited this mine in person. He seemed a little uneasy about something in that quarter; but no one knew what: he was a silent man. The third evening, after he dismounted Long Tom, he received private notice that an order was coming down from the commander-in-chief to assault the bastion. He shrugged his shoulders, but said nothing. That same night the colonel and one of his lieutenants stole out of the trenches, and by the help of a pitch-dark, windy night, got under the bastion unperceived, and crept round it, and made their observations, and got safe back. About noon down came General Raimbaut.

"Well, colonel, you are to have your way at last. Your bastion is to be stormed this afternoon previous to the general assault. Why, how is this? you don't seem enchanted?"

"I am not."

"Why, it was you who pressed for the assault."

"At the right time, general, not the wrong. In five days I undertake to blow that bastion into the air. To assault it now would be to waste our men."

General Raimbaut thought this excess of caution a great piece of perversity in Achilles. They were alone, and he said a little peevishly, —

"Is not this to blow hot and cold on the same thing?"

"No, general," was the calm reply. "Not on the same thing. I blew hot upon timorous counsels; I blow cold on rash ones. General, last night Lieutenant Fleming and I were under that bastion; and all round it."

"Ah! my prudent colonel, I thought we should not talk long without your coming out in your true light. If ever a man secretly enjoyed risking his life, it is you."

"No, general," said Dujardin looking gloomily down; "I enjoy neither that nor anything else. Live or die, it is all one to me; but to the lives of my soldiers I am not indifferent, and never will be while I live. My apparent rashness of last night was pure prudence."

Raimbaut's eye twinkled with suppressed irony. "No doubt!" said he; "no doubt!"

The impassive colonel would not notice the other's irony; he went calmly on: —

"I suspected something; I went to confute, or confirm that suspicion. I confirmed it."

Rat! tat! tat! tat! tat! tat! tat! was heard a drum. Relieving guard in the mine.

Colonel Dujardin interrupted himself.

"That comes apropos," said he. "I expect one proof more from that quarter. Sergeant, send me the sentinel they are relieving."

Sergeant La Croix soon came back, as pompous as a hen with one chick, predominating with a grand military air over a droll figure that chattered with cold, and held its musket in hands clothed in great mittens. Dard.

La Croix marched him up as if he had been a file; halted him like a file, sang out to him as to a file, stentorian and unintelligible, after the manner of sergeants.

"Private No. 4."

DARD. P-p-p-present!

LA CROIX. Advance to the word of command, and speak to the colonel.

The shivering figure became an upright statue directly, and carried one of his mittens to his forehead. Then, suddenly recognizing the rank of the gray-haired officer, he was morally shaken, but remained physically erect, and stammered, —

"Colonel! — general! — colonel!"

"Don't be frightened, my lad. But look at the general and answer me."

"Yes! general! colonel!" and he levelled his eye dead at the general, as he would a bayonet at a foe, being so commanded.

"Now answer in as few syllables as you can."

"Yes! general — colonel."

"You have been on guard in the mine."

"Yes, general."

"What did you see there?"

"Nothing; it was night down there."

"What did you feel?"

"Cold! I — was — in — water — hugh!"

"Did you hear nothing, then?"

"Yes."

"What?"

"Bum! bum! bum!"

"Are you sure you did not hear particles of earth fall at the end of the trench?"

"I think it did, and this (touching his musket) sounded of its own accord."

"Good! you have answered well; go."

"Sergeant, I did not miss a word," cried Dard, exulting. He thought he had passed a sort of military college examination. The sergeant was awe-struck and disgusted at his familiarity, speaking to him before the great: he pushed Private Dard hastily out of the presence, and bundled him into the trenches.

"Are you countermined, then?" asked General Raimbaut.

"I think not, general; but the whole bastion is. And we found it had been opened in the rear, and lately half a dozen broad roads cut through the masonry."

"To let in re-enforcements?"

"Or to let the men run out in ease of an assault. I have seen from the first an able hand behind that part of the defences. If we assault the bastion, they will pick off as many of us as they can with their muskets then they will run for it, and fire a train, and blow it and us into the air."

"Colonel, this is serious. Are you prepared to lay this statement before the commander-in-chief?"

"I am, and I do so through you, the general of my division. I even beg you to say, as from me, that the assault will be mere suicide — bloody and useless."

General Raimbaut went off to headquarters in some haste, a thorough convert to Colonel Dujardin's opinion. Meantime the colonel went slowly to his tent. At the mouth of it a corporal, who was also his body-servant, met him, saluted, and asked respectfully if there were any orders.

"A few minutes' repose, Francois, that is all. Do not let me be disturbed for an hour."

"Attention!" cried Francois. "Colonel wants to sleep."

The tent was sentinelled, and Dujardin was alone with the past.

Then had the fools, that took (as fools will do) deep sorrow for sullenness, seen the fiery soldier droop, and his wan face fall into haggard lines, and his martial figure shrink, and heard his stout heart sigh! He took a letter from his bosom: it was almost worn to pieces. He had read it a thousand times, yet he read it again. A part of the sweet sad words ran thus: —

"We must bow. We can never be happy together on earth; let us make Heaven our friend. This is still left us, — not to blush for our love; to do our duty, and to die."

"How tender, but how firm," thought Camille. "I might agitate, taunt, grieve her I love, but I could not shake her. No! God and the saints to my aid! they saved me from a crime I now shudder at. And they have given me the good chaplain: he prays with me, he weeps for me. His prayers still my beating heart. Yes, poor suffering angel! I read your will in these tender, but bitter, words: you prefer duty to love. And one day you will forget me; not yet awhile, but it will be so. It wounds me when I think of it, but I must bow. Your will is sacred. I must rise to your level, not drag you to mine."

Then the soldier that had stood between two armies in a hail of bullets, and fired a master-shot, took a little book of offices in one hand, — the chaplain had given it him, — and fixed his eyes upon the pious words, and clung like a child to the pious words, and kissed his lost wife's letter, and tried hard to be like her he loved: patient, very patient, till the end should come.

"Qui vive?" cried the sentinel outside to a strange officer.

"France," was his reply. He then asked the sentinel, "Where is the colonel commanding the brigade?"

The sentinel lowered his voice, "Asleep, my officer," said he; for the new-comer carried two epaulets.

"Wake him," said the officer in a tone of a man used to command on a large scale.

Dujardin heard, and did not choose a stranger should think he was asleep in broad day. He came hastily out of the tent, therefore, with Josephine's letter in his hand, and, in the very act of conveying it to his bosom, found himself face to face with — her husband.

Did you ever see two duellists cross rapiers?

How unlike a theatrical duel! How smooth and quiet the bright blades are! they glide into contact. They are polished and slippery, yet they hold each other. So these two men's eyes met, and fastened: neither spoke: each searched the other's face keenly. Raynal's countenance, prepared as he was for this meeting, was like a stern statue's. The other's face flushed, and his heart raged and sickened at sight of the man, that, once his comrade and benefactor, was now possessor of the woman he loved. But the figures of both stood alike haughty, erect, and immovable, face to face.

Colonel Raynal saluted Colonel Dujardin ceremoniously. Colonel Dujardin returned the salute in the same style.

"You thought I was in Egypt," said Raynal with grim significance that caught Dujardin's attention, though he did not know quite how to interpret it.

He answered mechanically, "Yes, I did."

"I am sent here by General Bonaparte to take a command," explained Raynal.

"You are welcome. What command?"

"Yours."

"Mine?" cried Dujardin, his forehead flushing with mortification and anger. "What, is it not enough that you take my" — He stopped then.

"Come, colonel," said the other calmly, "do not be unjust to an old comrade. I take your demi-brigade; but you are promoted to Raimbaut's brigade. The exchange is to be made tomorrow."

"Was it then to announce to me my promotion you came to my quarters?" and Camille looked with a strange mixture of feelings at his old comrade.

"That was the first thing, being duty, you know."

"What? have you anything else to say to me, then?"

"I have."

"Is it important? for my own duties will soon demand me."

"It is so important that, command or no command, I should have come further than the Rhine to say it to you."

Let a man be as bold as a lion, a certain awe still waits upon doubt and mystery; and some of this vague awe crept over Camille Dujardin at Raynal's mysterious speech, and his grave, quiet, significant manner.

Had he discovered something, and what? For Josephine's sake, more than his own, Camille was on his guard directly.

Raynal looked at him in silence a moment.

"What?" said he with a slight sneer, "has it never occurred to you that I *must* have a serious word to say to you? First, let me put you a question: did they treat you well at my house? at the chateau de Beaurepaire?"

"Yes," faltered Camille.

"You met, I trust, all the kindness and care due to a wounded soldier and an officer of merit. It would annoy me greatly if I thought you were not treated like a brother in my house."

Colonel Dujardin writhed inwardly at this view of matters. He could not reply in few words. This made him hesitate.

His inquisitor waited, but, receiving no reply, went on, "Well, colonel, have you shown the sense of gratitude we had a right to look for in return? In a word, when you left Beaurepaire, had your conscience nothing to reproach you with?"

Dujardin still hesitated. He scarcely knew what to think or what to say. But he thought to himself, "Who has told him? does he know all?"

"Colonel Dujardin, I am the husband of Josephine, the son of Madame de Beaurepaire, and the brother of Rose. You know very well what brings me here. Your answer?"

"Colonel Raynal, between men of honor, placed as you and I are, few words should pass, for words are idle. You will never prove to me that I have wronged you: I shall never convince you that I have not. Let us therefore close this painful interview in the way it is sure to close. I am at your service, at any hour and place you please."

"And pray is that all the answer you can think of?" asked Raynal somewhat scornfully.

"Why, what other answer can I give you?"

"A more sensible, a more honest, and a less boyish one. Who doubts that you can fight, you silly fellow? haven't I seen you? I want you to show me a much higher sort of courage: the courage to repair a wrong, not the paltry valor to defend one."

"I really do not understand you, sir. How can I undo what is done?"

"Why, of course you cannot. And therefore I stand here ready to forgive all that is past; not without a struggle, which you don't seem to appreciate."

Camille was now utterly mystified. Raynal continued, "But of course it is upon condition that you consent to heal the wound you have made. If you refuse — hum! but you will not refuse."

"But what is it you require of me?" inquired Camille impatiently.

"Only a little common honesty. This is the case: you have seduced a young lady."

"Sir!" cried Camille angrily.

"What is the matter? The word is not so bad as the crime, I take it. You have seduced her, and under circumstances — But we won't speak of them, because I am resolved to keep cool. Well, sir, as you said just now, it's no use crying over spilled milk; you can't unseduce the little fool; so you must marry her."

"M — m — marry her?" and Dujardin flushed all over, and his heart beat, and he stared in Raynal's face.

"Why, what is the matter again? If she has played the fool, it was with you, and no other man: it is not as if she was depraved. Come, my lad, show a little generosity! Take the consequences of your own act — or your share of it — don't throw it all on the poor feeble woman. If she has loved you too much, you are the man of all others that should forgive her. Come, what do you say?"

This was too much for Camille; that Raynal should come and demand of him to marry his own wife, for so he understood the proposal. He stared at Raynal in silence ever so long, and even when he spoke it was only to mutter, "Are you out of your senses, or am I?"

At this it cost Raynal a considerable effort to restrain his wrath. However, he showed himself worthy of the office he had undertaken. He contained himself, and submitted to argue the matter. "Why, colonel," said he, "is it such a misfortune to marry poor Rose? She is young, she is lovely, she has many good qualities, and she would have walked straight to the end of her days but for you."

Now here was another surprise for Dujardin, another mystification.

"Rose de Beaurepaire?" said he, putting his hand to his head, as if to see whether his reason was still there.

"Yes, Rose de Beaurepaire — Rose Dujardin that ought to be, and that is to be, if you please."

"One word, monsieur: is it of Rose we have been talking all this time?"

Raynal nearly lost his temper at this question, and the cold, contemptuous tone with which it was put; but he gulped down his ire.

"It is," said he.

"One question more. Did she tell you I had — I had" —

"Why, as to that, she was in no condition to deny she had fallen, poor girl; the evidence was too strong. She did not reveal her seducer's name; but I had not far to go for that."

"One question more," said Dujardin, with a face of anguish. "Is it Jos — is it Madame Raynal's wish I should marry her sister?"

"Why, of course," said Raynal, in all sincerity, assuming that naturally enough as a matter of course; "if you have any respect for *her* feelings, look on me as her envoy in this matter."

At this Camille turned sick with disgust; then rage and bitterness swelled his heart. A furious impulse seized him to expose Josephine on the spot. He overcame that, however, and merely said, "She wishes me to marry her sister, does she? very well then, I decline."

Raynal was shocked. "Oh," said he, sorrowfully, "I cannot believe this of you; such heartlessness as this is not written in your face; it is contradicted by your past actions."

"I refuse," said Dujardin, hastily; and to tell the truth, not sorry to inflict some pain on the honest soldier who had unintentionally driven the iron so deep into his own soul.

"And I," said Raynal, losing his temper, "insist, in the name of my dear Josephine" —

"Perdition!" snarled Dujardin, losing his self-command in turn.

"And of the whole family."

"And I tell you I will never marry her. Upon my honor, never."

"Your honor! you have none. The only question is would you rather marry her — or die."

"Die, to be sure."

"Then die you shall."

"Ah!" said Dujardin; "did I not tell you we were wasting time?

"Let us waste no more then. *when* and *where*?"

"At the rear of the commander-in-chief's tent; when you like."

"This afternoon, then — at five."

"At five."

"Seconds?"

"What for?"

"You are right. They are only in the way of men who carry sabres; and besides the less gossip the better. Good-by, till five," and the two saluted one another with grim ceremony; and Raynal turned on his heel.

Camille stood transfixed; a fierce, guilty joy throbbed in his heart. His rival had quarrelled with him, had insulted him, had challenged him. It was not his fault. The sun shone bright now upon his cold despair. An hour ago life offered nothing. A few hours more, and then joy beyond expression, or an end of all. Death or Josephine! Then he remembered that this very Josephine wished to marry him to Rose. Then he remembered Raynal had saved his life. Cold chills crossed his breaking heart. Of all that could happen to him death alone seemed a blessing without alloy.

He stood there so torn with conflicting passions, that he noted neither the passing hours nor the flying bullets.

He was only awakened from his miserable trance by the even tread of soldiers marching towards him; he looked up and there were several officers coming along the edge of the trench, escorted by a corporal's guard.

He took a step or two to meet them. After the usual salutes, one of the three colonels delivered a large paper, with a large seal, to Dujardin. He read it out to his captains and lieutenants, who had assembled at sight of the cocked hats and full uniforms.

"Attack by the army tomorrow upon all the lines. Attack of the bastion St. Andre this evening. The 22d, the 24th, and 12th brigades will furnish the contingents; the operation will be conducted by one of the colonels of the second division, to be appointed by General Raimbaut."

"Aha!" sounded a voice like a trombone at the reader's elbow. "I am just in the nick of time. When, colonel, when?"

"At five this evening, Colonel Raynal."

"There," said Raynal, in a half-whisper, to Dujardin; "could they choose no hour but that?"

"Do not be uneasy," replied Dujardin, under his breath. He explained aloud — "the assault will not take place, gentlemen; the bastion is mined."

"What of that? half of them are mined. We will take our engineers in with us," said Raynal.

"Such an assault will be a useless massacre," resumed Dujardin. "I reconnoitred the bastion last night, and saw their preparations for blowing us to the devil; and General Raimbaut, at my request, is even now presenting my remarks to the commander-in-chief, and enforcing them. There will be no assault. In a day or two we shall blow the bastion, mines, and all into the air."

At this moment Raynal caught sight of a gray-haired officer coming at some distance. "There *is* General Raimbaut," said he. "I will go and pay my respects to him." General Raimbaut shook his hand warmly, and welcomed him to the army. They were old and warm friends. "And you are come at the right time," said he. "It will soon be as hot here as in Egypt."

Raynal laughed and said all the better.

General Raimbaut now joined the group of officers, and entered at once in the business which had brought him. Addressing himself to Colonel Dujardin, first he informs that officer he had presented his observations to the commander-in-chief, who had given them the attention they merited.

Colonel Dujardin bowed.

"But," continued General Raimbaut, "they are overruled by imperious circumstances, some of which he did not reveal; they remain in his own breast. However, on the eve of a general attack, which he cannot postpone, that bastion must be disarmed, otherwise it would be too fatal to all the storming parties. It is a painful necessity." He added, "Tell Colonel Dujardin I count greatly on the courage and discipline of his brigade, and on his own wise measures."

Colonel Dujardin bowed. Then he whispered in the other's ear, "Both will alike be wasted."

The other colonels waved their hats in triumph at the commander-in-chief's decision, and Raynal's face showed he looked on Dujardin as a sort of spoil-sport happily defeated.

"Well, then, gentlemen," said General Raimbaut, "we begin by settling the contingents to be furnished by your several brigades. Say, an equal number from each. The sum total shall be settled by Colonel Dujardin, who has so long and ably baffled the bastion at this post."

Colonel Dujardin bowed stiffly and not very graciously. In his heart he despised these old fogies, compounds of timidity and rashness.

"So, how many men in all, colonel?" asked General Raimbaut.

"The fewer the better," replied the other solemnly, "since" — and then discipline tied his tongue.

"I understand you," said the old man. "Shall we say eight hundred men?"

"I should prefer three hundred. They have made a back door to the bastion, and the means of flight at hand will put flight into their heads. They will pick off some of our men as we go at them. When the rest jump in they will jump out, and" — He paused.

"Why, he knows all about it before it comes," said one of the colonels naively.

"I do. I see the whole operation and its result before me, as I see this hand. Three hundred men will do."

"But, general," objected Raynal, "you are not beginning at the beginning. The first thing in these cases is to choose the officer to command the storming party."

"Yes, Raynal, unquestionably; but you must be aware that is a painful and embarrassing part of my duty, especially after Colonel Dujardin's remarks."

"Ah, bah!" cried Raynal. "He is prejudiced. He has been digging a thundering long mine here, and now you are going to make his child useless. We none of us like that. But when he gets the colors in his hand, and the storming column at his back, his misgivings will all go to the wind, and the enemy after them, unless he has been committing some crime, and is very much changed from what I knew him four years ago."

"Colonel Raynal," said one of the other colonels, politely but firmly, "pray do not assume that Colonel Dujardin is to lead the column; there are three other claimants. General Raimbaut is to select from us four."

"Yes, gentlemen, and in a service of this kind I would feel grateful to you all if you would relieve me of that painful duty."

"Gentlemen," said Dujardin, with an imperceptible sneer, "the general means to say this: the operation is so glorious that he could hardly without partiality assign the command to either of us four claimants. Well, then, let us cast lots."

The proposal was received by acclamation.

"The general will mark a black cross on one lot, and he who draws it wins the command."

The young colonels prepared their lots with almost boyish eagerness. These fiery spirits were sick to death of lying and skulking in the trenches. They flung their lots into the hat. After them, who should approach the hat, lot in hand, but Raynal. Dujardin instantly interfered, and held his arm as he was in the act of dropping in his lot.

"What is the matter?" said Raynal, sharply.

"This is our affair, Colonel Raynal. You have no command in this army."

"I beg your pardon, sir, I have yours."

"Not till tomorrow."

"Why, you would not take such a pettifogging advantage of an old comrade as that."

"Tell him the day ends at twelve o'clock," said one of the colonels interested by this strange strife.

"Ah!" cried Raynal, triumphantly; "but no," said he, altering his tone, "let us leave that sort of argument to lawyers. I have come a good many miles to fight with you, general; and now you must decide to pay me this little compliment on my arrival, or put a bitter affront on me — choose!"

While the old general hesitated, Camille replied, "Since you take that tone there can be but one answer. You are too great a credit to the French army for even an apparent slight to be put on you here. The rule, I think, is, that one of the privates shall hold the hat. — Hallo! Private Dard, come here — there — hold this hat."

"Yes, colonel. — Lord, here is my young mistress's husband!"

"Silence!"

And they began to draw, and, in the act of drawing, a change of manner was first visible in these gay and ardent spirits.

"It is not I," said one, throwing away his lot.

"Nor I."

"It is I," said Raynal; then with sudden gravity, "I am the lucky one."

And now that the honor and the danger no longer floated vaguely over four heads, but had fixed on one, a sudden silence and solemnity took the place of eager voices.

It was first broken by Private Dard saying, with foolish triumph, "And I held the hat for you, colonel."

"Ah, Raynal!" said General Raimbaut, sorrowfully, "it was not worth while to come from Egypt for this."

Raynal made no reply to this. He drew out his watch, and said calmly, he had no time to lose; he must inspect the detachments he was to command. "Besides," said he, "I have some domestic arrangements to make. Hitherto on these occasions I was a bachelor, now I am married." General Raimbaut could not help sighing. Raynal read this aright, and turned to him, "A droll marriage, my old friend; I'll tell you all about it if ever I have the time. It began with a purchase, general, and ends with — with a bequest, which I might as well write now, and so have nothing to think of but duty afterwards. Where can I write?"

"Colonel Dujardin will lend you his tent, I am sure."

"Certainly."

"And, messieurs," said Raynal, "if I waste time you need not. You can pick me my men from your brigades. Give me a strong spice of old hands."

The colonels withdrew on this, and General Raimbaut walked sadly and thoughtfully towards the battery. Dujardin and Raynal were left alone.

"This postpones our affair, sir."

"Yes, Raynal."

"Have you writing materials in your tent?"

"Yes; on the table."

"You are quite sure the bastion is mined, comrade?"

This unexpected word and Raynal's gentle appeal touched Dujardin deeply. It was in a broken voice he replied that he was unfortunately too sure of it.

Raynal received this reply as a sentence of death, and without another word walked slowly into Dujardin's tent.

Dujardin's generosity was up in arms; he followed Raynal, and said eagerly, "Raynal, for Heaven's sake resign this command!"

"Allow me to write to my wife, colonel," was the cold reply.

Camille winced at this affront, and drew back a moment; but his nobler part prevailed. He seized Raynal by the wrist. "You shall not affront me, you cannot affront me. You go to certain death I tell you, if you attack that bastion."

"Don't be a fool, colonel," said Raynal: "somebody must lead the men."

"Yes; but not you. Who has so good a right to lead them as I, their colonel?"

"And be killed in my place, eh?"

"I know the ground better than you," said Camille. "Besides, who cares for me? I have no friends, no family. But you are married — and so many will mourn if you" —

Raynal interrupted him sternly. "You forget, sir, that Rose de Beaurepaire is my sister, when you tell me you have no tie to life." He added, with wonderful dignity and sobriety, "Allow me to write to my wife, sir; and, while I write, reflect that you can embitter an old comrade's last moments by persisting in your refusal to restore his sister the honor you have robbed her of."

And leaving the other staggered and confused by this sudden blow, he retired into Dujardin's tent, and finding writing materials on a little table that was there, sat down to pen a line to Josephine.

Camille knew to whom he was writing, and a jealous pang passed through him.

What he wrote ran thus, —

"A bastion is to be attacked at five. I command. Colonel Dujardin proposed we should draw lots, and I lost. The service is honorable, but the result may, I fear, give you some pain. My dear wife, it is our fate. I was not to have time to make you know, and perhaps love me. God bless you."

In writing these simple words, Raynal's hard face worked, and his mustache quivered, and once he had to clear his eye with his hand to form the letters. He, the man of iron.

He who stood there, leaning on his scabbard and watching the writer, saw this, and it stirred all that was great and good in that grand though passionate heart of his.

"Poor Raynal!" thought he, "you were never like that before on going into action. He is loath to die. Ay, and it is a coward's trick to let him die. I shall have her, but shall I have her esteem? What will the army say? What will my conscience say? Oh! I feel already it will gnaw my heart to death; the ghost of that brave fellow — once my dear friend, my rival now, by no fault of his — will rise between her and me, and reproach me with my bloody inheritance. The heart never deceives; I feel it now whispering in my ear: 'Skulking captain, white-livered soldier, that stand behind a parapet while a better man does your work! you assassinate the husband, but the rival conquers you.' There, he puts his hand to his eyes. What shall I do?"

"Colonel," said a low voice, and at the same time a hand was laid on his shoulder.

It was General Raimbaut. The general looked pale and distressed.

"Come apart, colonel, for Heaven's sake! One word, while he is writing. Ah! that was an unlucky idea of yours."

"Of mine, general?"

"'Twas you proposed to cast lots."

"Good God! so it was."

"I thought of course it was to be managed so that Raynal should not be the one. Between ourselves, what honorable excuse can we make?"

"None, general."

"The whole division will be disgraced, and forgive me if I say a portion of the discredit will fall on you."

"Help me to avert that shame then," cried Camille, eagerly.

"Ah! that I will: but how?"

"Take your pencil and write — 'I authorize Colonel Dujardin to save the honor of the colonels of the second division.'"

The general hesitated. He had never seen an order so worded. But at last he took out his pencil and wrote the required order, after his own fashion; i.e., in milk and water: —

On account of the singular ability and courage with which Colonel Dujardin has conducted the operations against the Bastion St. Andre, a discretionary power is given him at the moment of assault to carry into effect such measures, as, without interfering with the commander-in-chief's order, may sustain his own credit, and that of the other colonels of the second division.

RAIMBAUT, General of Division.

Camille put the paper into his bosom.

"Now, general, you may leave all to me. I swear to you, Raynal shall not die — shall not lead this assault."

"Your hand, colonel. You are an honor to the French armies. How will you do it?"

"Leave it to me, general, it shall be done."

"I feel it will, my noble fellow: but, alas! I fear not without risking some valuable life or other, most likely your own. Tell me!"

"General, I decline."

"You refuse me, sir?"

"Yes; this order gives me a discretionary power. I will hand back the order at your command; but modify it I will not. Come, sir, you veteran generals have been unjust to me, and listened to me too little all through this siege, but at last you have honored me. This order is the greatest honor that was ever done me since I wore a sword.".

"My poor colonel!"

"Let me wear it intact, and carry it to my grave."

"Say no more! One word — Is there anything on earth I can do for you, my brave soldier?"

"Yes, general. Be so kind as to retire to your quarters; there are reasons why you ought not to be near this post in half an hour."

"I go. Is there *nothing* else?"

"Well, general, ask the good priest Ambrose, to pray for all those who shall die doing their duty to their country this afternoon."

They parted. General Raimbaut looked back more than once at the firm, intrepid figure that stood there unflinching, on the edge of the grave. But *he* never took his eye off Raynal. The next minute the sad letter was finished, and Raynal walked out of the tent, and confronted the man he had challenged to single combat.

I have mentioned elsewhere that Colonel Dujardin had eyes strangely compounded of battle and love, of the dove and the hawk. And these, softened by a noble act he meditated, now rested on Raynal with a strange expression of warmth and goodness. This strange gaze struck Raynal, so far at least as this; he saw it was no hostile eye. He was glad of that, for his own heart was calmed and softened by the solemn prospect before him.

"We, too, have a little account to settle before I order out the men," said he, calmly, "and I can't give you a long credit. I am pressed for time."

"Our quarrel is at an end. When duty sounds the recall, a soldier's heart leaves private feuds. See! I come to you without anger and ill-will. Just now my voice was loud, my manner, I dare say, offensive, and menacing even, and that always tempts a brave fellow like you to resist. But now, you see, I am harmless as a woman. We are alone. Humbug to the winds! I know that you are the only man in this army fit to command a division. I know that when you say the assault of that bastion is death, death it is. To the point then; now that my manner is no longer irritating, now that I am going to die, Camille Dujardin, my old comrade, have you the heart to refuse me? am I to die unhappy?"

"No; no: I will do whatever you like."

"You will marry that poor girl, then?"

"Yes."

"Aha! did not I always say he was a good fellow? Clench the nail; give me your honor."

"I give you my honor to marry her, if I live."

"You take a load off me; may Heaven reward you. In one hour those poor women, whose support I had promised to be, will lose their protector; but I give them another in you. We shall not leave that family in tears, Rose in shame, and your child without a name."

Dujardin stared at the speaker. What new and devilish deception was this?

"My child!" he faltered. "What child?"

"Ah," said Raynal, "what a fool I was! That is the first thing I ought to have told you. Poor little fellow! I surprised him in his cradle; his mother and Josephine were rocking him, and singing over him. Oh! it was a scene, I can tell you. My poor wife had been ill for some time, and was so weakened by it, that I frightened her into a fit, stealing a march on her that way. She fainted away. Perhaps it is as well she did; for I — I did not know what to think; it looked ugly; but while she lay at our feet insensible, I forced the truth from Rose; she owned the boy was hers."

While Raynal told him this strange story, Camille turned hot and cold. First came a thrill of glowing joy; he had some clew to all this: he was a father; that child was Josephine's and his; the next moment he froze within. So Josephine had not only gulled her husband, but him, too; she had refused him the sad consolation of knowing he had a child. Cruelty, calculation, and baseness unexampled! Here was a creature who could sacrifice anything and anybody to her comfort, to the peace and sordid smoothness of her domestic life. She stood between two men — a thing. Between two truths — a double lie.

His heart, in one moment, turned against her like a stone. A musket-bullet through the body does not turn life to death quicker than Raynal turned his rival's love to despair and scorn:

that love which neither wounds, absence, prison, nor even her want of constancy had prevailed to shake.

"Out of my bosom!" he cried — "out of it, in this world and the next!"

He forgot, in his lofty rage, who stood beside him.

"What? — what?" cried Raynal.

"No matter," said Camille; "only I esteem *you*, Raynal. You are truth; you are a man, and deserve a better lot."

"Don't say that," replied Raynal, quite misunderstanding him. "It is a soldier's end: I never desired nor hoped a better: only, of course, I feel sad. You are a happy fellow, to have a child and to live to see it, and her you love."

"Oh, yes, I am very happy," replied the poor fellow, his lip quivering.

"Watch over all those poor women, comrade, and sometimes speak to them of me. It is foolish, but we like to be remembered."

"Yes! but do not let us speak of that. Raynal, you and I were lieutenants together; do you remember saving my life in the Arno?"

"Yes."

"Then promise me, if you should live, to remember not our quarrel of *today*, nor anything; but only those early days, *and this afternoon.*"

"I do."

"Your hand, comrade."

"There, comrade, there."

They wrung one another's hands, and turned away and hid their faces from each other, for their eyes were moist.

"This won't do, comrade, I must go. I shall attack from your position. So I shall go down the line, and bring the men up. Meantime, pick me your detachment. Give me a good spice of veterans. I shall get one word with you before we go out. God bless you!"

"God bless you, Raynal!"

The moment Raynal was gone, Camille beckoned a lieutenant to him, and ordered half the brigade to form in a strong column on both sides Death's Alley.

His eye fell upon private Dard, as luck would have it. "Come here," said he. Dard came and saluted.

"Have you anybody at Beaurepaire that would be sorry if you were killed?"

"Yes, colonel! Jacintha, that used to make your broth, colonel."

"Take this line to Colonel Raynal. You will find him with the

12th brigade."

He wrote a few lines in pencil, folded them, and Dard went off with them, little dreaming that the colonel of his brigade was taking the trouble to save his life, because he came from Beaurepaire. Colonel Dujardin then went into his tent, and closed the aperture, and took the good book the priest had given him, and prayed humbly, and forgave all the world.

Then he sat down, his head in his hands, and thought of his child, and how hard it was he must die and never see him. Then he lighted a candle, and sealed up his orders of valor, and wrote a line, begging that they might be sent to his sister. He also sealed up his purse, and left a memorandum that the contents should be given to disabled soldiers of his brigade upon their being invalided.

Then he took out Josephine's letter. "Poor coward," he said, "let me not be unkind. See, I burn your letter, lest it should be found, and disturb the peace you prize so highly. I, too, shall soon be at peace." He lighted the letter, and dropped it on the ground: it burned slowly away. He eyed it, despairingly. "Ay," said he, "you perish, last record of an unhappy love: and even so pass away my life; my hopes of glory, and my dreams of love; it all ends *today*: at nine and twenty."

He put his white handkerchief to his eyes. Josephine had given it him. He cried a little.

When he had done crying, he put his white handkerchief in his bosom, and the whole man was transformed beyond language to express. Powder does not change more when it catches fire. He rose that moment and went like a flash of lightning out of the tent. The next, he came down between the lines of the strong column that stood awaiting orders in Death's Alley.

"Attention!" cried the sergeants; "the colonel!"

There was a dead silence, for the bare sight of that erect and inspired figure made the men's bosoms thrill with the certainty of great deeds to come: the light of battle was in his eye. No longer the moody colonel, but a thunderbolt of war, red-hot, and waiting to be launched.

"Officers, sergeants, soldiers, a word with you!"

La Croix. Attention!

"Do you know what passed here five minutes ago?"

"The attack of the bastion was settled!" cried a captain.

"It was; and who was to lead the assault? do you know that?"

"No."

"A colonel *from Egypt*."

At that there was a groan from the men.

"With detachments from the other brigades."

"AH!" an angry roar.

Colonel Dujardin walked quickly down between the two lines, looking with his fiery eye into the men's eyes on his right. Then he came back on the other side, and, as he went, he lighted those men's eyes with his own. It was a torch passing along a line of ready gas-lights.

"The work to us!" he cried in a voice like a clarion (it fired the hearts as his eye had fired the eyes) — "The triumph to strangers! Our fatigues and our losses have not gained the brigade the honor of going out at those fellows that have killed so many of our comrades."

A fierce groan broke from the men.

"What! shall the colors of another brigade and not ours fly from that bastion this afternoon?"

"No! no!" in a roar like thunder.

"Ah! you are of my mind. Attention! the attack is fixed for five o'clock. Suppose you and I were to carry the bastion ten minutes before the colonel from Egypt can bring his men upon the ground."

At this there was a fierce burst of joy and laughter; the strange laughter of veterans and born invincibles. Then a yell of exulting assent, accompanied by the thunder of impatient drums, and the rattle of fixing bayonets.

The colonel told off a party to the battery.

"Level the guns at the top tier. Fire at my signal, and keep firing over our heads, till you see our colors on the place."

He then darted to the head of the column, which instantly formed behind him in the centre of Death's Alley.

"The colors! No hand but mine shall hold them *today*."

They were instantly brought him: his left hand shook them free in the afternoon sun.

A deep murmur of joy rolled out from the old hands at the now unwonted sight. Out flashed the colonel's sword like steel lightning. He pointed to the battery.

Bang! bang! bang! bang! went his cannon, and the smoke rolled over the trenches. At the same moment up went the colors waving, and the colonel's clarion voice pealed high above all: —

"Twenty-fourth brigade — FORWARD!"

They went so swiftly out of the trenches that they were not seen through their own smoke until they had run some sixty yards. As soon as they were seen, coming on like devils through their own smoke, two thousand muskets were levelled at them from the Prussian line. It was not a rattle of small arms — it was a crash, and the men fell fast: but in a moment they were seen to spread out like a fan, and to offer less mark, and when the fan closed again, it half encircled the bastion. It was a French attack: part swarmed at it in front like bees, part swept round the glacis and flanked it. They were seen to fall in numbers, shot down from the embrasures. But the living took the place of the dead: and the fight ranged evenly there. Where are the colors? Towards the rear there. The colonel and a hundred men are fighting hand to hand with the Prussians, who have charged out at the back doors of the bastion. Success there, and the bastion must fall — both sides know this.

The colors disappeared. There was a groan from the French lines. The colors reappeared, and close under the bastion.

And now in front the attack was so hot, that often the Prussian gunners were seen to jump down, driven from their posts; and the next moment a fierce hurrah from the rear told that the French had won some great advantage there. The fire slackening told a similar tale and presently down came the Prussian flag-staff. That might be an accident. A few moments of thirsting expectation, and up went the colors of the 24th brigade upon the Bastion St. Andre.

The French army raised a shout that rent the sky, and their cannon began to play on the Prussian lines and between the bastion and the nearest fort, to prevent a recapture.

Sudden there shot from the bastion a cubic acre of fire: it carried up a heavy mountain of red and black smoke that looked solid as marble. There was a heavy, sullen, tremendous explosion that snuffed out the sound of the cannon, and paralyzed the French and Prussian gunners' hands, and checked the very beating of their hearts. Thirty thousand pounds of gunpowder were in that awful explosion. War itself held its breath, and both armies, like peaceable spectators, gazed wonder-struck, terror-struck. Great hell seemed to burst through the earth's crust, and to be rushing at heaven. Huge stones, cannons, corpses, and limbs of soldiers, were seen driven or falling through the smoke. Some of these last came quite clear of the ruins, ay, into the French and Prussian lines, that even the veterans put their hands to their eyes. Raynal felt something patter on him from the sky — it was blood — a comrade's perhaps.

The smoke cleared. Where, a moment before, the great bastion stood and fought, was a monstrous pile of blackened, bloody stones and timbers, with dismounted cannon sticking up here and there.

And, rent and crushed to atoms beneath the smoking mass, lay the relics of the gallant brigade, and their victorious colors.

CHAPTER XXII.

A few wounded soldiers of the brigade lay still till dusk. Then they crept back to the trenches. These had all been struck down or disabled short of the bastion. Of those that had taken the place no one came home.

Raynal, after the first stupefaction, pressed hard and even angrily for an immediate assault on the whole Prussian line. Not they. It was on paper that the assault should be at daybreak tomorrow. Such leaders as they were cannot *improvise*.

Rage and grief in his heart, Raynal waited chafing in the trenches till five minutes past midnight. He then became commander of the brigade, gave his orders, and took thirty men out to creep up to the wreck of the bastion, and find the late colonel's body.

Going for so pious a purpose, he was rewarded by an important discovery. The whole Prussian lines had been abandoned since sunset, and, mounting cautiously on the ramparts, Raynal saw the town too was evacuated, and lights and other indications on a rising ground behind it convinced him that the Prussians were in full retreat, probably to effect that junction with other forces which the assault he had recommended would have rendered impossible.

They now lighted lanterns, and searched all over and round the bastion for the poor colonel, in the rear of the bastion they found many French soldiers, most of whom had died by the bayonet. The Prussian dead had all been carried off.

Here they found the talkative Sergeant La Croix. The poor fellow was silent enough now. A terrible sabre-cut on the skull. The colonel was not there. Raynal groaned, and led the way on to the bastion. The ruins still smoked. Seven or eight bodies were discovered by an arm or a foot protruding through the masses of masonry. Of these some were Prussians; a proof that some devoted hand had fired the train, and destroyed both friend and foe.

They found the tube of Long Tom sticking up, just as he had shown over the battlements that glorious day, with this exception, that a great piece was knocked off his lip, and the slice ended in a long, broad crack.

The soldiers looked at this. "That is our bullet's work," said they. Then one old veteran touched his cap, and told Raynal gravely, he knew where their beloved colonel was. "Dig here, to the bottom," said he. "*He lies beneath his work.*"

Improbable and superstitious as this was, the hearts of the soldiers assented to it.

Presently there was a joyful cry outside the bastion. A rush was made thither. But it proved to be only Dard, who had discovered that Sergeant La Croix's heart still beat. They took him up carefully, and carried him gently into camp. To Dard's delight the surgeon pronounced him curable. For all that, he was three days insensible, and after that unfit for duty. So they sent him home invalided, with a hundred francs out of the poor colonel's purse.

Raynal reported the evacuation of the place, and that Colonel Dujardin was buried under the bastion, and soon after rode out of the camp.

The words Camille had scratched with a pencil, and sent him from the edge of the grave, were few but striking.

"A dead man takes you once more by the hand. My last thought, thank God, is France. For her sake and mine, Raynal. *Go for General Bonaparte*. Tell him, from a dying soldier, the Rhine is a river to these generals, but to him a field of glory. He will lay out our lives, not waste them."

There was nothing to hinder Raynal from carrying out this sacred request: for the 24th brigade had ceased to exist: already thinned by hard service, it was reduced to a file or two by the fatal bastion. It was incorporated with the 12th; and Raynal rode heavy at heart to Paris, with a black scarf across his breast.

CHAPTER XXIII.

You see now into what a fatal entanglement two high-minded young ladies were led, step by step, through yielding to the natural foible of their sex — the desire to hide everything painful from those they love, even at the expense of truth.

A nice mess they made of it with their amiable dishonesty. And pray take notice that after the first White Lie or two, circumstances overpowered them, and drove them on against their will. It was no small part of all their misery that they longed to get back to truth and could not.

We shall see presently how far they succeeded in that pious object, for the sake of which they first entered on concealments. But first a word is due about one of the victims of their amiable, self-sacrificing lubricity. Edouard Riviere fell in one night, from happiness and confidence, such as till that night he had never enjoyed, to deep and hopeless misery.

He lost that which, to every heart capable of really loving, is the greatest earthly blessing, the woman he adored. But worse than that, he lost those prime treasures of the masculine soul, belief in human goodness, and in female purity. To him no more could there be in nature a candid eye, a virtuous ready-mantling cheek: for frailty and treachery had put on these signs of virtue and nobility. Henceforth, let him live a hundred years, whom could he trust or believe in?

Here was a creature whose virtues seemed to make frailty impossible: treachery, doubly impossible: a creature whose very faults — for faults she had — had seemed as opposite to treachery as her very virtues were. Yet she was all frailty and falsehood.

He passed in that one night of anguish from youth to age. He went about his business like a leaden thing. His food turned tasteless. His life seemed ended. Nothing appeared what it had been. The very landscape seemed cut in stone, and he a stone in the middle of it, and his heart a stone in him. At times, across that heavy heart came gushes of furious rage and bitter mortification; his heart was broken, and his faith was gone, for his vanity had been stabbed as fiercely as his love. "Georges Dandin!" he would cry, "curse her! curse her!" But love and misery overpowered these heats, and froze him to stone again.

The poor boy pined and pined. His clothes hung loose about him; his face was so drawn with suffering, you would not have known him. He hated company. The things he was expected to talk about! — he with his crushed heart. He could not. He would not. He shunned all the world; he went alone like a wounded deer. The good doctor, on his return from Paris, called on him to see if he was ill: since he had not come for days to the chateau. He saw the doctor coming and bade the servant say he was not in the village.

He drew down the blind, that he might never see the chateau again. He drew it up again: he could not exist without seeing it. "She will be miserable, too," he cried, gnashing his teeth. "She will see whether she has chosen well." At other times, all his courage, and his hatred, and his wounded vanity, were drowned in his love and its despair, and then he bowed his head, and sobbed and cried as if his heart would burst. One morning he was so sobbing with his head on the table, when his landlady tapped at his door. He started up and turned his head away from the door.

"A young woman from Beaurepaire, monsieur."

"From Beaurepaire?" his heart gave a furious leap. "Show her in."

He wiped his eyes and seated himself at a table, and, all in a flutter, pretended to be the state's.

It was not Jacintha, as he expected, but the other servant. She made a low reverence, cast a look of admiration on him, and gave him a letter. His eye darted on it: his hand trembled as he took it. He turned away again to open it. He forced himself to say, in a tolerably calm voice, "I will send an answer."

The letter was apparently from the baroness de Beaurepaire; a mere line inviting him to pay her a visit. It was written in a tremulous hand. Edouard examined the writing, and saw directly it was written by Rose.

Being now, naturally enough, full of suspicion, he set this down as an attempt to disguise her hand. "So," said he, to himself, "this is the game. The old woman is to be drawn into it, too. She is to help to make Georges Dandin of me. I will go. I will baffle them all. I will expose this nest of depravity, all ceremony on the surface, and voluptuousness and treachery below. O God! who could believe that creature never loved me! They shall none of them see my weakness. Their benefactor shall be still their superior. They shall see me cold as ice, and bitter as gall."

But to follow him farther just now, would be to run too far in advance of the main story. I must, therefore, return to Beaurepaire, and show, amongst other things, how this very letter came to be written.

When Josephine and Rose awoke from that startled slumber that followed the exhaustion of that troubled night, Rose was the more wretched of the two. She had not only dishonored herself, but stabbed the man she loved.

Josephine, on the other hand, was exhausted, but calm. The fearful escape she had had softened down by contrast her more distant terrors.

She began to shut her eyes again, and let herself drift. Above all, the doctor's promise comforted her: that she should go to Paris with him, and have her boy.

This deceitful calm of the heart lasted three days.

Carefully encouraged by Rose, it was destroyed by Jacintha.

Jacintha, conscious that she had betrayed her trust, was almost heart-broken. She was ashamed to appear before her young mistress, and, coward-like, wanted to avoid knowing even how much harm she had done.

She pretended toothache, bound up her face, and never stirred from the kitchen. But she was not to escape: the other servant came down with a message: "Madame Raynal wanted to see her directly."

She came quaking, and found Josephine all alone.

Josephine rose to meet her, and casting a furtive glance round the room first, threw her arms round Jacintha's neck, and embraced her with many tears.

"Was ever fidelity like yours? how *could* you do it, Jacintha? and how can I ever repay it? But, no; it is too base of me to accept such a sacrifice from any woman."

Jacintha was so confounded she did not know what to say. But it was a mystification that could not endure long between two women, who were both deceived by a third. Between them they soon discovered that it must have been Rose who had sacrificed herself.

"And Edouard has never been here since," said Josephine.

"And never will, madame."

"Yes, he shall! there must be some limit even to my feebleness, and my sister's devotion. You shall take a line to him from me. I will write it this moment."

The letter was written. But it was never sent. Rose found Josephine and Jacintha together; saw a letter was being written, asked to see it; on Josephine's hesitating, snatched it out of her hand, read it, tore it to pieces, and told Jacintha to leave the room. She hated the sight of poor Jacintha, who had slept at the very moment when all depended on her watchfulness.

"So you were going to send to HIM, unknown to me."

"Forgive me, Rose." Rose burst out crying.

"O Josephine! is it come to this? Would you deceive *me*?"

"You have deceived *me*! Yes! it has come to that. I know all. Twill not consent to destroy *all* I love."

She then begged hard for leave to send the letter.

Rose gave an impetuous refusal. "What could you say to him? foolish thing, don't you know him, and his vanity? When you had exposed yourself to him, and showed him I had insulted him for you, do you think he would forgive me? No! this is to make light of my love — to make me waste the sacrifice I have made. I feel that sacrifice as much as you do, more perhaps, and I would rather die in a convent than waste that night of shame and agony. Come, promise me, no more attempts of that kind, or we are sisters no more, friends no more, one heart and one blood no more."

The weaker nature, weakened still more by ill-health and grief, was terrified into submission, or rather temporized. "Kiss me then," said Josephine, "and love me to the end. Ah, if I was only in my grave!"

Rose kissed her with many sighs, but Josephine smiled. Rose eyed her with suspicion. That deep smile; what did it mean? She had formed some resolution. "She is going to deceive me somehow," thought Rose.

From that day she watched Josephine like a spy. Confidence was gone between them. Suspicion took its place.

Rose was right in her misgivings. The moment Josephine saw that Edouard's happiness and Rose's were to be sacrificed for her whom nothing could make happy, the poor thing said to herself, *"I can die."*

And that was the happy thought that made her smile.

The doctor gave her laudanum: he found she could not sleep: and he thought it all-important that she should sleep.

Josephine, instead of taking these small doses, saved them all up, secreted them in a phial, and so, from the sleep of a dozen nights, collected the sleep of death: and now she was tranquil. This young creature that could not bear to give pain to any one else, prepared her own death with a calm resolution the heroes of our sex have not often equalled. It was so little a thing to her to strike Josephine. Death would save her honor, would spare her the frightful alternative of deceiving her husband, or of telling him she was another's. "Poor Raynal," said she to herself, "it is so cruel to tie him to a woman who can never be to him what he deserves. Rose would then prove her innocence to Edouard. A few tears for a weak, loving soul, and they would all be happy and forget her."

One day the baroness, finding herself alone with Rose and Dr.

Aubertin, asked the latter what he thought of Josephine's state.

"Oh, she was better: had slept last night without her usual narcotic."

The baroness laid down her knitting and said, with much meaning, "And I tell you, you will never cure her body till you can cure her mind. My poor child has some secret sorrow."

"Sorrow!" said Aubertin, stoutly concealing the uneasiness these words created, "what sorrow?"

"Oh, she has some deep sorrow. And so have you, Rose."

"Me, mamma! what *do* you mean?"

The baroness's pale cheek flushed a little. "I mean," said she, "that my patience is worn out at last; I cannot live surrounded by secrets. Raynal's gloomy looks when he left us, after staying but one hour; Josephine ill from that day, and bursting into tears at every word; yourself pale and changed, hiding an unaccountable sadness under forced smiles — Now, don't interrupt me. Edouard, who was almost like a son, gone off, without a word, and never comes near us now."

"Really you are ingenious in tormenting yourself. Josephine is ill! Well, is it so very strange? Have you never been ill? Rose is pale! you *are* pale, my dear; but she has nursed her sister for a month; is it a wonder she has lost color? Edouard is gone a journey, to inherit his uncle's property: a million francs. But don't you go and fall ill, like Josephine; turn pale, like Rose; and make journeys in the region of fancy, after Edouard Riviere, who is tramping along on the vulgar high road."

This tirade came from Aubertin, and very clever he thought himself. But he had to do with a shrewd old lady, whose suspicions had long smouldered; and now burst out. She said quietly, "Oh, then Edouard is not in this part of the world. That alters the case: where *is* he?"

"In Normandy, probably," said Rose, blushing.

The baroness looked inquiringly towards Aubertin. He put on an innocent face and said nothing.

"Very good," said the baroness. "It's plain I am to learn nothing from you two. But I know somebody who will be more communicative. Yes: this uncomfortable smiling, and unreasonable crying, and interminable whispering; these appearances of the absent, and disappearances of the present; I shall know this very day what they all mean."

"Really, I do not understand you."

"Oh, never mind; I am an old woman, and I am in my dotage. For all that, perhaps you will allow me two words alone with my daughter."

"I retire, madame," and he disappeared with a bow to her, and an anxious look at Rose. She did not need this; she clenched her teeth, and braced herself up to stand a severe interrogatory.

Mother and daughter looked at one another, as if to measure forces, and then, instead of questioning her as she had intended, the baroness sank back in her chair and wept aloud. Rose was all unprepared for this. She almost screamed in a voice of agony, "O mamma! mamma! O God! kill me where I stand for making my mother weep!"

"My girl," said the baroness in a broken voice, and with the most touching dignity, "may you never know what a mother feels who finds herself shut out from her daughters' hearts. Sometimes I think it is my fault; I was born in a severer age. A mother nowadays seems to be a sort of elder sister. In my day she was something more. Yet I loved my mother as well, or better than I did my sisters. But it is not so with those I have borne in my bosom, and nursed upon my knee."

At this Rose flung herself, sobbing and screaming, at her mother's knees. The baroness was alarmed. "Come, dearest, don't cry like that. It is not too late to take your poor old mother into your confidence. What is this mystery? and why this sorrow? How comes it I intercept at every instant glances that were not intended for me? Why is the very air loaded with signals and secrecy? (Rose replied only by sobs.) Is some deceit going on? (Rose sobbed.) Am I to have no reply but these sullen sobs? will you really tell me nothing?"

"I've nothing to tell," sobbed Rose.

"Well, then, will you do something for me?"

Such a proposal was not only a relief, but a delight to the deceiving but loving daughter. She started up crying, "Oh, yes, mamma; anything, everything. Oh, thank you!" In the ardor of her gratitude, she wanted to kiss her mother; but the baroness declined the embrace politely, and said, coldly and bitterly, "I shall not ask much; I should not venture now to draw largely on your affection; it's only to write a few lines for me."

Rose got paper and ink with great alacrity, and sat down all beaming, pen in hand.

The baroness dictated the letter slowly, with an eye gimleting her daughter all the time.

"Dear — Monsieur — Riviere."

The pen fell from Rose's hand, and she turned red and then pale.

"What! write to him?"

"Not in your own name; in mine. But perhaps you prefer to give me the trouble."

"Cruel! cruel!" sighed Rose, and wrote the words as requested.

The baroness dictated again, —

"Oblige me by coming here at your very earliest convenience."

"But, mamma, if he is in Normandy," remonstrated Rose, fighting every inch of the ground.

"Never you mind where he is," said the baroness. "Write as I request."

"Yes, mamma," said Rose with sudden alacrity; for she had recovered her ready wit, and was prepared to write anything, being now fully resolved the letter should never go.

"Now sign my name." Rose complied. "There; now fold it, and address it to his lodgings." Rose did so; and, rising with a cheerful air, said she would send Jacintha with it directly.

She was half across the room when her mother called her quietly back.

"No, mademoiselle," said she sternly. "You will give me the letter. I can trust neither the friend of twenty years, nor the servant that stayed by me in adversity, nor the daughter I suffered for and nursed. And why don't I trust you? Because *you have told me a lie*."

At this word, which in its coarsest form she had never heard from those high-born lips till then, Rose cowered like a hare.

"Ay, *a lie*," said the baroness. "I saw Edouard Riviere in the park but yesterday. I saw him. My old eyes are feeble, but they are not deceitful. I saw him. Send my breakfast to my own room. I come of an ancient race: I could not sit with liars; I should forget courtesy; you would see in my face how thoroughly I scorn you all." And she went haughtily out with the letter in her hand.

Rose for the first time, was prostrated. Vain had been all this deceit; her mother was not happy; was not blinded. Edouard might come and tell her his story. Then no power could keep Josephine silent. The plot was thickening; the fatal net was drawing closer and closer.

She sank with a groan into a chair, and body and spirit alike succumbed. But that was only for a little while. To this prostration succeeded a feverish excitement. She could not, would not, look Edouard in the face. She would implore Josephine to be silent; and she herself would fly from the chateau. But, if Josephine would not be silent? Why, then she would go herself to Edouard, and throw herself upon his honor, and tell him the truth. With this, she ran wildly up the stairs, and burst into Josephine's room so suddenly, that she caught her, pale as death, on her knees, with a letter in one hand and a phial of laudanum in the other.

CHAPTER XXIV.

Josephine conveyed the phial into her bosom with wonderful rapidity and dexterity, and rose to her feet. But Rose just saw her conceal something, and resolved to find out quietly what it was. So she said nothing about it, but asked Josephine what on earth she was doing.

"I was praying."

"And what is that letter?"

"A letter I have just received from Colonel Raynal."

Rose took the letter and read it. Raynal had written from Paris. He was coming to Beaurepaire to stay a month, and was to arrive that very day.

Then Rose forgot all about herself, and even what she had come for. She clung about her sister's neck, and implored her, for her sake, to try and love Raynal.

Josephine shuddered, and clung weeping to her sister in turn. For in Rose's arms she realized more powerfully what that sister would suffer if she were to die. Now, while they clung together, Rose felt something hard, and contrived just to feel it with her cheek. It was the phial.

A chill suspicion crossed the poor girl. The attitude in which she had found Josephine; the letter, the look of despair, and now this little bottle, which she had hidden. *Why hide it?* She resolved not to let Josephine out of her sight; at all events, until she had seen this little bottle, and got it away from her.

She helped her to dress, and breakfasted with her in the tapestried room, and dissembled, and put on gayety, and made light of everything but Josephine's health.

Her efforts were not quite in vain. Josephine became more composed; and Rose even drew from her a half promise that she would give Raynal and time a fair trial.

And now Rose was relieved of her immediate apprehensions for Josephine, but the danger of another kind, from Edouard, remained. So she ran into her bedroom for her bonnet and shawl, determined to take the strong measure of visiting Edouard at once, or intercepting him. While she was making her little toilet, she heard her mother's voice in the room. This was unlucky; she must pass through that room to go out. She sat down and fretted at this delay. And then, as the baroness appeared to be very animated, Rose went to the keyhole, and listened. Their mother was telling Josephine how she had questioned Rose, and how Rose had told her an untruth, and how she had made that young lady write to Edouard, etc.; in short, the very thing Rose wanted to conceal from Josephine.

Rose lost all patience, and determined to fly through the room and out before anybody could stop her. She heard Jacintha come in with some message, and thought that would be a good opportunity to slip out unmolested. So she opened the door softly. Jacintha, it seemed, had been volunteering some remark that was not well received, for the baroness was saying, sharply, "Your opinion is not asked. Go down directly, and bring him up here, to this room." Jacintha cast a look of dismay at Rose, and vanished.

Rose gathered from that look, as much as from the words, who the visitor was. She made a dart after Jacintha. But the room was a long one, and the baroness intercepted her: "No," said she, gravely, "I cannot spare you."

Rose stood pale and panting, but almost defiant. "Mamma," said she, "if it is Monsieur Riviere, I *must* ask your leave to retire. And you have neither love nor pity, nor respect for me, if you detain me."

"Mademoiselle!" was the stern reply, "I *forbid* you to move. Be good enough to sit there;" with which the baroness pointed imperiously to a sofa at the other side of the room. "Josephine, go to your room." Josephine retired, casting more than one anxious glance over her shoulder.

Rose looked this way and that in despair and terror; but ended by sinking, more dead than alive, into the seat indicated; and even as she drooped, pale and trembling, on that sofa, Edouard Riviere, worn and agitated, entered the room, and bowed low to them all, without a word.

The baroness looked at him, and then at her daughter, as much as to say, now I have got you; deceive me now if you can. "Rose, my dear," said this terrible old woman, affecting honeyed accents, "don't you see Monsieur Riviere?"

The poor girl at this challenge rose with difficulty, and courtesied humbly to Edouard.

He bowed to her, and stealing a rapid glance saw her pallor and distress; and that showed him she was not so hardened as he had thought.

"You have not come to see us lately," said the baroness, quietly, "yet you have been in the neighborhood."

These words puzzled Edouard. Was the old lady all in the dark, then? As a public man he had already learned to be on his guard; so he stammered out, "That he had been much occupied with public duties."

Madame de Beaurepaire despised this threadbare excuse too much to notice it at all. She went on as if he had said nothing. "Intimate as you were with us, you must have some reason for deserting us so suddenly."

"I have," said Edouard, gravely.

"What is it?"

"Excuse me," said Edouard, sullenly.

"No, monsieur, I cannot. This neglect, succeeding to a somewhat ardent pursuit of my daughter, is almost an affront. You shall, of course, withdraw yourself altogether, if you choose. But not without an explanation. This much is due to me; and, if you are a gentleman, you will not withhold it from me."

"If he is a gentleman!" cried Rose; "O mamma, do not you affront a gentleman, who never, never gave you nor me any ground of offence. Why affront the friends and benefactors we have lost by our own fault?"

"Oh, then, it is all your fault," said the baroness. "I feared as much."

"All my fault, all," said Rose; then putting her pretty palms together, and casting a look of abject supplication on Edouard, she murmured, "my temper!"

"Do not you put words into his mouth," said the shrewd old lady. "Come, Monsieur Riviere, be a man, and tell me the truth. What has she said to you? What has she done?"

By this time the abject state of terror the high-spirited Rose was in, and her piteous glances, had so disarmed Edouard, that he had not the heart to expose her to her mother.

"Madame," said he, stiffly, taking Rose's hint, "my temper and mademoiselle's could not accord."

"Why, her temper is charming: it is joyous, equal, and gentle."

"You misunderstand me, madame; I do not reproach Mademoiselle Rose. It is I who am to blame."

"For what?" inquired the baroness dryly.

"For not being able to make her love me."

"Oh! that is it! She did not love you?"

"Ask herself, madame," said Edouard, bitterly.

"Rose," said the baroness, her eye now beginning to twinkle, "were you really guilty of such a want of discrimination? Didn't you love monsieur?"

Rose flung her arms round her mother's neck, and said, "No, mamma, I did not love Monsieur Edouard," in an exquisite tone of love, that to a female ear conveyed the exact opposite of the words.

But Edouard had not that nice discriminating ear. He sighed deeply, and the baroness smiled. "You tell me that?" said she, "and you are crying!"

"She is crying, madame?" said Edouard, inquiringly, and taking a step towards them.

"Why, you see she is, you foolish boy. Come, I must put an end to this;" and she rose coolly from her seat, and begging Edouard to forgive her for leaving him a moment with his deadly enemy, went off with knowing little nods into Josephine's room; only, before she entered it, she turned, and with a maternal smile discharged this word at the pair.

"Babies!"

But between the alienated lovers was a long distressing silence. Neither knew what to say; and their situation was intolerable. At last Rose ventured in a timorous voice to say, "I thank you for your generosity. But I knew that you would not betray me."

"Your secret is safe for me," sighed Edouard. "Is there anything else I can do for you?"

Rose shook her head sadly.

Edouard moved to the door.

Rose bowed her head with a despairing moan. It took him by the heart and held him. He hesitated, then came towards her.

"I see you are sorry for what you have done to me who loved you so; and you loved me. Oh! yes, do not deny it, Rose; there was a time you loved me. And that makes it worse: to have given me such sweet hopes, only to crush both them and me. And is not this cruel of you to weep so and let me see your penitence — when it is too late?"

"Alas! how can I help my regrets? I have insulted so good a friend."

There was a sad silence. Then as he looked at her, her looks belied the charge her own lips had made against herself.

A light seemed to burst on Edouard from that high-minded, sorrow-stricken face.

"Tell me it is false!" he cried.

She hid her face in her hands — woman's instinct to avoid being read.

"Tell me you were misled then, fascinated, perverted, but that your heart returned to me. Clear yourself of deliberate deceit, and I will believe and thank you on my knees."

"Heaven have pity on us both!" cried poor Rose.

"On us! Thank you for saying on us. See now, you have not gained happiness by destroying mine. One word — do you love that man? — that Dujardin?"

"You know I do not."

"I am glad of that; since his life is forfeited; if he escapes my friend Raynal, he shall not escape me."

Rose uttered a cry of terror. "Hush! not so loud. The life of Camille! Oh! if he were to die, what would become of — oh, pray do not speak so loud."

"Own then that you *do* love him," yelled Edouard; "give me truth, if you have no love to give. Own that you love him, and he shall be safe. It is myself I will kill, for being such a slave as to love you still."

Rose's fortitude gave way.

"I cannot bear it," she cried despairingly; "it is beyond my strength; Edouard, swear to me you will keep what I tell you secret as the grave!"

"Ah!" cried Edouard, all radiant with hope, "I swear."

"Then you are under a delirium. I have deceived, but never wronged you; that unhappy child is not — Hush! *Here she comes.*"

The baroness came smiling out, and Josephine's wan, anxious face was seen behind her.

"Well," said the baroness, "is the war at an end? What, are we still silent? Let me try then what I can do. Edouard, lend me your hand."

While Edouard hesitated, Josephine clasped her hands and mutely supplicated him to consent. Her sad face, and the thought of how often she had stood his friend, shook his resolution. He held out his hand, but slowly and reluctantly.

"There is my hand," he groaned.

"And here is mine, mamma," said Rose, smiling to please her mother.

Oh! the mixture of feeling, when her soft warm palm pressed his. How the delicious sense baffled and mystified the cold judgment.

Josephine raised her eyes thankfully to heaven.

While the young lovers yet thrilled at each other's touch, yet could not look one another in the face, a clatter of horses' feet was heard.

"That is Colonel Raynal," said Josephine, with unnatural calmness. "I expected him *today.*"

The baroness was at the side window in a moment.

"It is he! — it is he!"

She hurried down to embrace her son.

Josephine went without a word to her own room. Rose followed her the next minute. But in that one minute she worked magic.

She glided up to Edouard, and looked him full in the face: not the sad, depressed, guilty-looking humble Rose of a moment before, but the old high-spirited, and some what imperious girl.

"You have shown yourself noble this day. I am going to trust you as only the noble are trusted. Stay in the house till I can speak to you."

She was gone, and something leaped within Edouard's bosom, and a flood of light seemed to burst in on him. Yet he saw no object clearly: but he saw light.

Rose ran into Josephine's room, and once more surprised her on her knees, and in the very act of hiding something in her bosom.

"What are you doing, Josephine, on your knees?" said she, sternly.

"I have a great trial to go through," was the hesitating answer.

Rose said nothing. She turned paler. She is deceiving me, thought she, and she sat down full of bitterness and terror, and, affecting not to watch Josephine, watched her.

"Go and tell them I am coming, Rose."

"No, Josephine, I will not leave you till this terrible meeting is over. We will encounter him hand in hand, as we used to go when our hearts were one, and we deceived others, but never each other."

At this tender reproach Josephine fell upon her neck and wept.

"I will not deceive you," she said. "I am worse than the poor doctor thinks me. My life is but a little candle that a breath may put out any day."

Rose said nothing, but trembled and watched her keenly.

"My little Henri," said Josephine imploringly, "what would you do with him — if anything should happen to me?"

"What would I do with him? He is mine. I should be his mother. Oh! what words are these: my heart! my heart!"

"No, dearest; some day you will be married, and owe all the mother to your children; and Henri is not ours only: he belongs to some one I have seemed unkind to. Perhaps he thinks me heartless. For I am a foolish woman; I don't know how to be virtuous, yet show a man my heart. But *then* he will understand me and forgive me. Rose, love, you will write to him. He will come to you. You will go together to the place where I shall be sleeping. You will show him my heart. You will tell him all my long love that lasted to the end. *You* need not blush to tell him all. I have no right. Then you will give him his poor Josephine's boy, and you will say to him, 'She never loved but you: she gives you all that is left of her, her child. She only prays you not to give him a bad mother.'"

Poor soul! this was her one bit of little, gentle jealousy; but it made her eyes stream. She would have put out her hand from the tomb to keep her boy's father single all his life.

"Oh! my Josephine, my darling sister," cried Rose, "why do you speak of death? Do you meditate a crime?"

"No; but it was on my heart to say it: it has done me good."

"At least, take me to your bosom, my well-beloved, that I may not *see* your tears."

"There — tears? No, you have lightened my heart. Bless you! bless you!"

The sisters twined their bosoms together in a long, gentle embrace. You might have taken them for two angels that flowed together in one love, but for their tears.

A deep voice was now heard in the sitting-room.

Josephine and Rose postponed the inevitable one moment more, by arranging their hair in the glass: then they opened the door, and entered the tapestried room.

Raynal was sitting on the sofa, the baroness's hand in his. Edouard was not there.

Colonel Raynal had given him a strange look, and said, "What, you here?" in a tone of voice that was intolerable.

Raynal came to meet the sisters. He saluted Josephine on the brow.

"You are pale, wife: and how cold her hand is."

"She has been ill this month past," said Rose interposing.

"You look ill, too, Mademoiselle Rose."

"Never mind," cried the baroness joyously, "you will revive them both."

Raynal made no reply to that.

"How long do you stay this time, a day?"

"A month, mother."

The doctor now joined the party, and friendly greetings passed between him and Raynal.

But ere long somehow all became conscious this was not a joyful meeting. The baroness could not alone sustain the spirits of the party, and soon even she began to notice that Raynal's replies were short, and that his manner was distrait and gloomy. The sisters saw this too, and trembled for what might be coming.

At last Raynal said bluntly, "Josephine, I want to speak to you alone."

The baroness gave the doctor a look, and made an excuse for going down-stairs to her own room. As she was going Josephine went to her and said calmly, —

"Mother, you have not kissed me *today*."

"There! Bless you, my darling!"

Raynal looked at Rose. She saw she must go, but she lingered, and sought her sister's eye: it avoided her. At that Rose ran to the doctor, who was just going out of the door.

"Oh! doctor," she whispered trembling, "don't go beyond the door. I found her praying. My mind misgives me. She is going to tell him — or something worse."

"What do you mean?"

"I am afraid to say all I dread. She could not be so calm if she meant to live. Be near! as I shall. She has a phial hid in her bosom."

She left the old man trembling, and went back.

"Excuse me," said she to Raynal, "I only came to ask Josephine if she wants anything."

"No! — yes! — a glass of eau sucree."

Rose mixed it for her. While doing this she noticed that Josephine shunned her eye, but Raynal gazed gently and with an air of pity on her.

She retired slowly into Josephine's bedroom, but did not quite close the door.

Raynal had something to say so painful that he shrank from plunging into it. He therefore, like many others, tried to creep into it, beginning with something else.

"Your health," said he, "alarms me. You seem sad, too. I don't understand that. You have no news from the Rhine, have you?"

"Monsieur!" said Josephine scared.

"Do not call me monsieur, nor look so frightened. Call me your friend. I am your sincere friend."

"Oh, yes; you always were."

"Thank you. You will give me a dearer title before we part this time."

"Yes," said Josephine in a low whisper, and shuddered.

"Have you forgiven me frightening you so that night?"

"Yes."

"It was a shock to me, too, I can tell you. I like the boy. She professed to love him, and, to own the truth, I loathe all treachery and deceit. If I had done a murder, I would own it. A lie doubles every crime. But I took heart; we are all selfish, we men; of the two sisters one was all innocence and good faith; and she was the one I had chosen."

At these words Josephine rose, like a statue moving, and took a phial from her bosom and poured the contents into the glass.

But ere she could drink it, if such was her intention, Raynal, with his eyes gloomily lowered, said, in a voice full of strange solemnity, —

"I went to the army of the Rhine."

Josephine put down the glass directly, though without removing her hand from it.

"I see you understand me, and approve. Yes, I saw that your sister would be dishonored, and I went to the army and saw her seducer."

"You saw *him*. Oh, I hope you did not go and speak to him of — of this?"

"Why, of course I did."

Josephine resolved to know the worst at once. "May I ask," said she, "what you told him?"

"Why, I told him all I had discovered, and pointed out the course he must take; he must marry your sister at once. He refused. I challenged him. But ere we met, I was ordered to lead a forlorn hope against a bastion. Then, seeing me go to certain death, the noble fellow pitied me. I mean this is how I understood it all at the time; at any rate, he promised to marry Rose if he should live."

Josephine put out her hand, and with a horrible smile said, "I thank you; you have saved the honor of our family;" and with no more ado, she took the glass in her hand to drink the fatal contents.

But Raynal's reply arrested her hand. He said solemnly, "No, I have not. Have you no inkling of the terrible truth? Do not fiddle with that glass: drink it, or leave it alone; for, indeed, I need all your attention."

He took the glass out of her patient hand, and with a furtive look at the bedroom-door, drew her away to the other end of the room; "and," said he, "I could not tell your mother, for she knows nothing of the girl's folly; still less Rose, for I see she loves him still, or why is she so pale? Advise me, now, whilst we are alone. Colonel Dujardin was *comparatively* indifferent to *you*. Will you undertake the task? A rough soldier like me is not the person to break the terrible tidings to that poor girl."

"What tidings? You confuse, you perplex me. Oh! what does this horrible preparation mean?"

"It means he will never marry your sister; he will never see her more."

Then Raynal walked the room in great agitation, which at once communicated itself to his hearer. But the loving heart is ingenious in avoiding its dire misgivings.

"I see," said she; "he told you he would never visit Beaurepaire again. He was right."

Raynal shook his head sorrowfully.

"Ah, Josephine, you are far from the truth. I was to attack the bastion. It was mined by the enemy, and he knew it. He took advantage of my back being turned. He led his men out of the trenches; he assaulted the bastion at the head of his brigade. He took it."

"Ah, it was noble; it was like him."

"The enemy, retiring, blew the bastion into the air, and Dujardin — is dead."

"Dead!" said Josephine, in stupefied tones, as if the word conveyed no meaning to her mind, benumbed and stunned by the blow.

"Don't speak so loud," said Raynal; "I hear the poor girl at the door. Ay, he took my place, and is dead."

"Dead!"

"Swallowed up in smoke and flames, overwhelmed and crushed under the ruins."

Josephine's whole body gave way, and heaved like a tree falling under the axe. She sank slowly to her knees, and low moans of agony broke from her at intervals. "Dead, dead, dead!"

"Is it not terrible?" he cried.

She did not see him nor hear him, but moaned out wildly, "Dead, dead, dead!" The bedroom-door was opened.

She shrieked with sudden violence, "Dead! ah, pity! the glass! the composing draught." She stretched her hands out wildly. Raynal, with a face full of concern, ran to the table, and got the glass. She crawled on her knees to meet it; he brought it quickly to her hand.

"There, my poor soul!"

Even as their hands met, Rose threw herself on the cup, and snatched it with fury from them both. She was white as ashes, and her eyes, supernaturally large, glared on Raynal with terror. "Madman!" she cried, "would you kill her?"

He glared back on her: what did this mean? Their eyes were fixed on each other like combatants for life and death; they did not see that the room was filling with people, that the doctor was only on the other side of the table, and that the baroness and

Edouard were at the door, and all looking wonderstruck at this strange sight — Josephine on her knees, and those two facing each other, white, with dilating eyes, the glass between them.

But what was that to the horror, when the next moment the patient Josephine started to her feet, and, standing in the midst, tore her hair by handfuls, out of her head.

"Ah, you snatch the kind poison from me!"

"Poison!"

"Poison!"

"Poison!" cried the others, horror-stricken.

"Ah! you won't let me die. Curse you all! curse you! I never had my own way in anything. I was always a slave and a fool. I have murdered the man I love — I love. Yes, my husband, do you hear? the man I love."

"Hush! daughter, respect my gray hairs."

"Your gray hairs! You are not so old in years as I am in agony. So this is your love, Rose! Ah, you won't let me die — won't you? *Then I'll do worse — I'll tell.*"

"He who is dead; you have murdered him amongst you, and I'll follow him in spite of you all — he was my betrothed. He struggled wounded, bleeding, to my feet. He found me married. News came of my husband's death; I married my betrothed."

"Married him!" exclaimed the baroness.

"Ah, my poor mother. And she kissed me so kindly just now — she will kiss me no more. Oh, I am not ashamed of marrying him. I am only ashamed of the cowardice that dared not do it in face of all the world. We had scarce been happy a fortnight, when a letter came from Colonel Raynal. He was alive. I drove my true husband away, wretch that I was. None but bad women have an atom of sense. I tried to do my duty to my legal husband. He was my benefactor. I thought it was my duty. Was it? I don't know: I have lost the sense of right and wrong. I turned from a living creature to a lie. He who had scattered benefits on me and all this house; he whom it was too little to love; he ought to have been adored: this man came here one night to wife proud, joyous, and warm-hearted. He found a cradle, and two women watching it. Now Edouard, now *monsieur*, do you see that life is *impossible* to me? One bravely accused herself: she was innocent. One swooned away like a guilty coward."

Edouard uttered an exclamation.

"Yes, Edouard, you shall not be miserable like me; she was guilty. You do not understand me yet, my poor mother — and she was so happy this morning — I was the liar, the coward, the double-faced wife, the miserable mother that denied her child. Now will you let me die? Now do you see that I can't and won't live upon shame and despair? Ah, Monsieur Raynal, my dear friend, you were always generous: you will pity and kill me. I have dishonored the name you gave me to keep: I am neither Beaurepaire nor Raynal. Do pray kill me, monsieur — Jean, do pray release me from my life!"

And she crawled to his knees and embraced them, and kissed his hand, and pleaded more piteously for death, than others have begged for life.

Raynal stood like a rock: he was pale, and drew his breath audibly, but not a word. Then came a sight scarce less terrible than Josephine's despair. The baroness, looking and moving twenty years older than an hour before, tottered across the room to Raynal.

"Sir, you whom I have called my son, but whom I will never presume so to call again, I thought I had lived long enough never to have to blush again. I loved you, monsieur. I prayed every day for you. But she who *was* my daughter was not of my mind. Monsieur, I have never knelt but to God and to my king, and I kneel to you: forgive us, sir, forgive us!"

She tried to go down on her knees. He raised her with his strong arm, but he could not speak. She turned on the others.

"So this is the secret you were hiding from me! This secret has not killed you all. Oh! I shall not live under its shame so long as you have. Chateau of Beaurepaire — nest of treason, ingratitude, and immodesty — I loathe you as much as once I loved you. I will go and hide my head, and die elsewhere."

"Stay, madame!" said he, in a voice whose depth and dignity was such that it seemed impossible to disobey it. "It was sudden — I was shaken — but I am myself again."

"Oh, show some pity!" cried Rose.

"I shall try to be just."

There was a long, trembling silence; and during that silence and terrible agitation, one figure stood firm among those quaking, beating hearts, like a rock with the waves breaking round it — the *man of principle* among the creatures of impulse.

He raised Josephine from her knees, and placed her all limp and powerless in an armchair. To her frenzy had now succeeded a sickness and feebleness like unto death.

"Widow Dujardin," said he, in a broken voice, "listen to me."

She moaned a sort of assent.

"Your mistake has been not trusting me. I was your friend,

and not a selfish friend. I was not enough in love with you to destroy your happiness. Besides, I despise that sort of love. If you had told me all, I would have spared you this misery. By the present law, civil contracts of marriage can be dissolved by mutual consent."

At this the baroness uttered some sign of surprise.

"Ah!" continued Raynal, sadly, "you are aristocrats, and cannot keep pace with the times. This very day our mere contract shall be formally dissolved. Indeed, it ceases to exist since both parties are resolved to withdraw from it. So, if you married Dujardin in a church, you are Madame Dujardin at this moment, and his child is legitimate. What does she say?"

This question was to Rose, for what Josephine uttered sounded like a mere articulate moan. But Rose's quick ear had caught words, and she replied, all in tears, "My poor sister is blessing you, sir. We all bless you."

"She does not understand my position," said Raynal. He then walked up to Josephine, and leaning over her arm, and speaking rather loud, under the impression that her senses were blunted by grief, he said, "Look here: Colonel Dujardin, your husband, deliberately, and with his eyes open, sacrificed his life for me, and for his own heroic sense of honor. Now, it is my turn. If that hero stood here, and asked me for all the blood in my body, I would give it him. He is gone; but, dying for me, he has left me his widow and his child; they remain under my wing. To protect them is my pride, and my only consolation. I am going to the mayor to annul our unlucky contract in due form, and make us brother and sister instead. But," turning to the baroness, "don't you think to escape me as your daughter has done: no, no, old lady, once a mother, always a mother. Stir from your son's home if you dare!"

And with these words, in speaking which his voice had recovered its iron firmness, he strode out at the door, superb in manhood and principle, and every eye turned with wonder and admiration after him. Even when he was gone they gazed at the door by which a creature so strangely noble had disappeared.

The baroness was about to follow him without taking any notice of Josephine. But Rose caught her by the gown. "O mother, speak to poor Josephine: bid her live."

The baroness only made a gesture of horror and disgust, and turned her back on them both.

Josephine, who had tottered up from her seat at Rose's words, sank heavily down again, and murmured, "Ah! the grave holds all that love me now."

Rose ran to her side. "Cruel Josephine! what, do not I love you? Mother, will you not help me persuade her to live? Oh! if she dies, I will die too; you will kill both your children."

Stern and indignant as the baroness was, yet these words pierced her heart. She turned with a piteous, half apologetic air to Edouard and Aubertin. "Gentlemen," said she, "she has been foolish, not guilty. Heaven pardons the best of us. Surely a mother may forgive her child." And with this nature conquered utterly; and she held out her arms, wide, wide, as is a mother's heart. Her two erring children rushed sobbing violently into them; and there was not a dry eye in the room for a long time.

After this, Josephine's heart almost ceased to beat. Fear and misgivings, and the heavy sense of deceit gnawing an honorable heart, were gone. Grief reigned alone in the pale, listless, bereaved widow.

The marriage was annulled before the mayor; and, three days afterwards, Raynal, by his influence, got the consummated marriage formally allowed in Paris.

With a delicacy for which one would hardly have given him credit, he never came near Beaurepaire till all this was settled; but he brought the document from Paris that made Josephine the widow Dujardin, and her boy the heir of Beaurepaire; and the moment she was really Madame Dujardin he avoided her no longer; and he became a comfort to her instead of a terror.

The dissolution of the marriage was a great tie between them. So much that, seeing how much she looked up to Raynal, the doctor said one day to the baroness, "If I know anything of human nature, they will marry again, provided none of you give her a hint which way her heart is turning."

They, who have habituated themselves to live for others, can suffer as well as do great things. Josephine kept alive. A passion such as hers, in a selfish nature, must have killed her.

Even as it was, she often said, "It is hard to live."

Then they used to talk to her of her boy. Would she leave him — Camille's boy — without a mother? And these words were never spoken to her quite in vain.

Her mother forgave her entirely, and loved her as before. Who could be angry with her long? The air was no longer heavy with lies. Wretched as she was, she breathed lighter. Joy and hope were gone. Sorrowful peace was coming. When the heart comes to this, nothing but Time can cure; but what will not Time do? What wounds have I seen him heal! His cures are incredible.

The little party sat one day, peaceful, but silent and sad, in the

Pleasaunce, under the great oak.

Two soldiers came to the gate. They walked feebly, for one was lame, and leaned upon the other, who was pale and weak, and leaned upon a stick.

"Soldiers," said Raynal, "and invalided."

"Give them food and wine," said Josephine.

Rose went towards them; but she had scarcely taken three steps ere she cried out, —

"It is Dard! it is poor Dard! Come in, Dard, come in."

Dard limped towards them, leaning upon Sergeant La Croix. A bit of Dard's heel had been shot away, and of La Croix's head.

Rose ran to the kitchen.

"Jacintha, bring out a table into the Pleasaunce, and something for two guests to eat."

The soldiers came slowly to the Pleasaunce, and were welcomed, and invited to sit down, and received with respect; for France even in that day honored the humblest of her brave.

Soon Jacintha came out with a little round table in her hands, and affected a composure which was belied by her shaking hands and her glowing cheek.

After a few words of homely welcome — not eloquent, but very sincere — she went off again with her apron to her eyes. She reappeared with the good cheer, and served the poor fellows with radiant zeal.

"What regiment?" asked Raynal.

Dard was about to answer, but his superior stopped him severely; then, rising with his hand to his forehead, he replied, with pride, "Twenty-fourth brigade, second company. We were cut up at Philipsburg, and incorporated with the 12th."

Raynal instantly regretted his question; for Josephine's eye fixed on Sergeant La Croix with an expression words cannot paint. Yet she showed more composure, real or forced, than he expected.

"Heaven sends him," said she. "My friend, tell me, were you — ah!"

Colonel Raynal interfered hastily. "Think what you do. He can tell you nothing but what we know, not so much, in fact, as we know; for, now I look at him, I think this is the very sergeant we found lying insensible under the bastion. He must have been struck before the bastion was taken even."

"I was, colonel, I was. I remember nothing but losing my senses, and feeling the colors go out of my hand."

"There, you see, he knows nothing," said Raynal.

"It was hot work, colonel, under that bastion, but it was hotter to the poor fellows that got in. I heard all about it from Private Dard here."

"So, then, it was you who carried the colors?"

"Yes, I was struck down with the colors of the brigade in my hand," cried La Croix.

"See how people blunder about, everything; they told me the colonel carried the colors."

"Why, of course he did. You don't think our colonel, the fighting colonel, would let me hold the colors of the brigade so long as he was alive. No; he was struck by a Prussian bullet, and he had just time to hand the colors to me, and point with his sword to the bastion, and down he went. It was hot work, I can tell you. I did not hold them long, not thirty seconds, and if we could know their history, they passed through more hands than that before they got to the Prussian flag-staff."

Raynal suddenly rose, and walked rapidly to and fro, with his hands behind him.

"Poor colonel!" continued La Croix. "Well, I love to think he died like a soldier, and not like some of my poor comrades, hashed to atoms, and not a volley fired over him. I hope they put a stone over him, for he was the best soldier and the best general in the army."

"O sir!" cried Josephine, "there is no stone even to mark the spot where he fell," and she sobbed despairingly.

"Why, how is this, Private Dard?" inquired La Croix, sternly.

Dard apologized for his comrade, and touching his own head significantly told them that since his wound the sergeant's memory was defective.

"Now, sergeant, didn't I tell you the colonel must have got the better of his wound, and got into the battery?"

"It's false, Private Dard; don't I know our colonel better than that? Would ever he have let those colors out of his hand, if there had been an ounce of life left in him?"

"He died at the foot of the battery, I tell you."

"Then why didn't we find him?"

Here Jacintha put in a word with the quiet subdued meaning of her class. "I can't find that anybody ever saw the colonel dead."

"They did not find him, because they did not look for him," said Sergeant La Croix.

"God forgive you, sergeant!" said Dard, with some feeling. "Not look for *our colonel*! We turned over every body that lay there, — full thirty there were, — and you were one of them."

"Only thirty! Why, we settled more Prussians than that, I'll swear."

"Oh! they carried off their dead."

"Ay! but I don't see why they should carry our colonel off. His epaulets was all the thieves could do any good with. Stop! yet I do, Private Dard; I have a horrible suspicion. No, I have not; it is a certainty. What! don't you see, ye ninny? Thunder and thousands of devils, here's a disgrace. Dogs of Prussians! they have got our colonel, they have taken him prisoner."

"O God bless them!" cried Josephine; "O God bless the mouth that tells me so! O sir, I am his wife, his poor heart-broken wife. You would not be so cruel as to mock my despair. Say again that he may be alive, pray, say it again!"

"His wife! Private Dard, why didn't you tell me? You tell me nothing. Yes, my pretty lady, I'll say it again, and I'll prove it. Here is an enemy in full retreat, would they encumber themselves with the colonel? If he was dead, they'd have whipped off his epaulets, and left him there. Alive? why not? Look at me: I am alive, and I was worse wounded than he was. They took me for dead, you see. Courage, madame! you will see him again, take an old soldier's word for it. Dard, attention! this is the colonel's wife."

She gazed on the speaker like one in a trance.

Every eye and every soul had been so bent on Sergeant La Croix that it was only now Raynal was observed to be missing. The next minute he came riding out of the stable-yard, and went full gallop down the road.

"Ah!" cried Rose, with a burst of hope; "he thinks so too; he has hopes. He is gone somewhere for information. Perhaps to Paris."

Josephine's excitement and alternations of hope and fear were now alarming. Rose held her hand, and implored her to try and be calm till they could see Raynal.

Just before dark he came riding fiercely home. Josephine flew down the stairs. Raynal at sight of her forgot all his caution. He waved his cocked hat in the air. She fell on her knees and thanked God. He gasped out, —

"Prisoner — exchanged for two Prussian lieutenants — sent home — they say he is in France!"

The tears of joy gushed in streams from her.

Some days passed in hope and joy inexpressible; but the good doctor was uneasy for Josephine. She was always listening with supernatural keenness and starting from her chair, and every fibre of her lovely person seemed to be on the quiver.

Nor was Rose without a serious misgiving. Would husband and wife ever meet? He evidently looked on her as Madame Raynal, and made it a point of honor to keep away from Beaurepaire.

They had recourse to that ever-soothing influence — her child. Madame Jouvenel was settled in the village, and Josephine visited her every day, and came back often with red eyes, but always soothed.

One day Rose and she went to Madame Jouvenel, and, entering the house without ceremony, found the nurse out, and no one watching the child.

"How careless!" said Rose.

Josephine stopped eagerly to kiss him. But instead of kissing him, she uttered a loud cry. There was a locket hanging round his neck.

It was a locket containing some of Josephine's hair and Camille's. She had given it him in the happy days that followed their marriage. She stood gasping in the middle of the room. Madame Jouvenel came running in soon after. Josephine, by a wonderful effort over herself, asked her calmly and cunningly, —

"Where is the gentleman who put this locket round my child's neck? I want to speak with him."

Madame Jouvenel stammered and looked confused.

"A soldier — an officer? — come, tell me!"

"Woman," cried Rose, "why do you hesitate?"

"What am I to do?" said Madame Jouvenel. "He made me swear never to mention his coming here. He goes away, or hides whenever you come. And since Madame does not love the poor wounded gentleman, what can he do better?"

"Not love him!" cried Rose: "why, she is his wife, his lawful wedded wife; he is a fool or a monster to run away for her. She loves him as no woman ever loved before. She pines for him. She dies for him."

The door of a little back room opened at these words of Rose, and there stood Camille, with his arm in a sling, pale and astounded, but great joy and wonder working in his face.

Josephine gave a cry of love that made the other two women weep, and in a moment they were sobbing for joy upon each other's neck.

Away went sorrow, doubt, despair, and all they had suffered. That one moment paid for all. And in that moment of joy and surprise, so great as to be almost terrible, perhaps it was well for Josephine that Camille, weakened by his wound, was quite overcome, and nearly fainted. She was herself just going into hysterics; but, seeing him quite overcome, she conquered them directly, and nursed, and soothed, and pitied, and encouraged him instead.

Then they sat hand in hand. Their happiness stopped their very breath. They could not speak. So Rose told him all. He never owned why he had slipped away when he saw them coming. He forgot it. He forgot all his hard thoughts of her. They took him home in the carriage. His wife would not let him out of her sight. For years and years after this she could hardly bear to let him be an hour out of her sight.

The world is wide; there may be a man in it who can paint the sudden bliss that fell on these two much suffering hearts; but I am not that man; this is beyond me; it was not only heaven, but heaven after hell.

Leave we the indescribable and the unspeakable for a moment, and go to a lighter theme.

The day Rose's character was so unexpectedly cleared, Edouard had no opportunity of speaking to her, or a reconciliation would have taken place. As it was, he went home intensely happy. But he did not resume his visits to the chateau. When he came to think calmly over it, his vanity was cruelly mortified. She was innocent of the greater offence; but how insolently she had sacrificed him, his love, and his respect, to another's interest.

More generous thoughts prevailed by degrees. And one day that her pale face, her tears, and her remorse got the better of his offended pride, he determined to give her a good lecture that should drown her in penitent tears; and then end by forgiving her. For one thing he could not be happy till he had forgiven her.

She walked into the room with a calm, dignified, stately air, and before he could utter one word of his grave remonstrance, attacked him thus: "You wish to speak to me, sir. If it is to apologize to me, I will save your vanity the mortification. I forgive you."

"*You* forgive *me!*" cried Edouard furiously.

"No violence, if you please," said the lady with cold hauteur. "Let us be friends, as Josephine and Raynal are. We cannot be anything more to one another now. You have wounded me too deeply by your jealous, suspicious nature."

Edouard gasped for breath, and was so far out-generalled that he accepted the place of defendant. "Wasn't I to believe your own lips? Did not Colonel Raynal believe you?"

"Oh, that's excusable. He did not know me. But you were my lover; you ought to have seen I was forced to deceive poor Raynal. How dare you believe your eyes; much more your ears, against my truth, against my honor; and then to believe such nonsense?" Then, with a grand assumption of superior knowledge, says she, "You little simpleton, how could the child be mine when I wasn't married at all?"

At this reproach, Edouard first stared, then grinned. "I forgot that," said he.

"Yes, and you forgot the moon isn't made of green cheese. However, if I saw you very humble, and very penitent, I might, perhaps, really forgive you — in time."

"No, forgive me at once. I don't understand your angelical, diabolical, incomprehensible sex: who on earth can? forgive me."

"Oh! oh! oh! oh!"

Lo! the tears that could not come at a remonstrance were flowing in a stream at his generosity.

"What is the matter now?" said he tenderly. She cried away, but at the same time explained, —

"What a f — f — foolish you must be not to see that it is I who am without excuse. You were my betrothed. It was to you I owed my duty; not my sister. I am a wicked, unhappy girl. How you must hate me!"

"I adore you. There, no more forgiving on either side. Let our only quarrel be who shall love the other best."

"Oh, I know how that will be," said the observant toad. "You will love me best till you have got me; and then I shall love you best; oh, ever so much."

However, the prospect of loving best did not seem disagreeable to her; for with this announcement she deposited her head on his shoulder, and in that attitude took a little walk with him up and down the Pleasaunce: sixty times; about eight miles.

These two were a happy pair. This wayward, but generous heart never forgot her offence, and his forgiveness. She gave herself to him heart and soul, at the altar, and well she redeemed her vow. He rose high in political life: and paid the penalty of that sort of ambition; his heart was often sore. But by his own hearth sat comfort and ever ready sympathy. Ay, and patient industry to read blue-books, and a ready hand and brain to write diplomatic notes for him, off which the mind glided as from a ball of ice.

In thirty years she never once mentioned the servants to him.

"Oh, let eternal honor crown her name!"

It was only a little bit of heel that Dard had left in Prussia. More fortunate than his predecessor (Achilles), he got off with a slight but enduring limp. And so the army lost him.

He married Jacintha, and Josephine set them up in Bigot's,

(deceased) auberge. Jacintha shone as a landlady, and custom flowed in. For all that, a hankering after Beaurepaire was observable in her. Her favorite stroll was into the Beaurepaire kitchen, and on all fetes and grand occasions she was prominent in gay attire as a retainer of the house. The last specimen of her homely sagacity I shall have the honor to lay before you is a critique upon her husband, which she vented six years after marriage.

"My Dard," said she, "is very good as far as he goes. What he has felt himself, that he can feel FOR: nobody better. You come to him with an empty belly, or a broken head, or all bleeding with a cut, or black and blue, and you shall find a friend. But if it is a sore heart, or trouble, and sorrow, and no hole in your carcass to show for it, you had better come to *me*; for you might as well tell your grief to a stone wall as to my man."

The baroness took her son Raynal to Paris, and there, with keen eye, selected him a wife. She proved an excellent one. It would have been hard if she had not, for the baroness with the severe sagacity of her age and sex, had set aside as naught a score of seeming angels, before she could suit herself with a daughter-in-law. At first the Raynals very properly saw little of the Dujardins; but when both had been married some years, the recollection of that fleeting and nominal connection waxed faint, while the memory of great benefits conferred on both sides remained lively as ever in hearts so great, and there was a warm, a sacred friendship between the two houses — a friendship of the ancient Greeks, not of the modern club-house.

Camille and Josephine were blessed almost beyond the lot of humanity: none can really appreciate sunshine but those who come out of the cold dark. And so with happiness. For years they could hardly be said to live like mortals: they basked in bliss. But it was a near thing; for they but just scraped clear of life-long misery, and death's cold touch grazed them both as they went.

Yet they had heroic virtues to balance White Lies in the great Judge's eye.

A wholesome lesson, therefore, and a warning may be gathered from this story: and I know many novelists who would have preached that lesson at some length in every other chapter, and interrupted the sacred narrative to do it. But when I read stories so mutilated, I think of a circumstance related by Mr. Joseph Miller.

"An Englishman sojourning in some part of Scotland was afflicted with many hairs in the butter, and remonstrated. He was told, in reply, that the hairs and the butter came from one source — the cow; and that the just and natural proportions hith-

erto observed, could not be deranged, and bald butter invented —
for ONE. 'So be it,' said the Englishman; 'but let me have the
butter in one plate, and the hairs in another.'"

Acting on this hint, I have reserved some admirable remarks,
reflections, discourses, and tirades, until the story should be
ended, and the other plate be ready for the subsidiary sermon.

And now that the proper time is come, that love of intruding
one's own wisdom in one's own person on the reader, which has
marred so many works of art, is in my case restrained — first, by
pure fatigue; secondly, because the moral of this particular story
stands out so clear in the narrative, that he who runs may read it
without any sermon at all.

Those who will not take the trouble to gather my moral from
the living tree, would not lift it out of my dead basket: would not
unlock their jaw-bones to bite it, were I to thrust it into their very
mouths.@

www.ingramcontent.com/pod-product-compliance
Lightning Source LLC
Chambersburg PA
CBHW021956010726
47494CB00003B/765